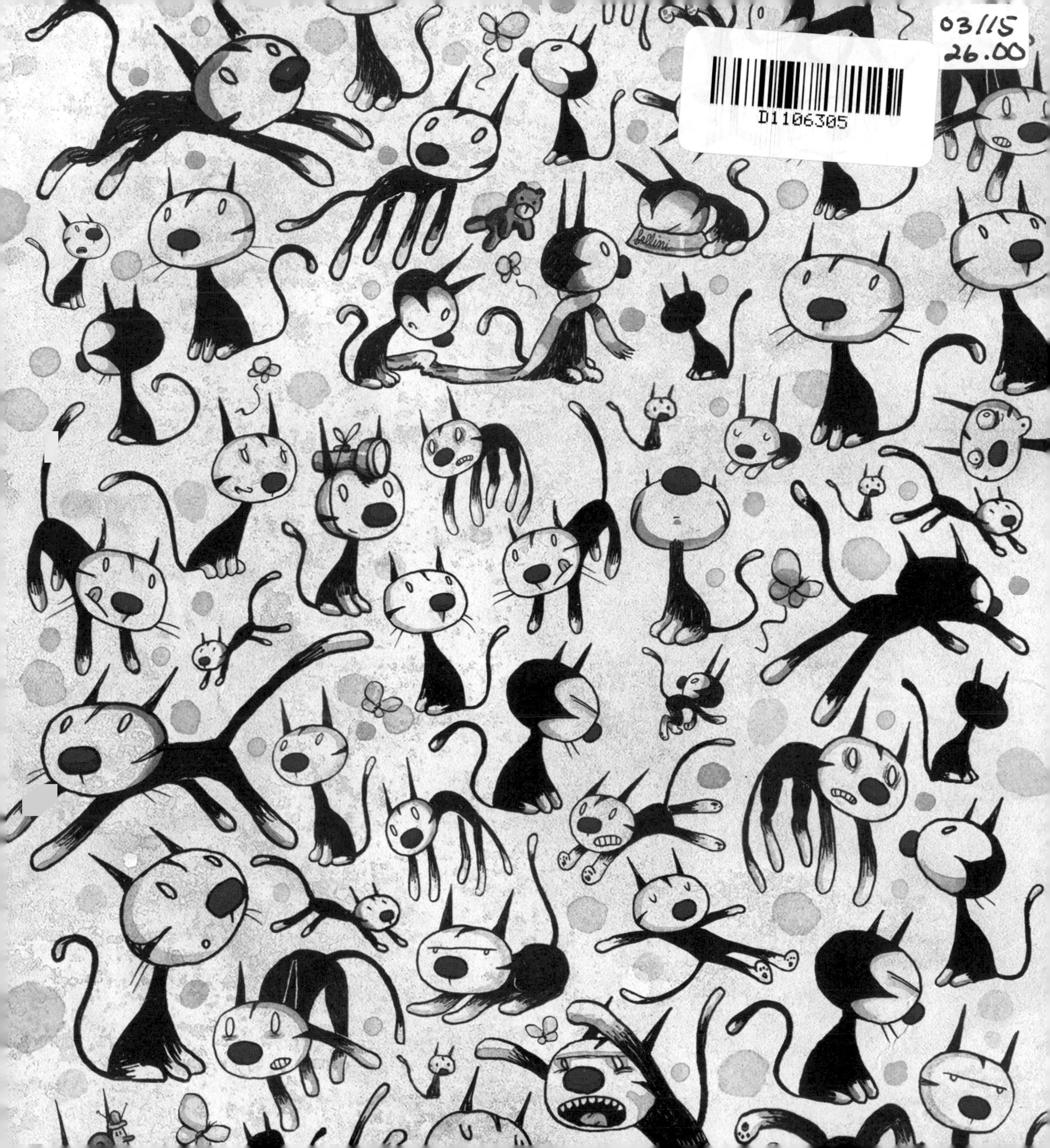

Dedicated to Angie for existing on this planet
and to Cristina for having existed.

First American edition published in 2014 by Enchanted Lion Books
351 Van Brunt Street, Brooklyn, NY 11231
English-language translation Copyright © 2014 by Mara Faye Lethem
English-language edition Copyright © 2014 by Enchanted Lion Books
Layout and design for the English-language edition by Sarah Klinger

Originally published in Spanish as *Macanudo 1* by Ediciones de la Flor S.R.L.
Copyright © 2004 by Ediciones de la Flor S.R.L, Buenos Aires, Argentina
All rights reserved under International and Pan-American Copyright Conventions
A CIP record is on file with the Library of Congress

Printed in China in February 2014 by South China Printing Co.

MACANUDO

Nº1

By LINIERS

TRANSLATED FROM THE SPANISH BY MARA LETHEM

Withdrawn from Collection

ENCHANTED LION BOOKS
NEW YORK

PROLOGUE

Anyone can draw a cat, anyone can draw a little girl, or a man with a hat, but not everyone can make that cat, that little girl, and that man with a hat different from any we've ever seen before and have them become part of our world, as if we knew them personally.

Liniers draws characters, and his characters are *macanudos*, which is to say they are extraordinary and awesome. And he draws them so well that they're all lovely. Even the ugly ones are so perfectly ugly that they're beautiful. Loners, with a pop innocence that's sometimes a bit perverse, they move elegantly between sadness and astonishment, like anonymous actors in small hand-crafted B movies.

Pencil, ink, and watercolors converge with poetry and the absurd in a world filled with surprises. Anything can happen in *Macanudo*. Its stories turn into silly jokes, told by someone who clearly appreciates the silliest things life has to offer.

Liniers draws a hard world with absolute delicacy. His is a melancholy joy located on the opposite pole from idiotic happiness. His work is lyrical and fun. He's a *macanudo* guy.

Maitena

"Surprise is the essence of humor, so the challenge of writing a comic strip is to surprise yourself." - Bill Watterson

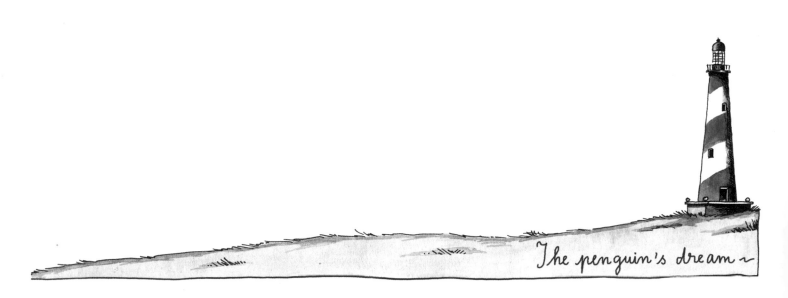

The penguin's dream

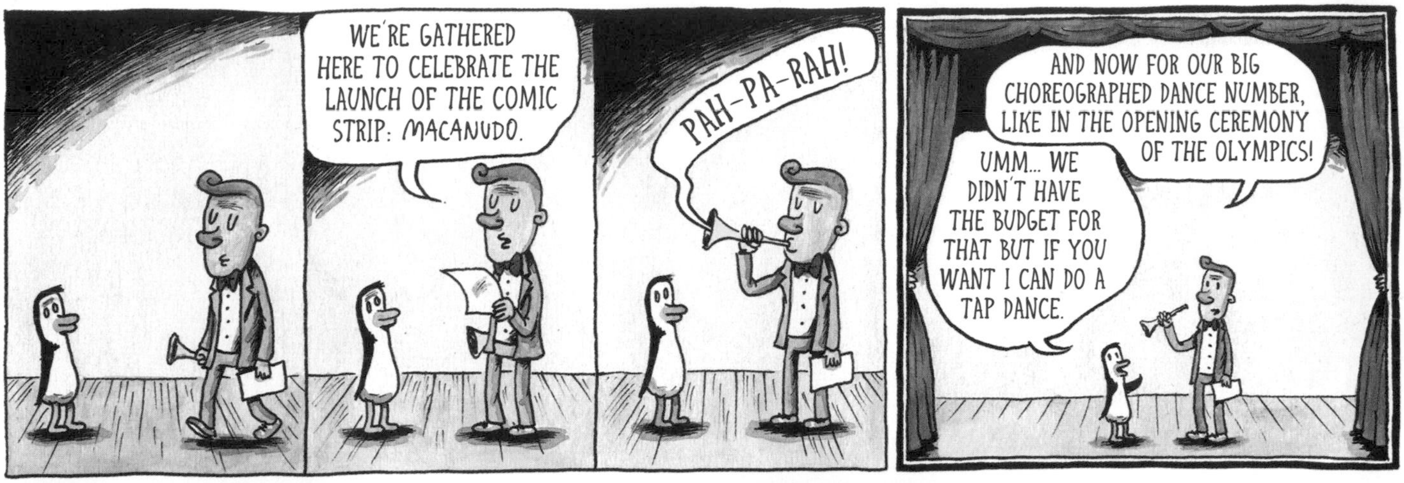
WE'RE GATHERED HERE TO CELEBRATE THE LAUNCH OF THE COMIC STRIP: MACANUDO.
PAH-PA-RAH!
AND NOW FOR OUR BIG CHOREOGRAPHED DANCE NUMBER, LIKE IN THE OPENING CEREMONY OF THE OLYMPICS!
UMM... WE DIDN'T HAVE THE BUDGET FOR THAT BUT IF YOU WANT I CAN DO A TAP DANCE.

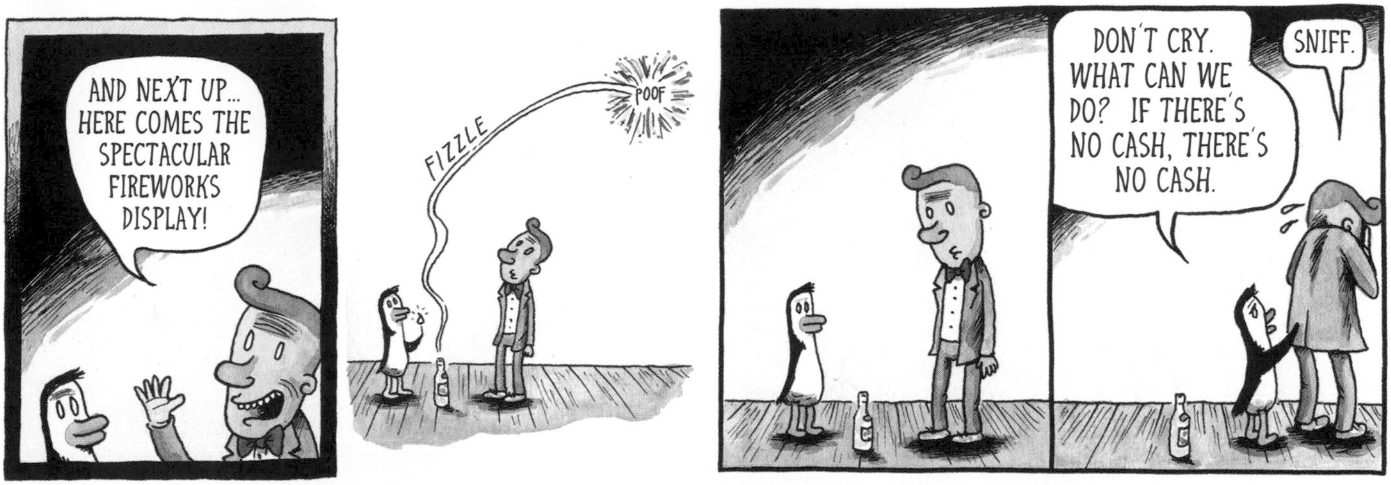
AND NEXT UP... HERE COMES THE SPECTACULAR FIREWORKS DISPLAY!
FIZZLE
POOF
DON'T CRY. WHAT CAN WE DO? IF THERE'S NO CASH, THERE'S NO CASH.
SNIFF.

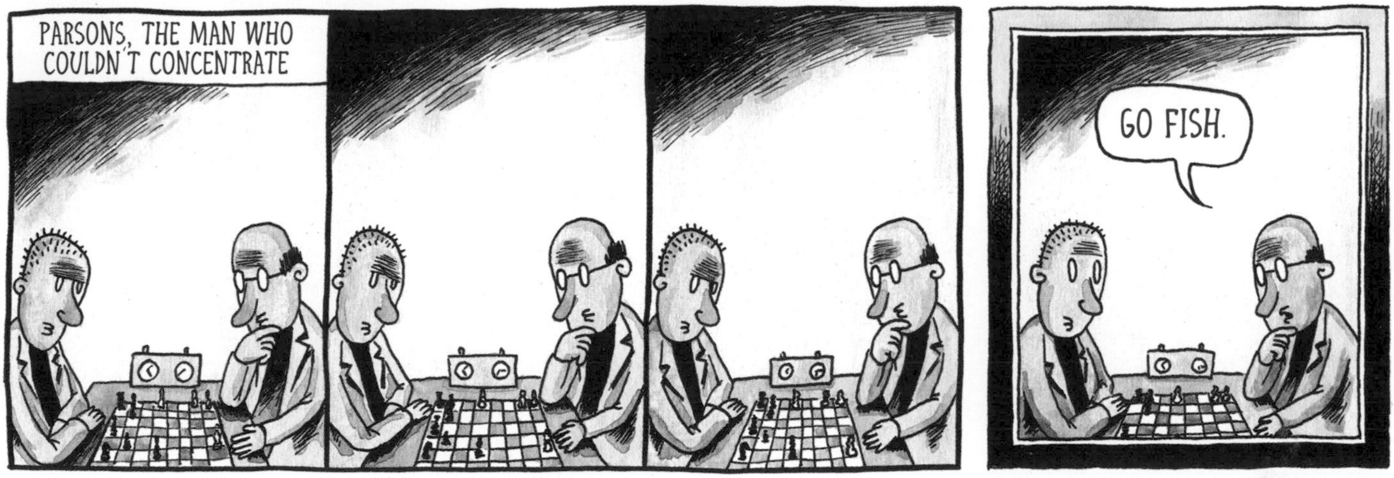
PARSONS, THE MAN WHO COULDN'T CONCENTRATE
GO FISH.

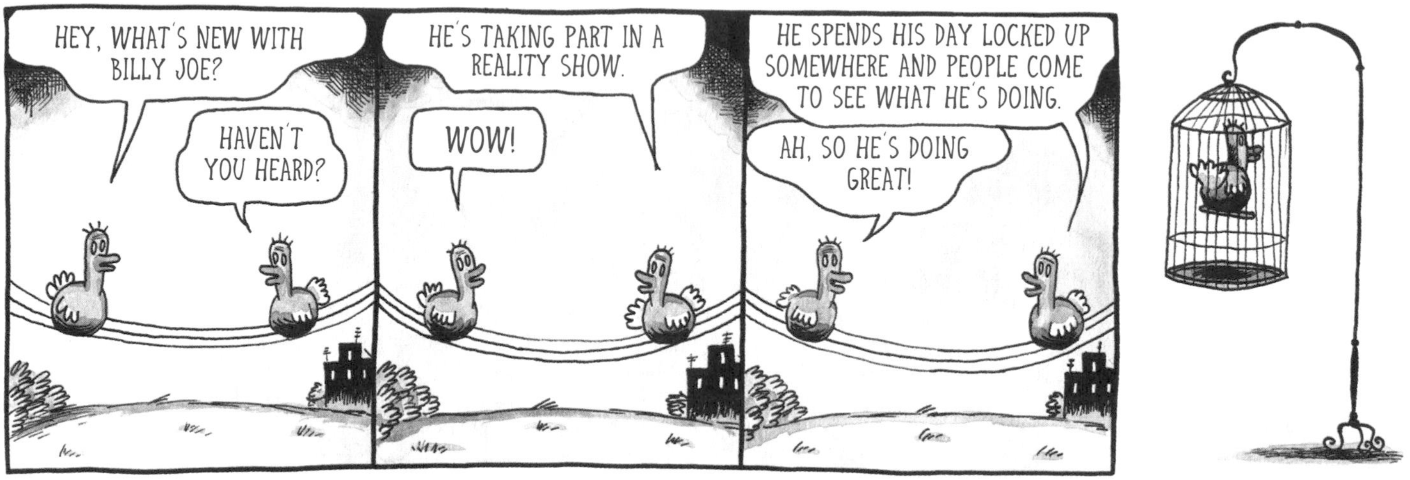
HEY, WHAT'S NEW WITH BILLY JOE?
HAVEN'T YOU HEARD?
HE'S TAKING PART IN A REALITY SHOW.
WOW!
HE SPENDS HIS DAY LOCKED UP SOMEWHERE AND PEOPLE COME TO SEE WHAT HE'S DOING.
AH, SO HE'S DOING GREAT!

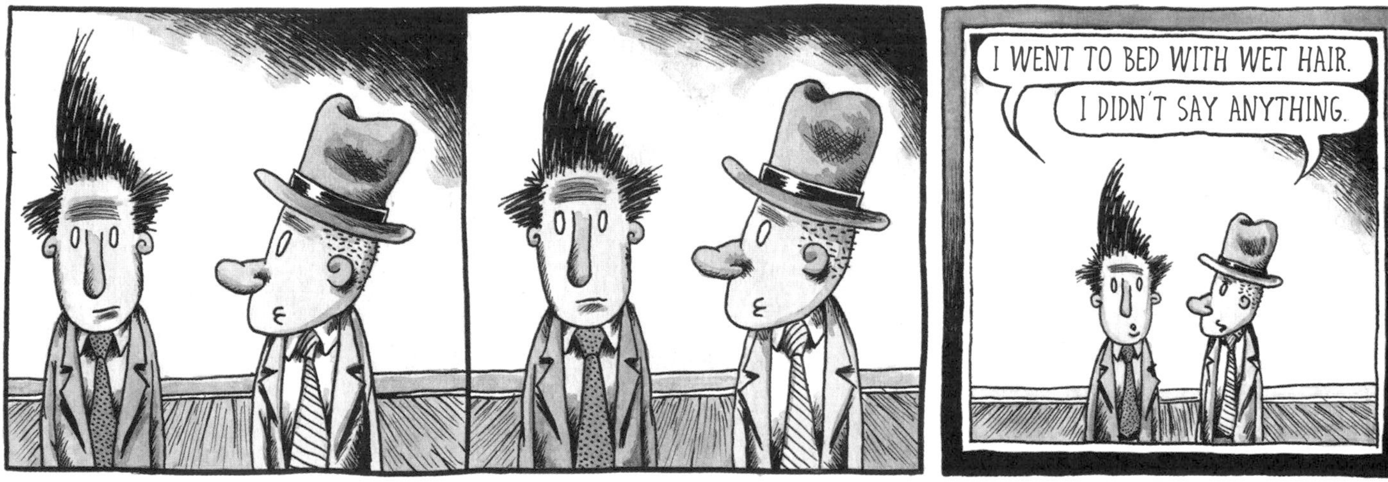
I WENT TO BED WITH WET HAIR.
I DIDN'T SAY ANYTHING.

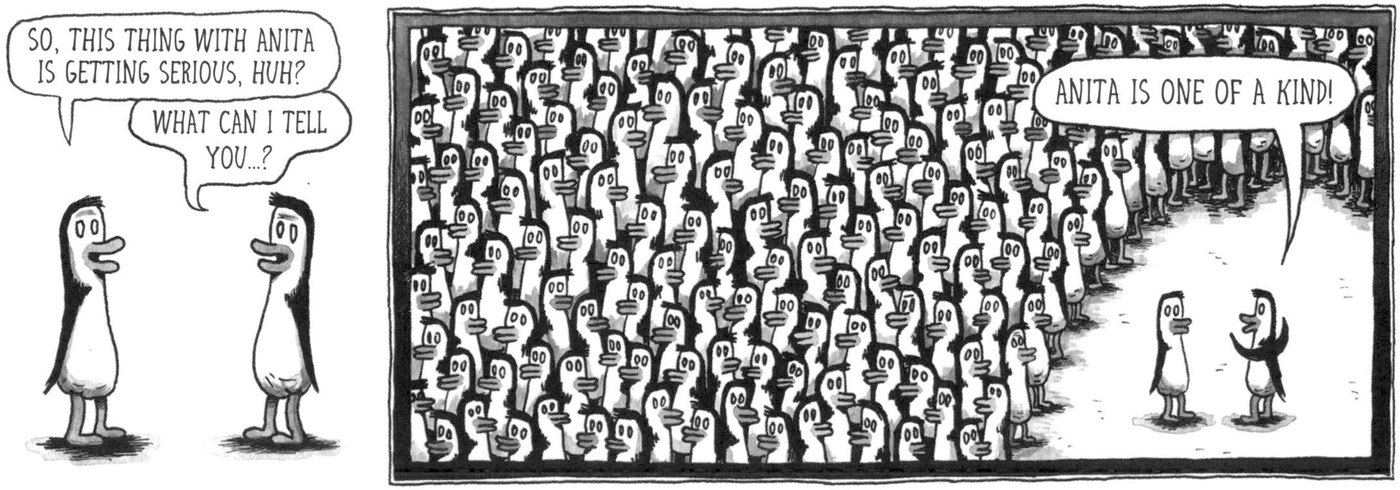
SO, THIS THING WITH ANITA IS GETTING SERIOUS, HUH?
WHAT CAN I TELL YOU...?
ANITA IS ONE OF A KIND!

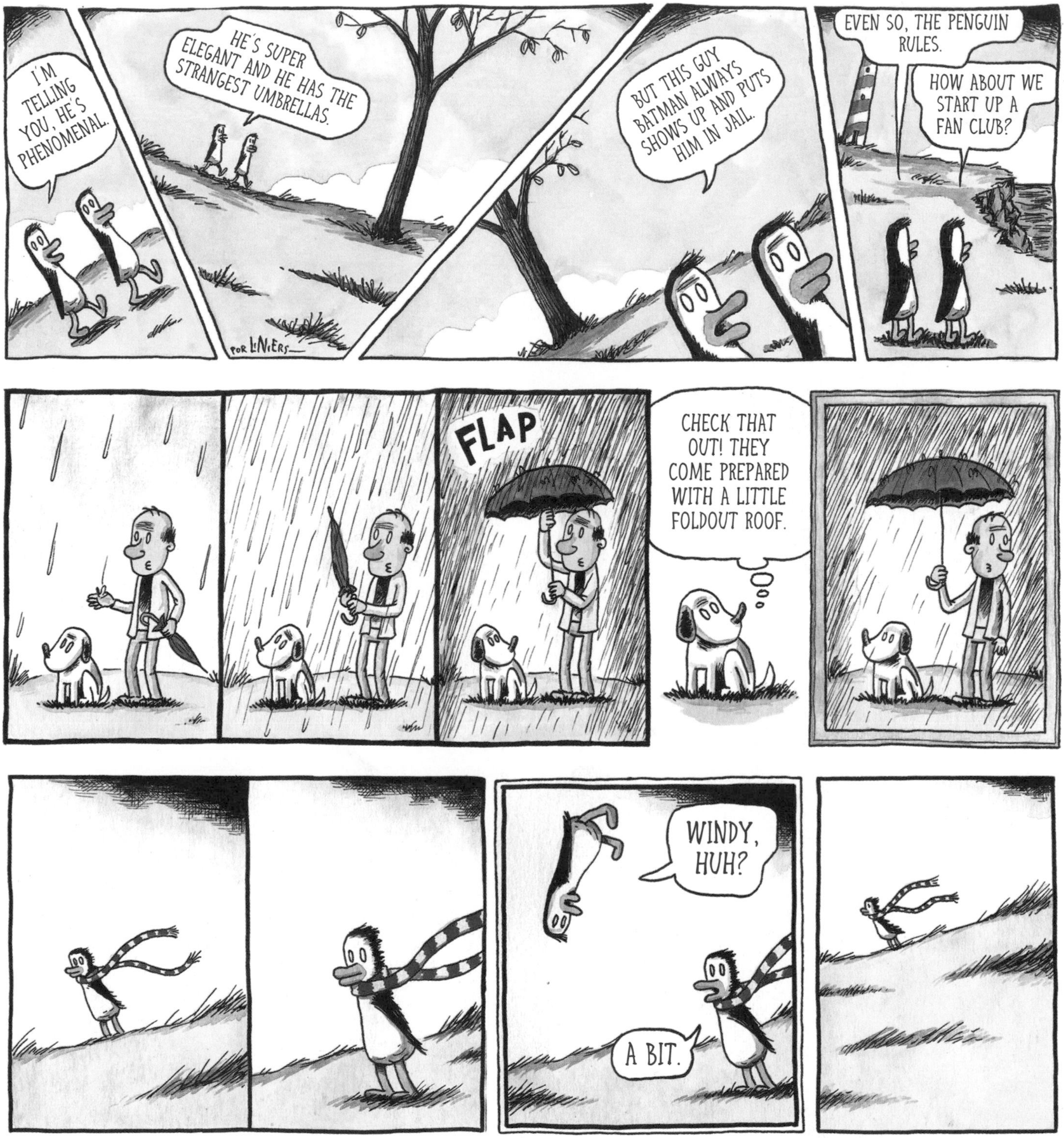
I'M TELLING YOU, HE'S PHENOMENAL.
HE'S SUPER ELEGANT AND HE HAS THE STRANGEST UMBRELLAS.
POR LINIERS
BUT THIS GUY BATMAN ALWAYS SHOWS UP AND PUTS HIM IN JAIL.
EVEN SO, THE PENGUIN RULES.
HOW ABOUT WE START UP A FAN CLUB?
FLAP
CHECK THAT OUT! THEY COME PREPARED WITH A LITTLE FOLDOUT ROOF.
WINDY, HUH?
A BIT.

LOOK, EDWARD, I LOVE YOU A LOT. YOU KNOW?
BUT I ALSO NEED MY SPACE. I'M VERY INDEPENDENT.
I WANT TO BE WITH YOU, BUT I DON'T WANT TO SEE YOU.
YOU KNOW WHAT, JOSEPHINE, I JUST DON'T UNDERSTAND YOU.
WHAT HAPPENED TO YOU?
I CUT MYSELF ON A PIECE OF GLASS.
SHUSH! AAAAAH! DON'T TELL ME! I DON'T WANT TO KNOW!
YOU KNOW WHAT YOUR PROBLEM IS? YOU NEVER FINISH ANYTHING!
AT FIRST YOU'RE ALL JAZZED UP BUT GRADUALLY YOU JUST TUNE OUT.
DO YOU KNOW WHAT YOU ARE? HUH?

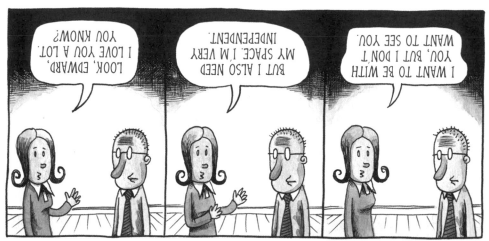

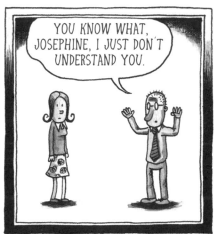

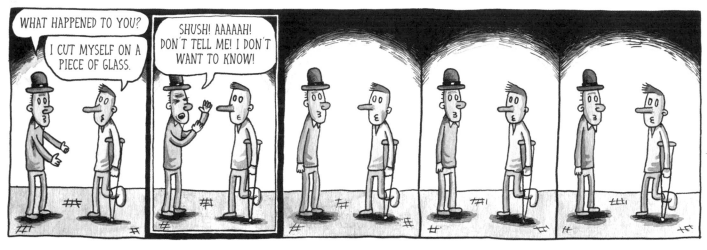

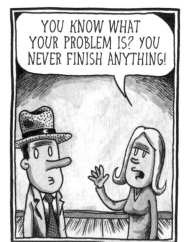

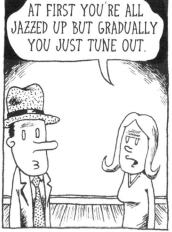

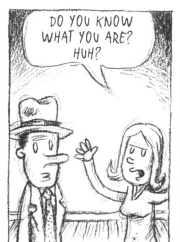

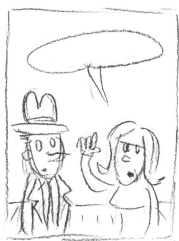

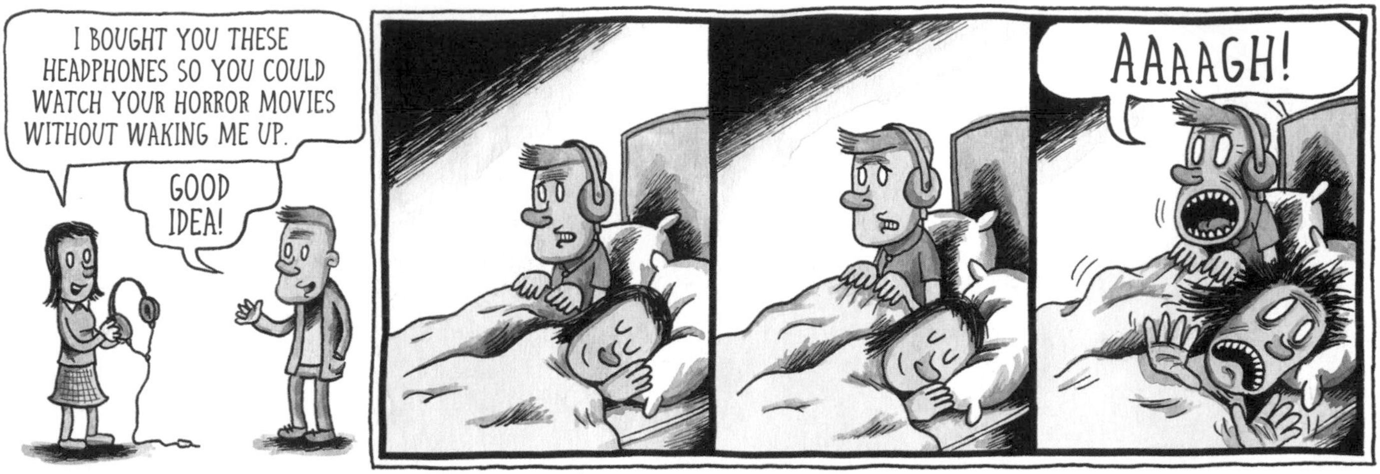
I BOUGHT YOU THESE HEADPHONES SO YOU COULD WATCH YOUR HORROR MOVIES WITHOUT WAKING ME UP.
GOOD IDEA!
AAAAGH!

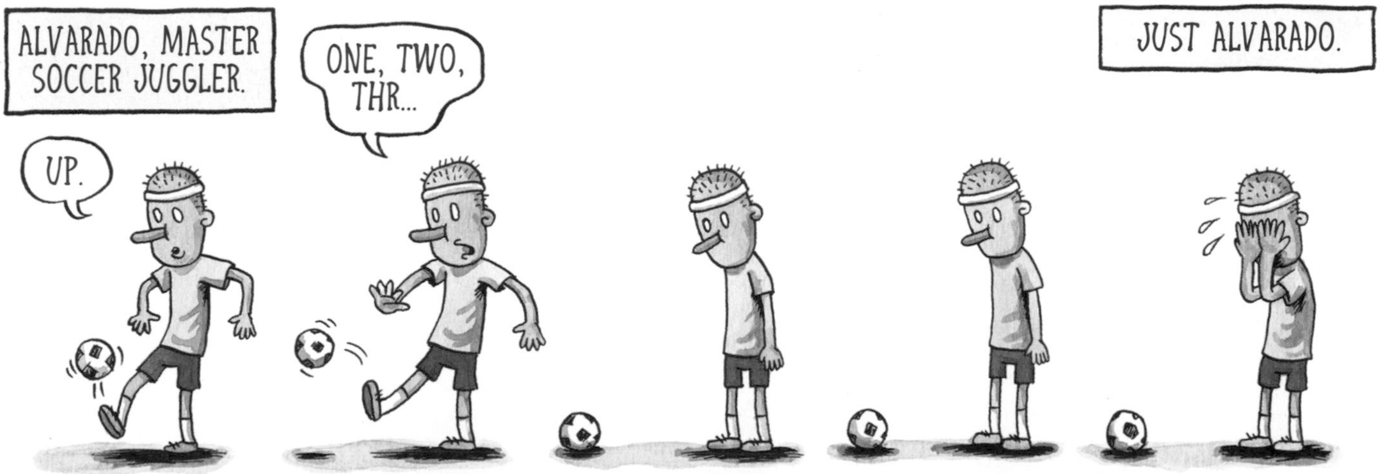
ALVARADO, MASTER SOCCER JUGGLER.
UP.
ONE, TWO, THR...
JUST ALVARADO.

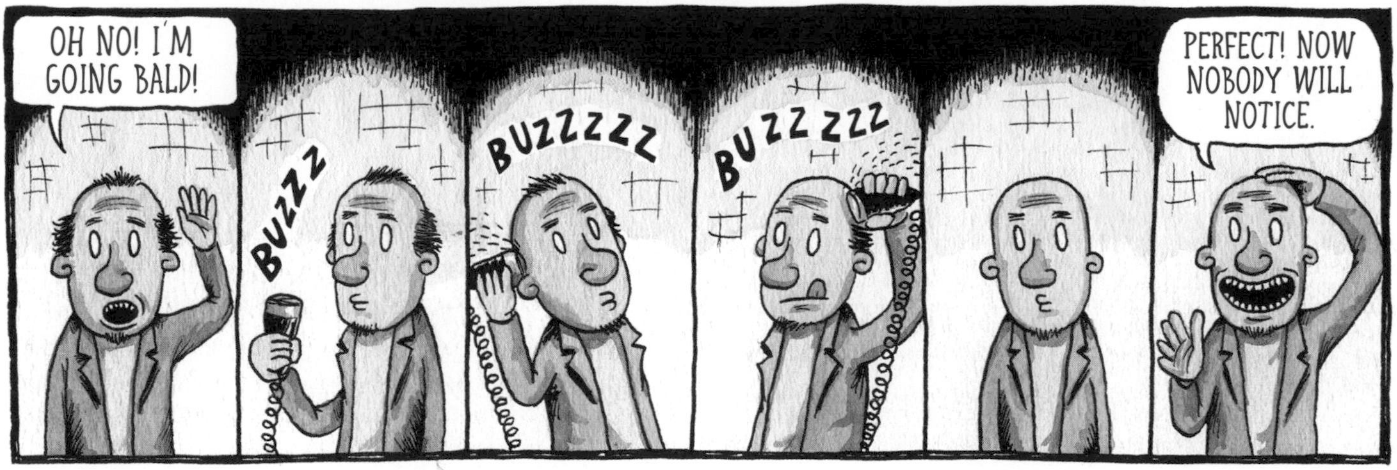
OH NO! I'M GOING BALD!
BUZZZ
BUZZZZZ
BUZZZZZ
PERFECT! NOW NOBODY WILL NOTICE.

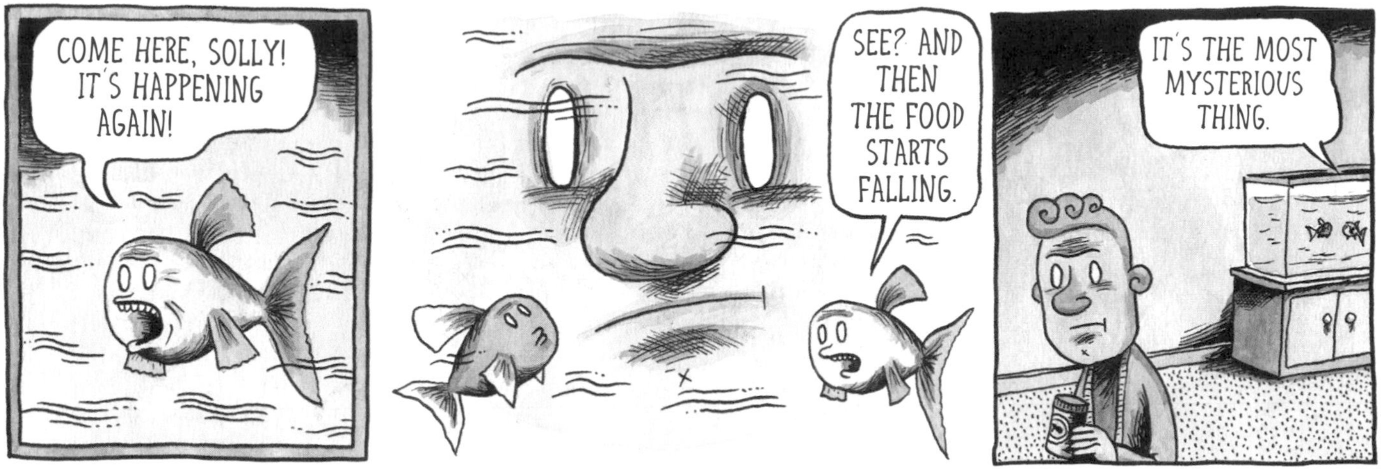
COME HERE, SOLLY! IT'S HAPPENING AGAIN!
SEE? AND THEN THE FOOD STARTS FALLING.
IT'S THE MOST MYSTERIOUS THING.

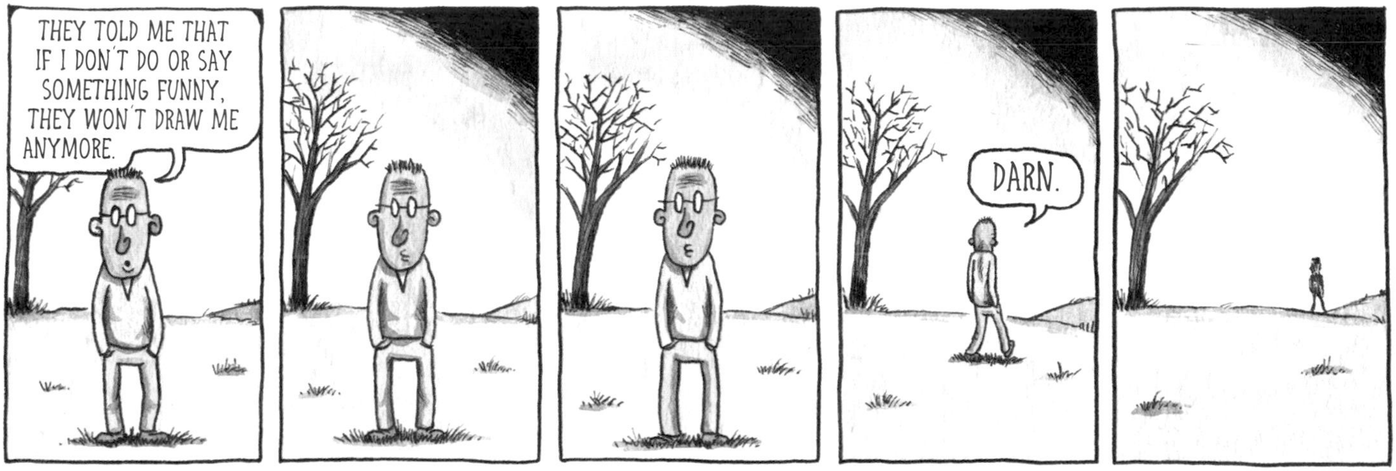
THEY TOLD ME THAT IF I DON'T DO OR SAY SOMETHING FUNNY, THEY WON'T DRAW ME ANYMORE.
DARN.

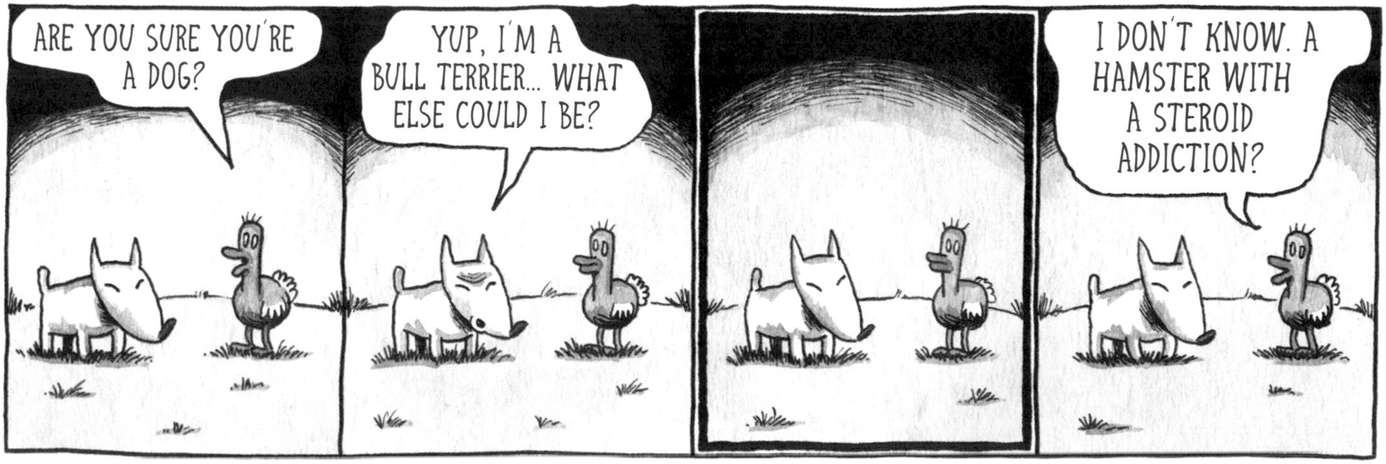
ARE YOU SURE YOU'RE A DOG?
YUP, I'M A BULL TERRIER... WHAT ELSE COULD I BE?
I DON'T KNOW. A HAMSTER WITH A STEROID ADDICTION?

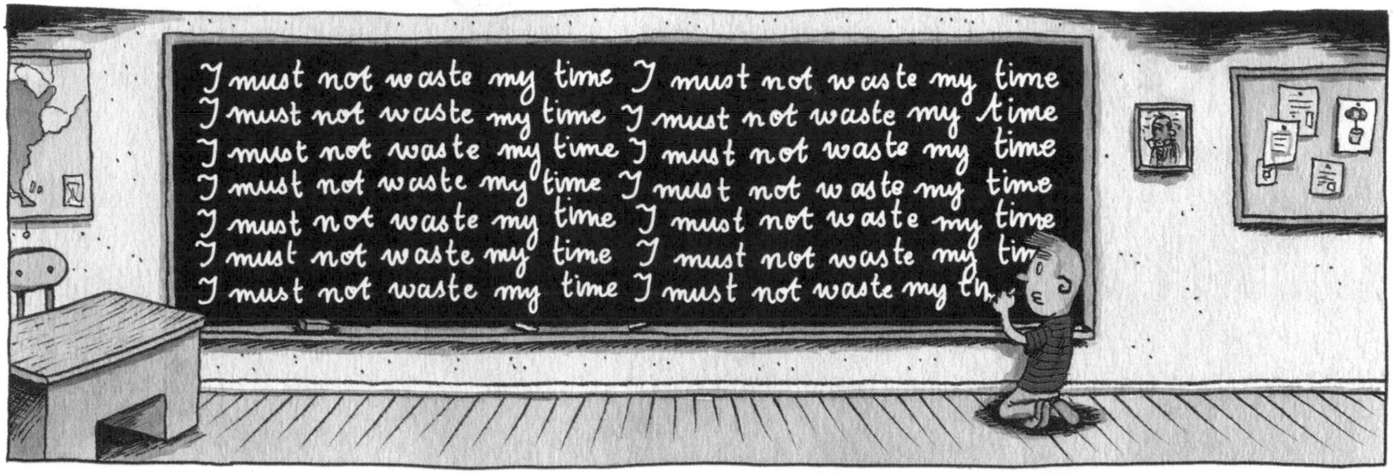
I must not waste my time I must not waste my time
I must not waste my time I must not waste my time
I must not waste my time I must not waste my time
I must not waste my time I must not waste my time
I must not waste my time I must not waste my time
I must not waste my time I must not waste my tim
I must not waste my time I must not waste my ti

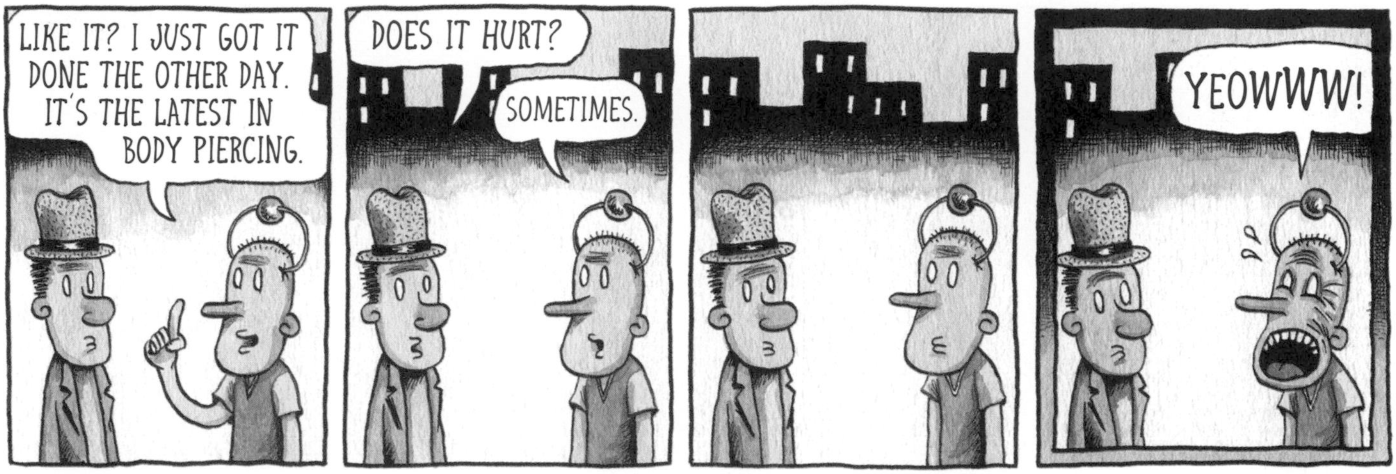
LIKE IT? I JUST GOT IT DONE THE OTHER DAY. IT'S THE LATEST IN BODY PIERCING.
DOES IT HURT?
SOMETIMES.
YEOWWW!

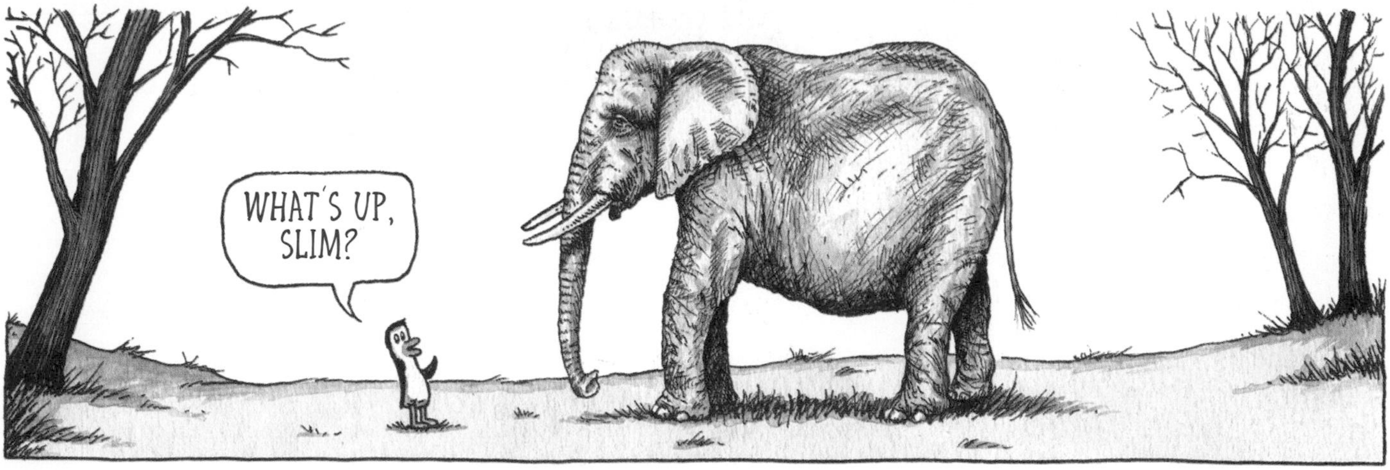
WHAT'S UP, SLIM?

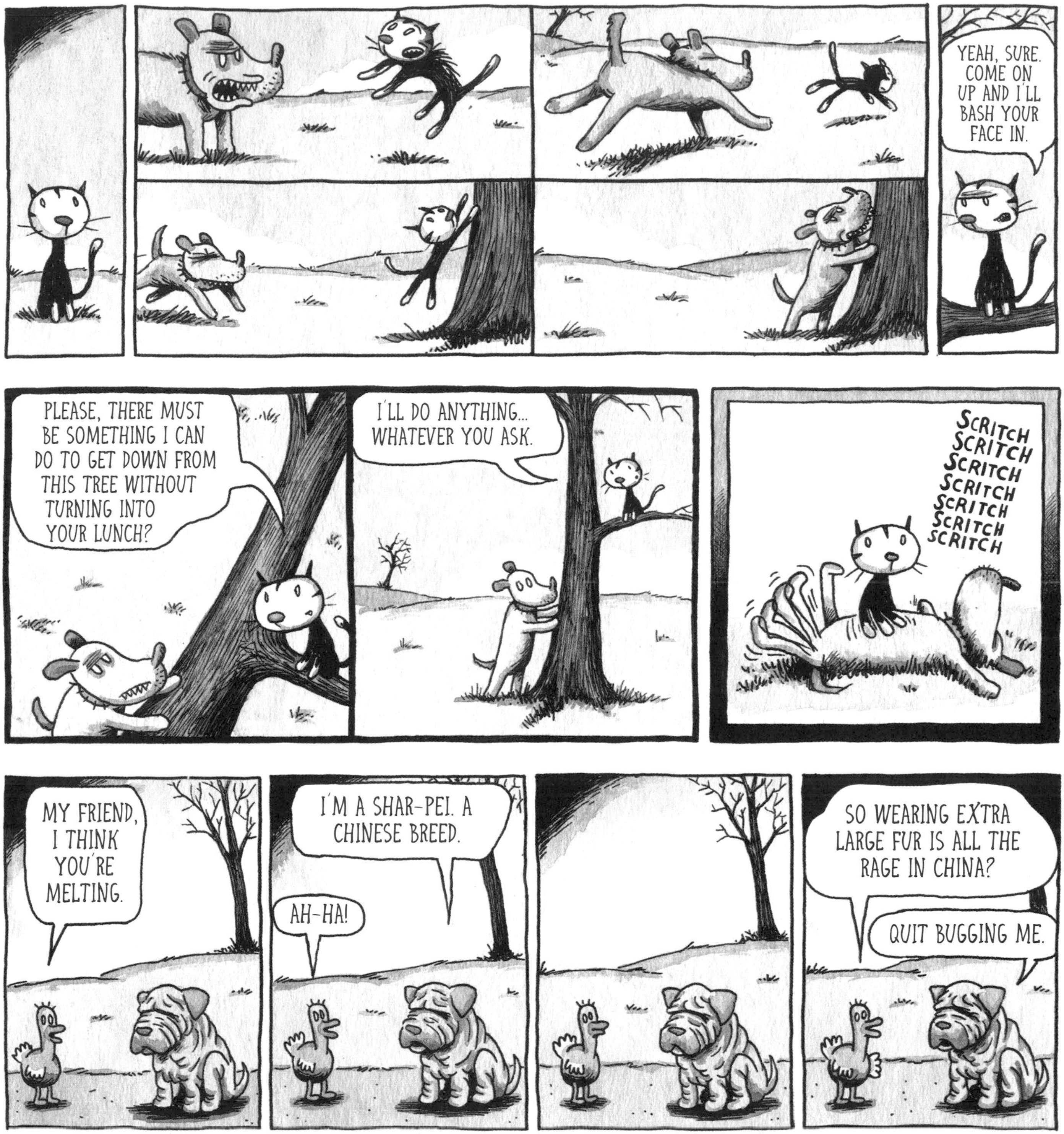
YEAH, SURE. COME ON UP AND I'LL BASH YOUR FACE IN.
PLEASE, THERE MUST BE SOMETHING I CAN DO TO GET DOWN FROM THIS TREE WITHOUT TURNING INTO YOUR LUNCH?
I'LL DO ANYTHING... WHATEVER YOU ASK.
SCRITCH SCRITCH SCRITCH SCRITCH SCRITCH SCRITCH SCRITCH
MY FRIEND, I THINK YOU'RE MELTING.
I'M A SHAR-PEI. A CHINESE BREED.
AH-HA!
SO WEARING EXTRA LARGE FUR IS ALL THE RAGE IN CHINA?
QUIT BUGGING ME.

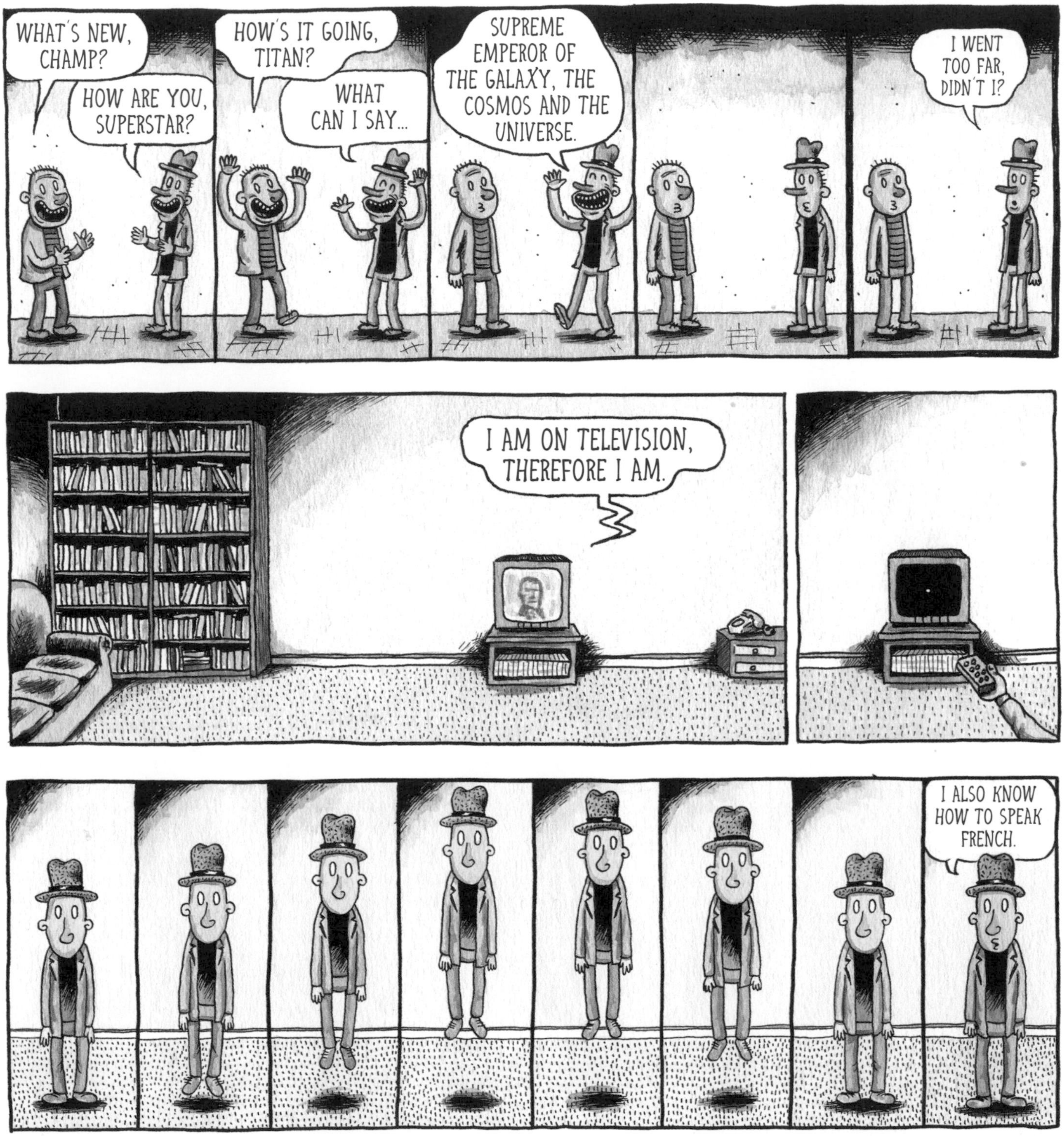
WHAT'S NEW, CHAMP?
HOW ARE YOU, SUPERSTAR?
HOW'S IT GOING, TITAN?
WHAT CAN I SAY...
SUPREME EMPEROR OF THE GALAXY, THE COSMOS AND THE UNIVERSE.
I WENT TOO FAR, DIDN'T I?
I AM ON TELEVISION, THEREFORE I AM.
I ALSO KNOW HOW TO SPEAK FRENCH.

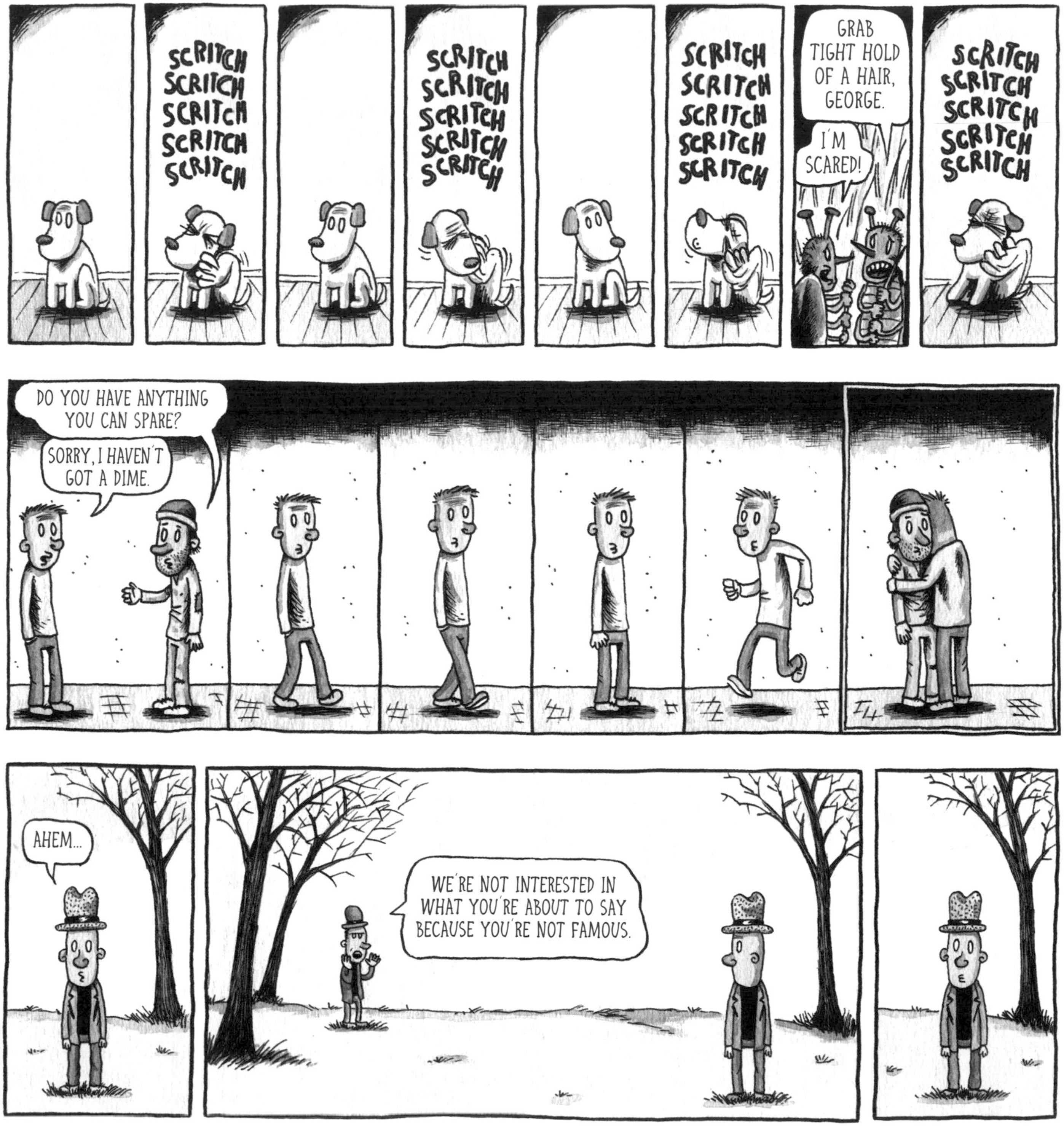
SCRITCH SCRITCH SCRITCH SCRITCH SCRITCH
SCRITCH SCRITCH SCRITCH SCRITCH SCRITCH
SCRITCH SCRITCH SCRITCH SCRITCH SCRITCH
GRAB TIGHT HOLD OF A HAIR, GEORGE.
I'M SCARED!
SCRITCH SCRITCH SCRITCH SCRITCH SCRITCH
DO YOU HAVE ANYTHING YOU CAN SPARE?
SORRY, I HAVEN'T GOT A DIME.
AHEM...
WE'RE NOT INTERESTED IN WHAT YOU'RE ABOUT TO SAY BECAUSE YOU'RE NOT FAMOUS.

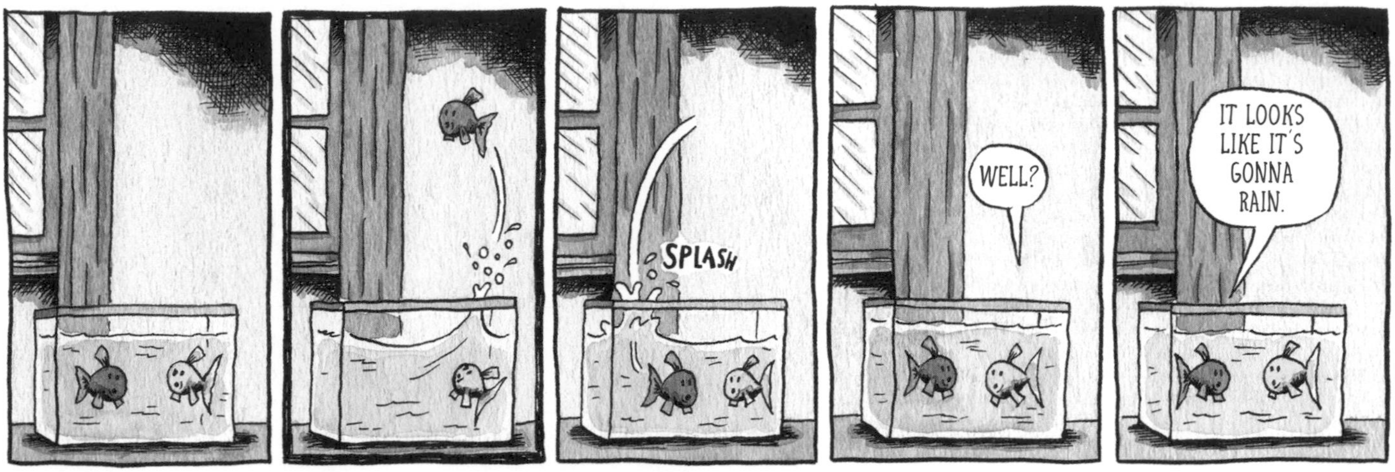
SPLASH
WELL?
IT LOOKS LIKE IT'S GONNA RAIN.

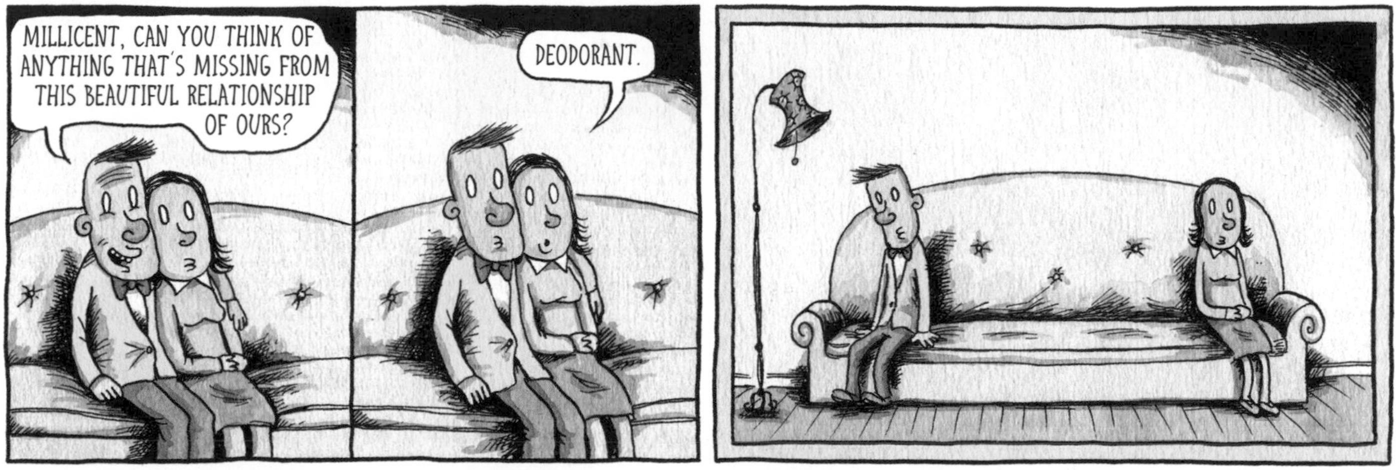
MILLICENT, CAN YOU THINK OF ANYTHING THAT'S MISSING FROM THIS BEAUTIFUL RELATIONSHIP OF OURS?
DEODORANT.

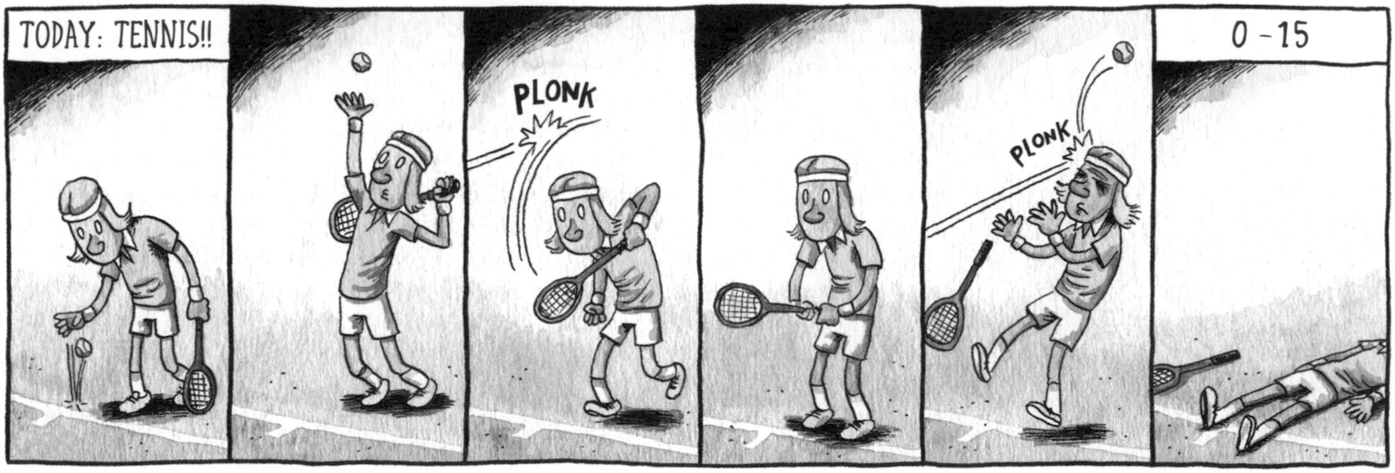
TODAY: TENNIS!!
PLONK
PLONK
0 -15

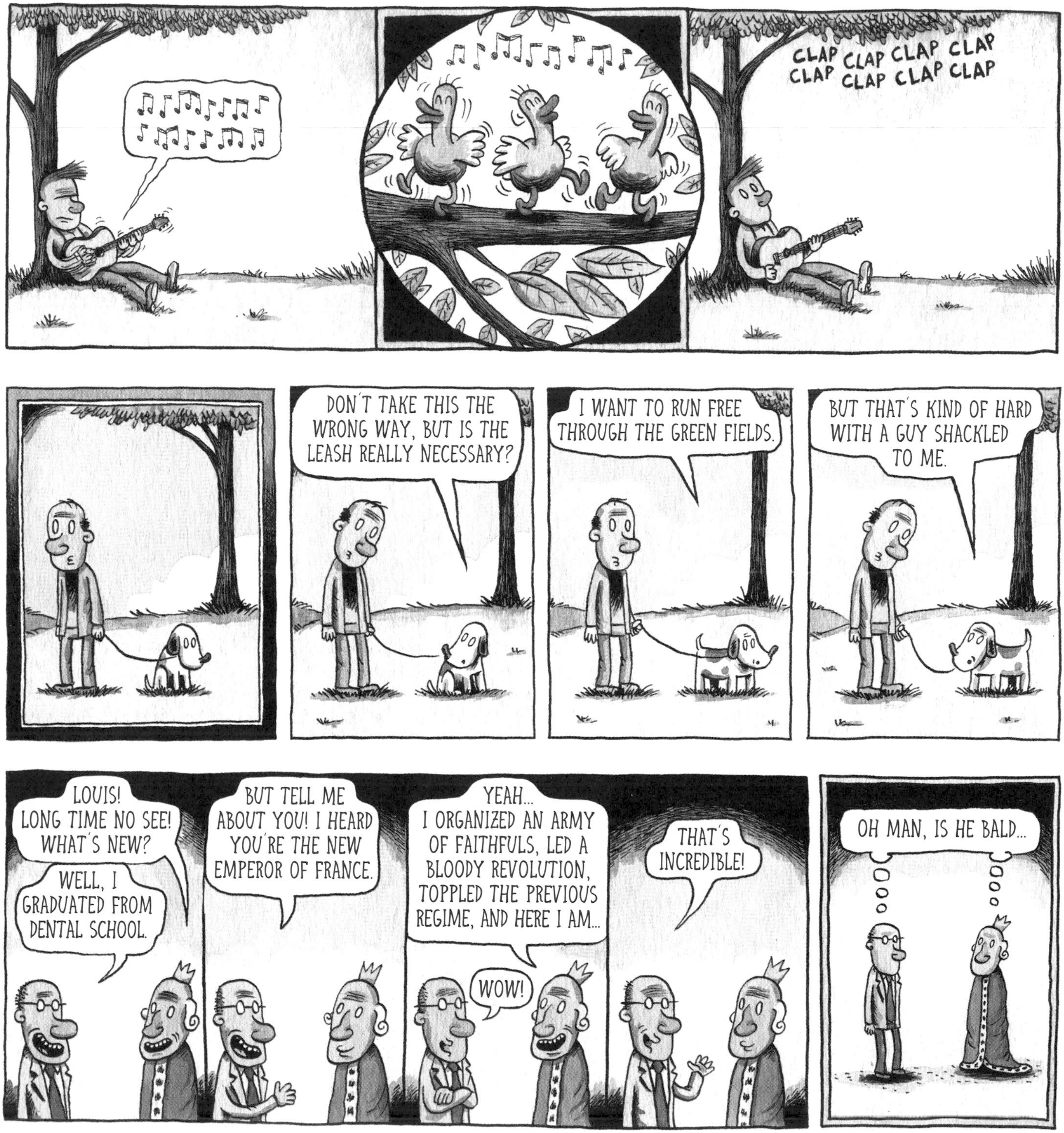
CLAP CLAP CLAP CLAP
CLAP CLAP CLAP CLAP
DON'T TAKE THIS THE WRONG WAY, BUT IS THE LEASH REALLY NECESSARY?
I WANT TO RUN FREE THROUGH THE GREEN FIELDS.
BUT THAT'S KIND OF HARD WITH A GUY SHACKLED TO ME.
LOUIS! LONG TIME NO SEE! WHAT'S NEW?
WELL, I GRADUATED FROM DENTAL SCHOOL.
BUT TELL ME ABOUT YOU! I HEARD YOU'RE THE NEW EMPEROR OF FRANCE.
YEAH... I ORGANIZED AN ARMY OF FAITHFULS, LED A BLOODY REVOLUTION, TOPPLED THE PREVIOUS REGIME, AND HERE I AM...
WOW!
THAT'S INCREDIBLE!
OH MAN, IS HE BALD...

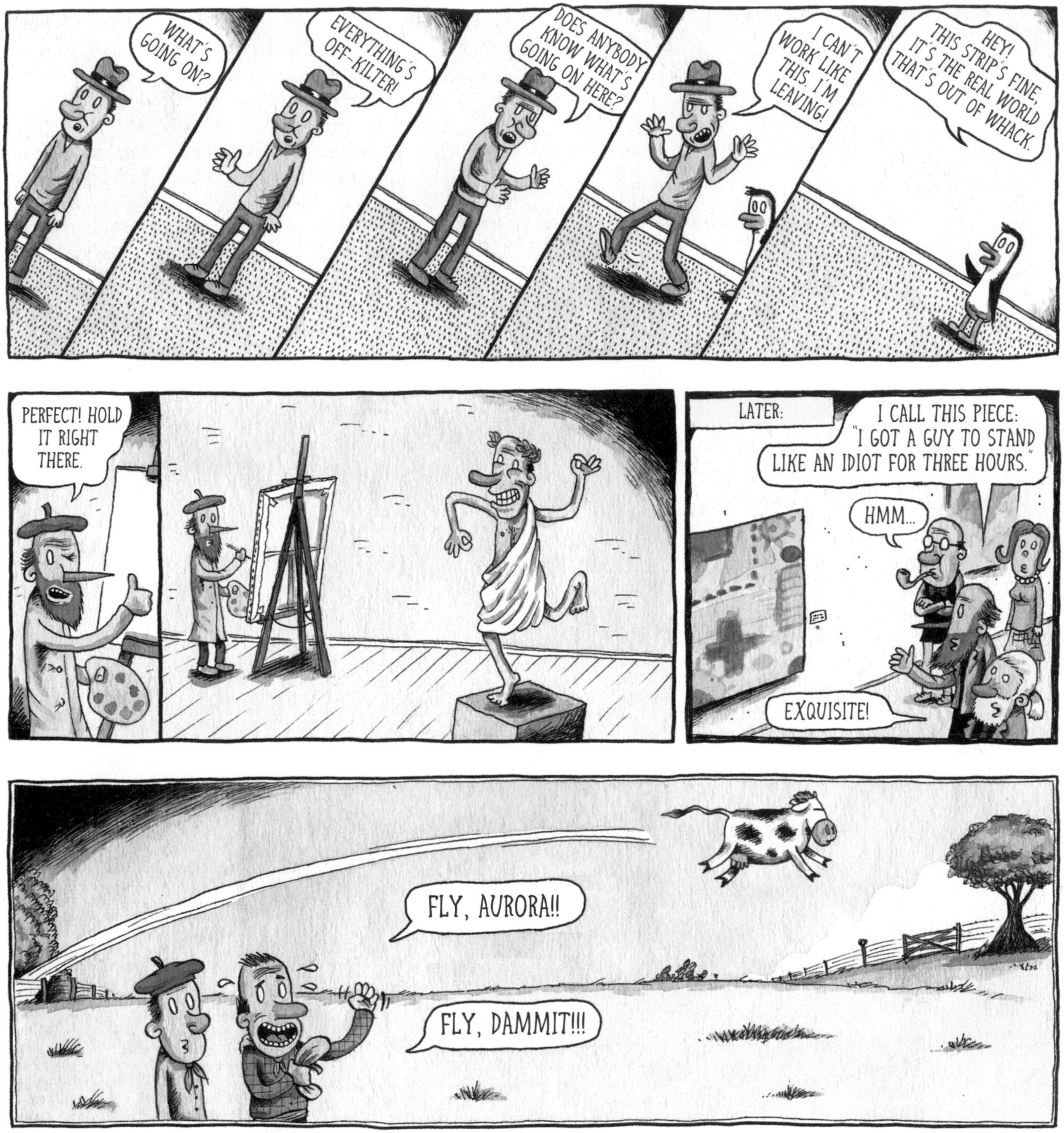
WHAT'S GOING ON?
EVERYTHING'S OFF-KILTER!
DOES ANYBODY KNOW WHAT'S GOING ON HERE?
I CAN'T WORK LIKE THIS. I'M LEAVING!
HEY! THIS STRIP'S FINE. IT'S THE REAL WORLD THAT'S OUT OF WHACK.
PERFECT! HOLD IT RIGHT THERE.
LATER:
I CALL THIS PIECE: "I GOT A GUY TO STAND LIKE AN IDIOT FOR THREE HOURS."
HMM...
EXQUISITE!
FLY, AURORA!!
FLY, DAMMIT!!!

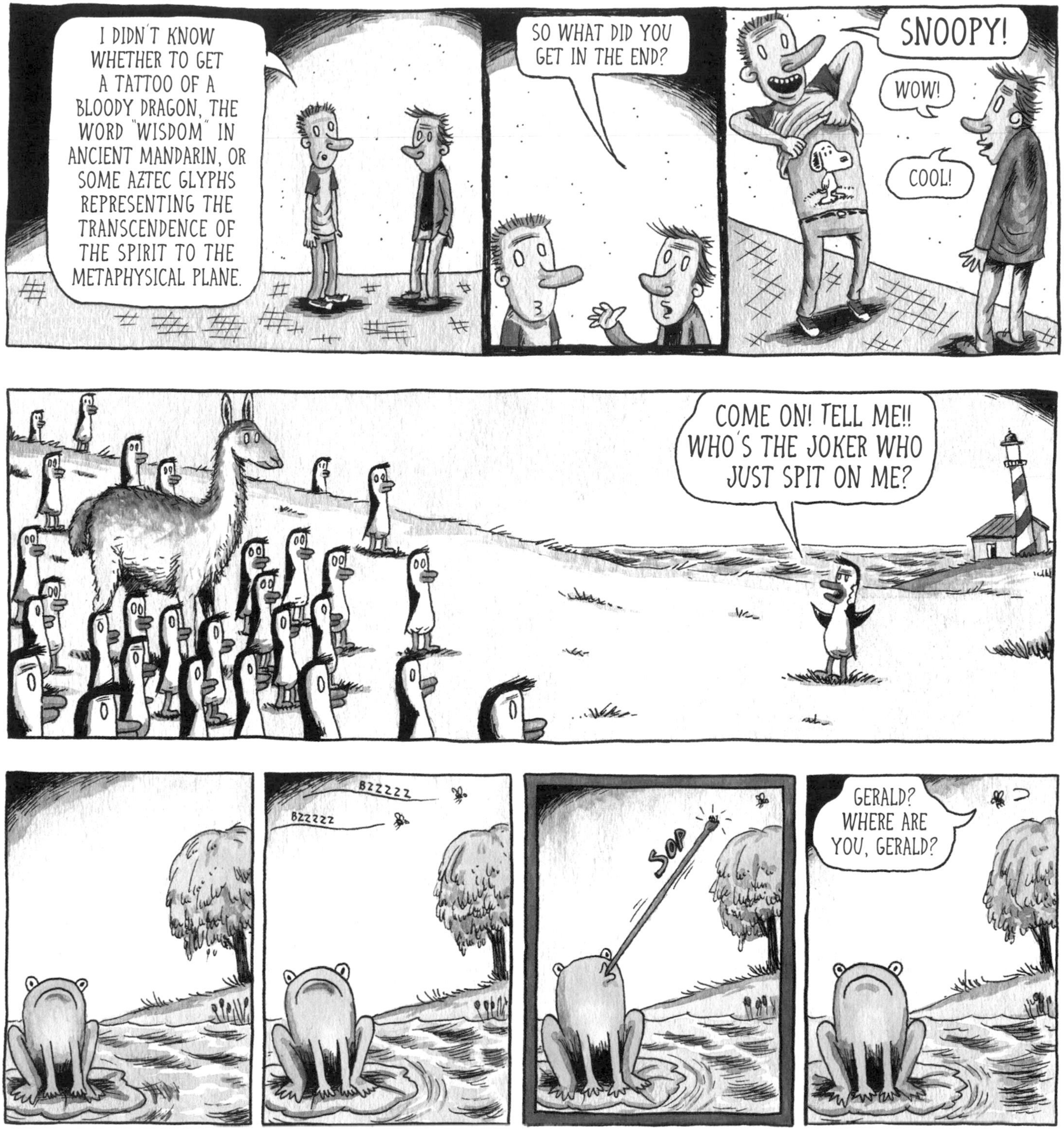
I DIDN'T KNOW WHETHER TO GET A TATTOO OF A BLOODY DRAGON, THE WORD "WISDOM" IN ANCIENT MANDARIN, OR SOME AZTEC GLYPHS REPRESENTING THE TRANSCENDENCE OF THE SPIRIT TO THE METAPHYSICAL PLANE.
SO WHAT DID YOU GET IN THE END?
SNOOPY!
WOW!
COOL!
COME ON! TELL ME!! WHO'S THE JOKER WHO JUST SPIT ON ME?
BZZZZZ
BZZZZZ
SOP
GERALD? WHERE ARE YOU, GERALD?

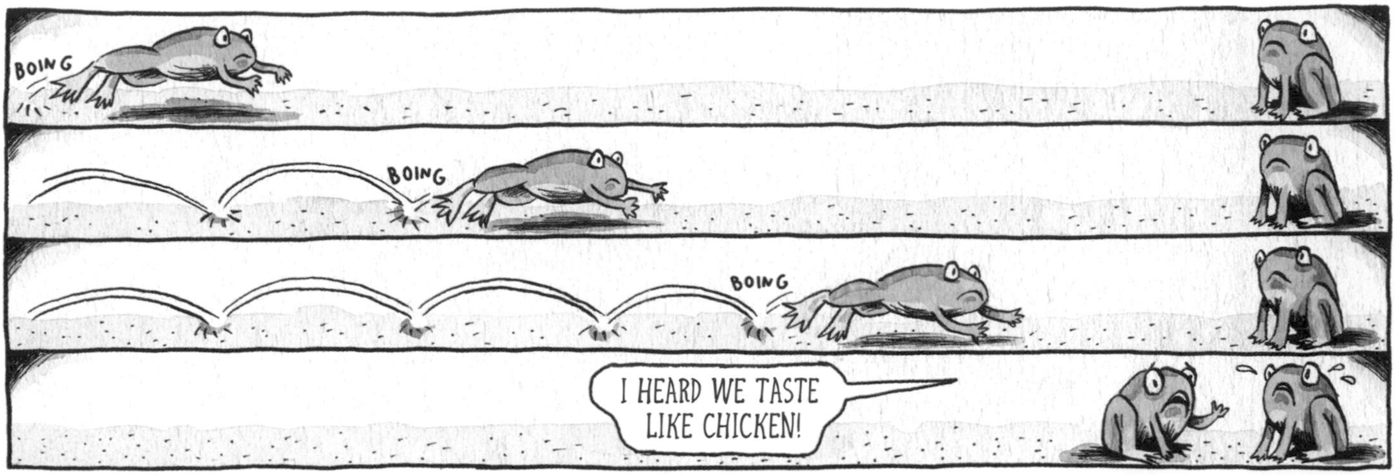
BOING
BOING
BOING
I HEARD WE TASTE LIKE CHICKEN!

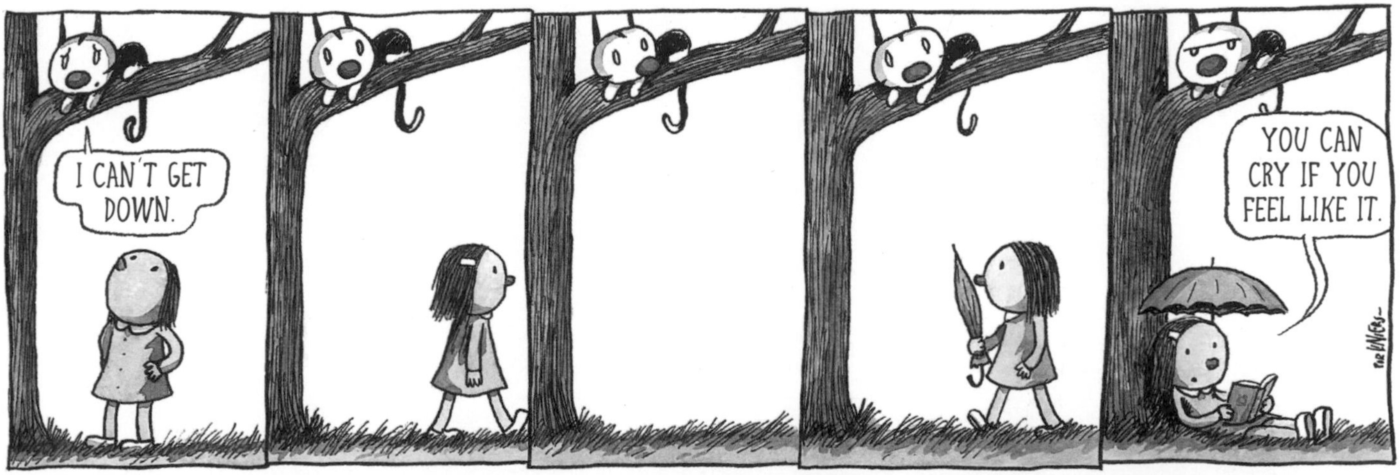
I CAN'T GET DOWN.
YOU CAN CRY IF YOU FEEL LIKE IT.

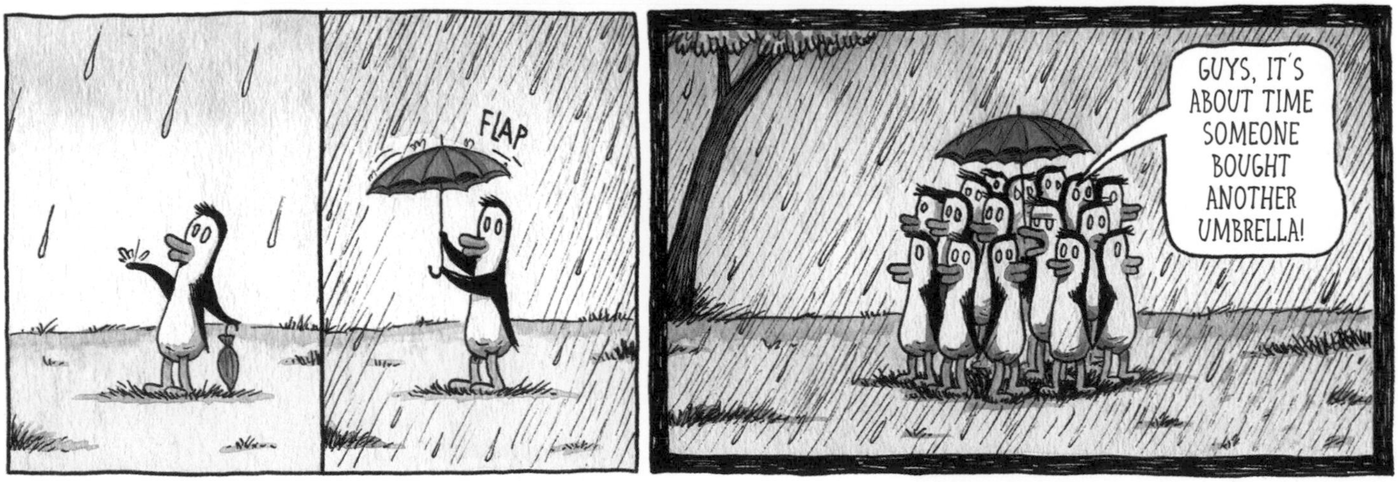
FLAP
GUYS, IT'S ABOUT TIME SOMEONE BOUGHT ANOTHER UMBRELLA!

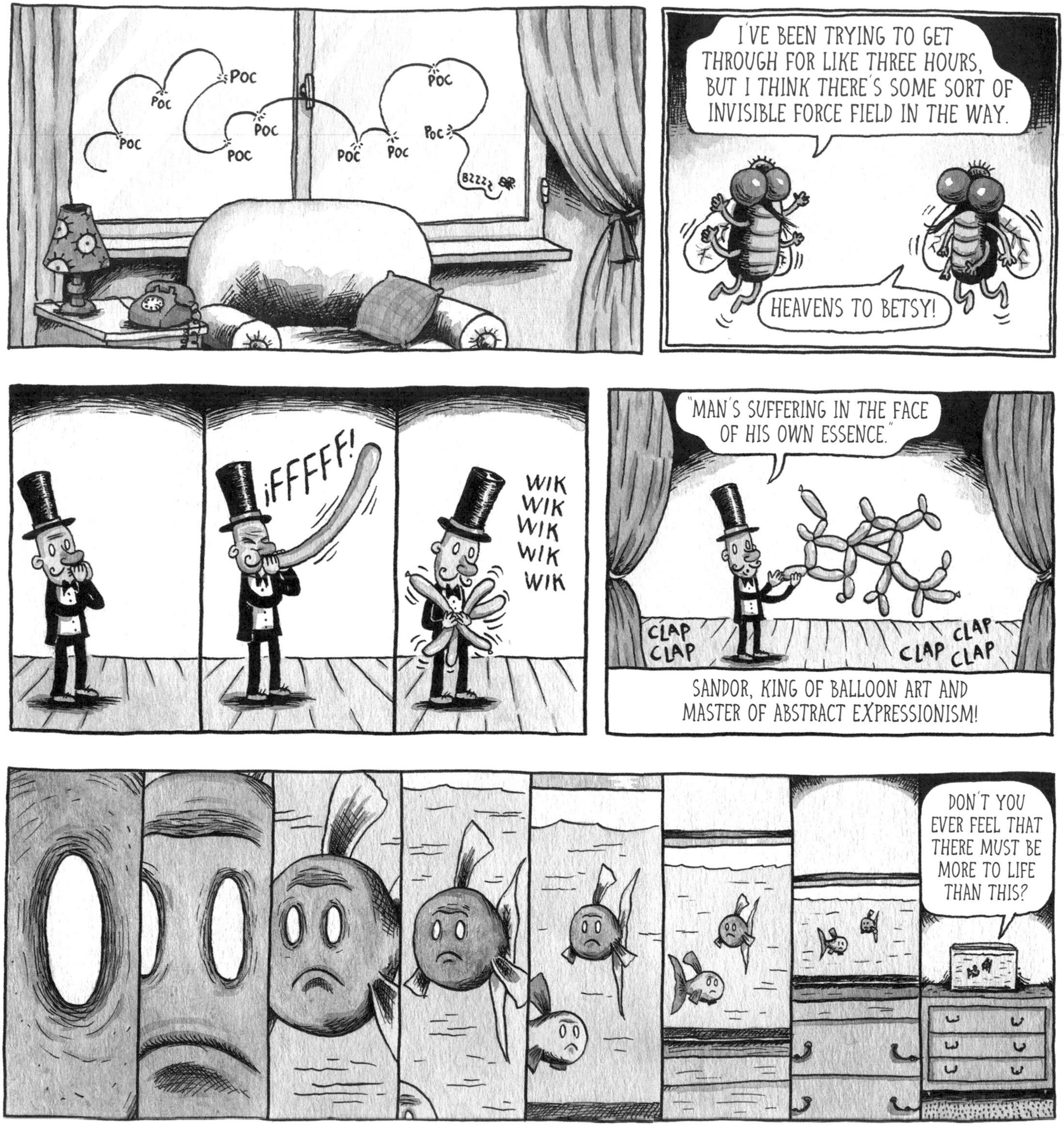
POC
POC
POC
POC
POC
POC
POC
POC
POC
BZZZZ
I'VE BEEN TRYING TO GET THROUGH FOR LIKE THREE HOURS, BUT I THINK THERE'S SOME SORT OF INVISIBLE FORCE FIELD IN THE WAY.
HEAVENS TO BETSY!
¡FFFFF!
WIK WIK WIK WIK WIK
"MAN'S SUFFERING IN THE FACE OF HIS OWN ESSENCE."
CLAP CLAP
CLAP CLAP CLAP CLAP
SANDOR, KING OF BALLOON ART AND MASTER OF ABSTRACT EXPRESSIONISM!
DON'T YOU EVER FEEL THAT THERE MUST BE MORE TO LIFE THAN THIS?

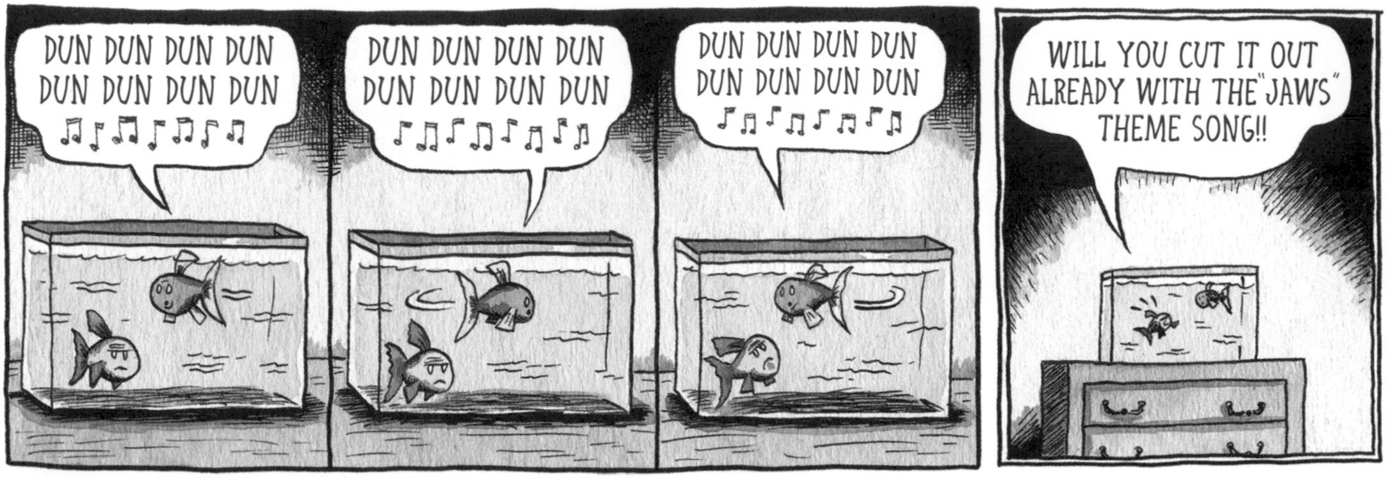
DUN DUN DUN DUN DUN DUN DUN DUN
DUN DUN DUN DUN DUN DUN DUN DUN
DUN DUN DUN DUN DUN DUN DUN DUN
WILL YOU CUT IT OUT ALREADY WITH THE "JAWS" THEME SONG!!

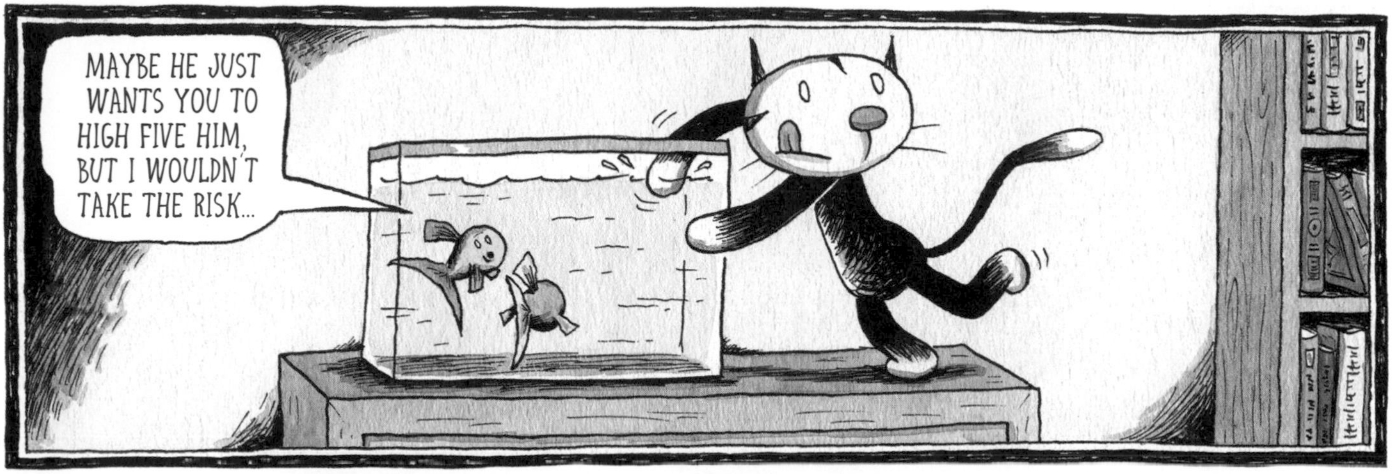
MAYBE HE JUST WANTS YOU TO HIGH FIVE HIM, BUT I WOULDN'T TAKE THE RISK...

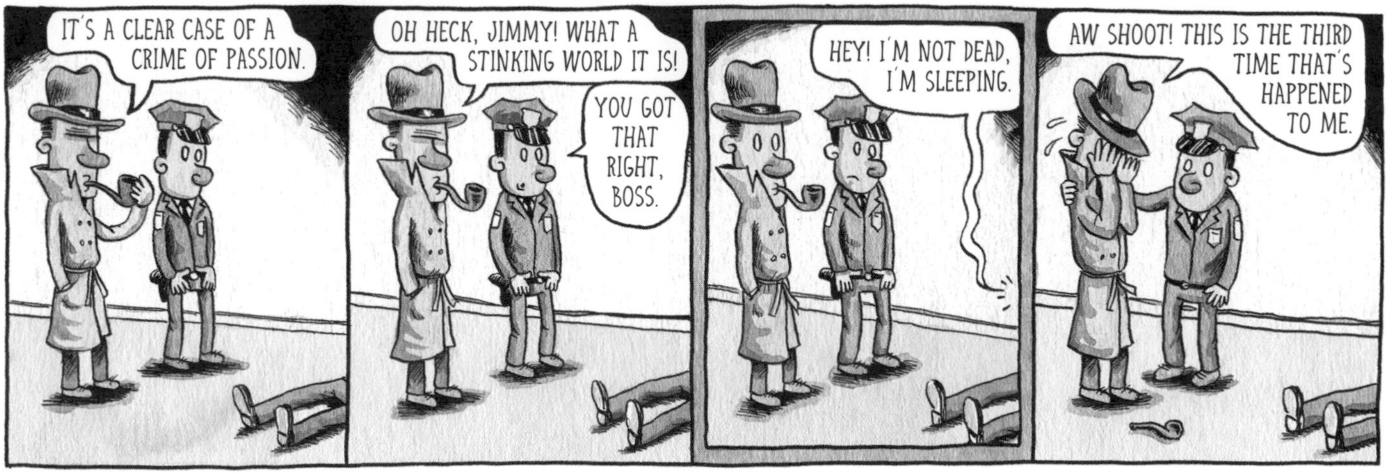
IT'S A CLEAR CASE OF A CRIME OF PASSION.
OH HECK, JIMMY! WHAT A STINKING WORLD IT IS!
YOU GOT THAT RIGHT, BOSS.
HEY! I'M NOT DEAD, I'M SLEEPING.
AW SHOOT! THIS IS THE THIRD TIME THAT'S HAPPENED TO ME.

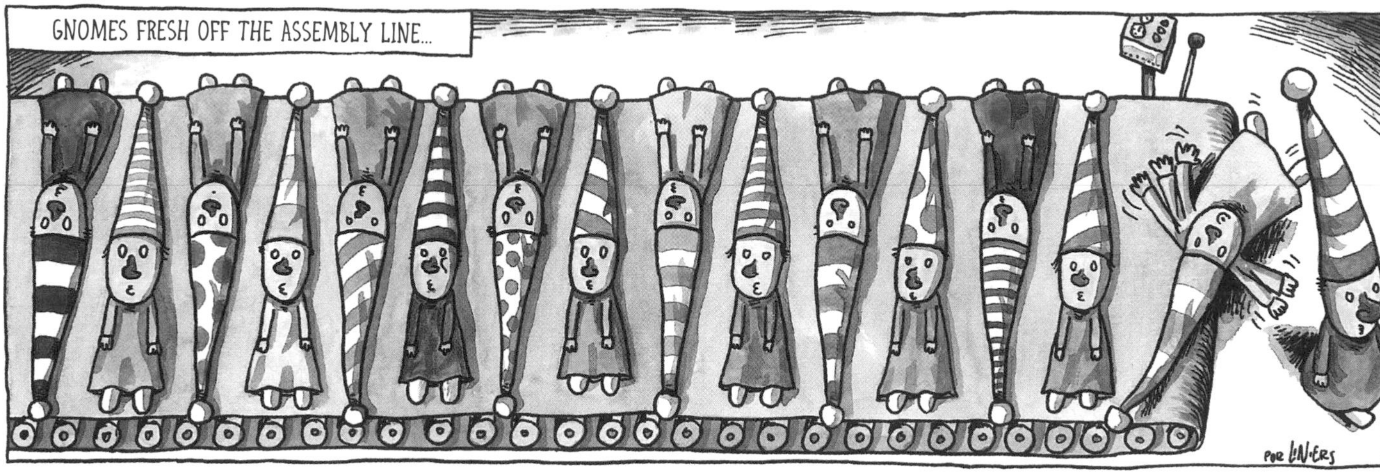
GNOMES FRESH OFF THE ASSEMBLY LINE...
POR LINIERS

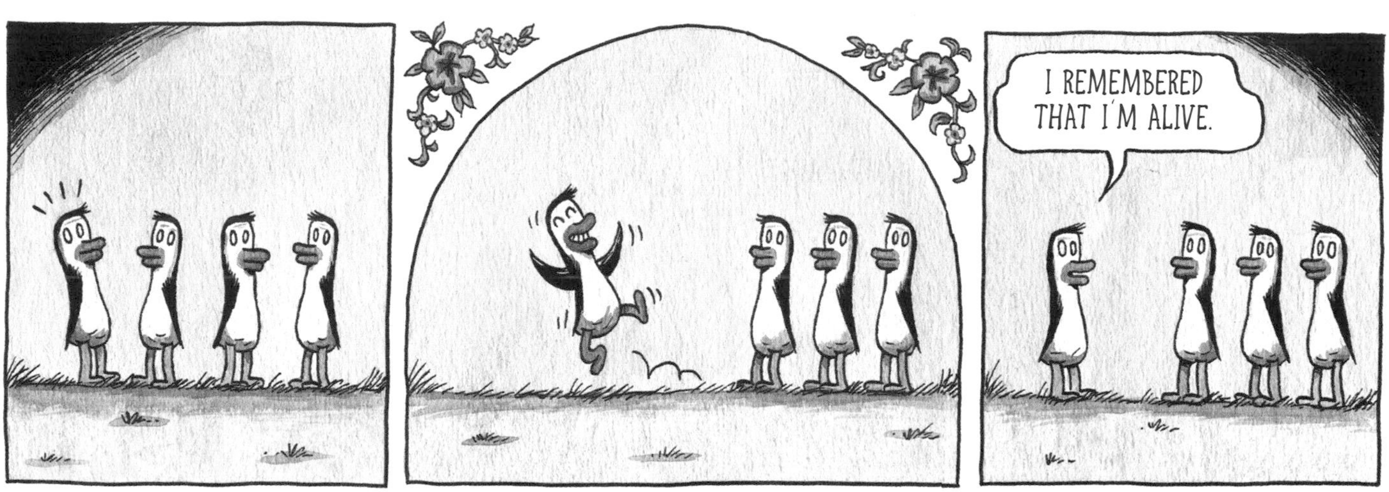
I REMEMBERED THAT I'M ALIVE.

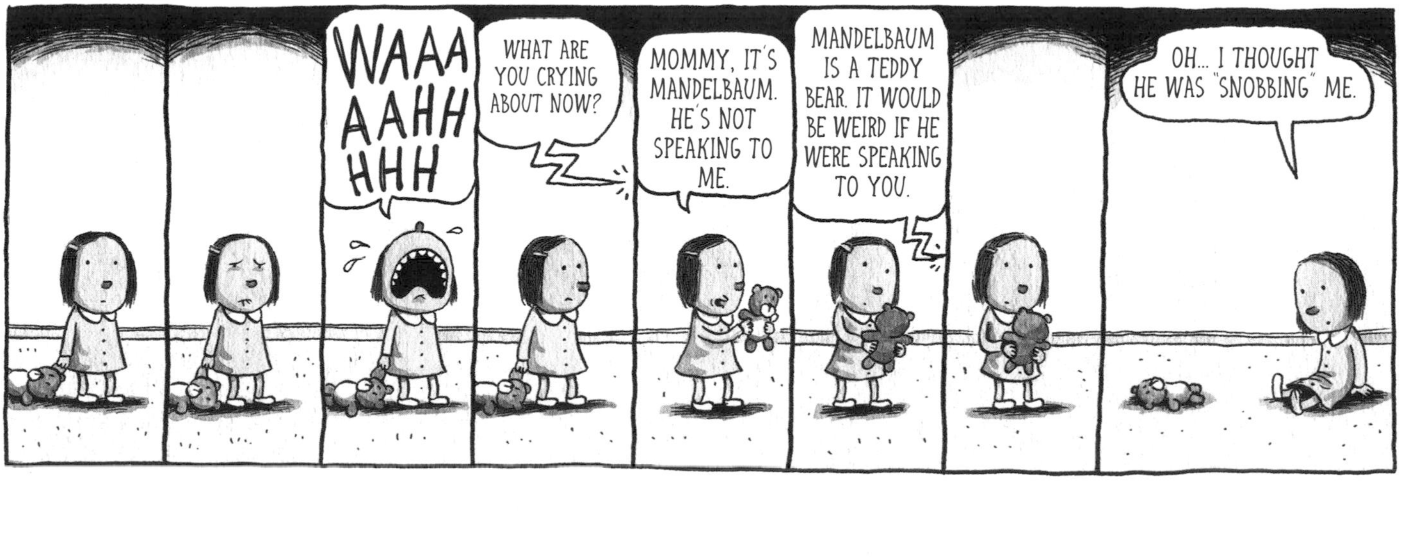
WAAAAAHHHHH
WHAT ARE YOU CRYING ABOUT NOW?
MOMMY, IT'S MANDELBAUM. HE'S NOT SPEAKING TO ME.
MANDELBAUM IS A TEDDY BEAR. IT WOULD BE WEIRD IF HE WERE SPEAKING TO YOU.
OH... I THOUGHT HE WAS "SNOBBING" ME.

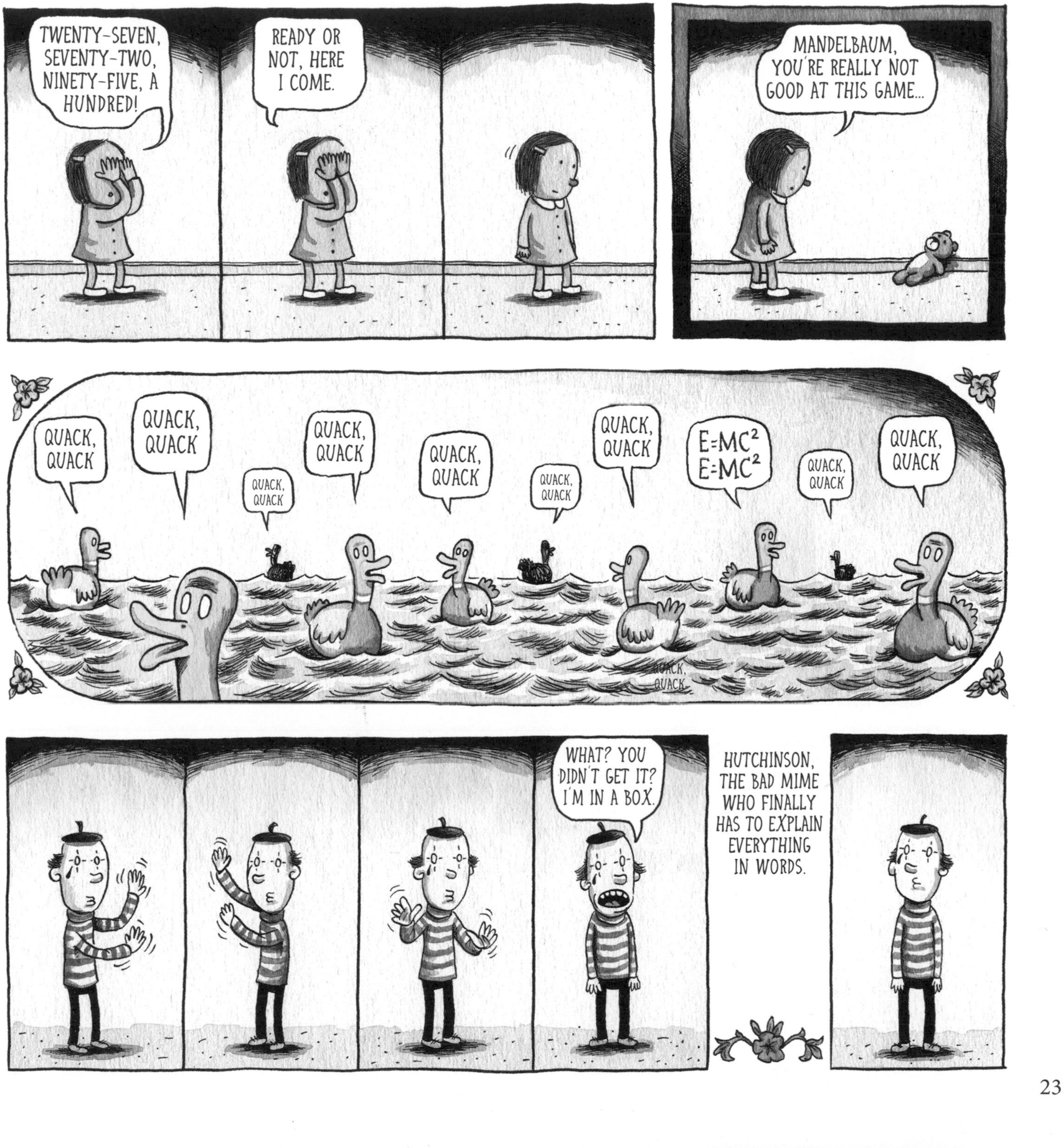
TWENTY-SEVEN, SEVENTY-TWO, NINETY-FIVE, A HUNDRED!
READY OR NOT, HERE I COME.
MANDELBAUM, YOU'RE REALLY NOT GOOD AT THIS GAME...
QUACK, QUACK
QUACK, QUACK
QUACK, QUACK
QUACK, QUACK
QUACK, QUACK
QUACK, QUACK
QUACK, QUACK
E=MC²
E=MC²
QUACK, QUACK
QUACK, QUACK
QUACK, QUACK
WHAT? YOU DIDN'T GET IT? I'M IN A BOX.
HUTCHINSON, THE BAD MIME WHO FINALLY HAS TO EXPLAIN EVERYTHING IN WORDS.

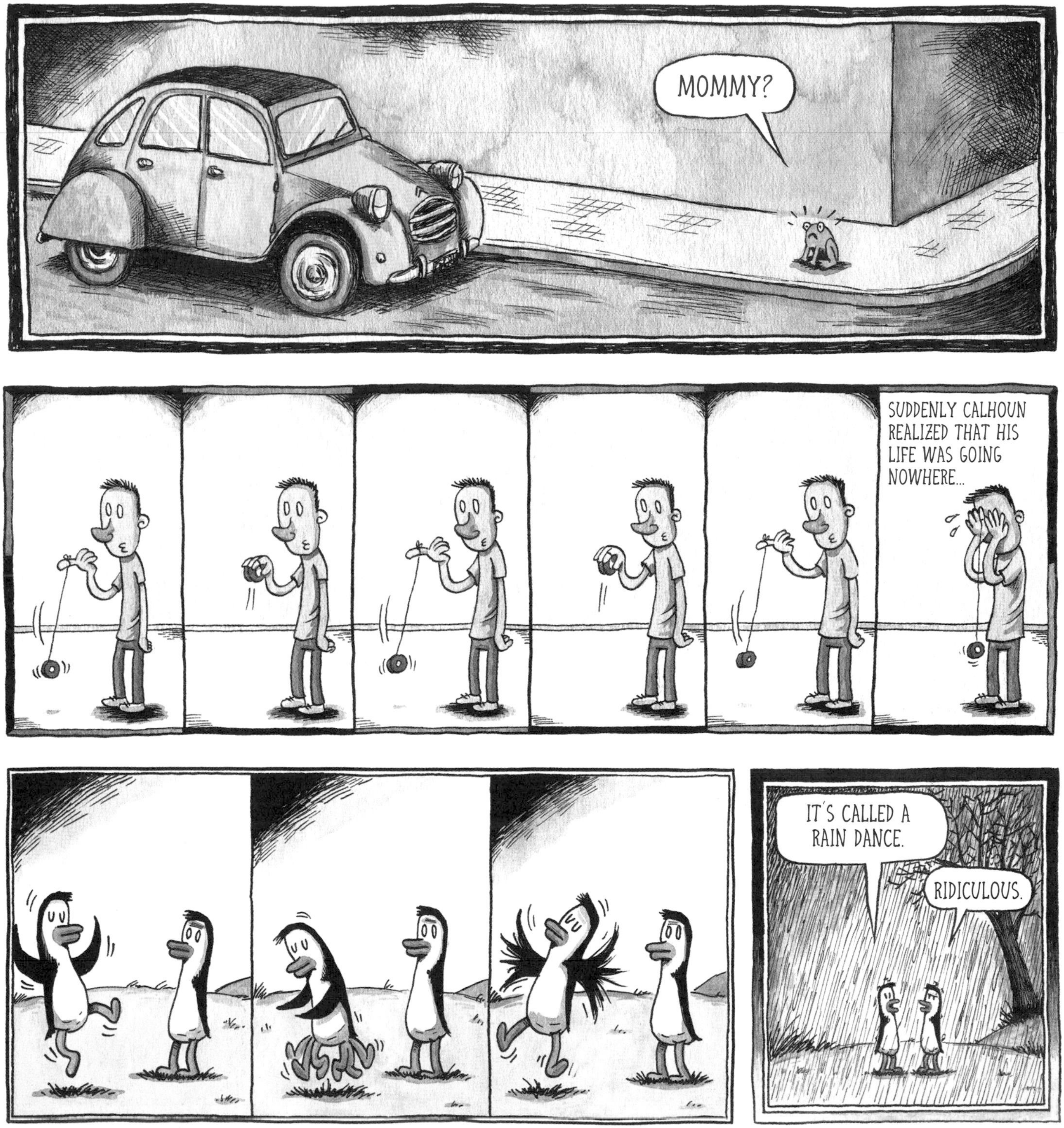
MOMMY?
SUDDENLY CALHOUN REALIZED THAT HIS LIFE WAS GOING NOWHERE...
IT'S CALLED A RAIN DANCE.
RIDICULOUS.

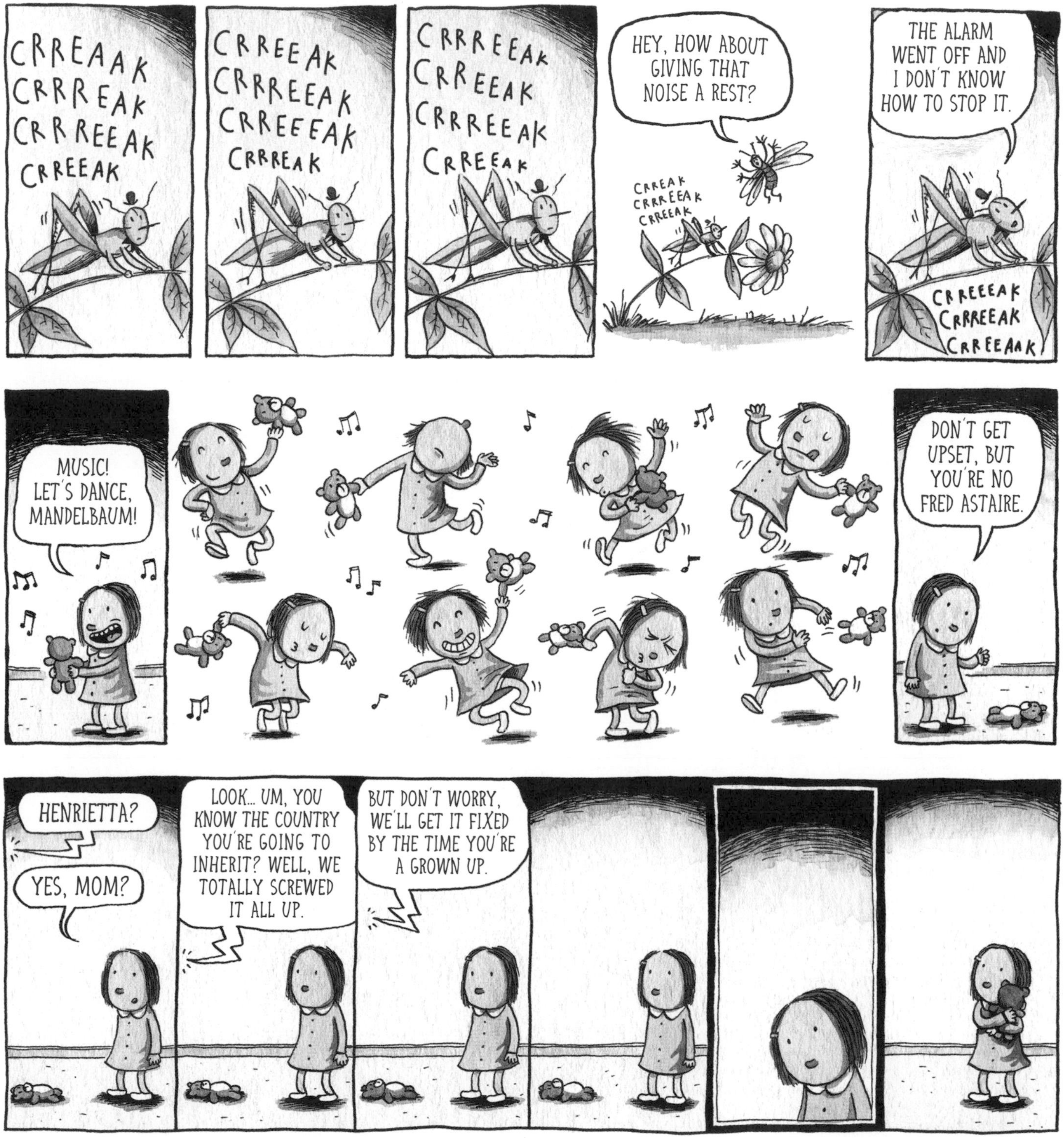
CRREAAK
CRRREAK
CRRREEAK
CRREEAK
CRREEAK
CRRREEAK
CRREEEEAK
CRRREAK
CRRREEAK
CRREEAK
CRRREEAK
CREEAK
HEY, HOW ABOUT GIVING THAT NOISE A REST?
CRREAK
CRRREEAK
CRREEAK
THE ALARM WENT OFF AND I DON'T KNOW HOW TO STOP IT.
CRREEEAK
CRRREEAK
CRREEAAK
MUSIC! LET'S DANCE, MANDELBAUM!
DON'T GET UPSET, BUT YOU'RE NO FRED ASTAIRE.
HENRIETTA?
YES, MOM?
LOOK... UM, YOU KNOW THE COUNTRY YOU'RE GOING TO INHERIT? WELL, WE TOTALLY SCREWED IT ALL UP.
BUT DON'T WORRY, WE'LL GET IT FIXED BY THE TIME YOU'RE A GROWN UP.

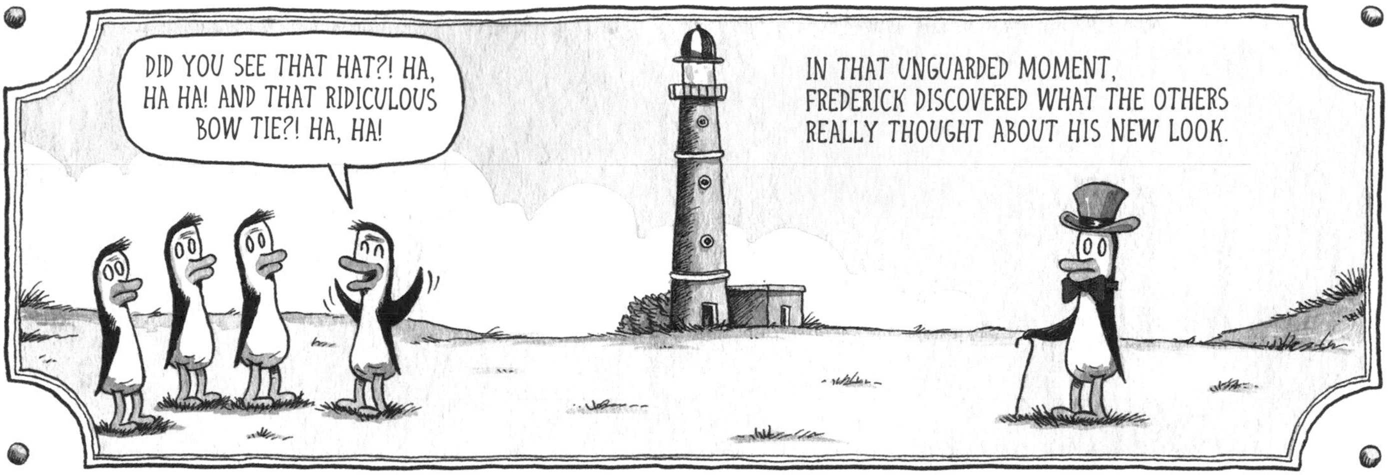
DID YOU SEE THAT HAT?! HA, HA HA! AND THAT RIDICULOUS BOW TIE?! HA, HA!
IN THAT UNGUARDED MOMENT, FREDERICK DISCOVERED WHAT THE OTHERS REALLY THOUGHT ABOUT HIS NEW LOOK.

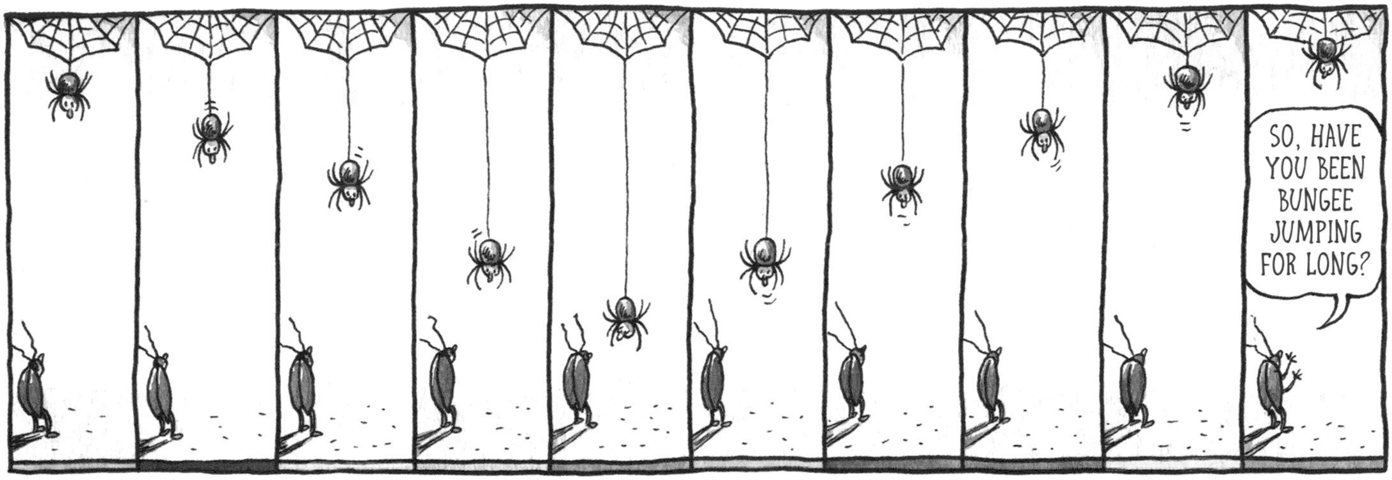
SO, HAVE YOU BEEN BUNGEE JUMPING FOR LONG?

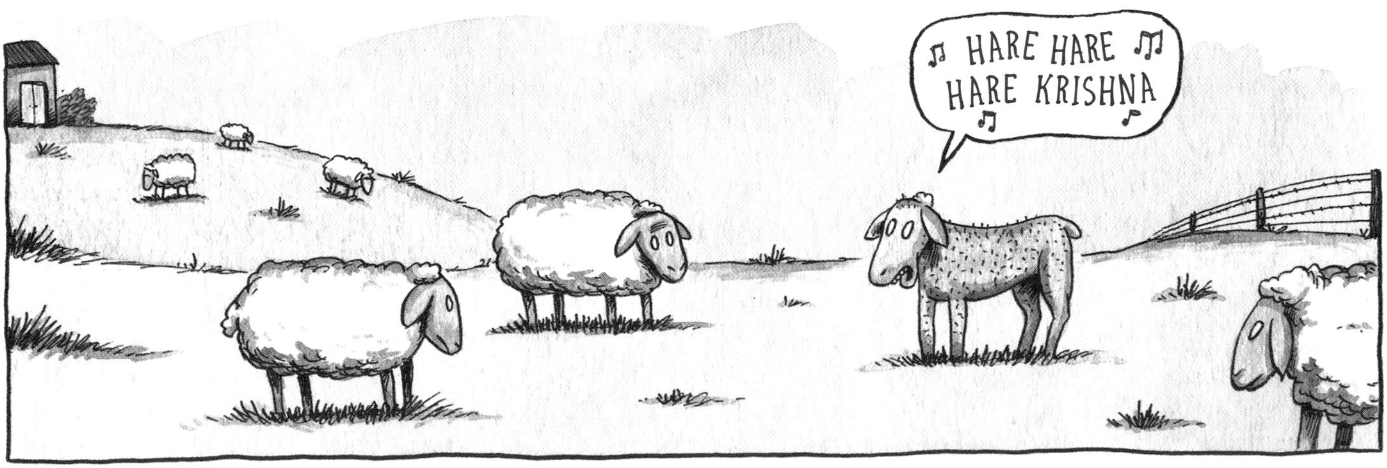
HARE HARE HARE KRISHNA

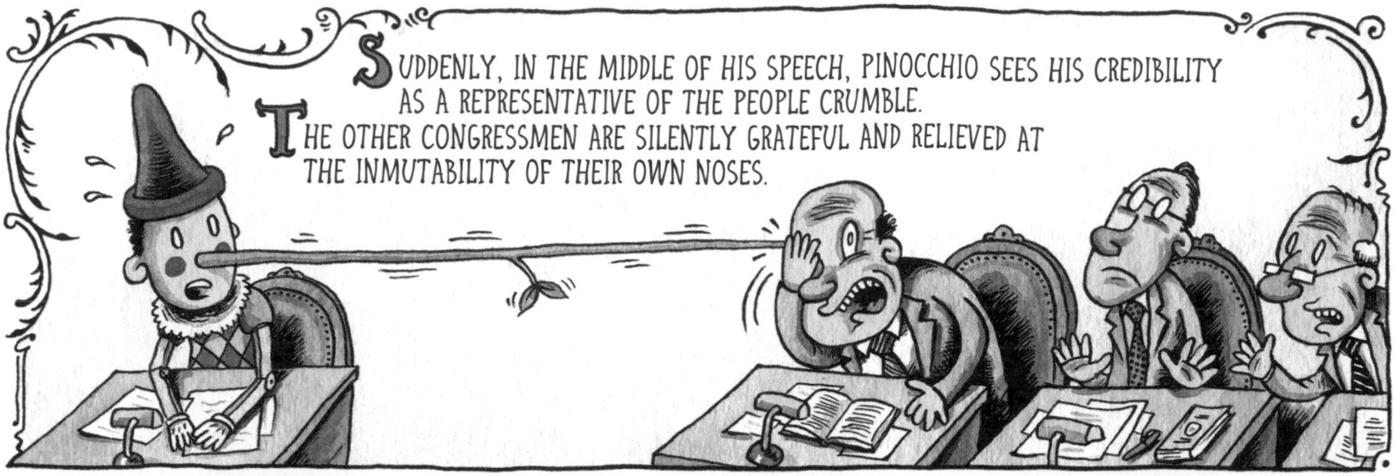
SUDDENLY, IN THE MIDDLE OF HIS SPEECH, PINOCCHIO SEES HIS CREDIBILITY AS A REPRESENTATIVE OF THE PEOPLE CRUMBLE.
THE OTHER CONGRESSMEN ARE SILENTLY GRATEFUL AND RELIEVED AT THE INMUTABILITY OF THEIR OWN NOSES.

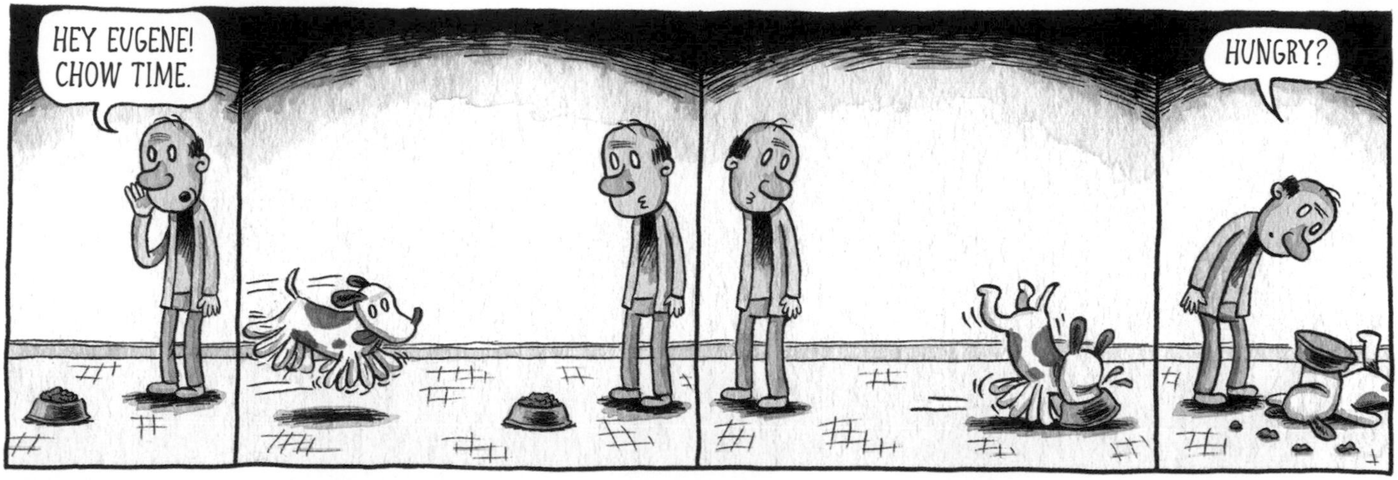
HEY EUGENE! CHOW TIME.
HUNGRY?

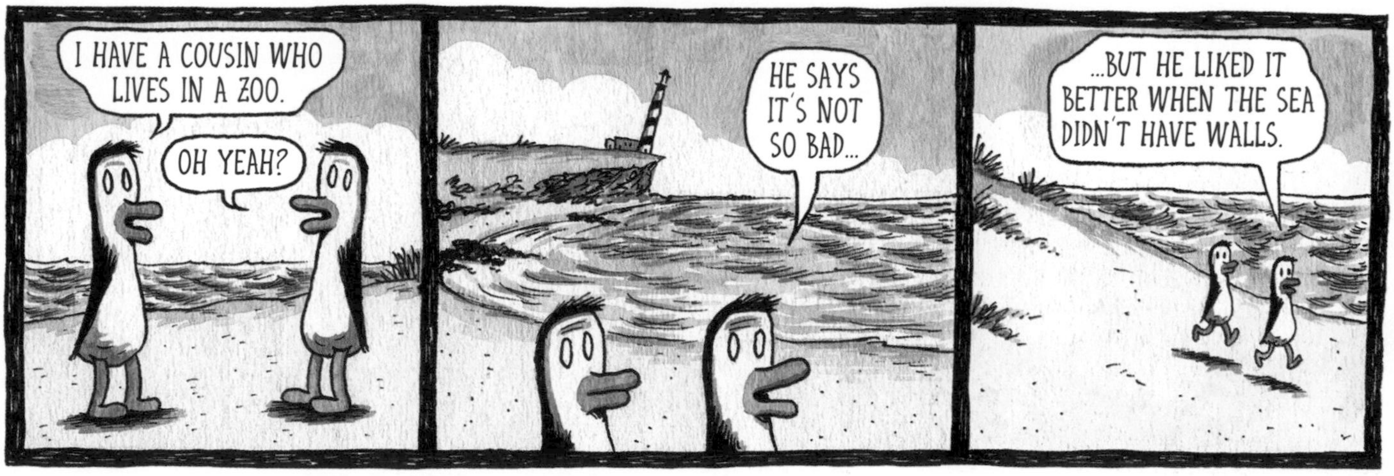
I HAVE A COUSIN WHO LIVES IN A ZOO.
OH YEAH?
HE SAYS IT'S NOT SO BAD...
...BUT HE LIKED IT BETTER WHEN THE SEA DIDN'T HAVE WALLS.

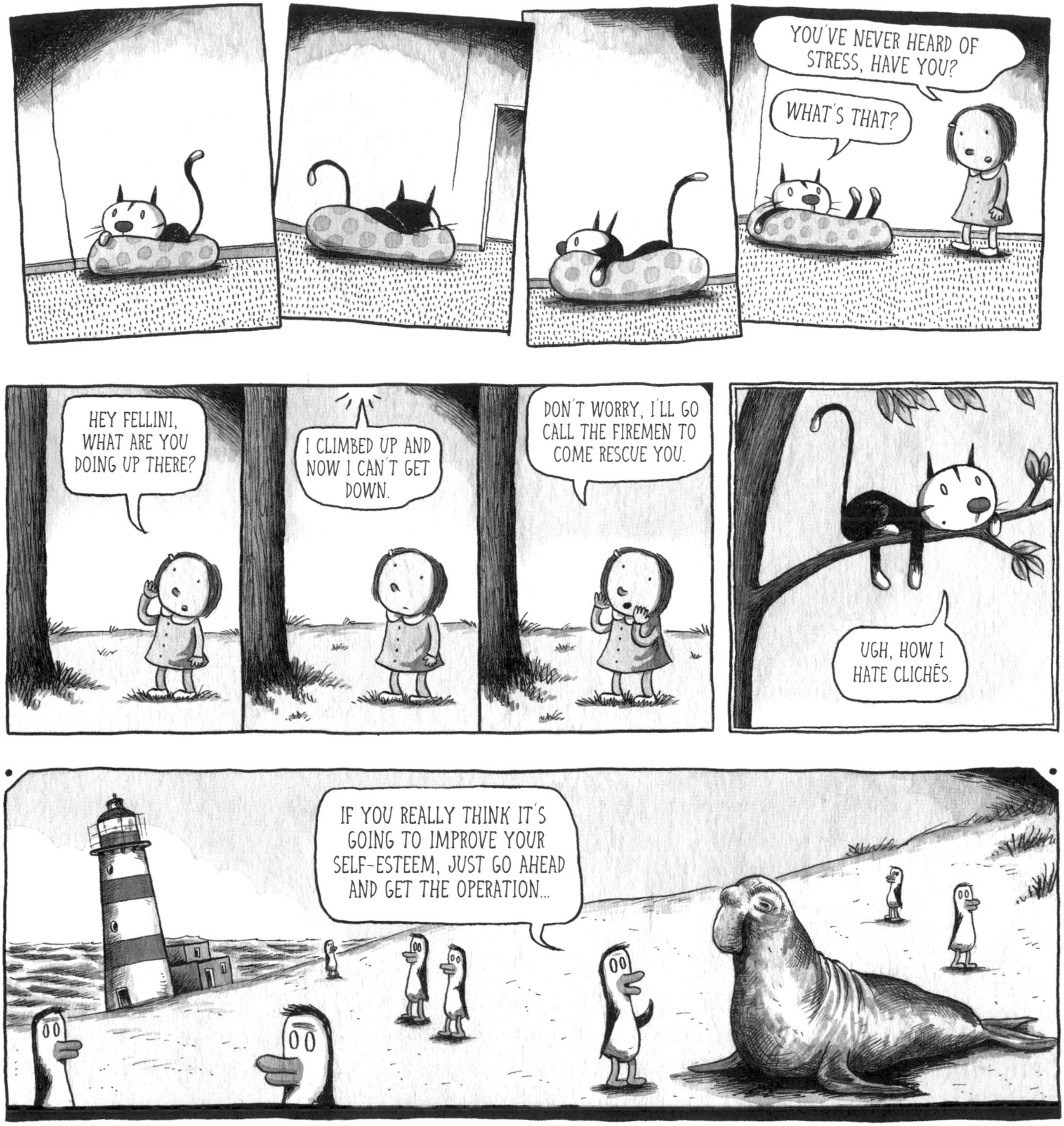
YOU'VE NEVER HEARD OF STRESS, HAVE YOU?
WHAT'S THAT?
HEY FELLINI, WHAT ARE YOU DOING UP THERE?
I CLIMBED UP AND NOW I CAN'T GET DOWN.
DON'T WORRY, I'LL GO CALL THE FIREMEN TO COME RESCUE YOU.
UGH, HOW I HATE CLICHÉS.
IF YOU REALLY THINK IT'S GOING TO IMPROVE YOUR SELF-ESTEEM, JUST GO AHEAD AND GET THE OPERATION...

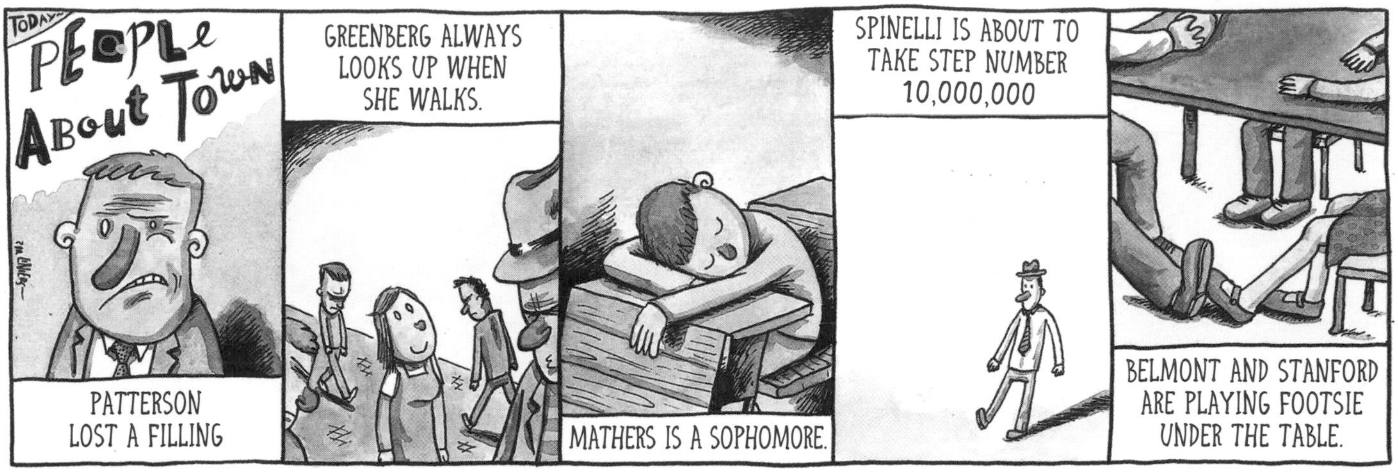
PEOPLE About Town
PATTERSON LOST A FILLING
GREENBERG ALWAYS LOOKS UP WHEN SHE WALKS.
MATHERS IS A SOPHOMORE.
SPINELLI IS ABOUT TO TAKE STEP NUMBER 10,000,000
BELMONT AND STANFORD ARE PLAYING FOOTSIE UNDER THE TABLE.

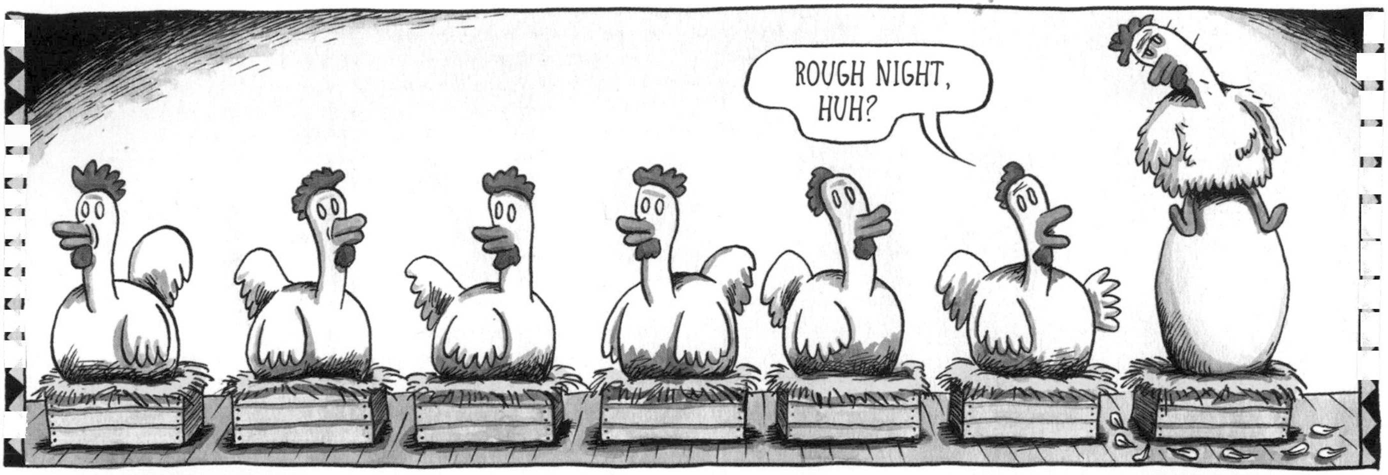
ROUGH NIGHT, HUH?

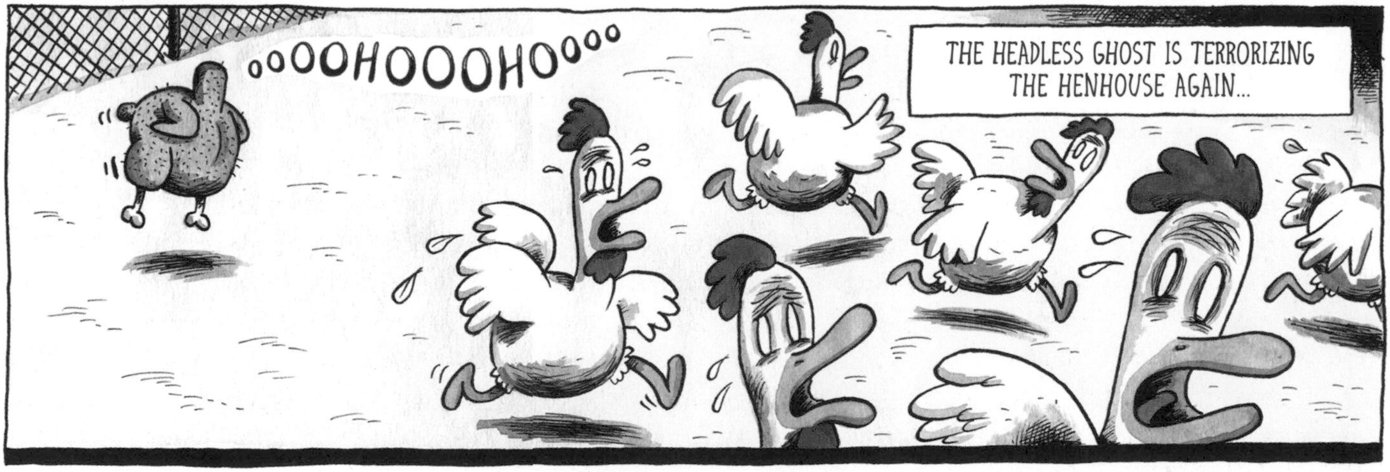
ooOOHOOOOHOooo
THE HEADLESS GHOST IS TERRORIZING THE HENHOUSE AGAIN...

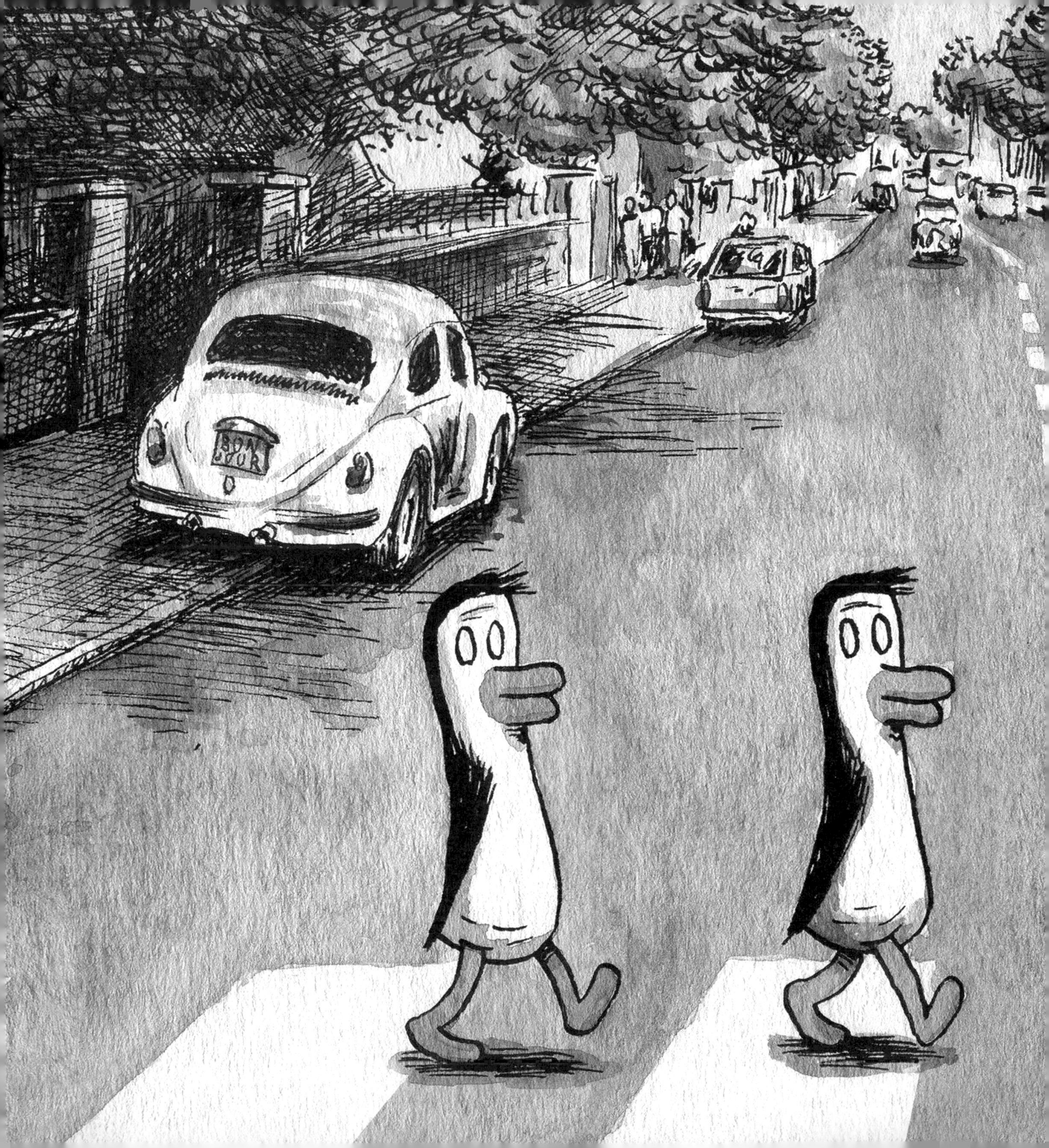
BON

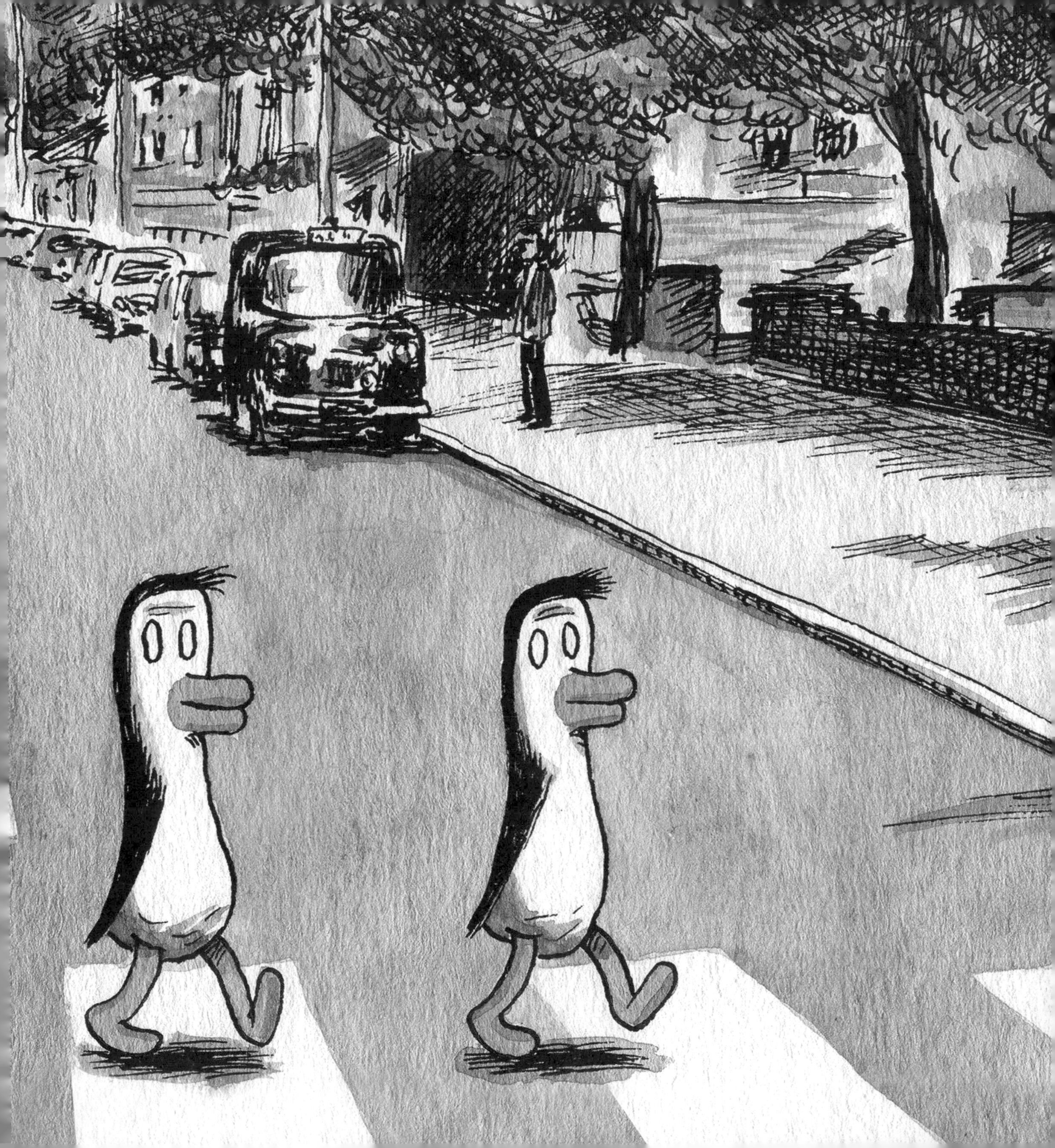

BENNETT

"NOTHING INTERESTING EVER HAPPENS IN MY LIFE, NOT A SINGLE THING WORTH EVEN MENTIONING..."

LOUIS THE HIPPO

"ALL RIGHT, I'M GONNA ASK THE NEXT GUY I SEE IF HE WANTS TO FORM A SUPERHERO DUO AND FIGHT ON THE SIDE OF GOOD AND JUSTICE..."

C'EST LA VIE!!

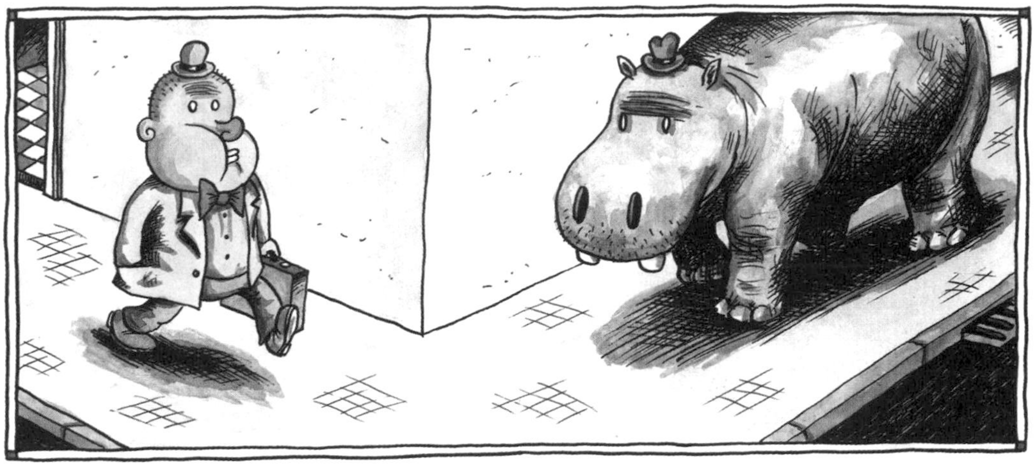

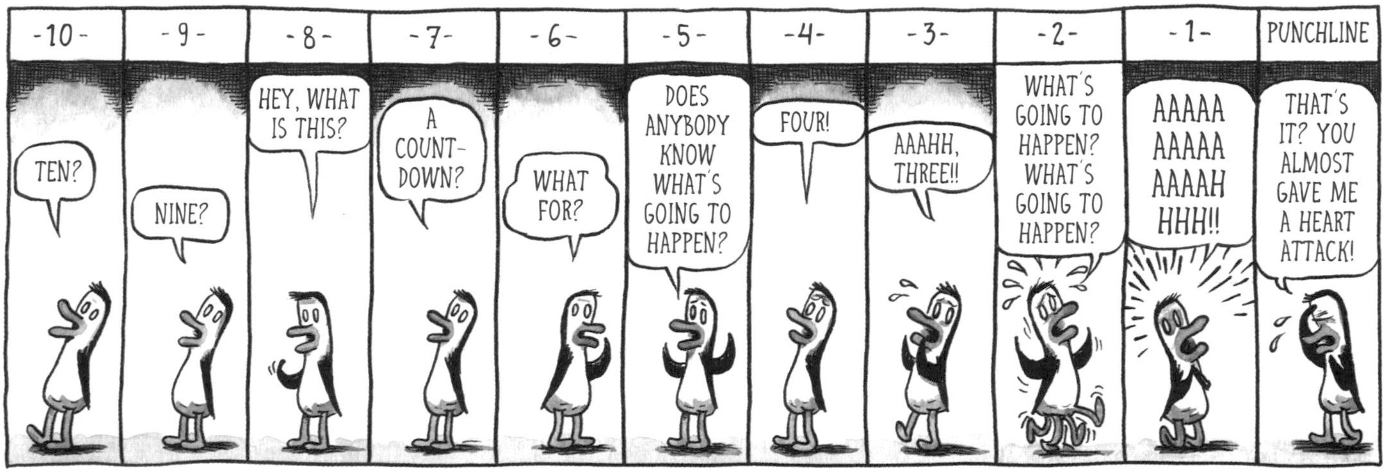
-10-
TEN?
-9-
NINE?
-8-
HEY, WHAT IS THIS?
-7-
A COUNT-DOWN?
-6-
WHAT FOR?
-5-
DOES ANYBODY KNOW WHAT'S GOING TO HAPPEN?
-4-
FOUR!
-3-
AAAHH, THREE!!
-2-
WHAT'S GOING TO HAPPEN? WHAT'S GOING TO HAPPEN?
-1-
AAAAA AAAAA AAAAH HHH!!
PUNCHLINE
THAT'S IT? YOU ALMOST GAVE ME A HEART ATTACK!

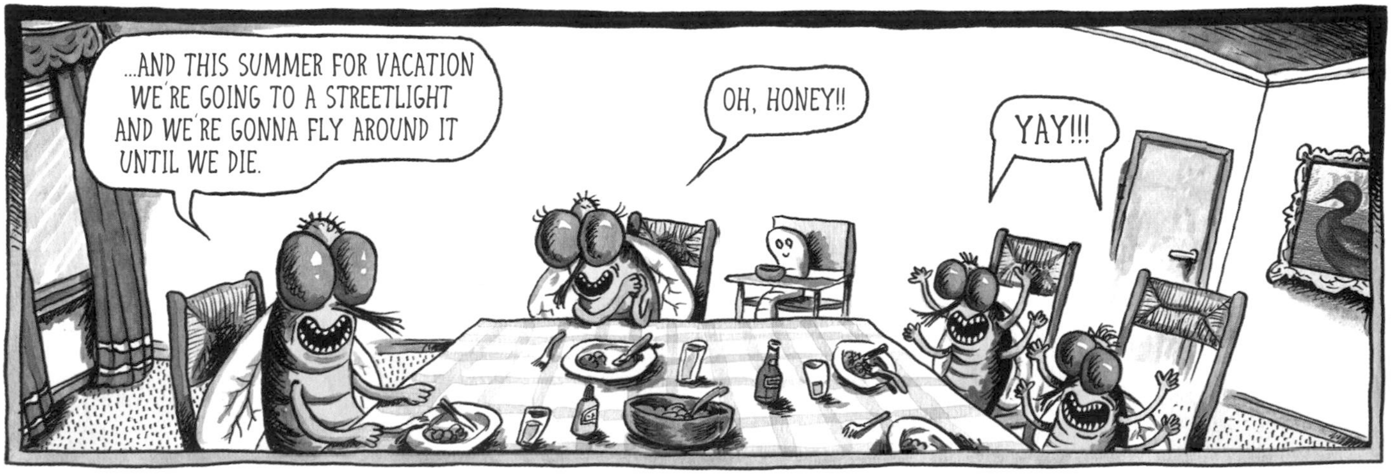
...AND THIS SUMMER FOR VACATION WE'RE GOING TO A STREETLIGHT AND WE'RE GONNA FLY AROUND IT UNTIL WE DIE.
OH, HONEY!!
YAY!!!

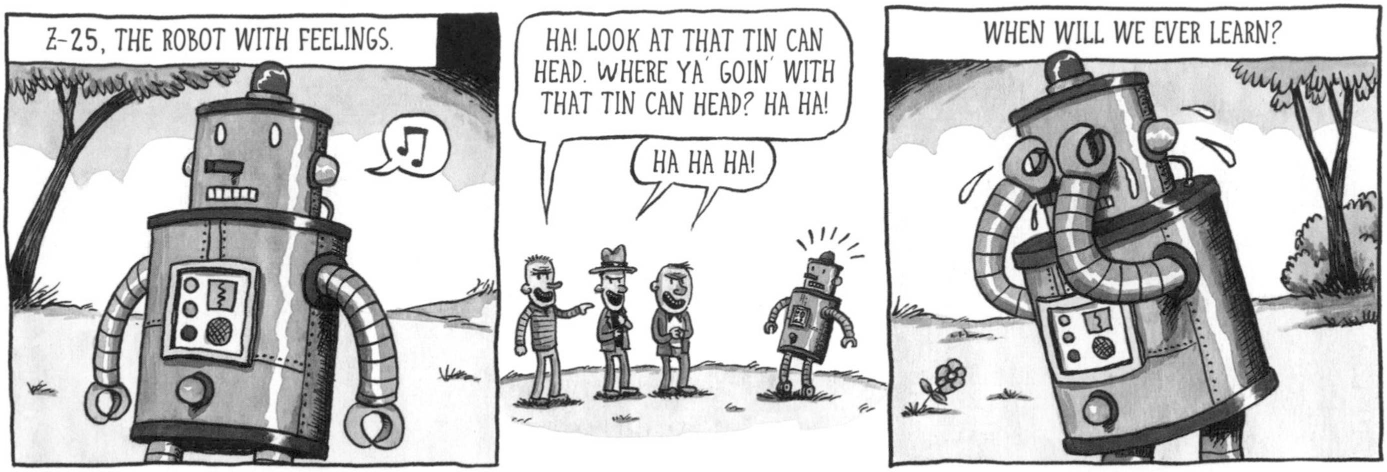
Z-25, THE ROBOT WITH FEELINGS.
HA! LOOK AT THAT TIN CAN HEAD. WHERE YA' GOIN' WITH THAT TIN CAN HEAD? HA HA!
HA HA HA!
WHEN WILL WE EVER LEARN?

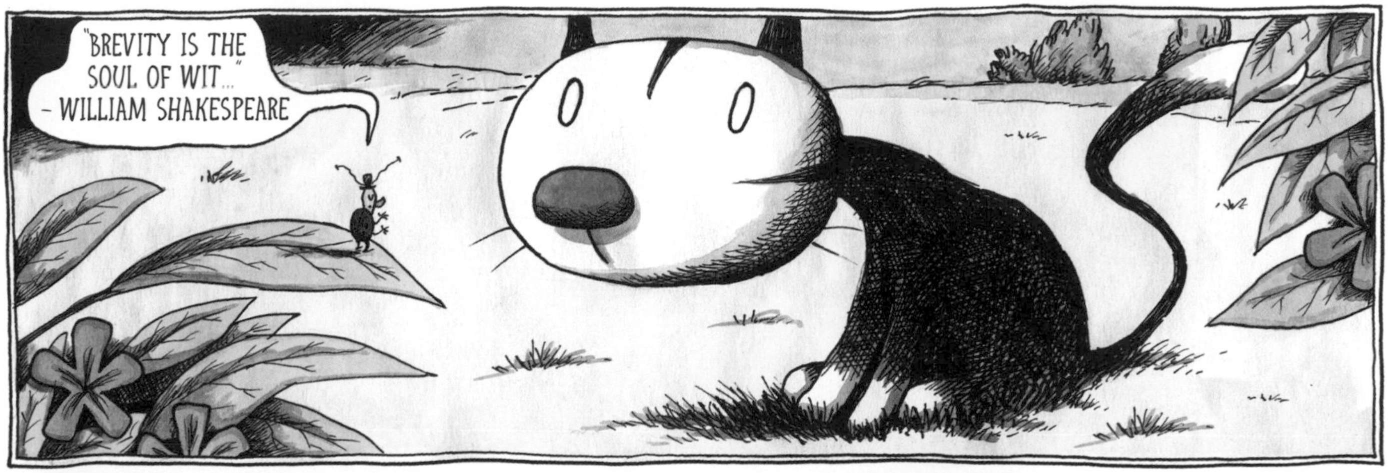
"BREVITY IS THE SOUL OF WIT..." - WILLIAM SHAKESPEARE

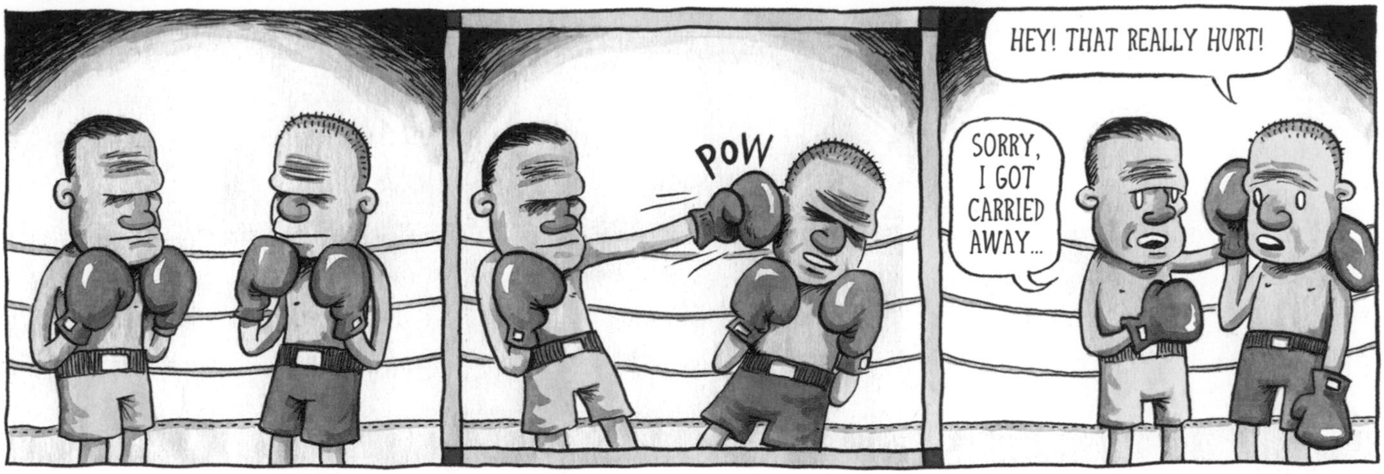
POW
HEY! THAT REALLY HURT!
SORRY, I GOT CARRIED AWAY...

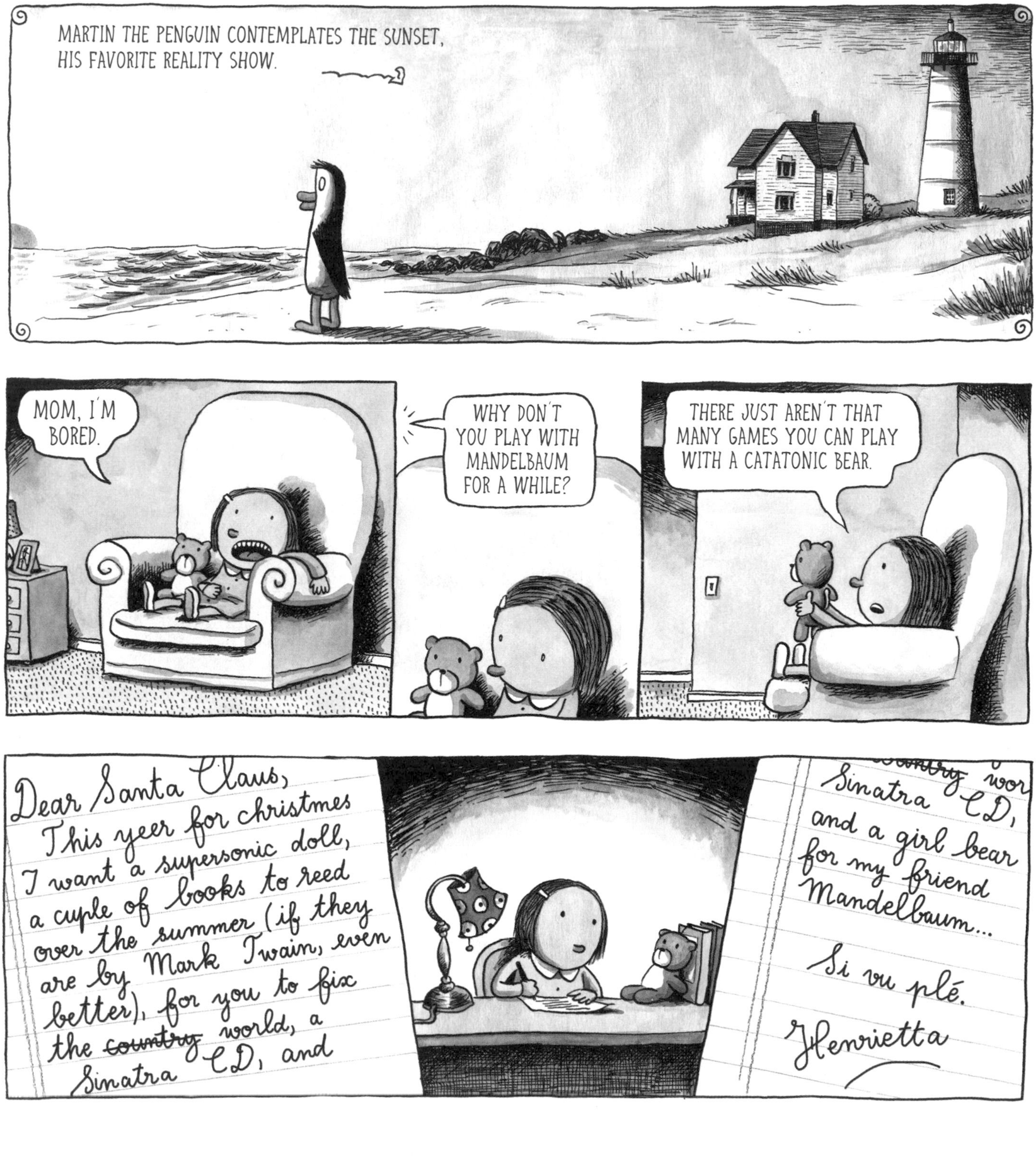
MARTIN THE PENGUIN CONTEMPLATES THE SUNSET, HIS FAVORITE REALITY SHOW.
MOM, I'M BORED.
WHY DON'T YOU PLAY WITH MANDELBAUM FOR A WHILE?
THERE JUST AREN'T THAT MANY GAMES YOU CAN PLAY WITH A CATATONIC BEAR.
Dear Santa Claus,
This yeer for christmes I want a supersonic doll, a cuple of books to reed over the summer (if they are by Mark Twain, even better), for you to fix the ~~country~~ world, a Sinatra CD, and
Sinatra CD, and a girl bear for my friend Mandelbaum...
Si vu plé.
Henrietta

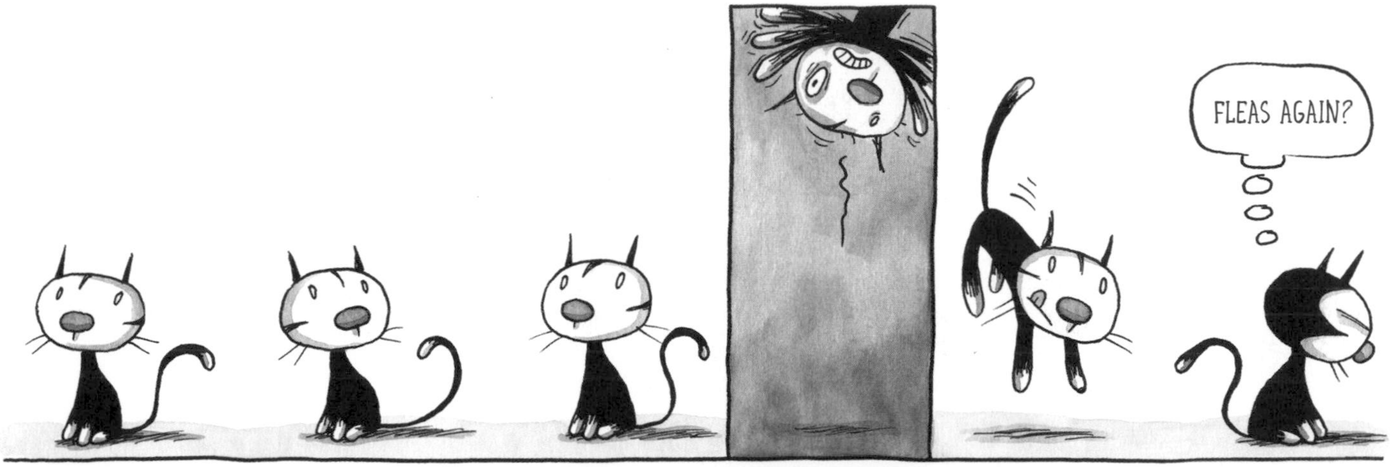
FLEAS AGAIN?

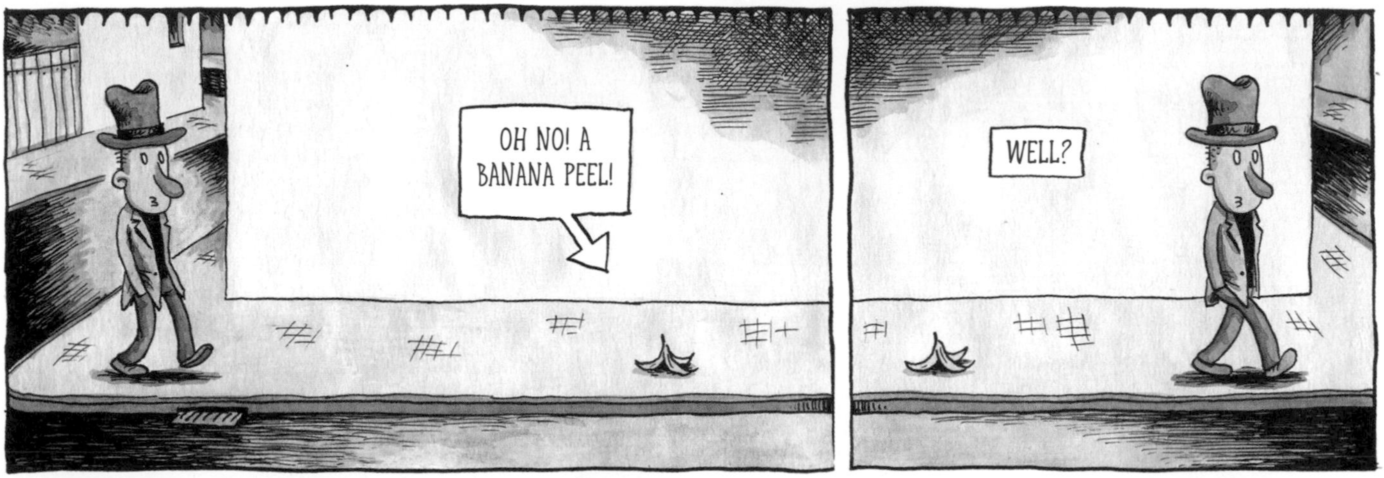
OH NO! A BANANA PEEL!
WELL?

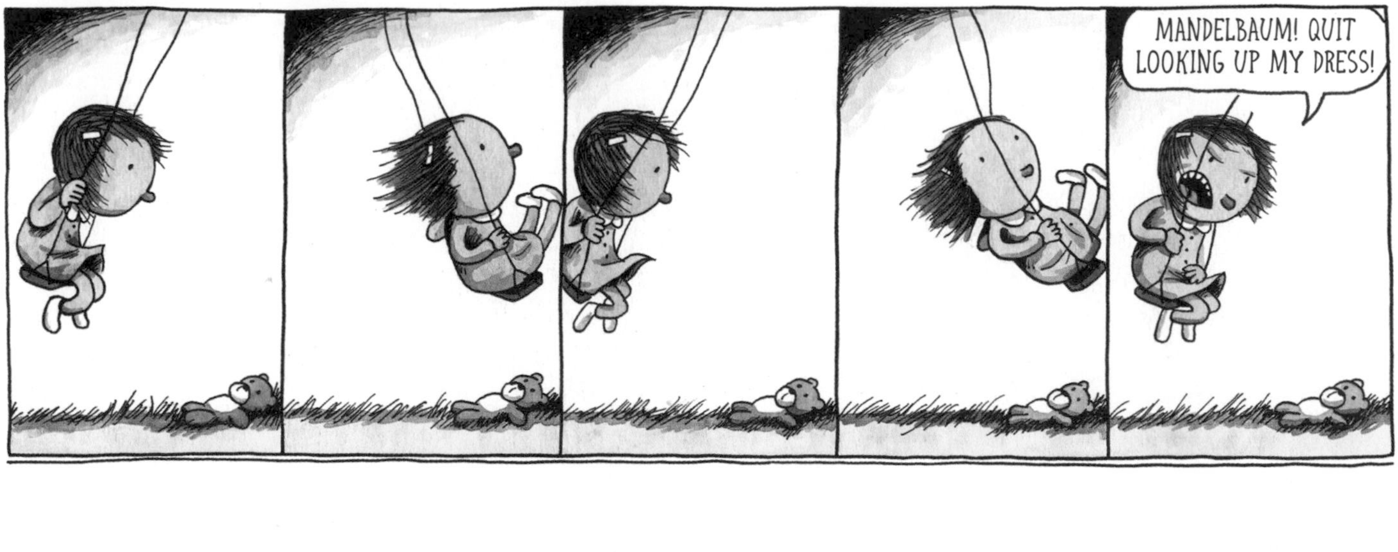
MANDELBAUM! QUIT LOOKING UP MY DRESS!

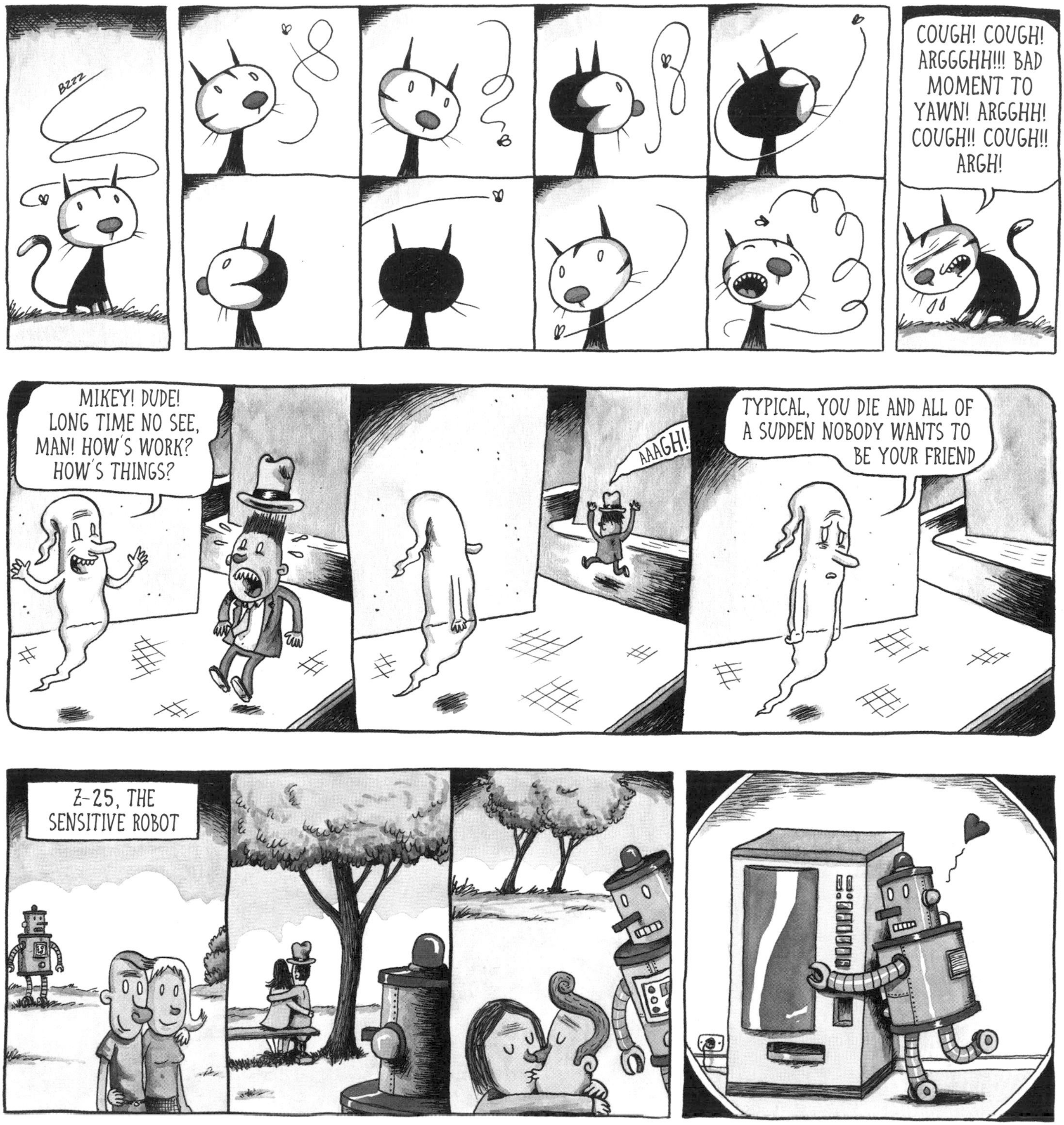
BZZZ
COUGH! COUGH! ARGGGHH!!! BAD MOMENT TO YAWN! ARGGHH! COUGH!! COUGH!! ARGH!
MIKEY! DUDE! LONG TIME NO SEE, MAN! HOW'S WORK? HOW'S THINGS?
AAAGH!
TYPICAL, YOU DIE AND ALL OF A SUDDEN NOBODY WANTS TO BE YOUR FRIEND
Z-25, THE SENSITIVE ROBOT

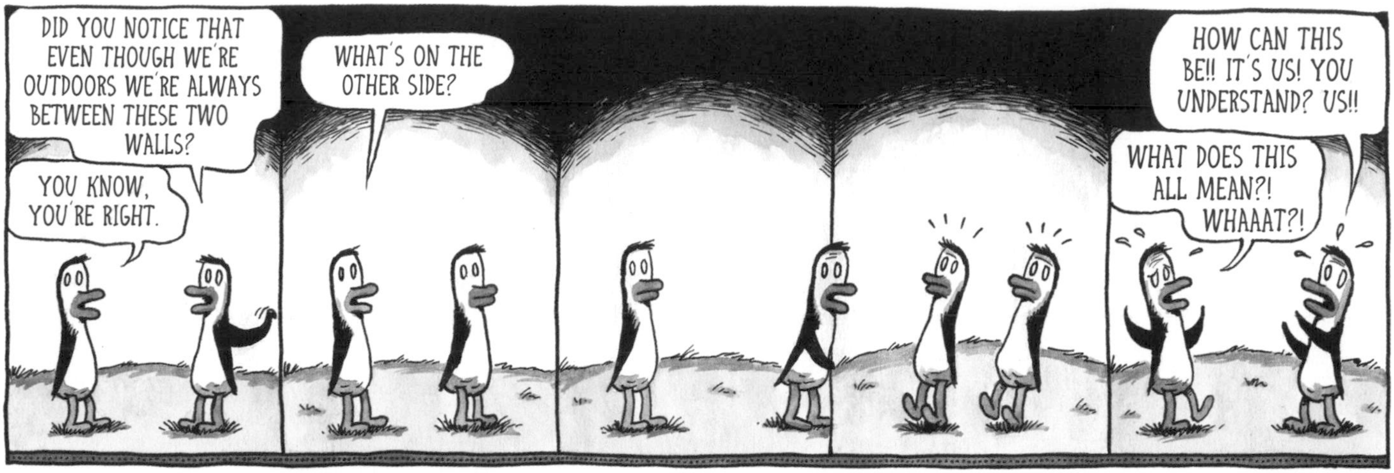
DID YOU NOTICE THAT EVEN THOUGH WE'RE OUTDOORS WE'RE ALWAYS BETWEEN THESE TWO WALLS?
YOU KNOW, YOU'RE RIGHT.
WHAT'S ON THE OTHER SIDE?
HOW CAN THIS BE!! IT'S US! YOU UNDERSTAND? US!!
WHAT DOES THIS ALL MEAN?! WHAAAT?!

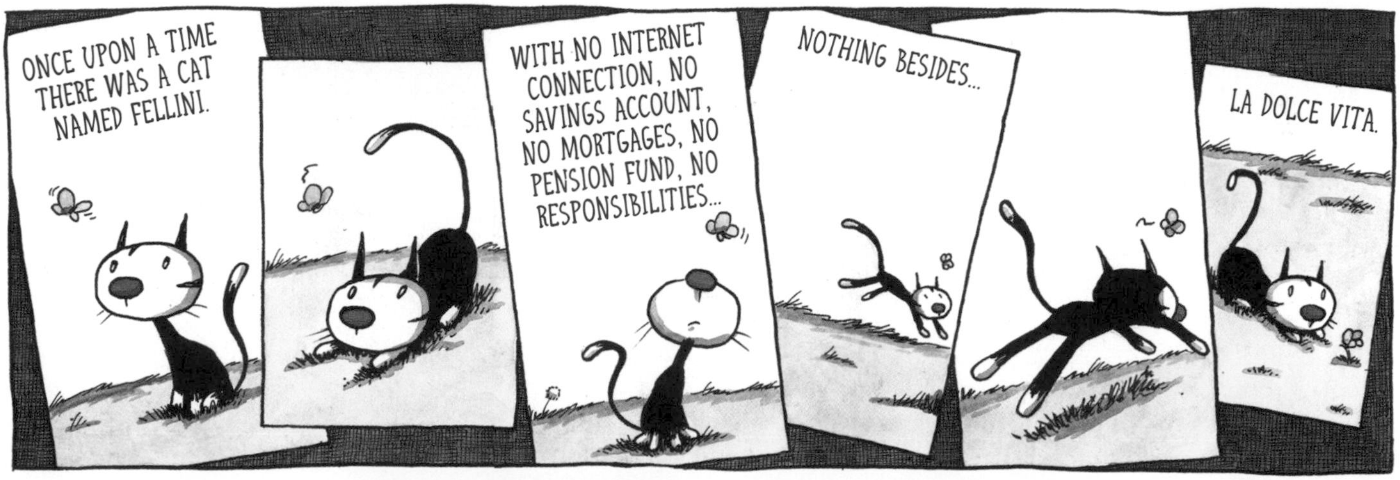
ONCE UPON A TIME THERE WAS A CAT NAMED FELLINI.
WITH NO INTERNET CONNECTION, NO SAVINGS ACCOUNT, NO MORTGAGES, NO PENSION FUND, NO RESPONSIBILITIES...
NOTHING BESIDES...
LA DOLCE VITA.

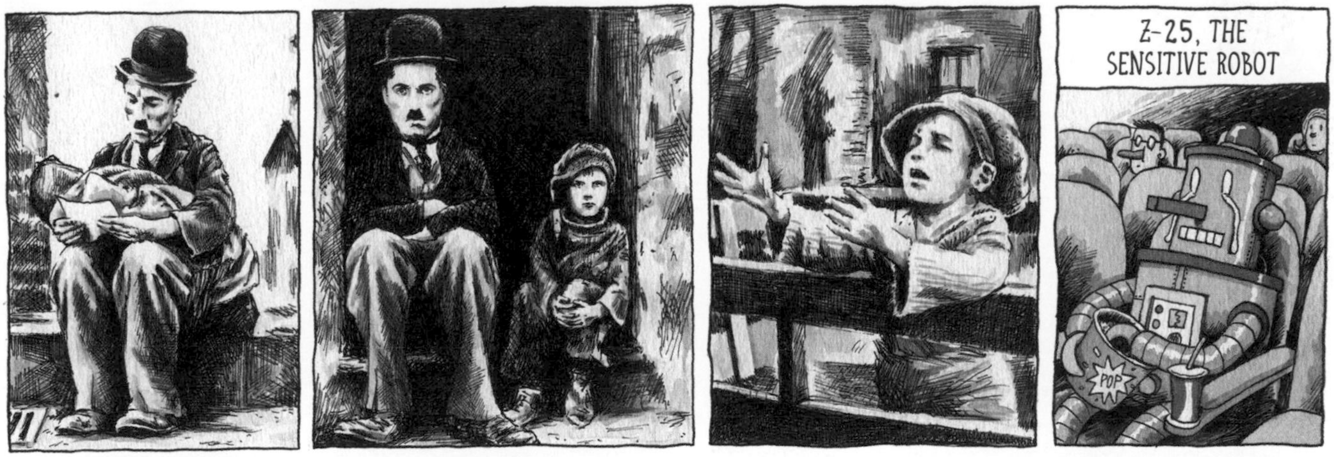
Z-25, THE SENSITIVE ROBOT
POP

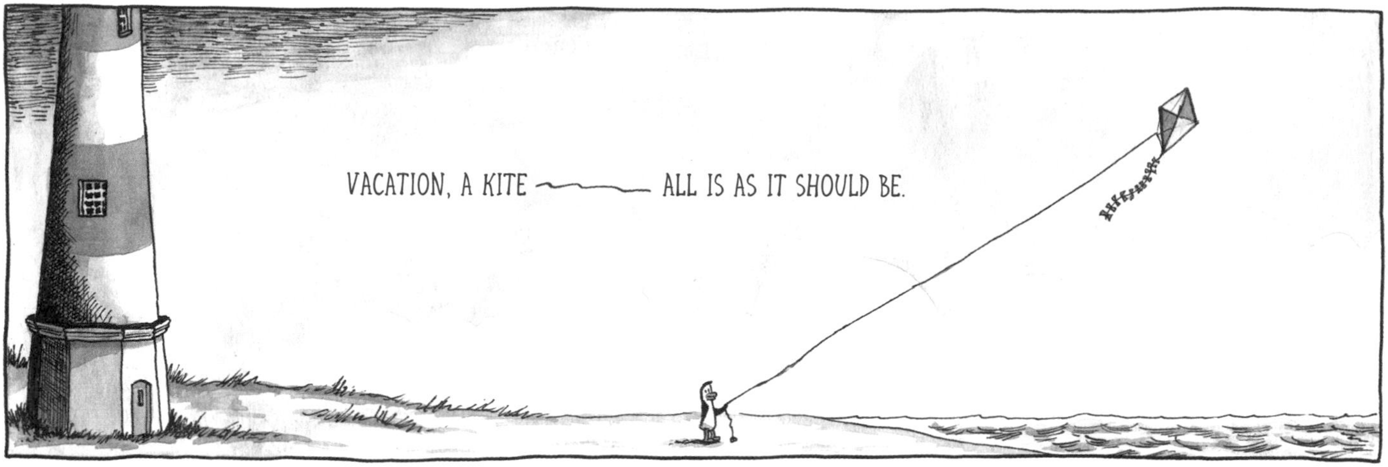
VACATION, A KITE ——— ALL IS AS IT SHOULD BE.

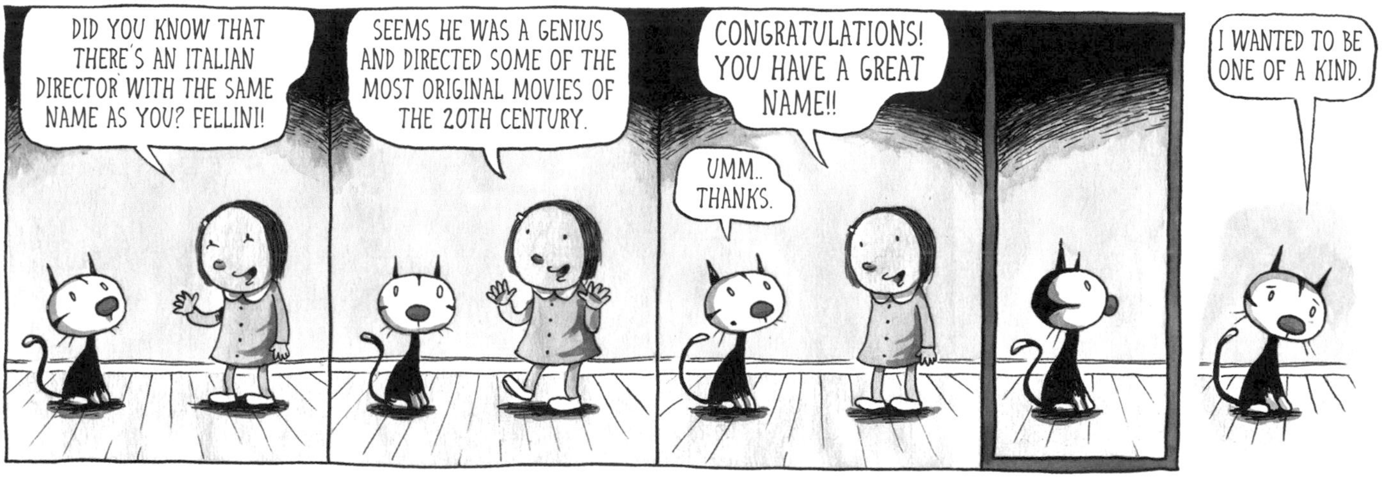
DID YOU KNOW THAT THERE'S AN ITALIAN DIRECTOR WITH THE SAME NAME AS YOU? FELLINI!
SEEMS HE WAS A GENIUS AND DIRECTED SOME OF THE MOST ORIGINAL MOVIES OF THE 20TH CENTURY.
CONGRATULATIONS! YOU HAVE A GREAT NAME!!
UMM.. THANKS.
I WANTED TO BE ONE OF A KIND.

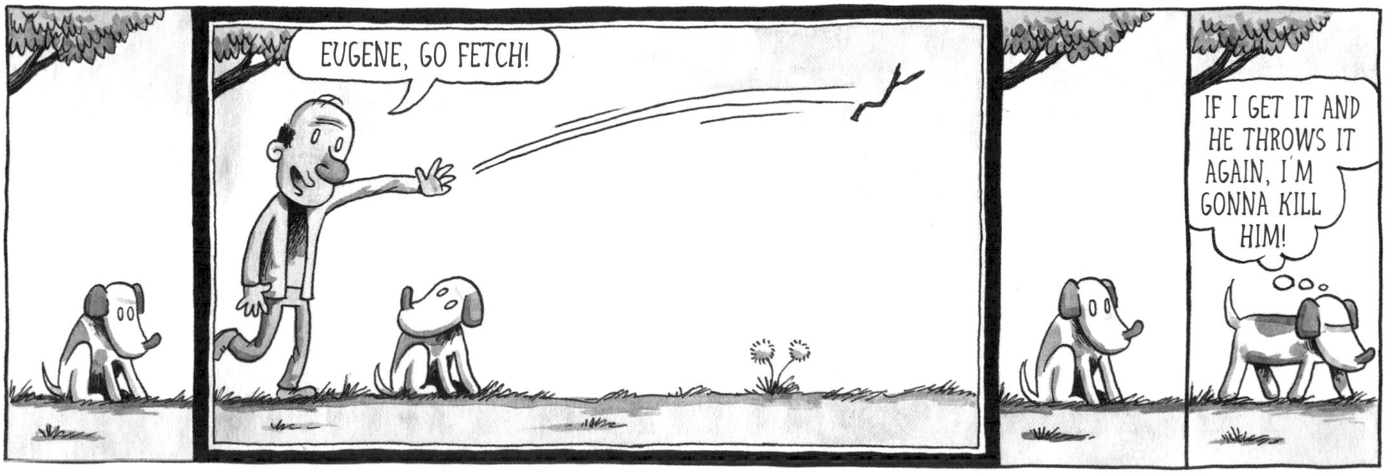
EUGENE, GO FETCH!
IF I GET IT AND HE THROWS IT AGAIN, I'M GONNA KILL HIM!

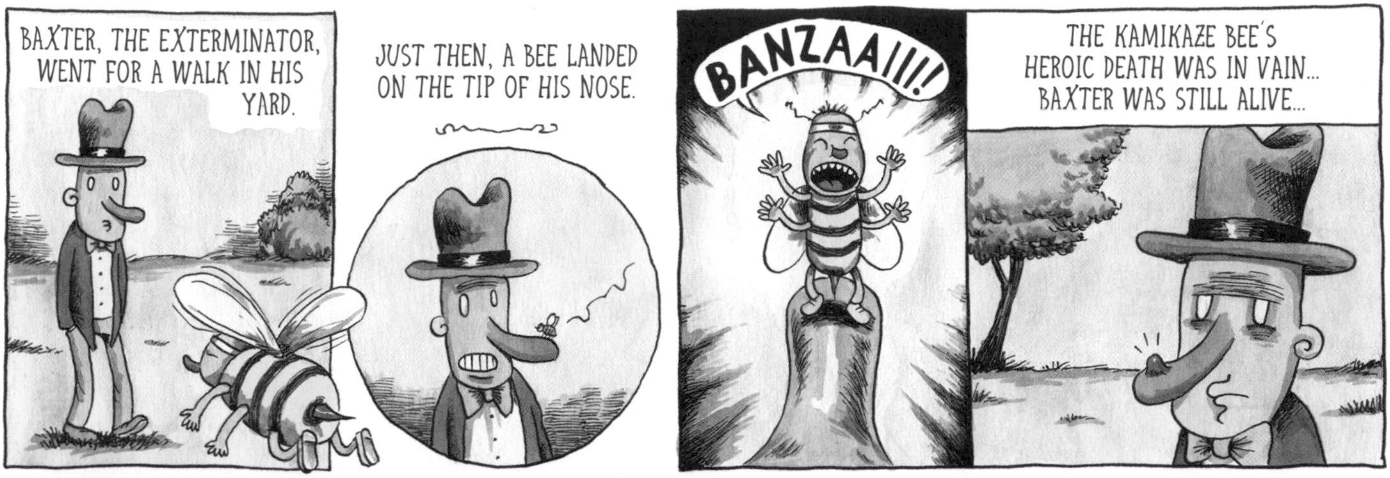
BAXTER, THE EXTERMINATOR, WENT FOR A WALK IN HIS YARD.
JUST THEN, A BEE LANDED ON THE TIP OF HIS NOSE.
BANZAAIII!
THE KAMIKAZE BEE'S HEROIC DEATH WAS IN VAIN... BAXTER WAS STILL ALIVE...

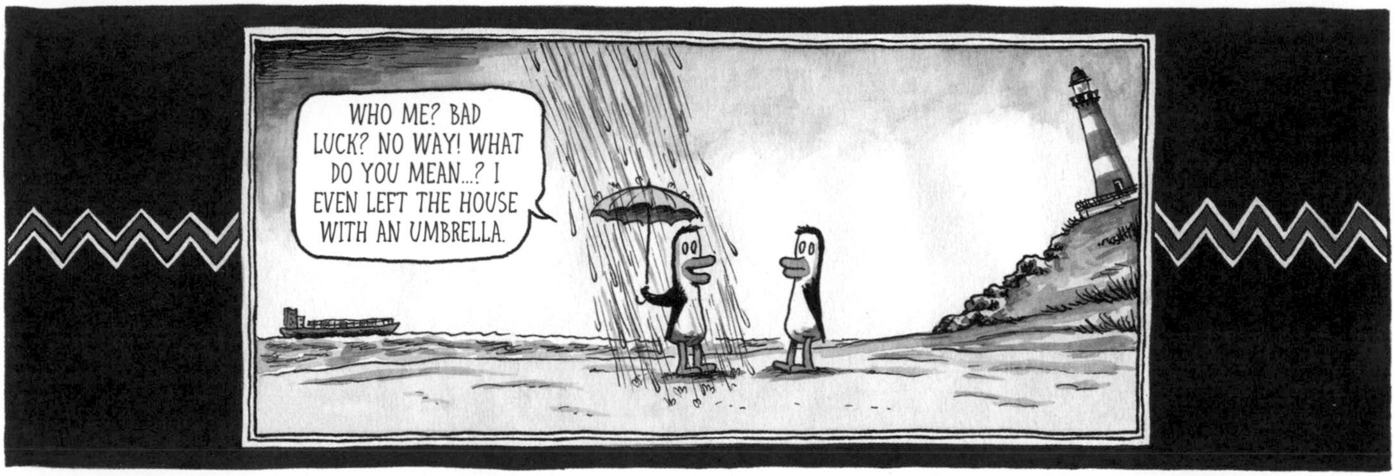
WHO ME? BAD LUCK? NO WAY! WHAT DO YOU MEAN...? I EVEN LEFT THE HOUSE WITH AN UMBRELLA.

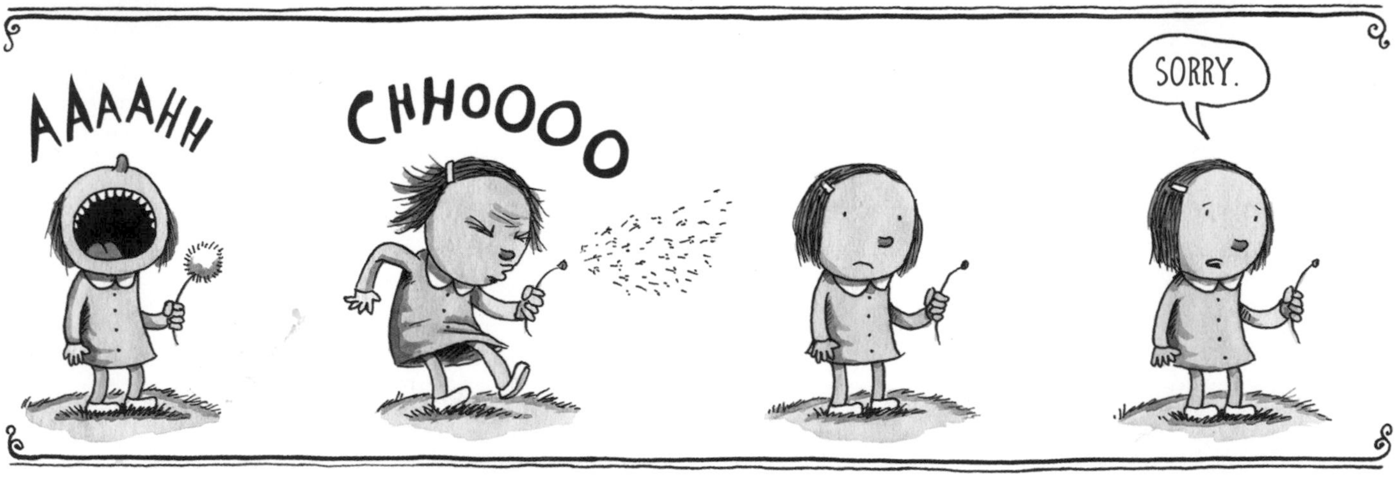
AAAAHH
CHHOOOO
SORRY.

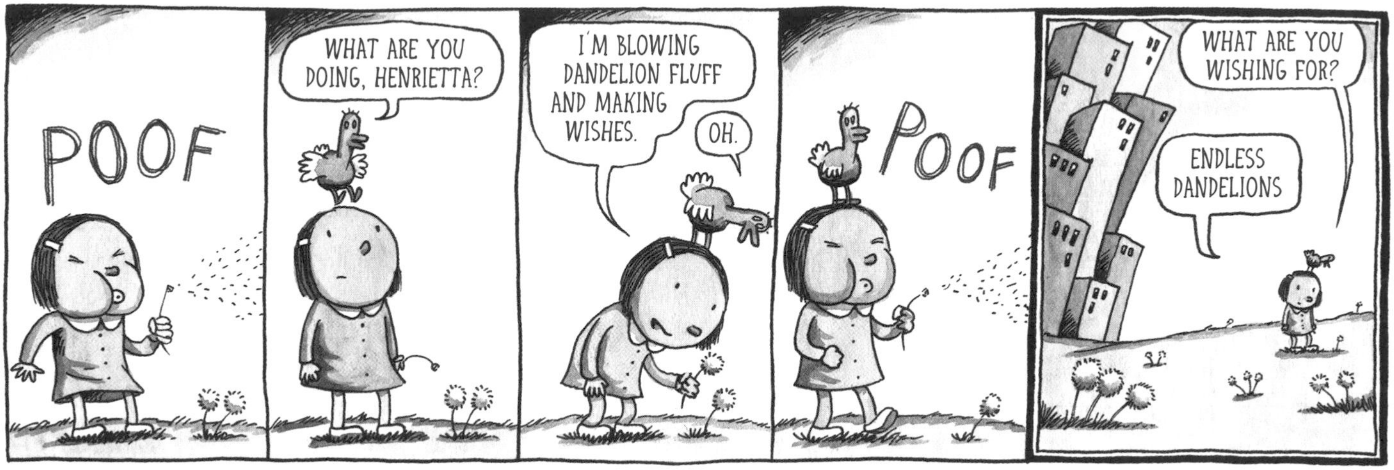
POOF
WHAT ARE YOU DOING, HENRIETTA?
I'M BLOWING DANDELION FLUFF AND MAKING WISHES.
OH.
POOF
WHAT ARE YOU WISHING FOR?
ENDLESS DANDELIONS

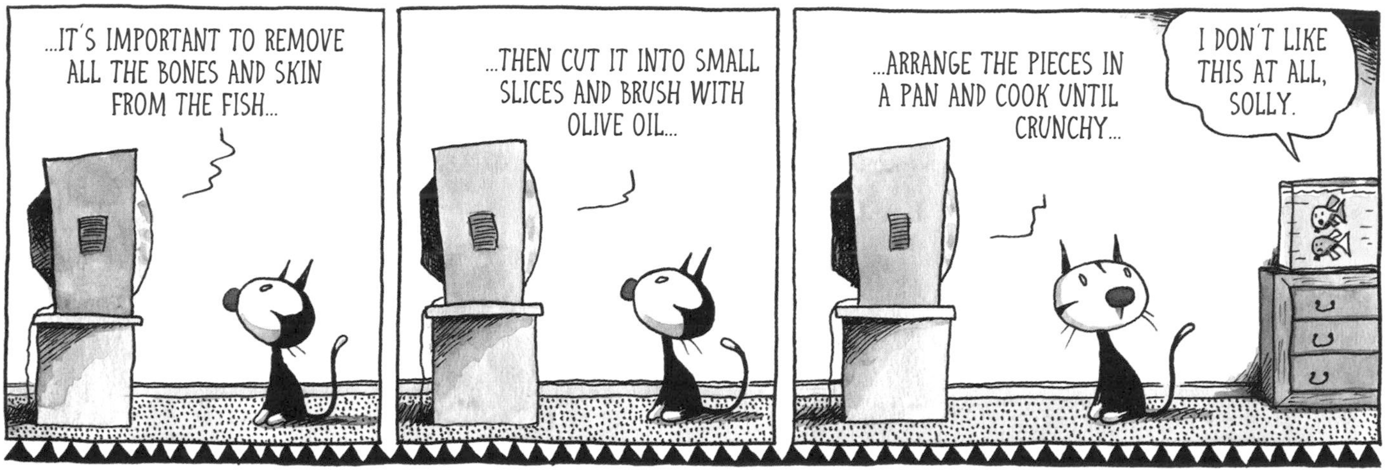
...IT'S IMPORTANT TO REMOVE ALL THE BONES AND SKIN FROM THE FISH...
...THEN CUT IT INTO SMALL SLICES AND BRUSH WITH OLIVE OIL...
...ARRANGE THE PIECES IN A PAN AND COOK UNTIL CRUNCHY...
I DON'T LIKE THIS AT ALL, SOLLY.

WHAT SHE'S THINKING: "OH! THIS IS SO ROMANTIC! I LOVE YOU SO MUCH, ALBERT!! I'M SO, SO HAPPY!!"

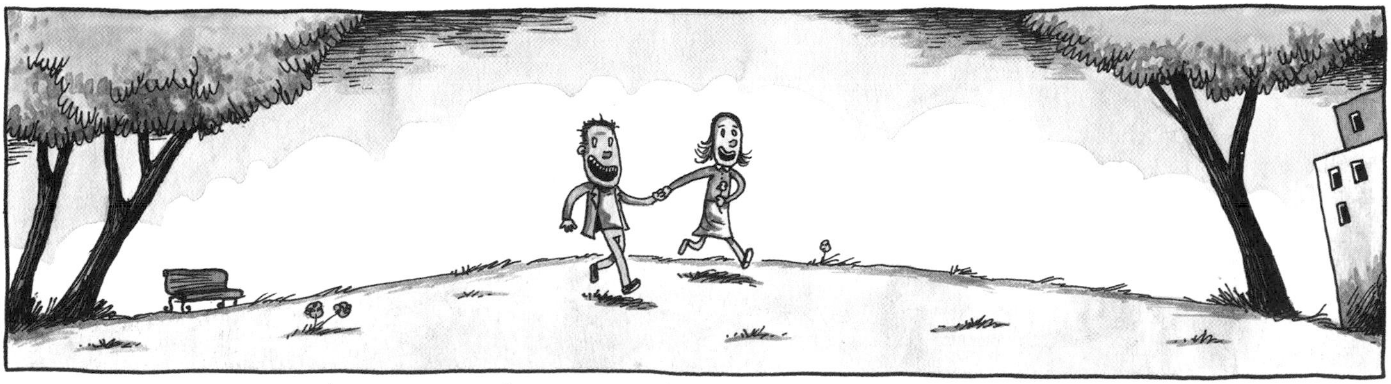

WHAT HE'S THINKING: "PLEASE DON'T LET ANYONE SEE ME. PLEASE DON'T..."

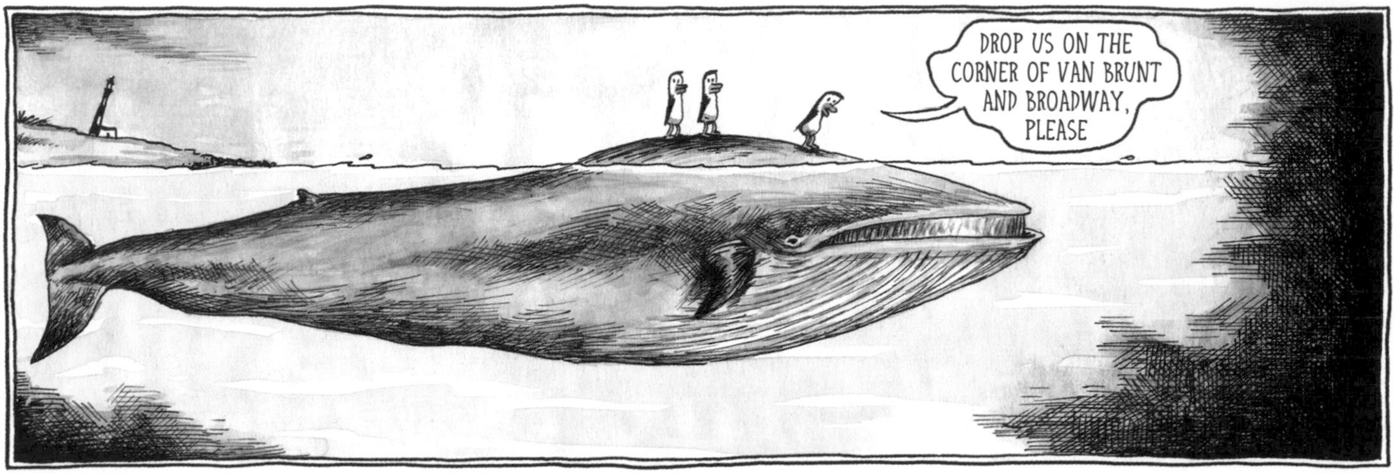
DROP US ON THE CORNER OF VAN BRUNT AND BROADWAY, PLEASE

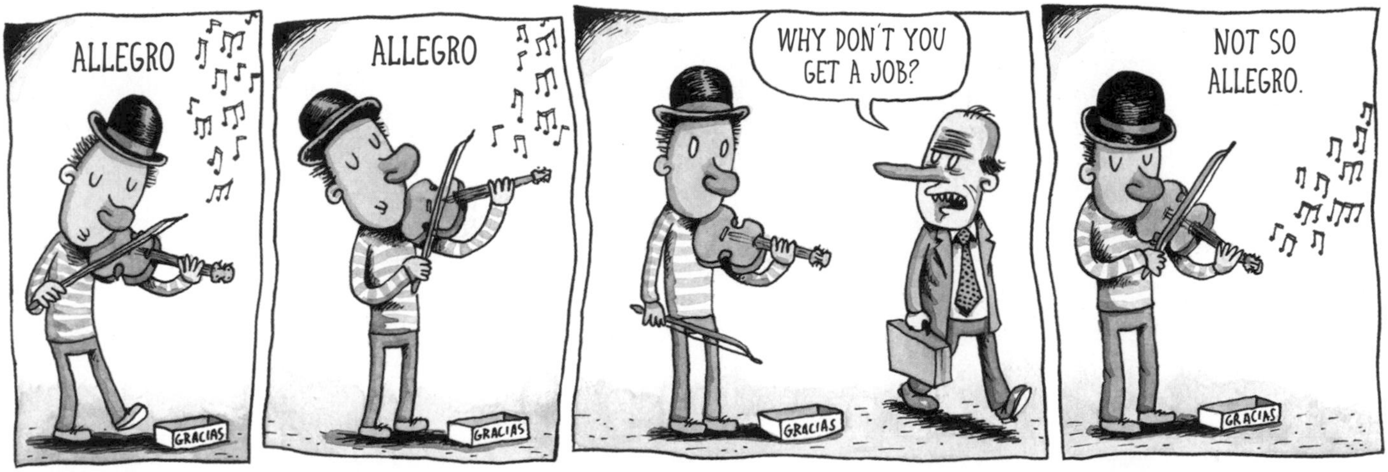
ALLEGRO
GRACIAS
ALLEGRO
GRACIAS
WHY DON'T YOU GET A JOB?
GRACIAS
NOT SO ALLEGRO.
GRACIAS

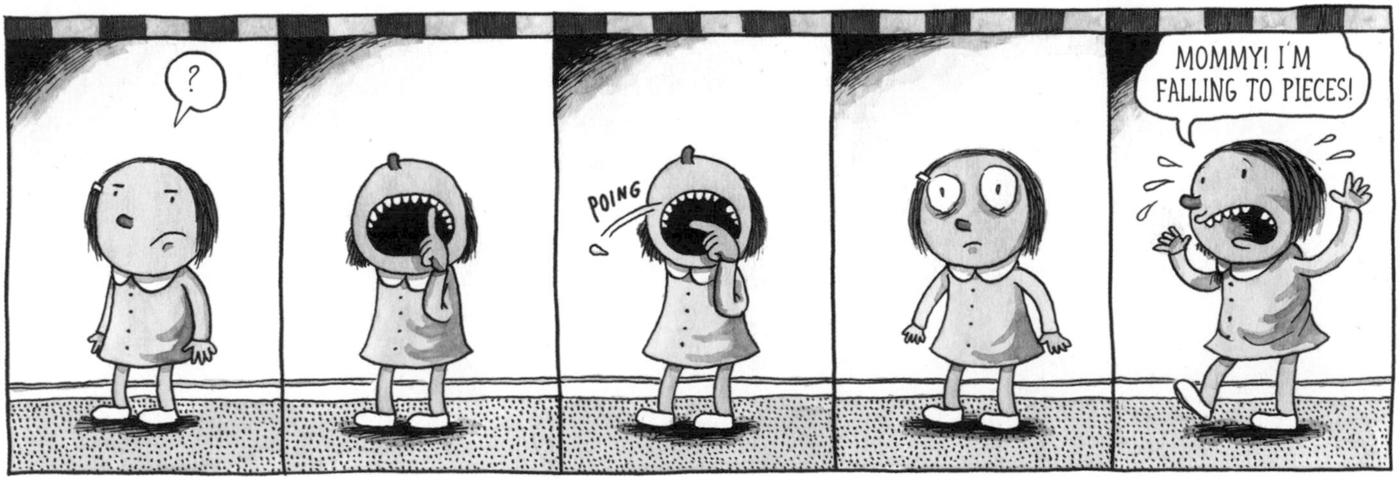
?
POING
MOMMY! I'M FALLING TO PIECES!

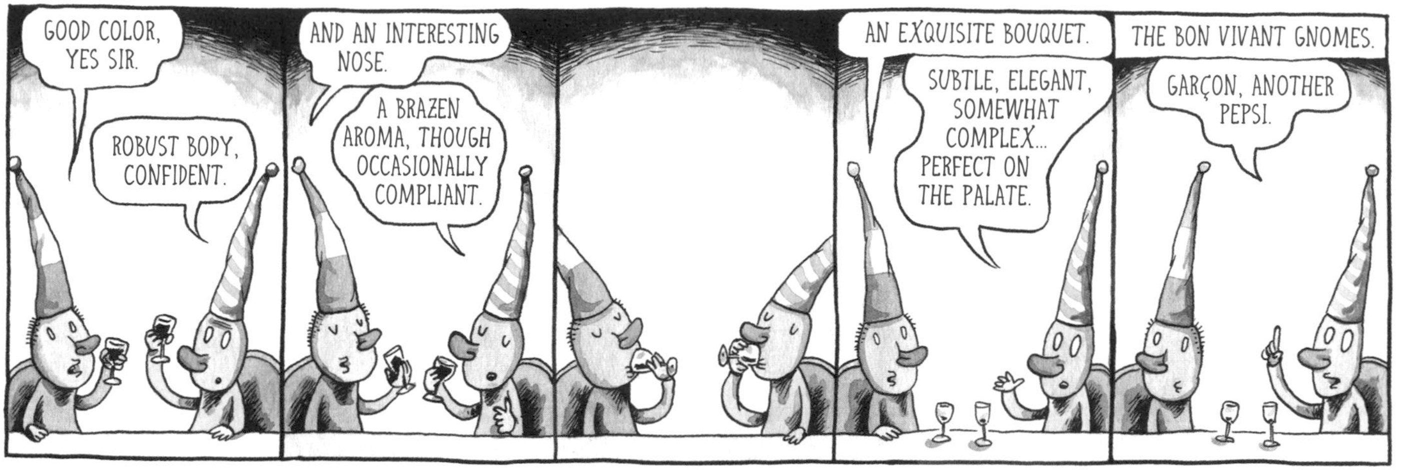
GOOD COLOR, YES SIR.
ROBUST BODY, CONFIDENT.
AND AN INTERESTING NOSE.
A BRAZEN AROMA, THOUGH OCCASIONALLY COMPLIANT.
AN EXQUISITE BOUQUET.
SUBTLE, ELEGANT, SOMEWHAT COMPLEX... PERFECT ON THE PALATE.
THE BON VIVANT GNOMES.
GARÇON, ANOTHER PEPSI.

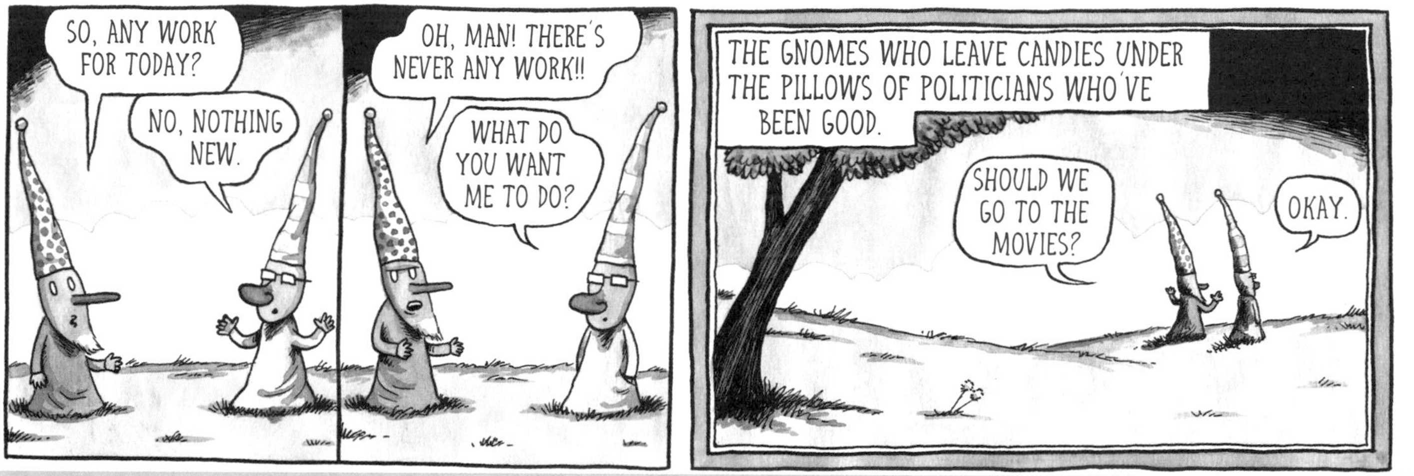
SO, ANY WORK FOR TODAY?
NO, NOTHING NEW.
OH, MAN! THERE'S NEVER ANY WORK!!
WHAT DO YOU WANT ME TO DO?
THE GNOMES WHO LEAVE CANDIES UNDER THE PILLOWS OF POLITICIANS WHO'VE BEEN GOOD.
SHOULD WE GO TO THE MOVIES?
OKAY.

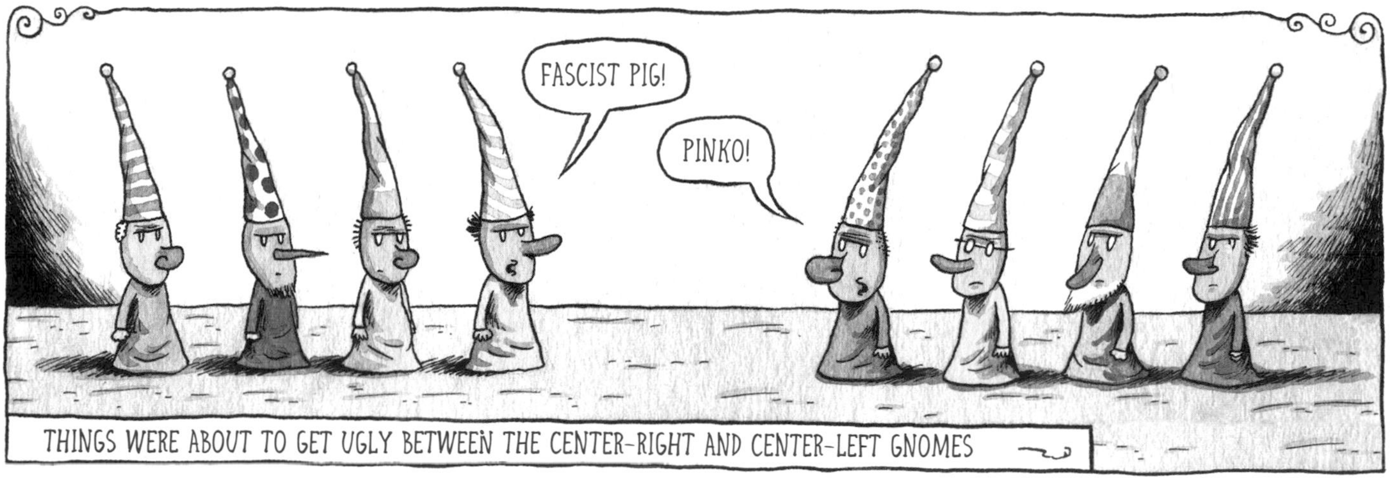
FASCIST PIG!
PINKO!
THINGS WERE ABOUT TO GET UGLY BETWEEN THE CENTER-RIGHT AND CENTER-LEFT GNOMES

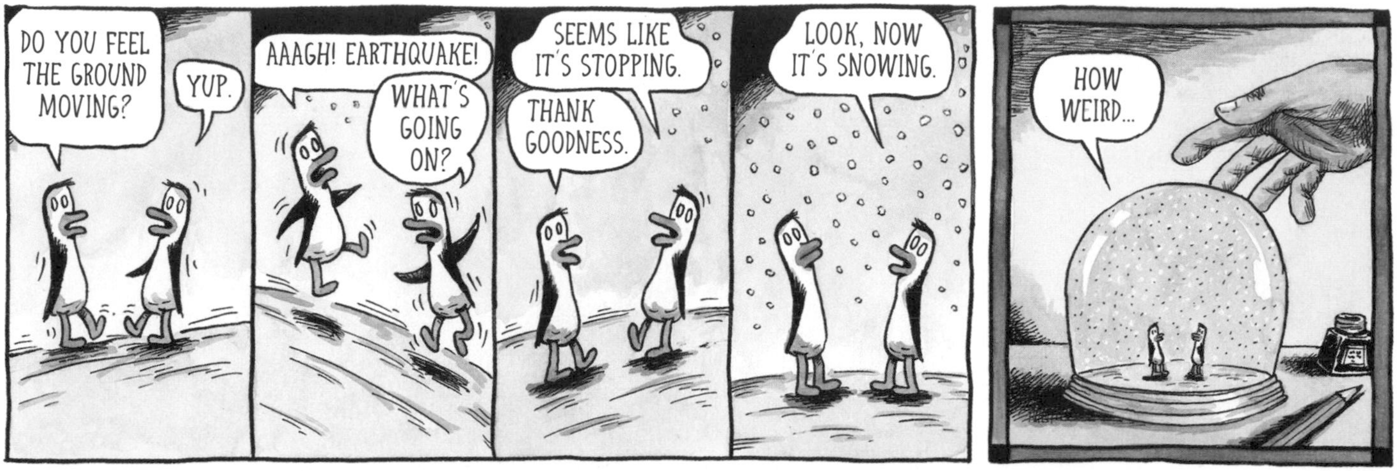
DO YOU FEEL THE GROUND MOVING?
YUP.
AAAGH! EARTHQUAKE!
WHAT'S GOING ON?
SEEMS LIKE IT'S STOPPING.
THANK GOODNESS.
LOOK, NOW IT'S SNOWING.
HOW WEIRD...

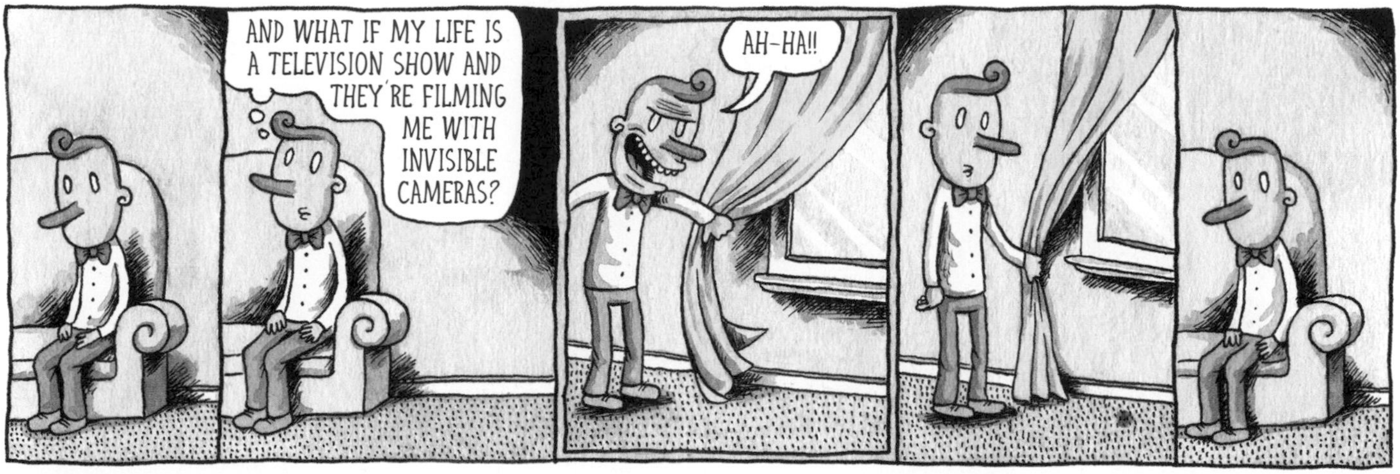
AND WHAT IF MY LIFE IS A TELEVISION SHOW AND THEY'RE FILMING ME WITH INVISIBLE CAMERAS?
AH-HA!!

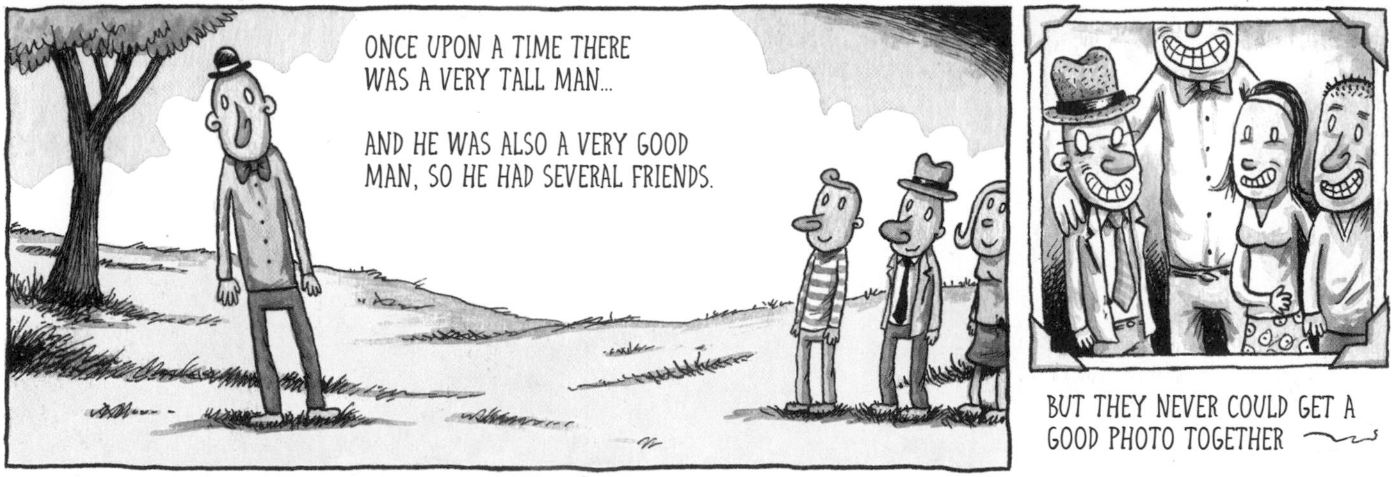
ONCE UPON A TIME THERE WAS A VERY TALL MAN...
AND HE WAS ALSO A VERY GOOD MAN, SO HE HAD SEVERAL FRIENDS.
BUT THEY NEVER COULD GET A GOOD PHOTO TOGETHER

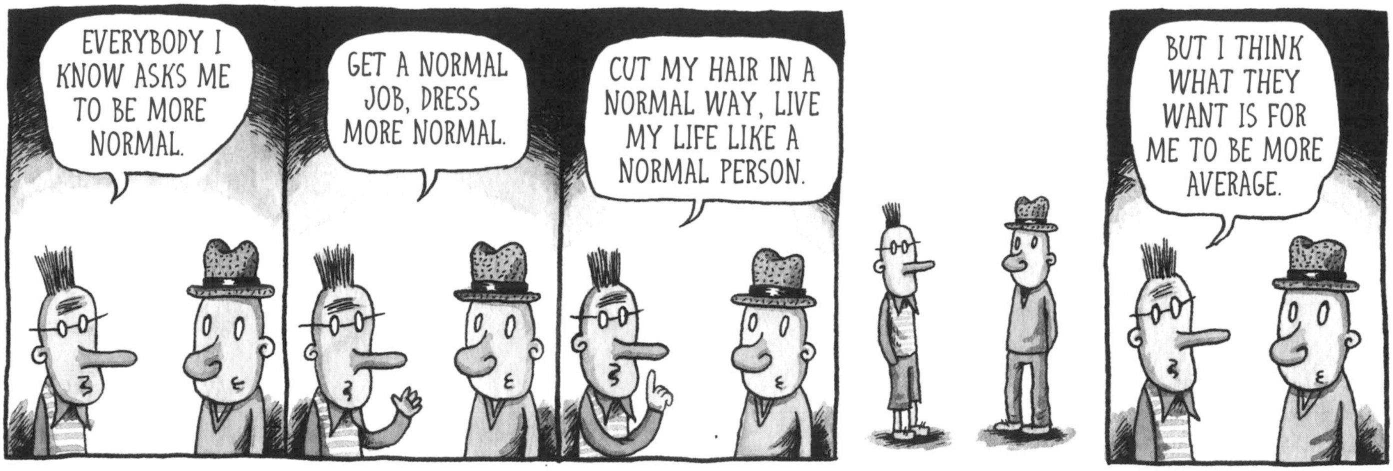
EVERYBODY I KNOW ASKS ME TO BE MORE NORMAL.
GET A NORMAL JOB, DRESS MORE NORMAL.
CUT MY HAIR IN A NORMAL WAY, LIVE MY LIFE LIKE A NORMAL PERSON.
BUT I THINK WHAT THEY WANT IS FOR ME TO BE MORE AVERAGE.

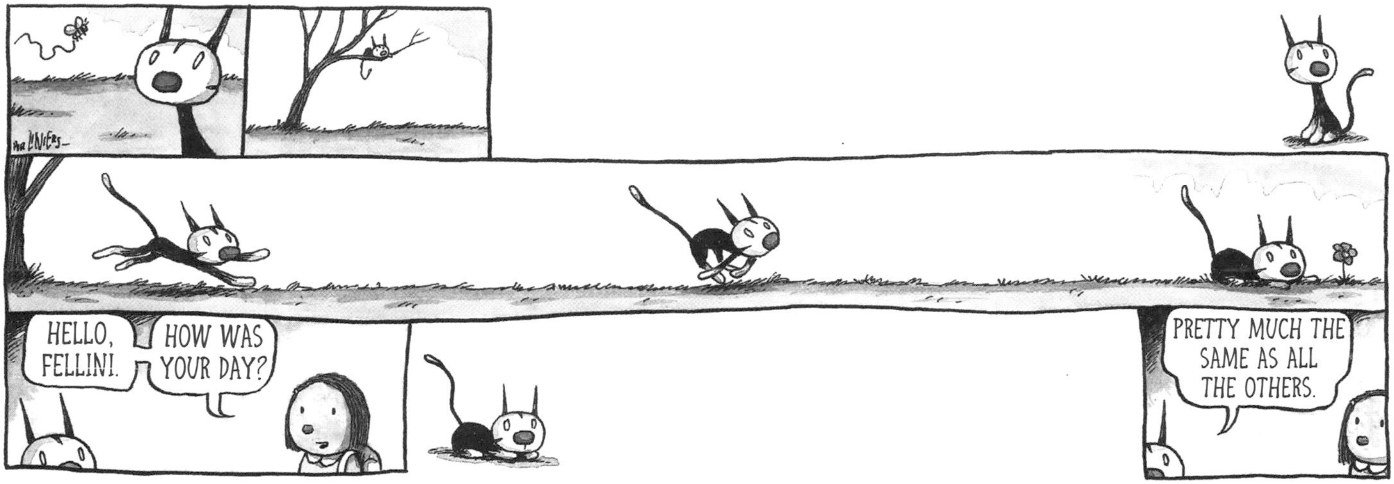
HELLO, FELLINI.
HOW WAS YOUR DAY?
PRETTY MUCH THE SAME AS ALL THE OTHERS.

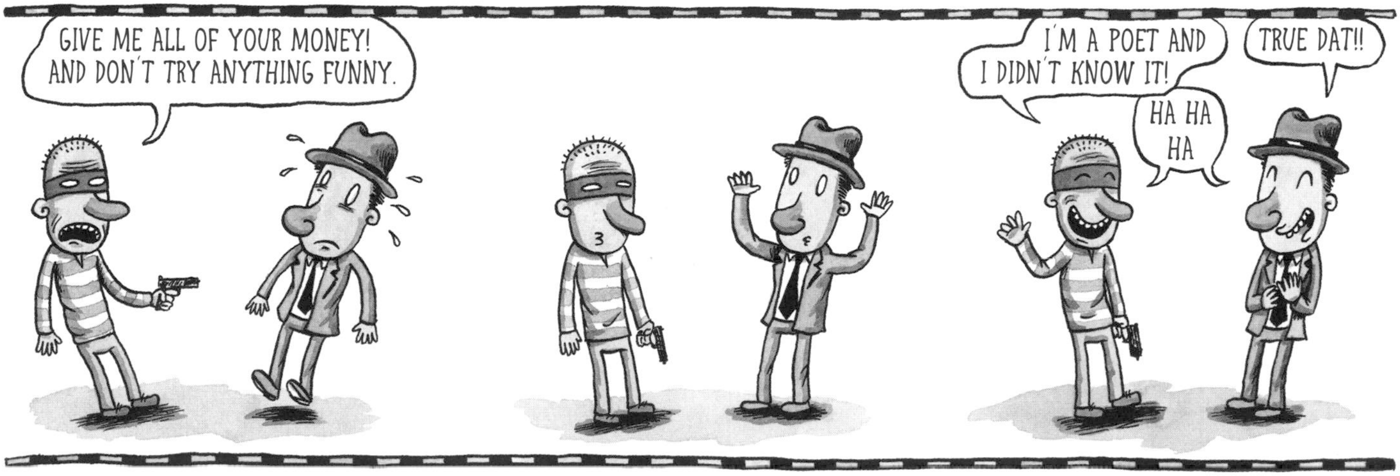
GIVE ME ALL OF YOUR MONEY! AND DON'T TRY ANYTHING FUNNY.
I'M A POET AND I DIDN'T KNOW IT!
TRUE DAT!!
HA HA HA

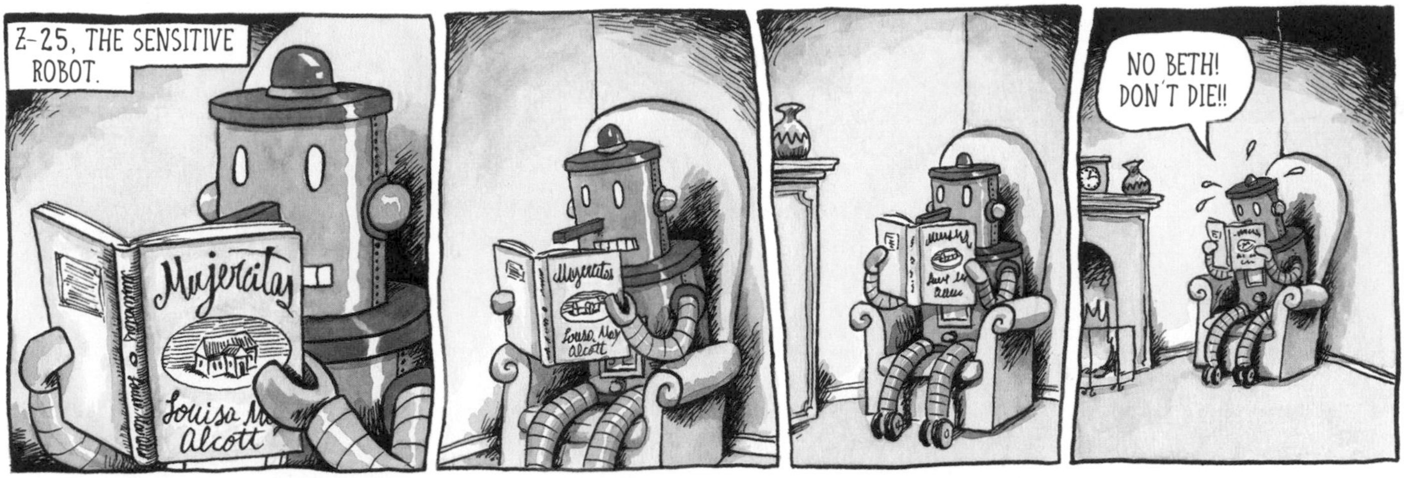
Z-25, THE SENSITIVE ROBOT.
NO BETH! DON'T DIE!!

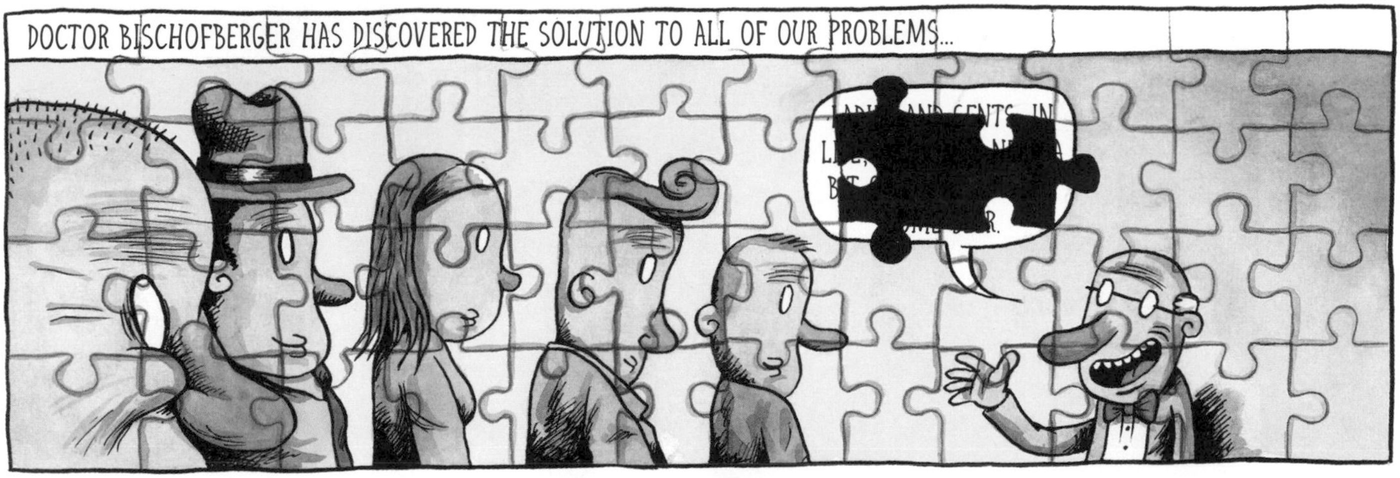
DOCTOR BISCHOFBERGER HAS DISCOVERED THE SOLUTION TO ALL OF OUR PROBLEMS...

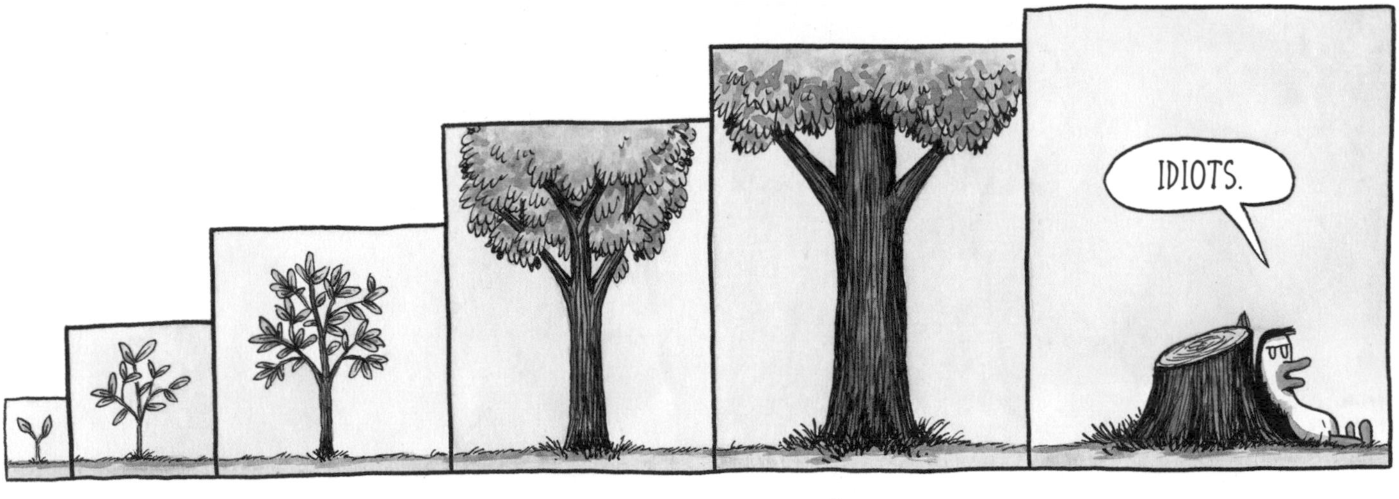
IDIOTS.

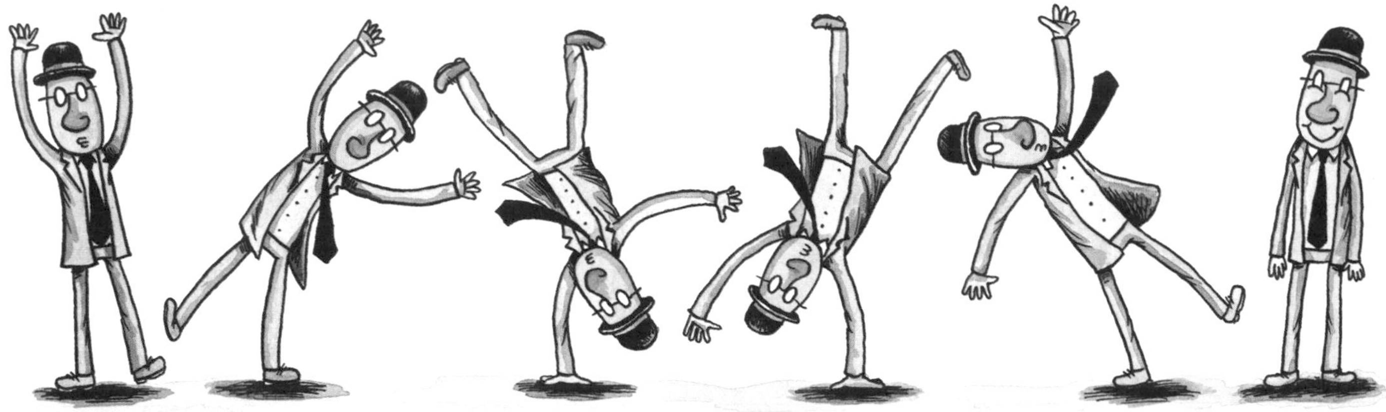

BARTELBY, ESQ. STILL REMEMBERS HOW FUN IT IS TO DO A CARTWHEEL.

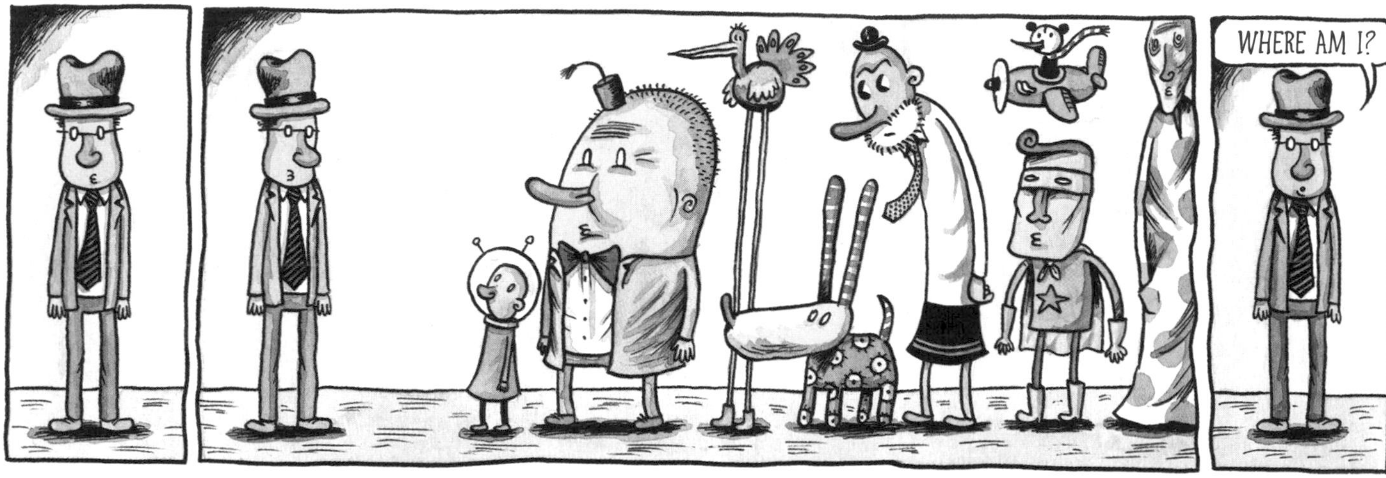
WHERE AM I?

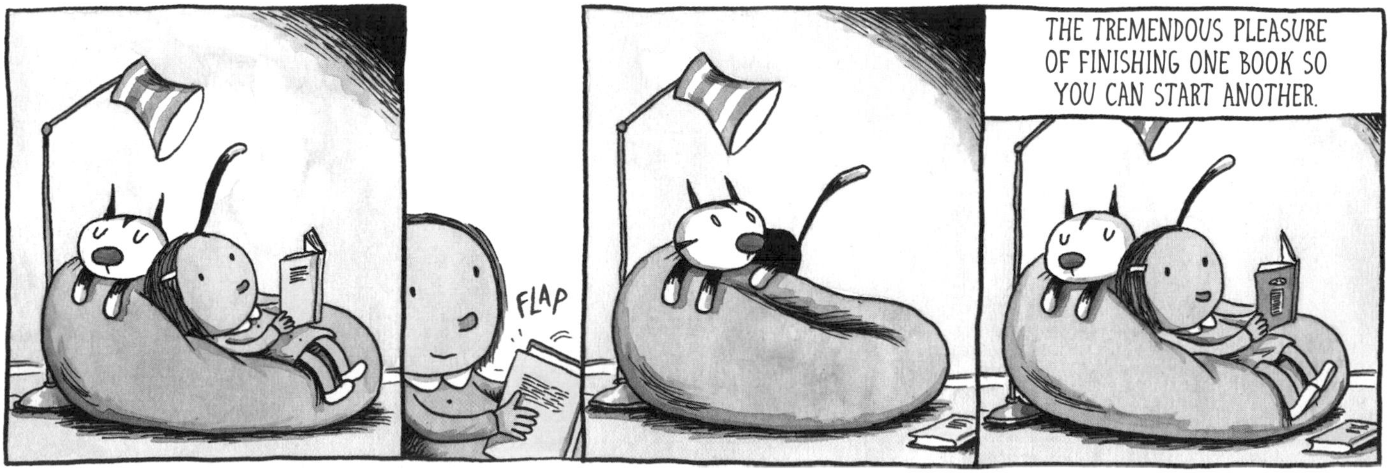
FLAP
THE TREMENDOUS PLEASURE OF FINISHING ONE BOOK SO YOU CAN START ANOTHER.

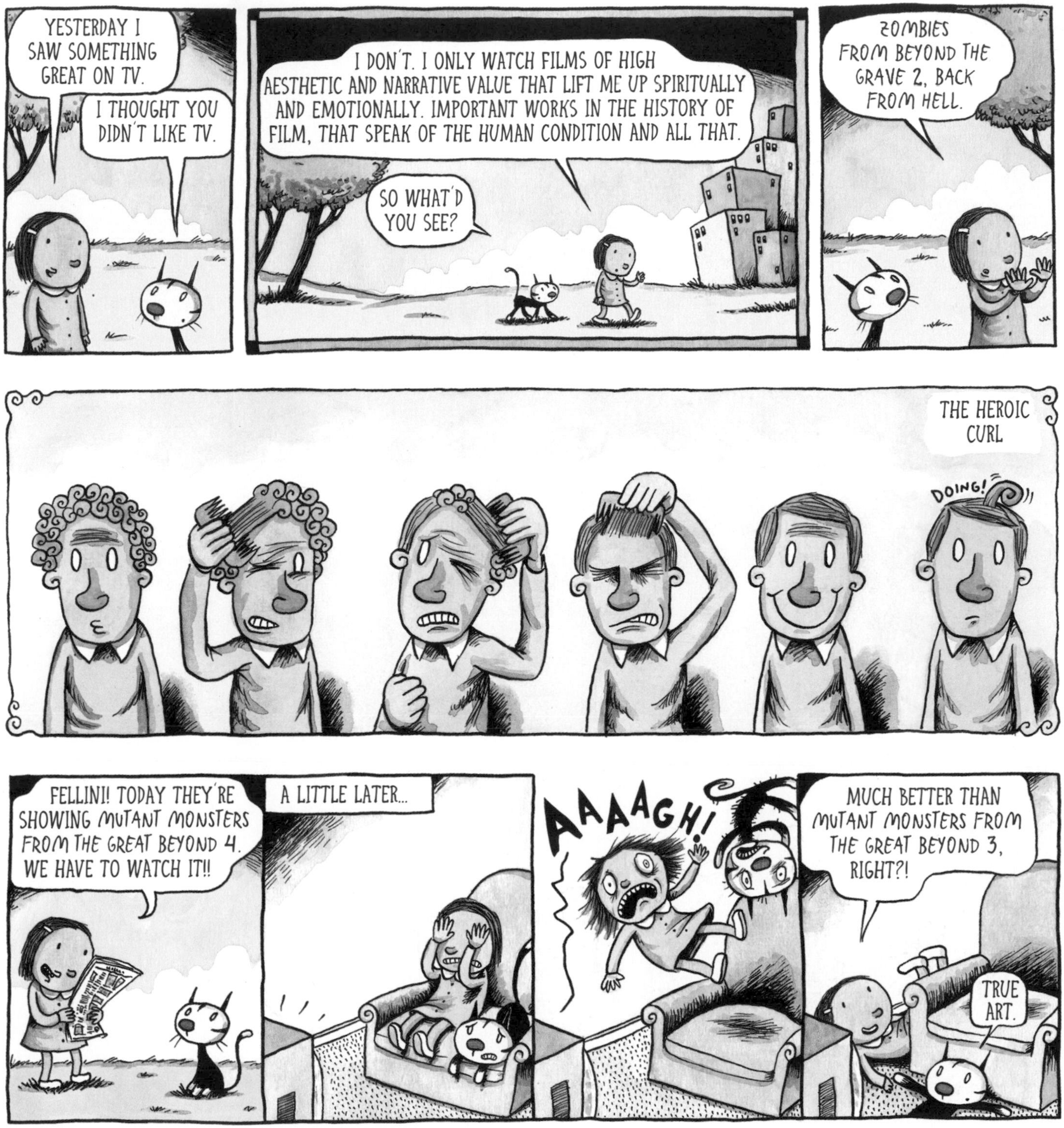
YESTERDAY I SAW SOMETHING GREAT ON TV.
I THOUGHT YOU DIDN'T LIKE TV.
I DON'T. I ONLY WATCH FILMS OF HIGH AESTHETIC AND NARRATIVE VALUE THAT LIFT ME UP SPIRITUALLY AND EMOTIONALLY. IMPORTANT WORKS IN THE HISTORY OF FILM, THAT SPEAK OF THE HUMAN CONDITION AND ALL THAT.
SO WHAT'D YOU SEE?
ZOMBIES FROM BEYOND THE GRAVE 2, BACK FROM HELL.
THE HEROIC CURL
DOING!
FELLINI! TODAY THEY'RE SHOWING MUTANT MONSTERS FROM THE GREAT BEYOND 4. WE HAVE TO WATCH IT!!
A LITTLE LATER...
AAAAGH!
MUCH BETTER THAN MUTANT MONSTERS FROM THE GREAT BEYOND 3, RIGHT?!
TRUE ART.

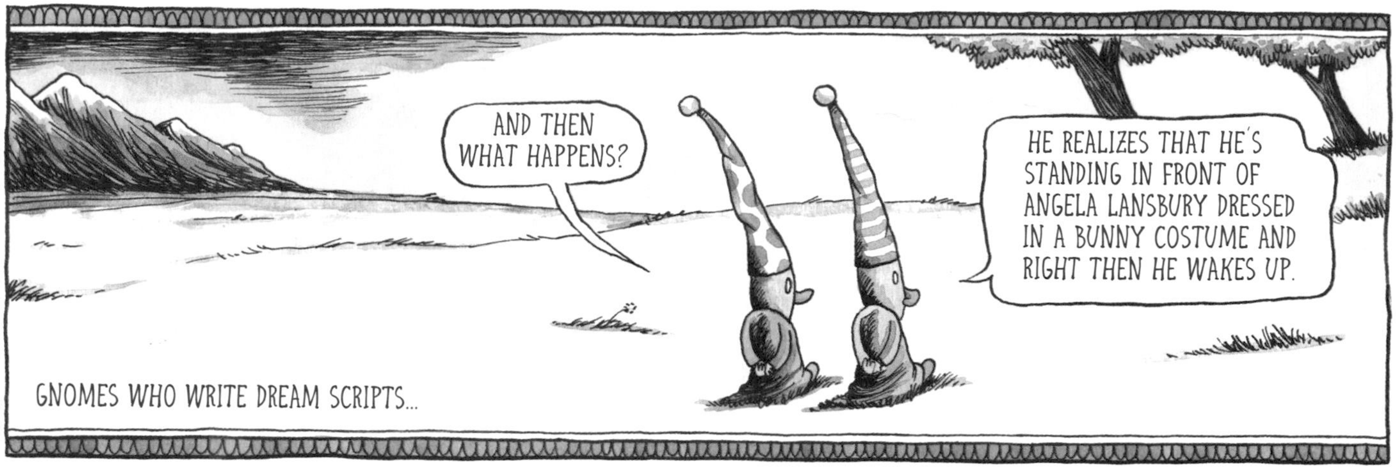
AND THEN WHAT HAPPENS?
HE REALIZES THAT HE'S STANDING IN FRONT OF ANGELA LANSBURY DRESSED IN A BUNNY COSTUME AND RIGHT THEN HE WAKES UP.
GNOMES WHO WRITE DREAM SCRIPTS...

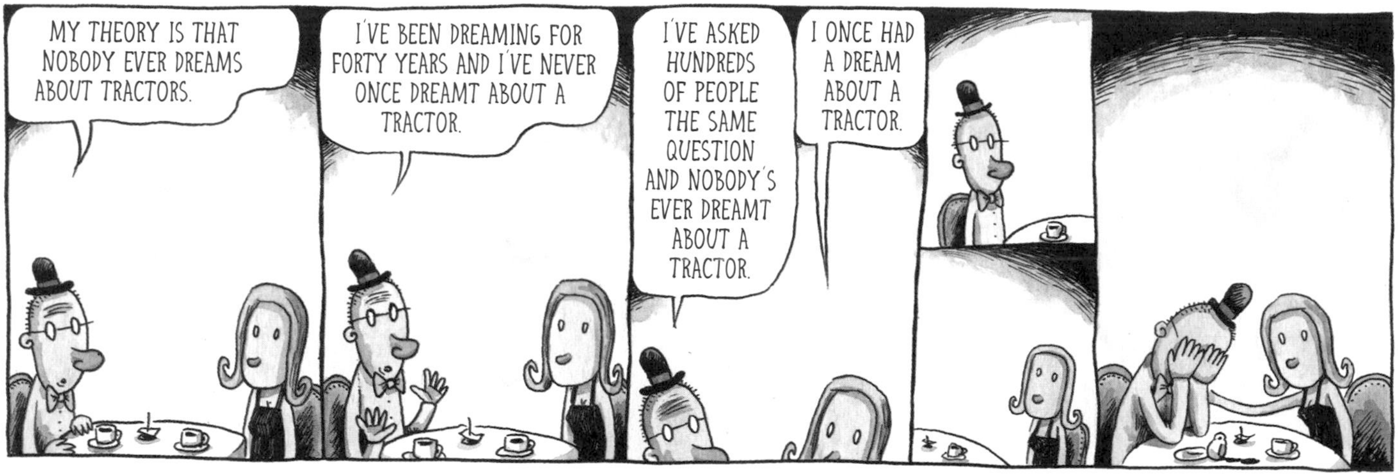
MY THEORY IS THAT NOBODY EVER DREAMS ABOUT TRACTORS.
I'VE BEEN DREAMING FOR FORTY YEARS AND I'VE NEVER ONCE DREAMT ABOUT A TRACTOR.
I'VE ASKED HUNDREDS OF PEOPLE THE SAME QUESTION AND NOBODY'S EVER DREAMT ABOUT A TRACTOR.
I ONCE HAD A DREAM ABOUT A TRACTOR.

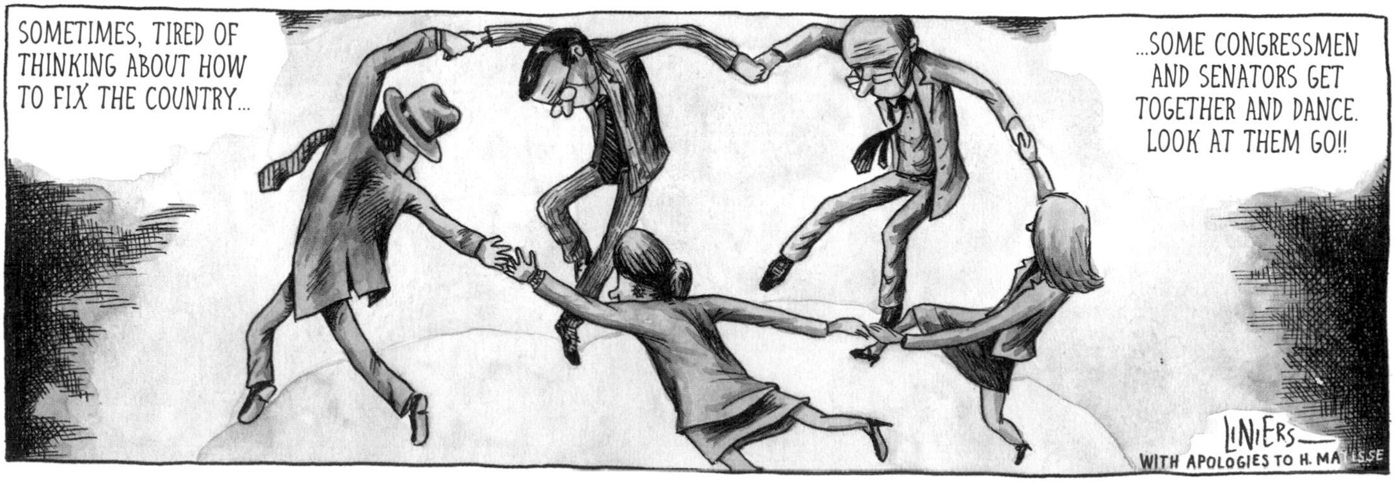
SOMETIMES, TIRED OF THINKING ABOUT HOW TO FIX THE COUNTRY...
...SOME CONGRESSMEN AND SENATORS GET TOGETHER AND DANCE. LOOK AT THEM GO!!
LINIERS
WITH APOLOGIES TO H. MATISSE

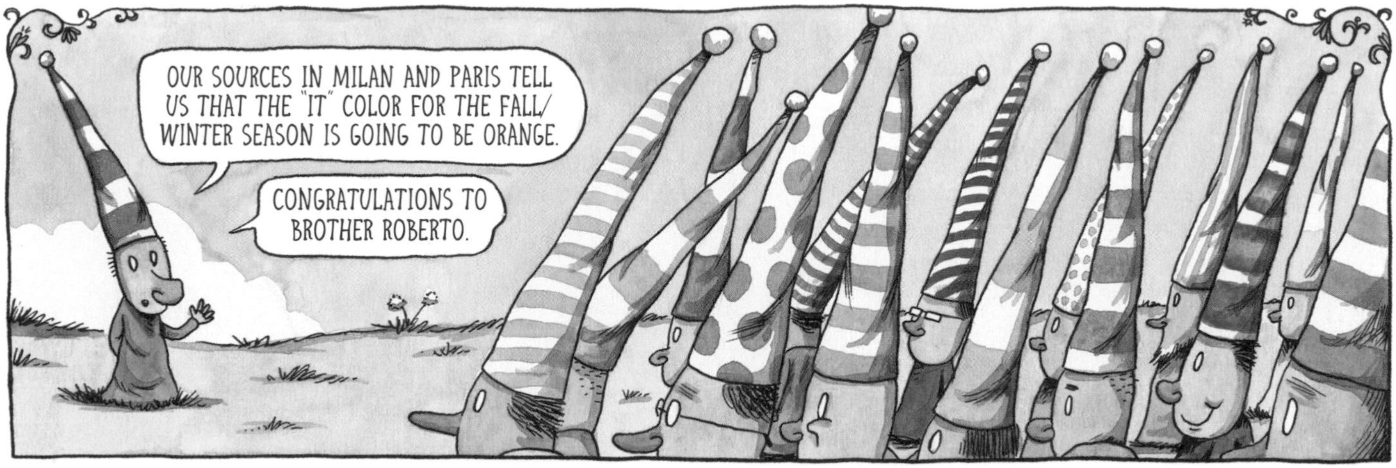
OUR SOURCES IN MILAN AND PARIS TELL US THAT THE "IT" COLOR FOR THE FALL/WINTER SEASON IS GOING TO BE ORANGE.
CONGRATULATIONS TO BROTHER ROBERTO.

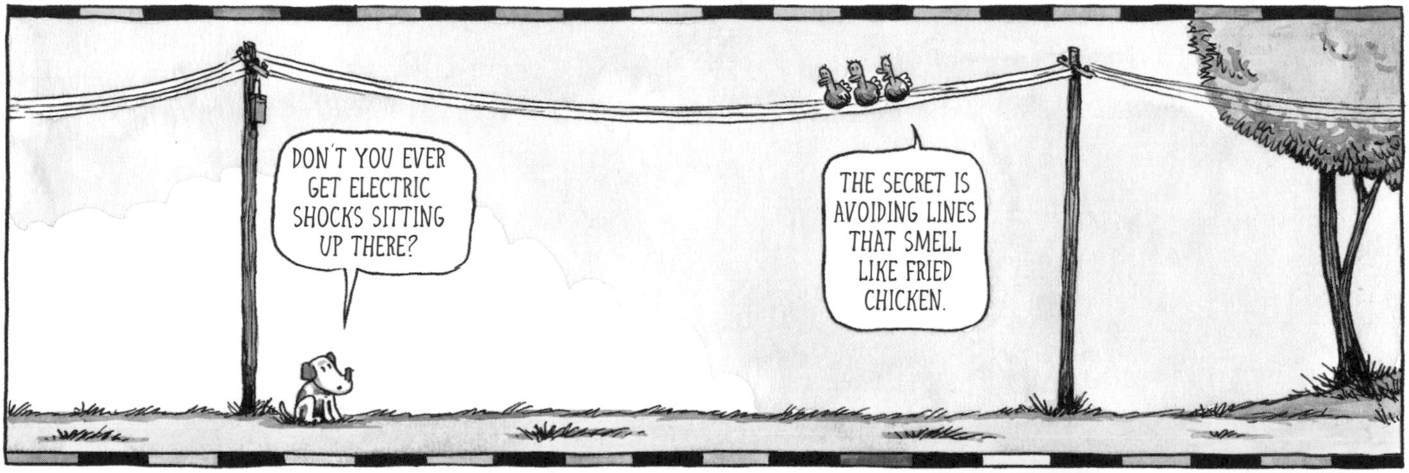
DON'T YOU EVER GET ELECTRIC SHOCKS SITTING UP THERE?
THE SECRET IS AVOIDING LINES THAT SMELL LIKE FRIED CHICKEN.

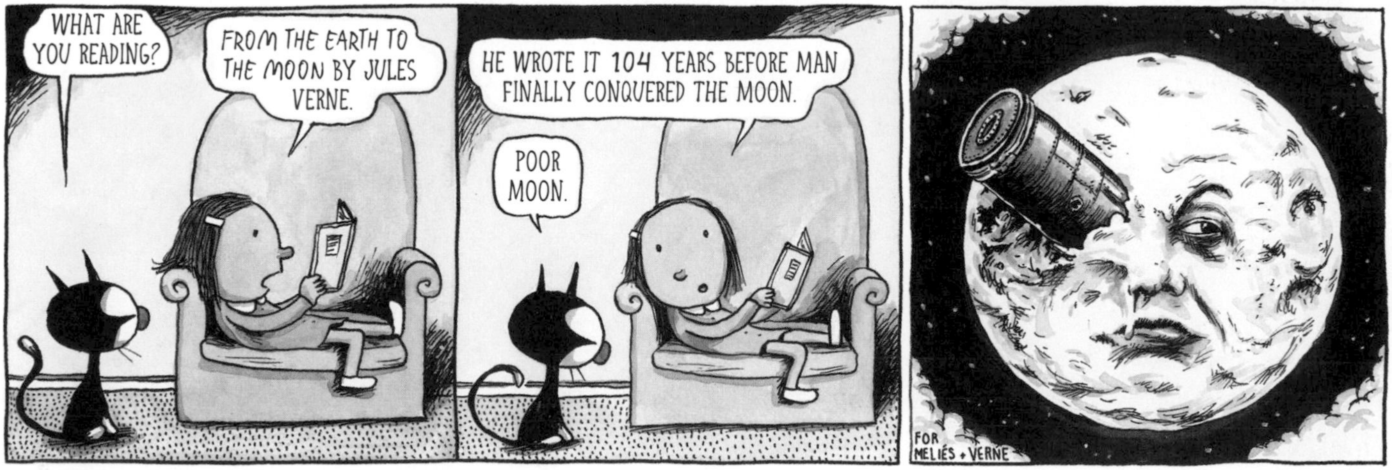
WHAT ARE YOU READING?
FROM THE EARTH TO THE MOON BY JULES VERNE.
HE WROTE IT 104 YEARS BEFORE MAN FINALLY CONQUERED THE MOON.
POOR MOON.
FOR MELIÉS + VERNE

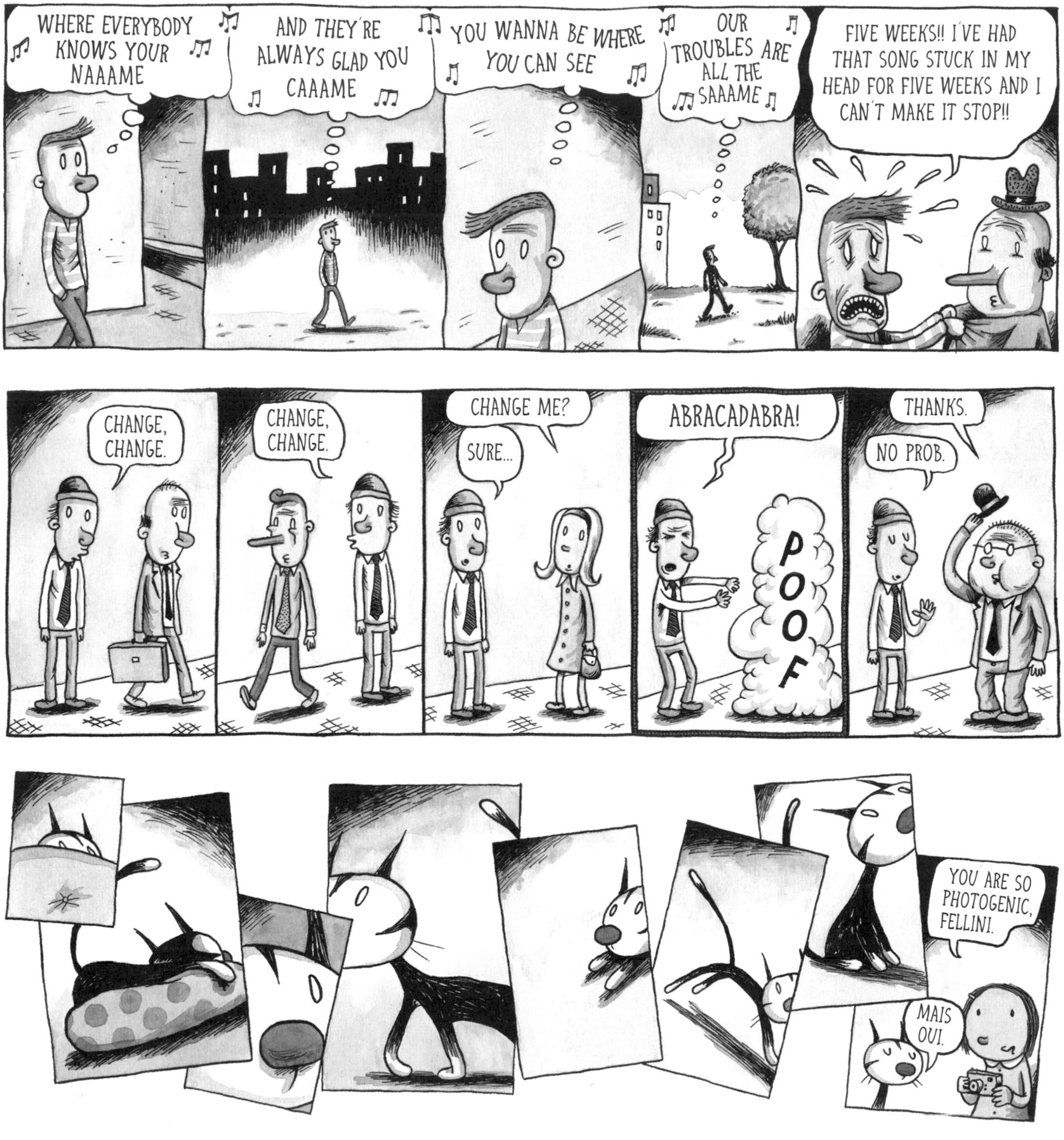
WHERE EVERYBODY KNOWS YOUR NAAAME
AND THEY'RE ALWAYS GLAD YOU CAAAME
YOU WANNA BE WHERE YOU CAN SEE
OUR TROUBLES ARE ALL THE SAAAME
FIVE WEEKS!! I'VE HAD THAT SONG STUCK IN MY HEAD FOR FIVE WEEKS AND I CAN'T MAKE IT STOP!!
CHANGE, CHANGE.
CHANGE, CHANGE.
CHANGE ME?
SURE...
ABRACADABRA!
POOF
THANKS.
NO PROB.
YOU ARE SO PHOTOGENIC, FELLINI.
MAIS OUI.

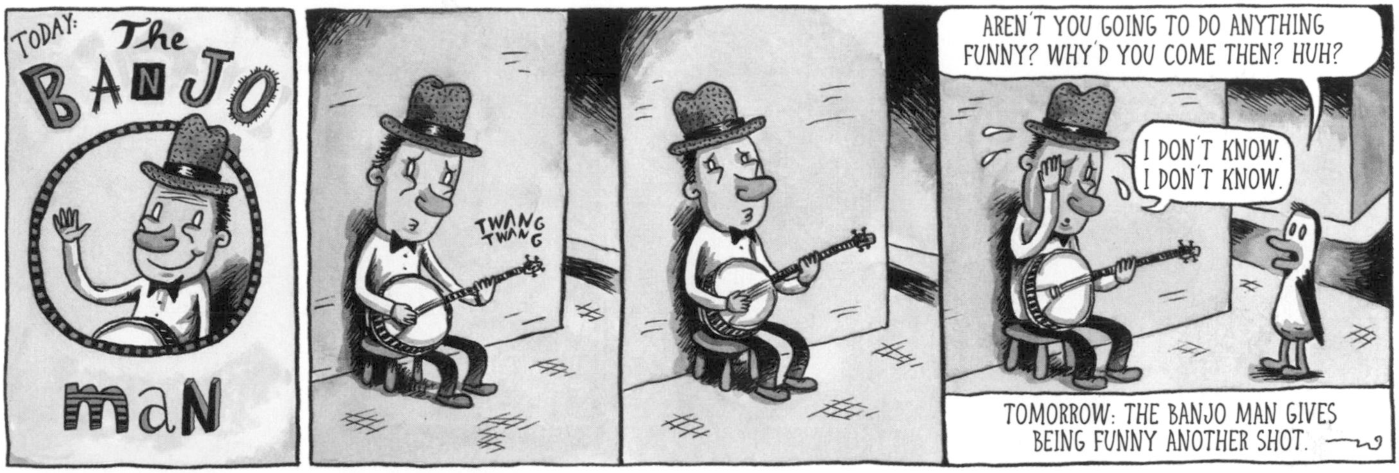
TODAY: The BANJO man
TWANG TWANG
AREN'T YOU GOING TO DO ANYTHING FUNNY? WHY'D YOU COME THEN? HUH?
I DON'T KNOW. I DON'T KNOW.
TOMORROW: THE BANJO MAN GIVES BEING FUNNY ANOTHER SHOT.

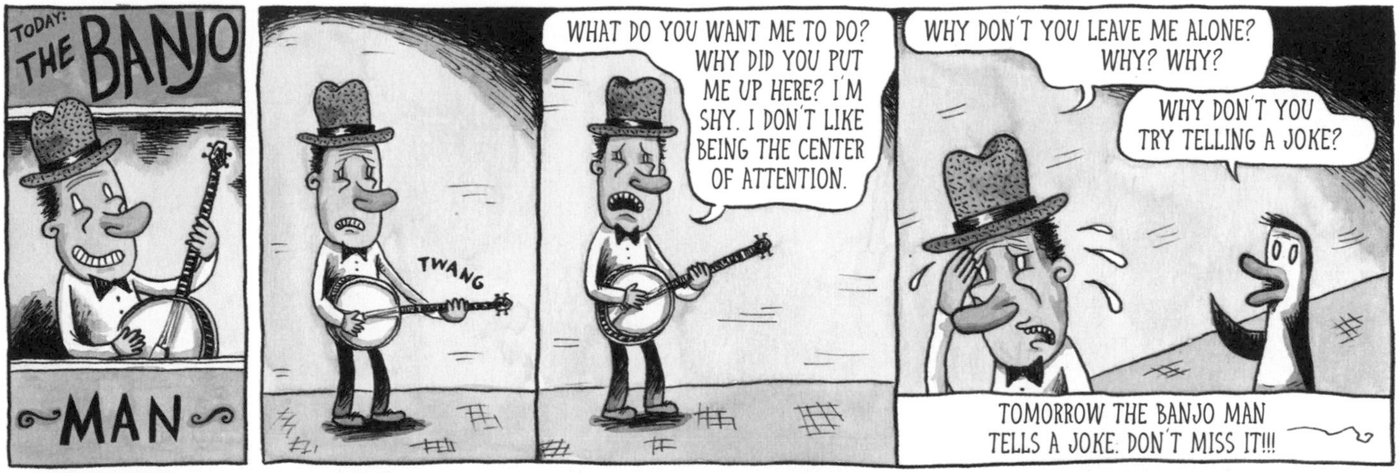
TODAY: THE BANJO MAN
TWANG
WHAT DO YOU WANT ME TO DO? WHY DID YOU PUT ME UP HERE? I'M SHY. I DON'T LIKE BEING THE CENTER OF ATTENTION.
WHY DON'T YOU LEAVE ME ALONE? WHY? WHY?
WHY DON'T YOU TRY TELLING A JOKE?
TOMORROW THE BANJO MAN TELLS A JOKE. DON'T MISS IT!!!

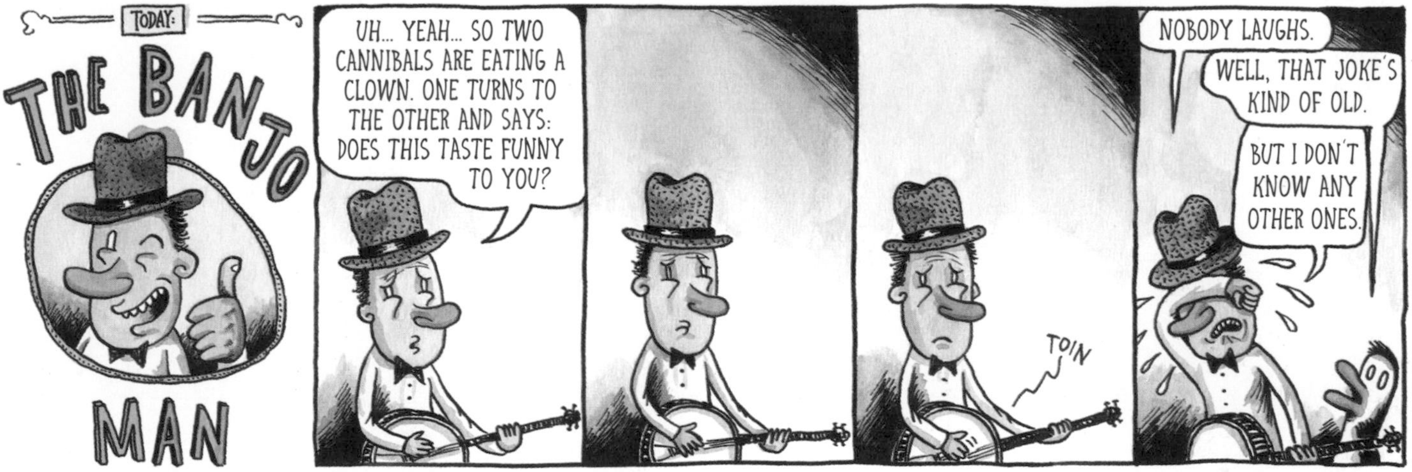
TODAY: THE BANJO MAN
UH... YEAH... SO TWO CANNIBALS ARE EATING A CLOWN. ONE TURNS TO THE OTHER AND SAYS: DOES THIS TASTE FUNNY TO YOU?
TOIN
NOBODY LAUGHS.
WELL, THAT JOKE'S KIND OF OLD.
BUT I DON'T KNOW ANY OTHER ONES.

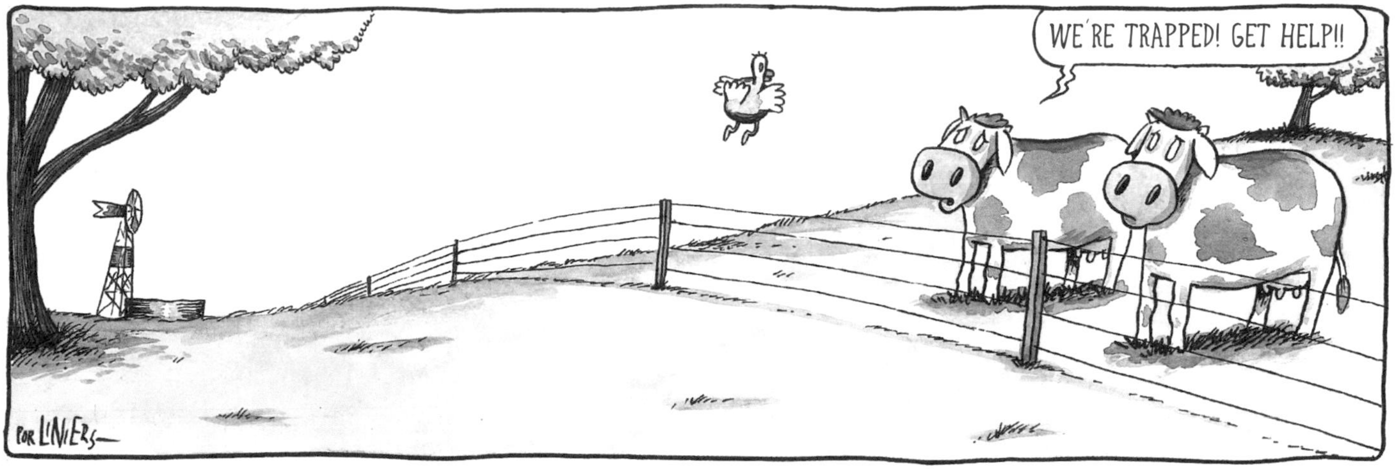
POR LINIERS
WE'RE TRAPPED! GET HELP!!

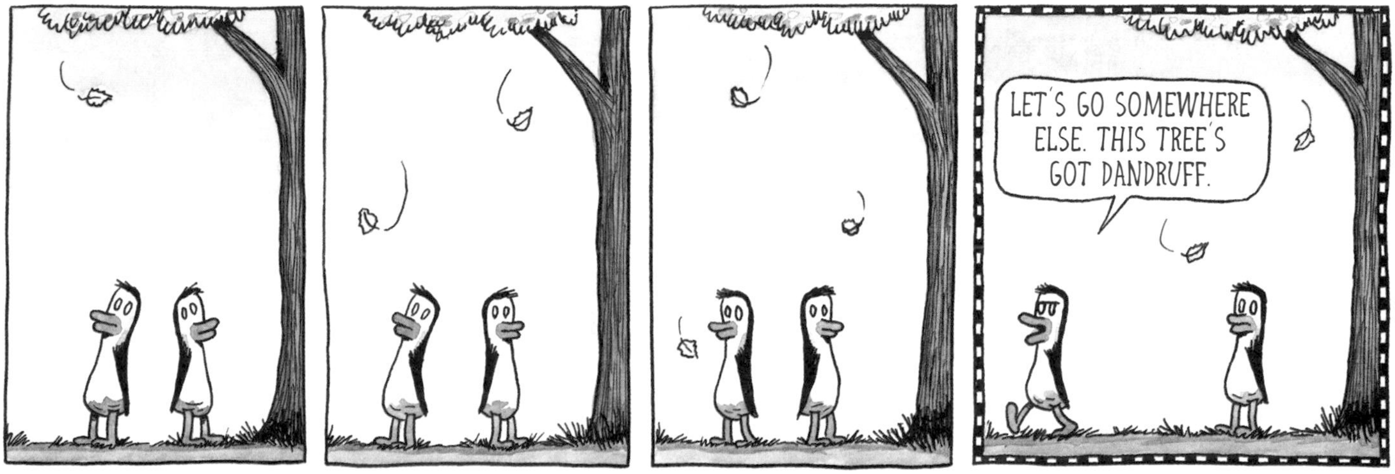
LET'S GO SOMEWHERE ELSE. THIS TREE'S GOT DANDRUFF.

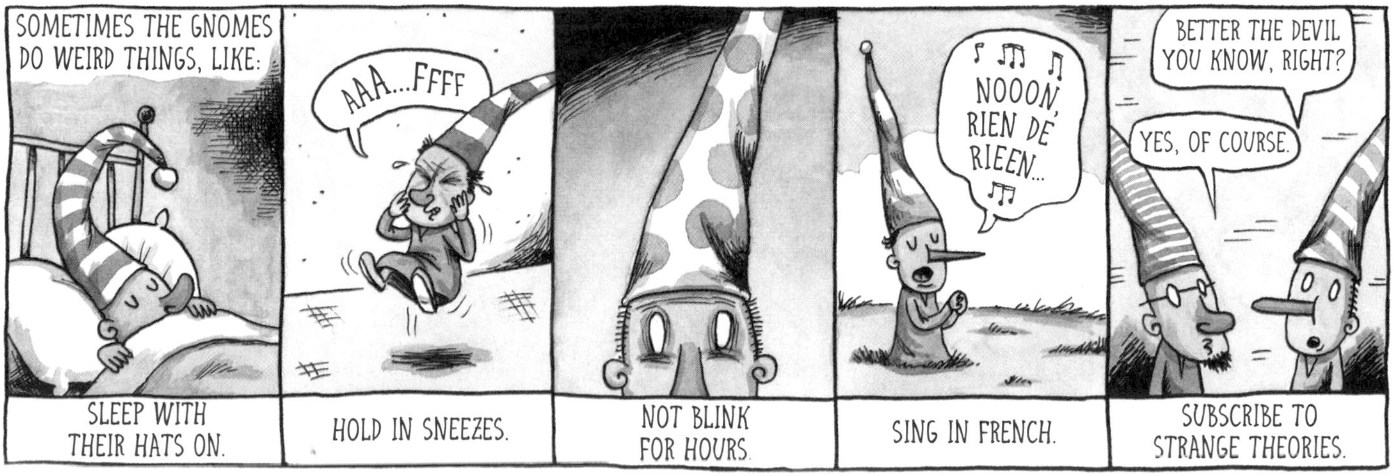
SOMETIMES THE GNOMES DO WEIRD THINGS, LIKE:
SLEEP WITH THEIR HATS ON.
AAA...FFFF
HOLD IN SNEEZES.
NOT BLINK FOR HOURS.
NOOON, RIEN DE RIEEN...
SING IN FRENCH.
BETTER THE DEVIL YOU KNOW, RIGHT?
YES, OF COURSE.
SUBSCRIBE TO STRANGE THEORIES.

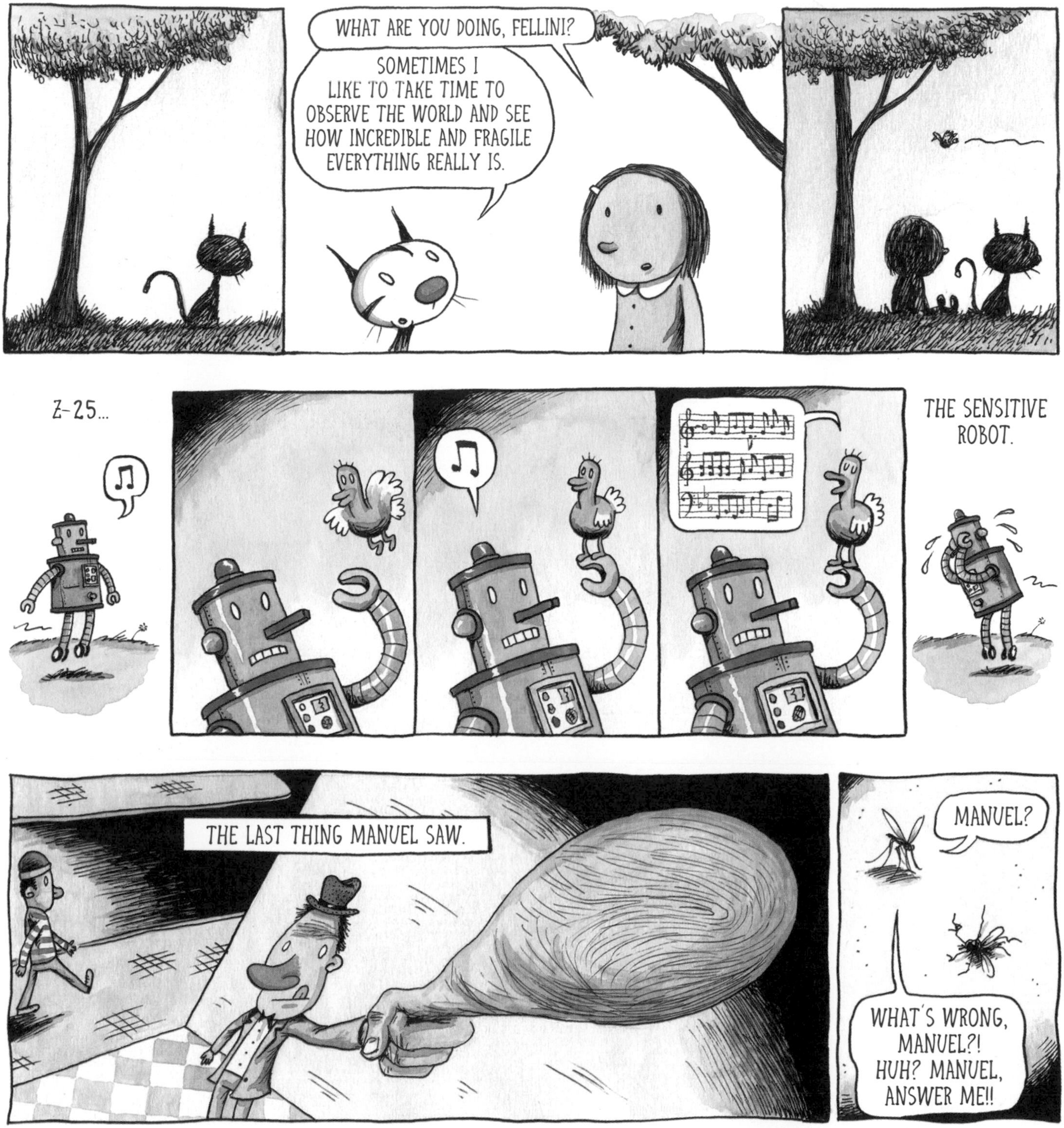

WHAT ARE YOU DOING, FELLINI?
SOMETIMES I LIKE TO TAKE TIME TO OBSERVE THE WORLD AND SEE HOW INCREDIBLE AND FRAGILE EVERYTHING REALLY IS.
Z-25...
THE SENSITIVE ROBOT.
THE LAST THING MANUEL SAW.
MANUEL?
WHAT'S WRONG, MANUEL?! HUH? MANUEL, ANSWER ME!!

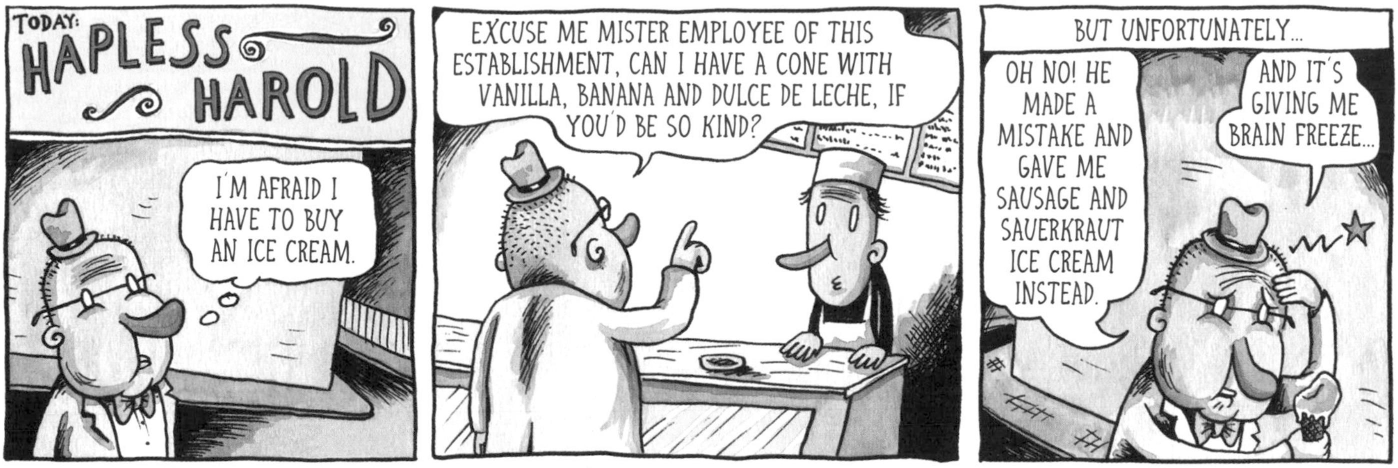
TODAY:
HAPLESS HAROLD
I'M AFRAID I HAVE TO BUY AN ICE CREAM.
EXCUSE ME MISTER EMPLOYEE OF THIS ESTABLISHMENT, CAN I HAVE A CONE WITH VANILLA, BANANA AND DULCE DE LECHE, IF YOU'D BE SO KIND?
BUT UNFORTUNATELY...
OH NO! HE MADE A MISTAKE AND GAVE ME SAUSAGE AND SAUERKRAUT ICE CREAM INSTEAD.
AND IT'S GIVING ME BRAIN FREEZE...

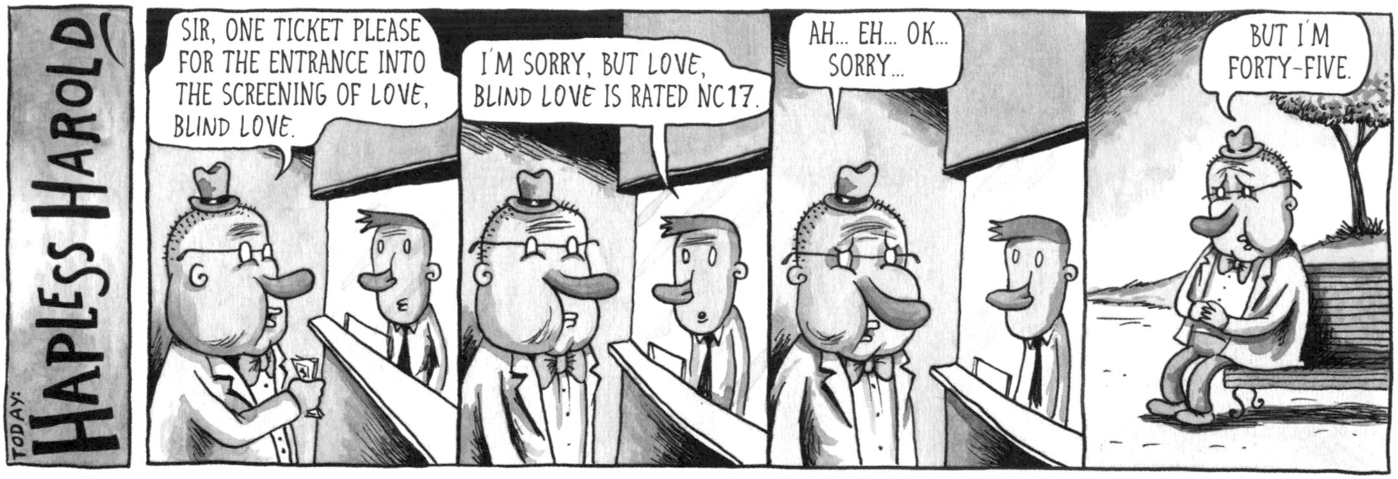
TODAY:
HAPLESS HAROLD
SIR, ONE TICKET PLEASE FOR THE ENTRANCE INTO THE SCREENING OF LOVE, BLIND LOVE.
I'M SORRY, BUT LOVE, BLIND LOVE IS RATED NC17.
AH... EH... OK... SORRY...
BUT I'M FORTY-FIVE.

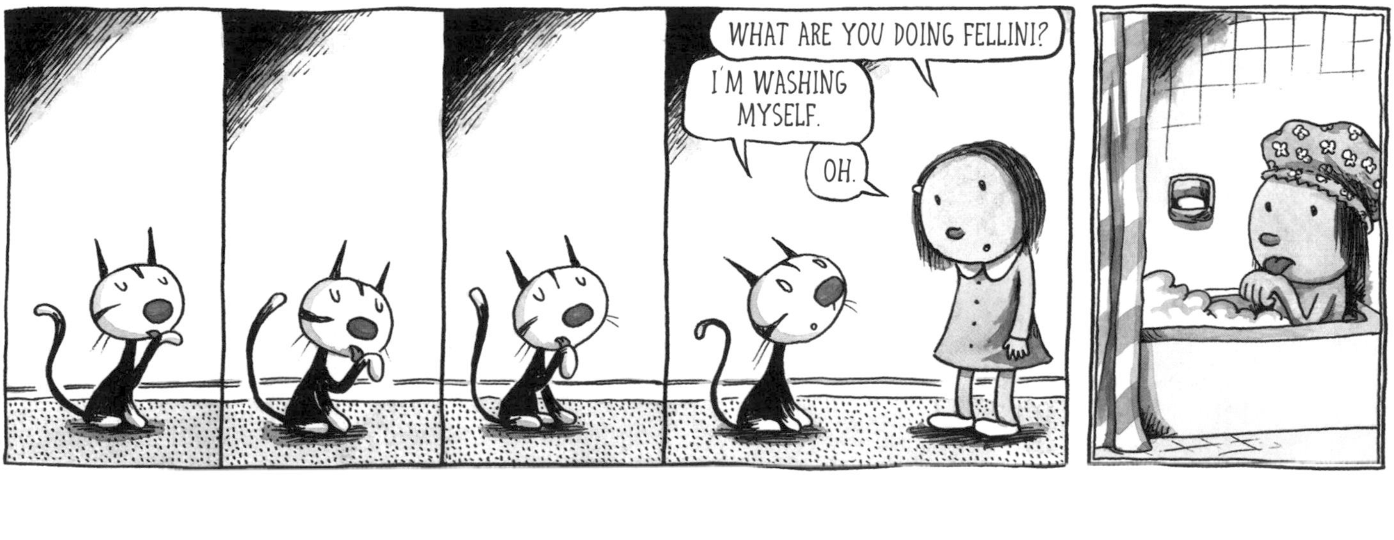
WHAT ARE YOU DOING FELLINI?
I'M WASHING MYSELF.
OH.

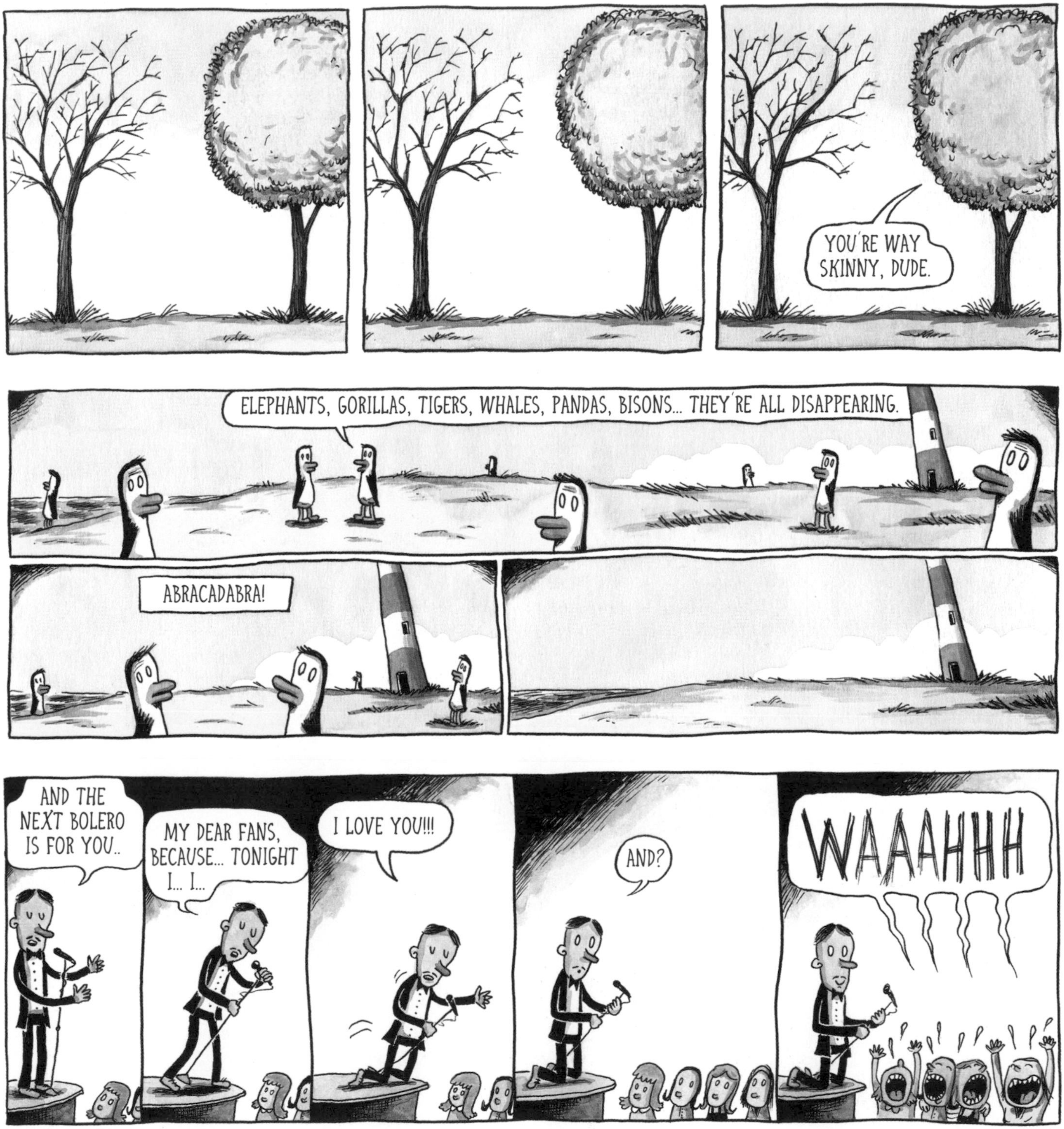
YOU'RE WAY SKINNY, DUDE.
ELEPHANTS, GORILLAS, TIGERS, WHALES, PANDAS, BISONS... THEY'RE ALL DISAPPEARING.
ABRACADABRA!
AND THE NEXT BOLERO IS FOR YOU..
MY DEAR FANS, BECAUSE... TONIGHT I... I...
I LOVE YOU!!!
AND?
WAAAHHH

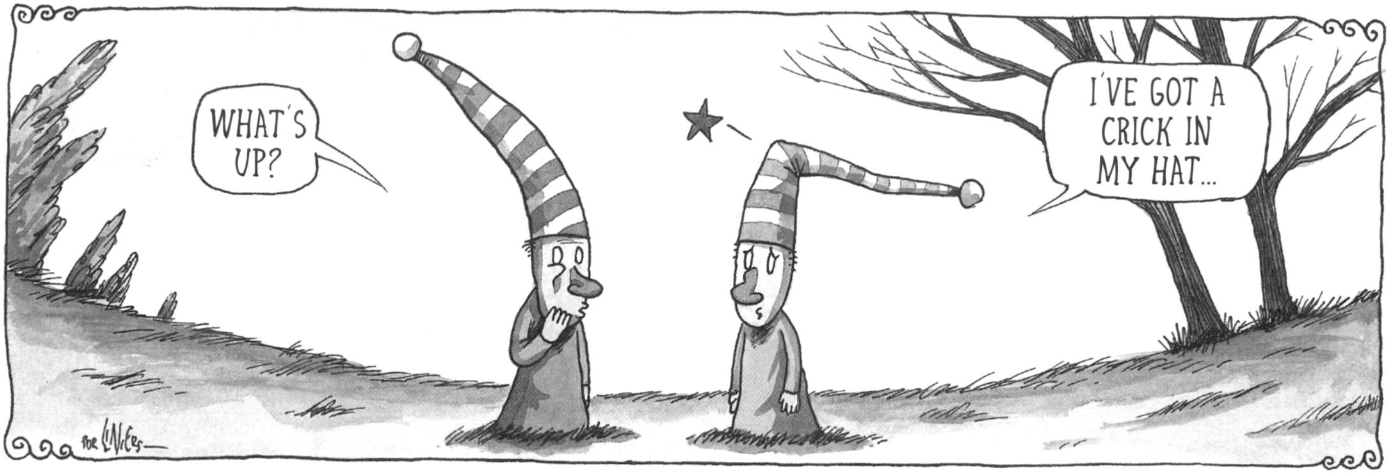
WHAT'S UP?
I'VE GOT A CRICK IN MY HAT...

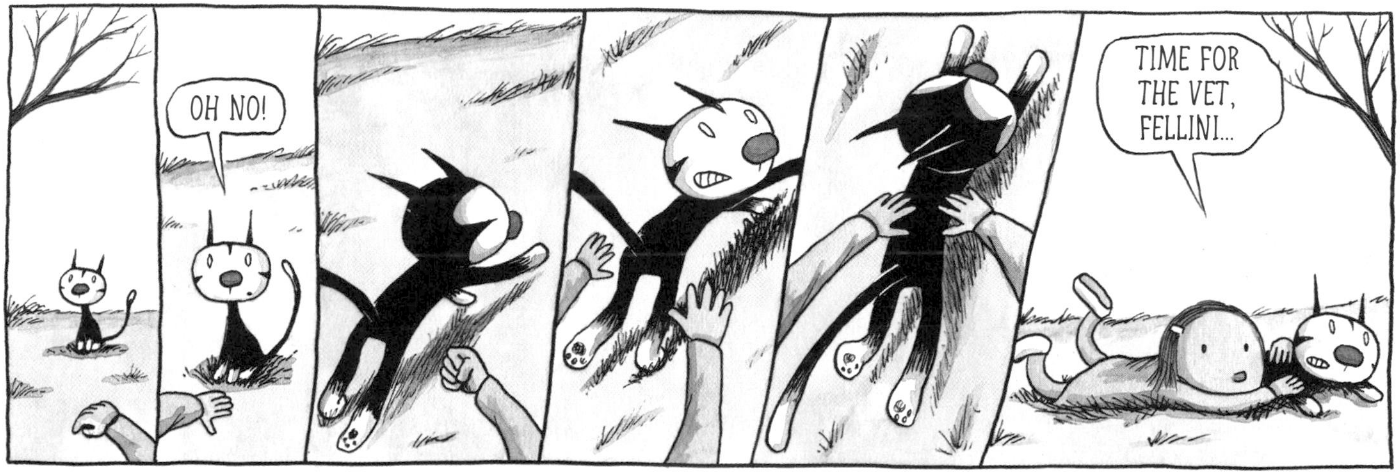
OH NO!
TIME FOR THE VET, FELLINI...

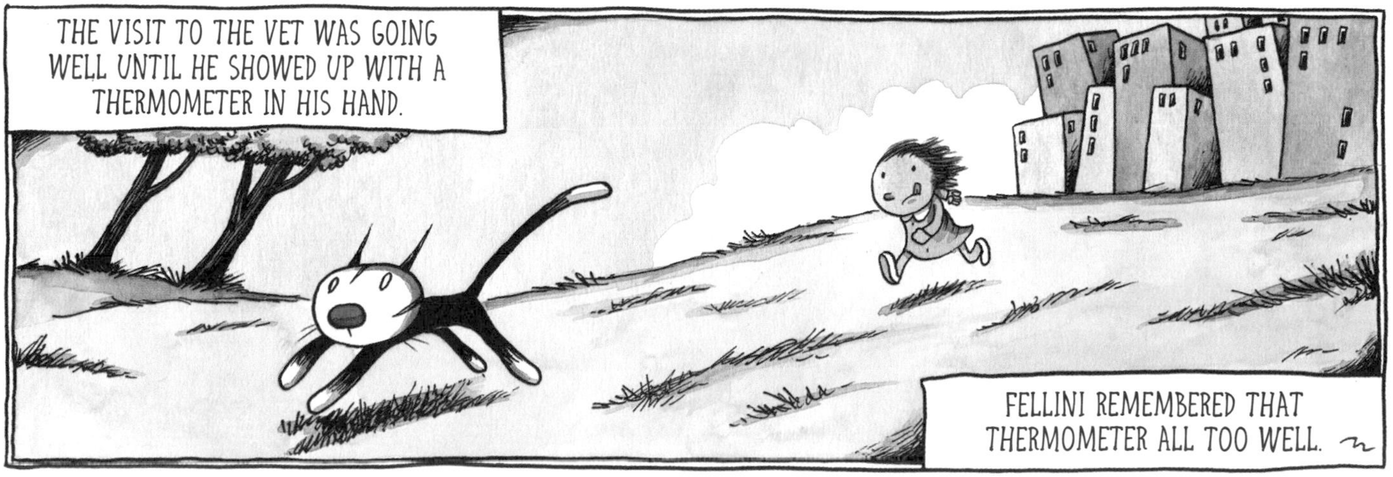
THE VISIT TO THE VET WAS GOING WELL UNTIL HE SHOWED UP WITH A THERMOMETER IN HIS HAND.
FELLINI REMEMBERED THAT THERMOMETER ALL TOO WELL.

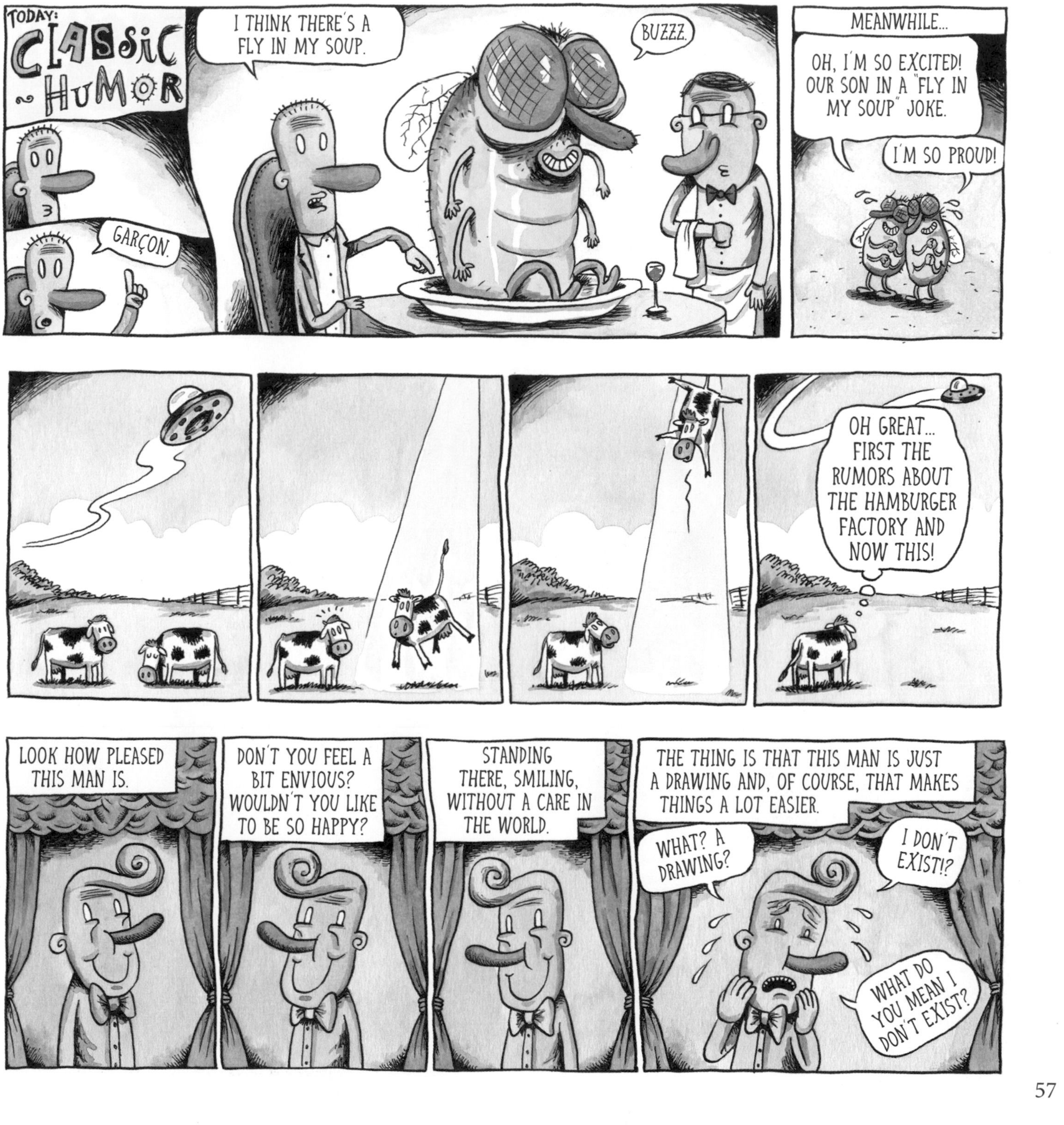
TODAY:
CLASSIC HUMOR
GARÇON.
I THINK THERE'S A FLY IN MY SOUP.
BUZZZ.
MEANWHILE...
OH, I'M SO EXCITED! OUR SON IN A "FLY IN MY SOUP" JOKE.
I'M SO PROUD!
OH GREAT... FIRST THE RUMORS ABOUT THE HAMBURGER FACTORY AND NOW THIS!
LOOK HOW PLEASED THIS MAN IS.
DON'T YOU FEEL A BIT ENVIOUS? WOULDN'T YOU LIKE TO BE SO HAPPY?
STANDING THERE, SMILING, WITHOUT A CARE IN THE WORLD.
THE THING IS THAT THIS MAN IS JUST A DRAWING AND, OF COURSE, THAT MAKES THINGS A LOT EASIER.
WHAT? A DRAWING?
I DON'T EXIST!?
WHAT DO YOU MEAN I DON'T EXIST?

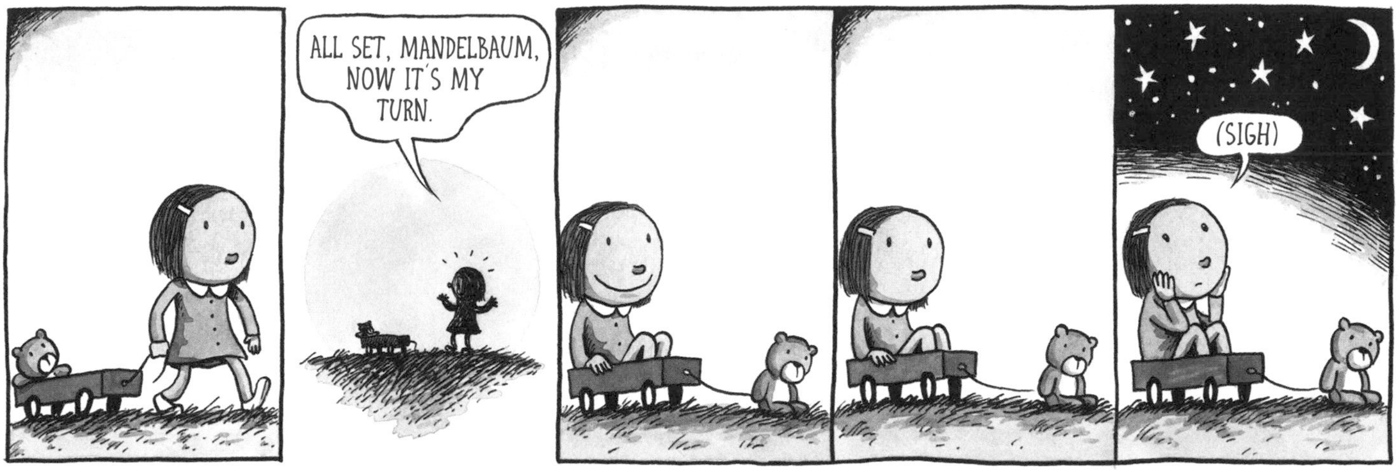
ALL SET, MANDELBAUM, NOW IT'S MY TURN.
(SIGH)

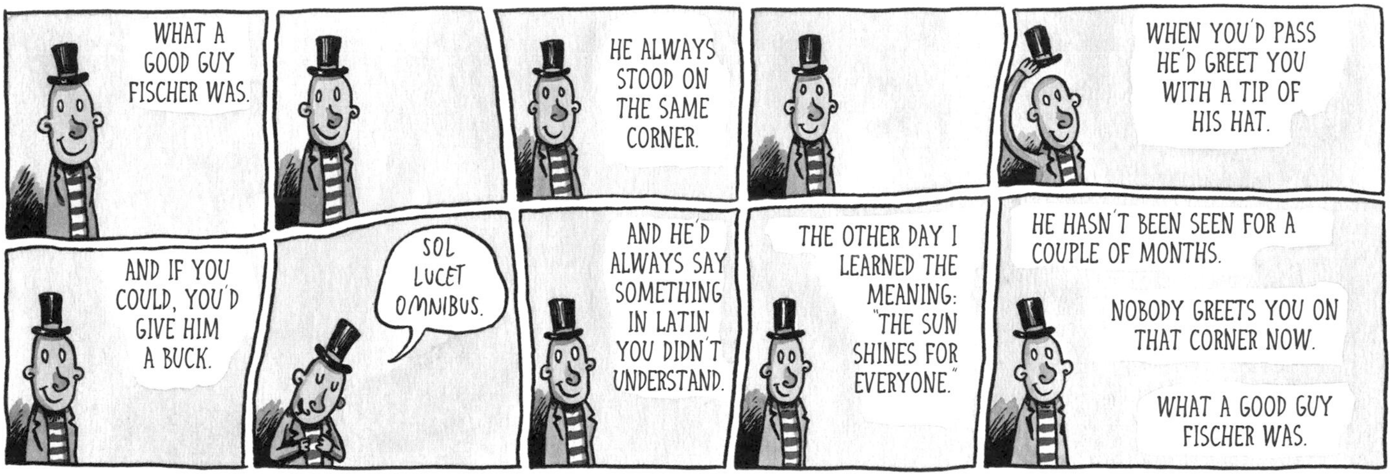
WHAT A GOOD GUY FISCHER WAS.
HE ALWAYS STOOD ON THE SAME CORNER.
WHEN YOU'D PASS HE'D GREET YOU WITH A TIP OF HIS HAT.
AND IF YOU COULD, YOU'D GIVE HIM A BUCK.
SOL LUCET OMNIBUS.
AND HE'D ALWAYS SAY SOMETHING IN LATIN YOU DIDN'T UNDERSTAND.
THE OTHER DAY I LEARNED THE MEANING: "THE SUN SHINES FOR EVERYONE."
HE HASN'T BEEN SEEN FOR A COUPLE OF MONTHS.
NOBODY GREETS YOU ON THAT CORNER NOW.
WHAT A GOOD GUY FISCHER WAS.

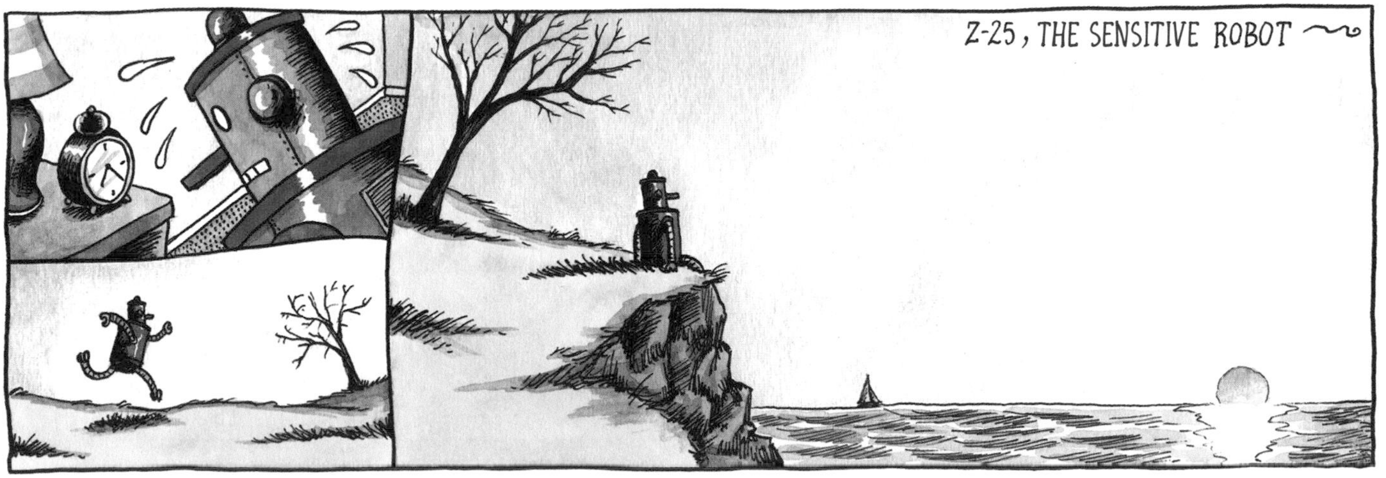
Z-25, THE SENSITIVE ROBOT

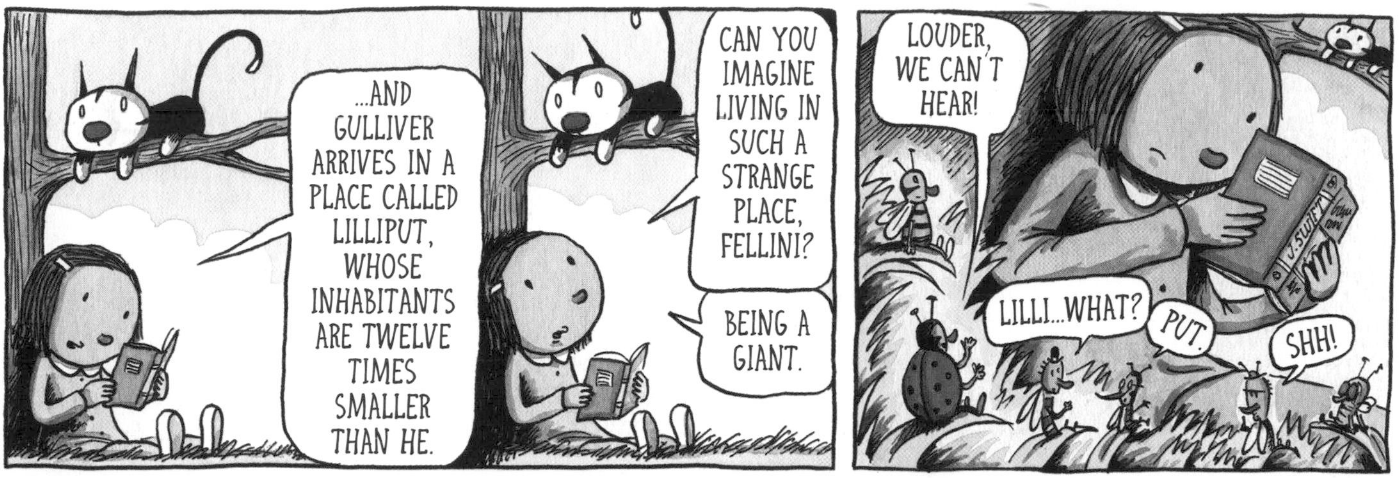
...AND GULLIVER ARRIVES IN A PLACE CALLED LILLIPUT, WHOSE INHABITANTS ARE TWELVE TIMES SMALLER THAN HE.
CAN YOU IMAGINE LIVING IN SUCH A STRANGE PLACE, FELLINI?
BEING A GIANT.
LOUDER, WE CAN'T HEAR!
LILLI...WHAT?
PUT.
SHH!

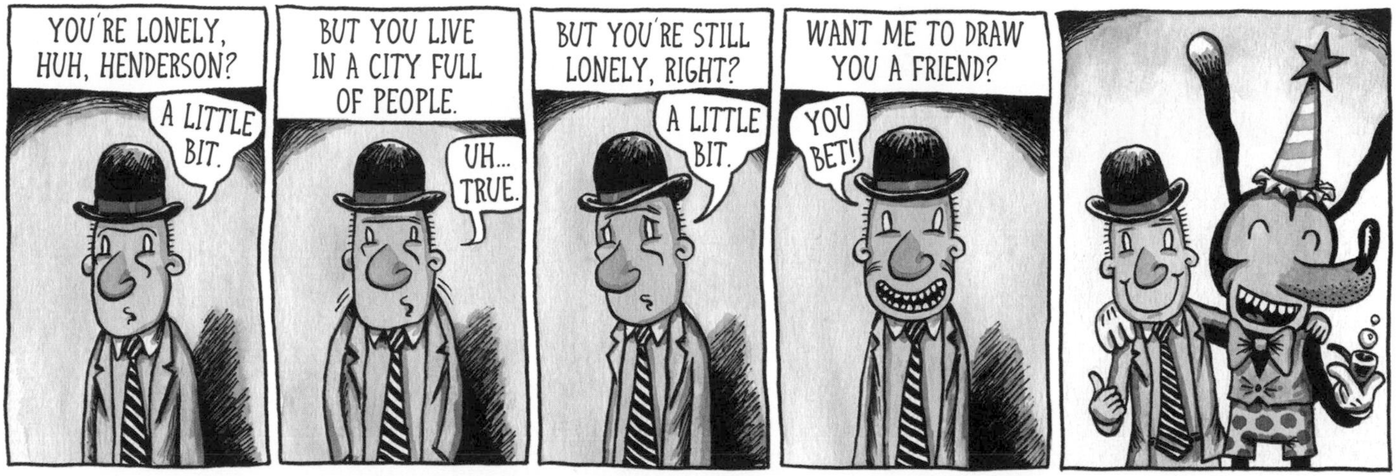
YOU'RE LONELY, HUH, HENDERSON?
A LITTLE BIT.
BUT YOU LIVE IN A CITY FULL OF PEOPLE.
UH... TRUE.
BUT YOU'RE STILL LONELY, RIGHT?
A LITTLE BIT.
WANT ME TO DRAW YOU A FRIEND?
YOU BET!

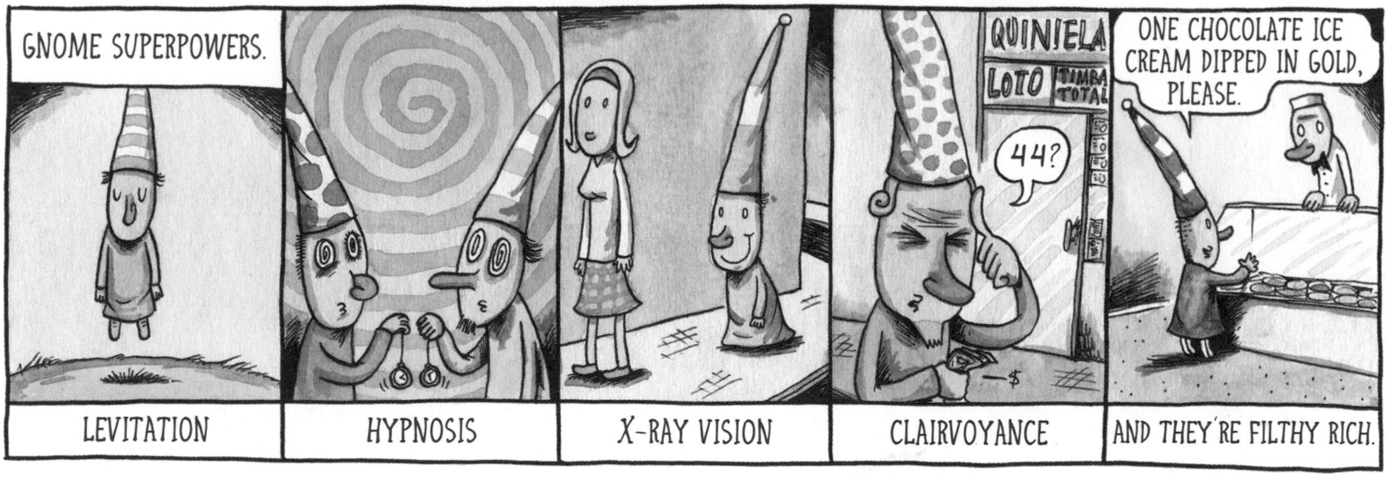
GNOME SUPERPOWERS.
LEVITATION
HYPNOSIS
X-RAY VISION
QUINIELA
LOTO
TIMBA TOTAL
44?
CLAIRVOYANCE
ONE CHOCOLATE ICE CREAM DIPPED IN GOLD, PLEASE.
AND THEY'RE FILTHY RICH.

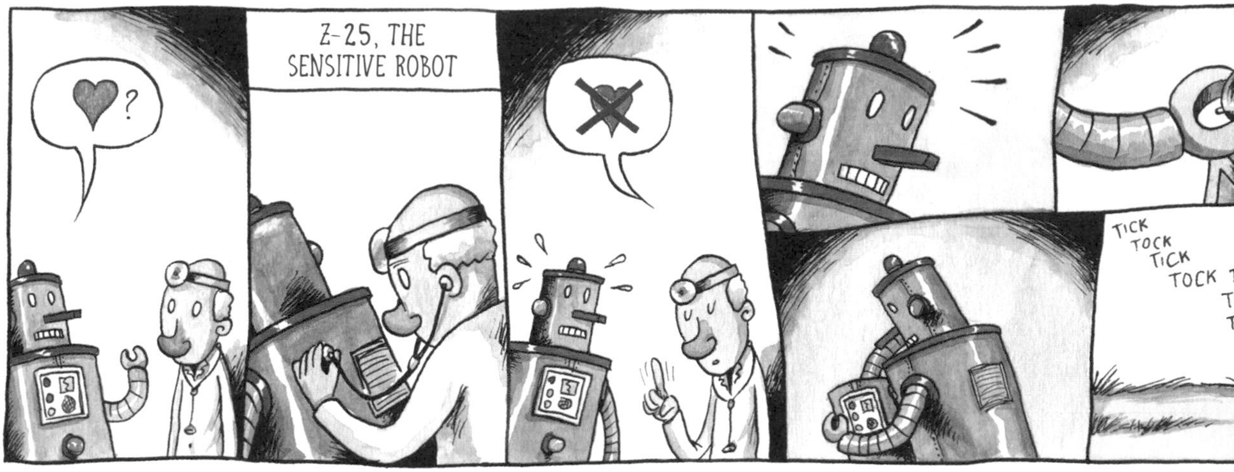
?
Z-25, THE SENSITIVE ROBOT
TICK TOCK TICK TOCK TICK TOCK TICK

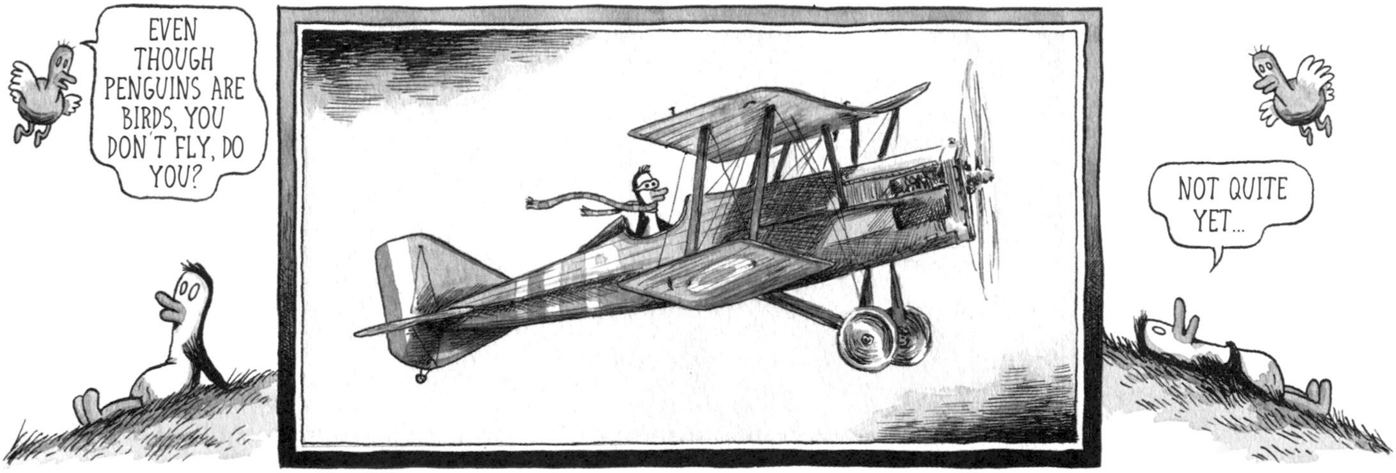
EVEN THOUGH PENGUINS ARE BIRDS, YOU DON'T FLY, DO YOU?
NOT QUITE YET...

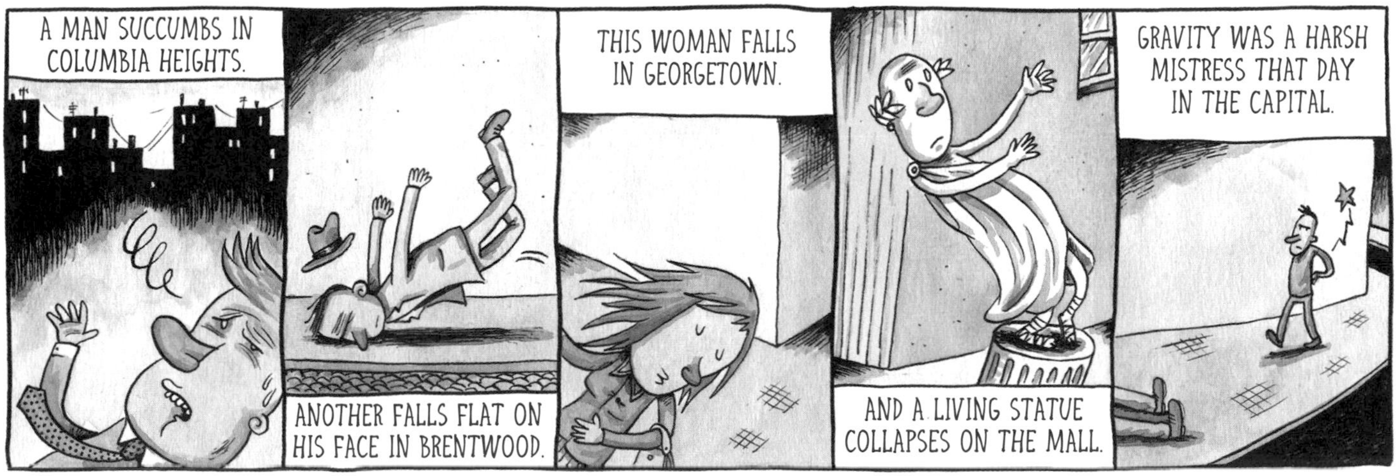
A MAN SUCCUMBS IN COLUMBIA HEIGHTS.
ANOTHER FALLS FLAT ON HIS FACE IN BRENTWOOD.
THIS WOMAN FALLS IN GEORGETOWN.
AND A LIVING STATUE COLLAPSES ON THE MALL.
GRAVITY WAS A HARSH MISTRESS THAT DAY IN THE CAPITAL.

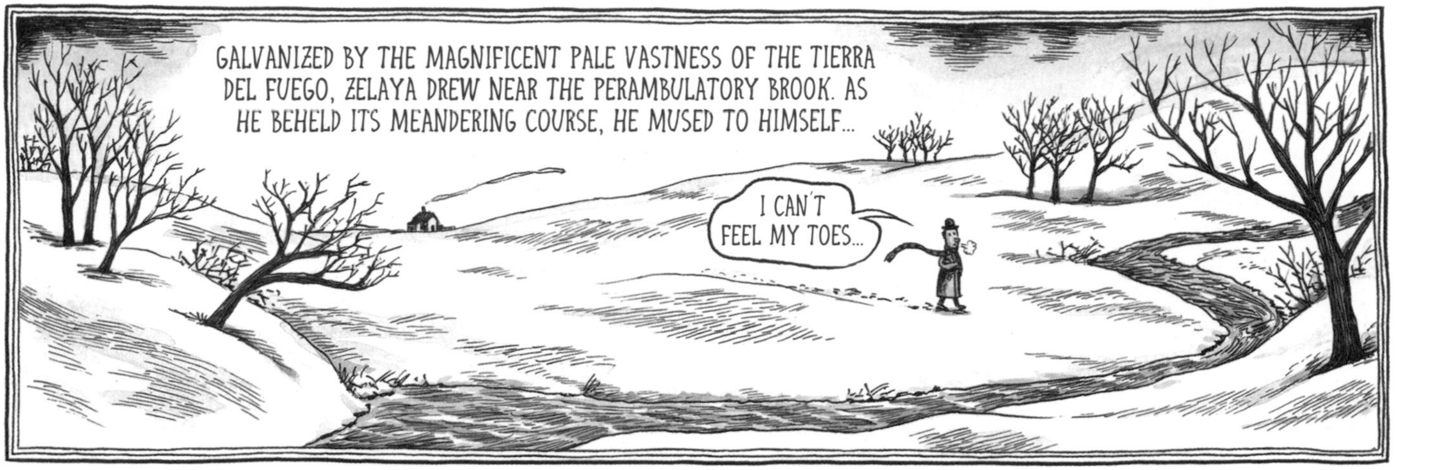
GALVANIZED BY THE MAGNIFICENT PALE VASTNESS OF THE TIERRA DEL FUEGO, ZELAYA DREW NEAR THE PERAMBULATORY BROOK. AS HE BEHELD ITS MEANDERING COURSE, HE MUSED TO HIMSELF...
I CAN'T FEEL MY TOES...

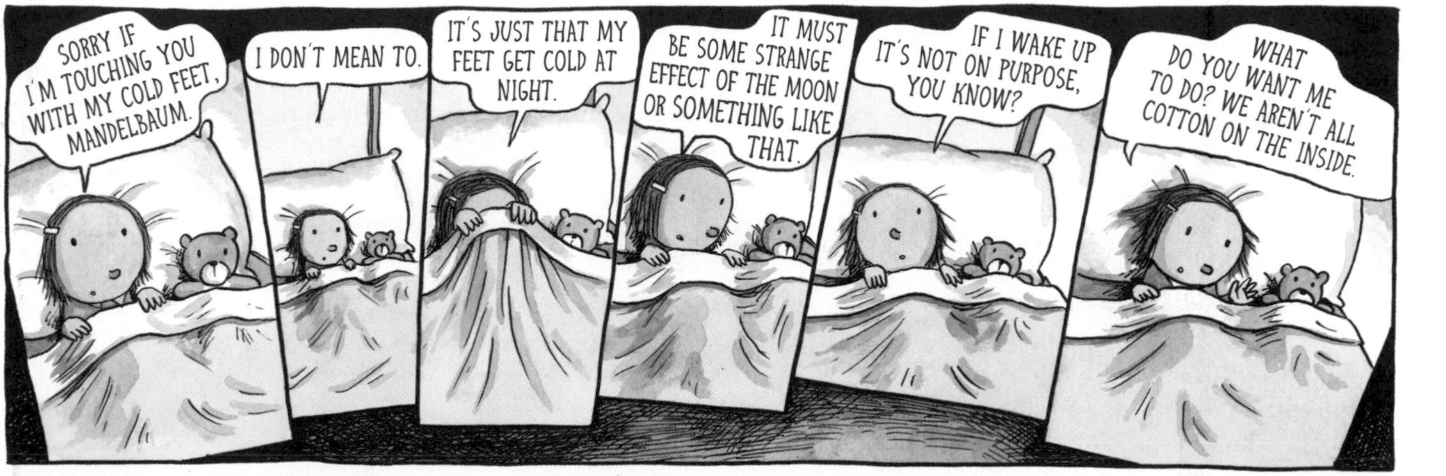
SORRY IF I'M TOUCHING YOU WITH MY COLD FEET, MANDELBAUM.
I DON'T MEAN TO.
IT'S JUST THAT MY FEET GET COLD AT NIGHT.
IT MUST BE SOME STRANGE EFFECT OF THE MOON OR SOMETHING LIKE THAT.
IF I WAKE UP IT'S NOT ON PURPOSE, YOU KNOW?
WHAT DO YOU WANT ME TO DO? WE AREN'T ALL COTTON ON THE INSIDE.

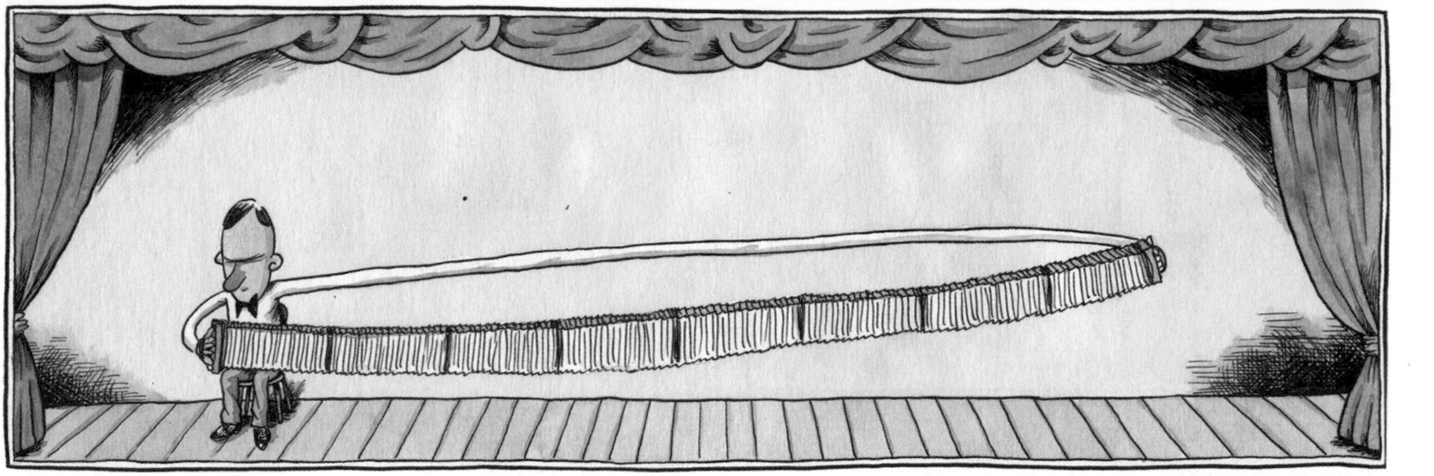

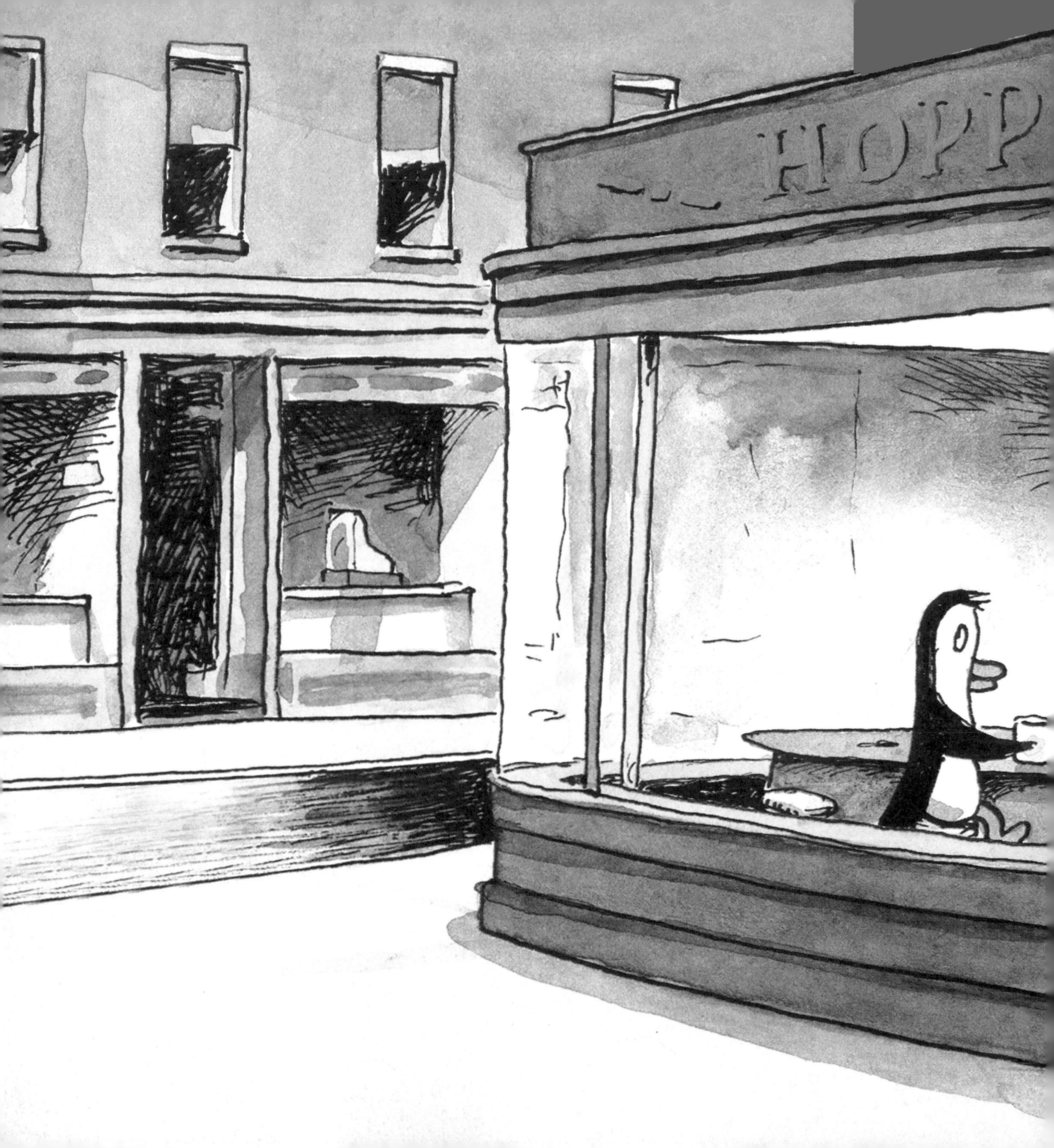
HOPP

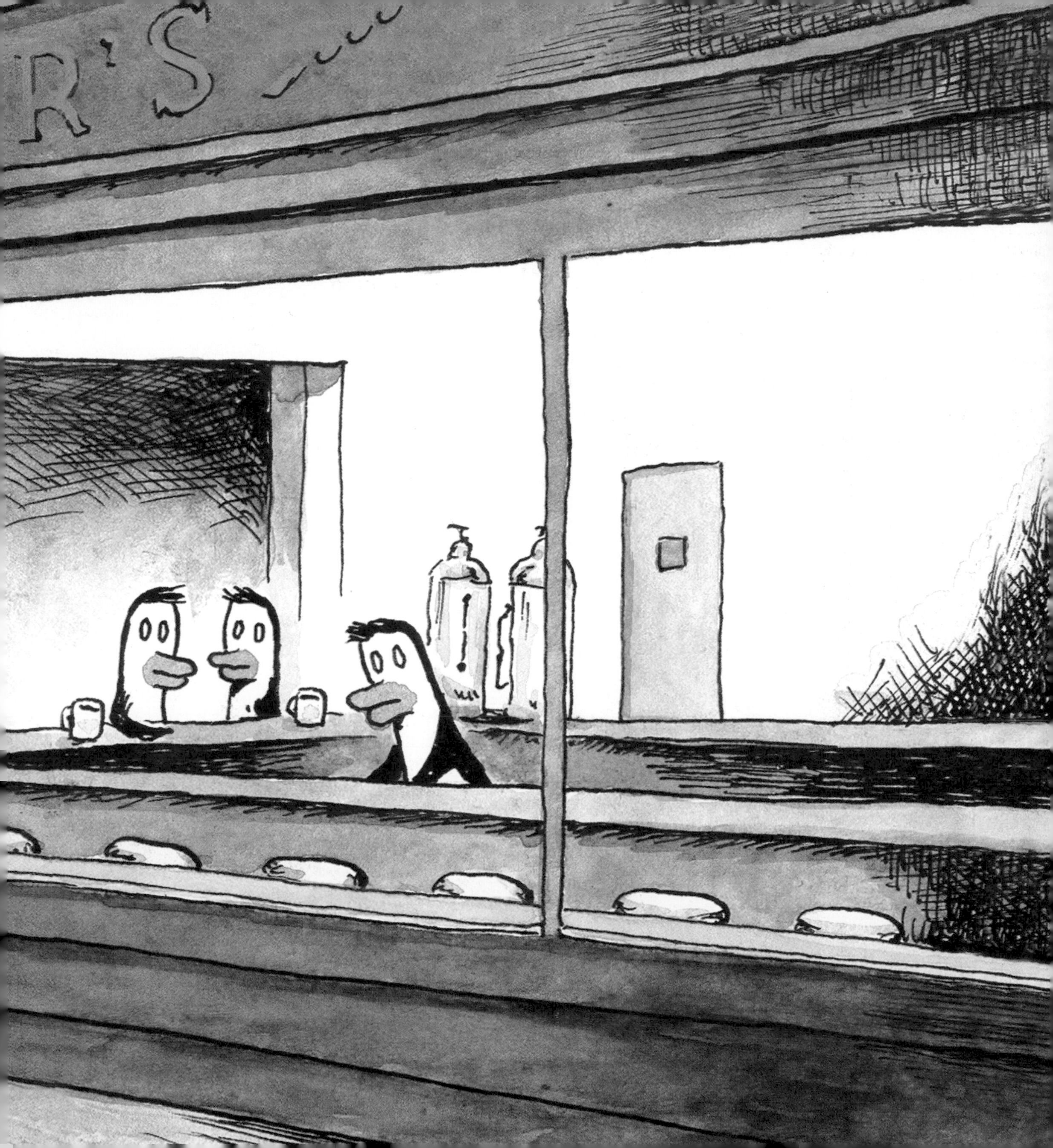
R'S

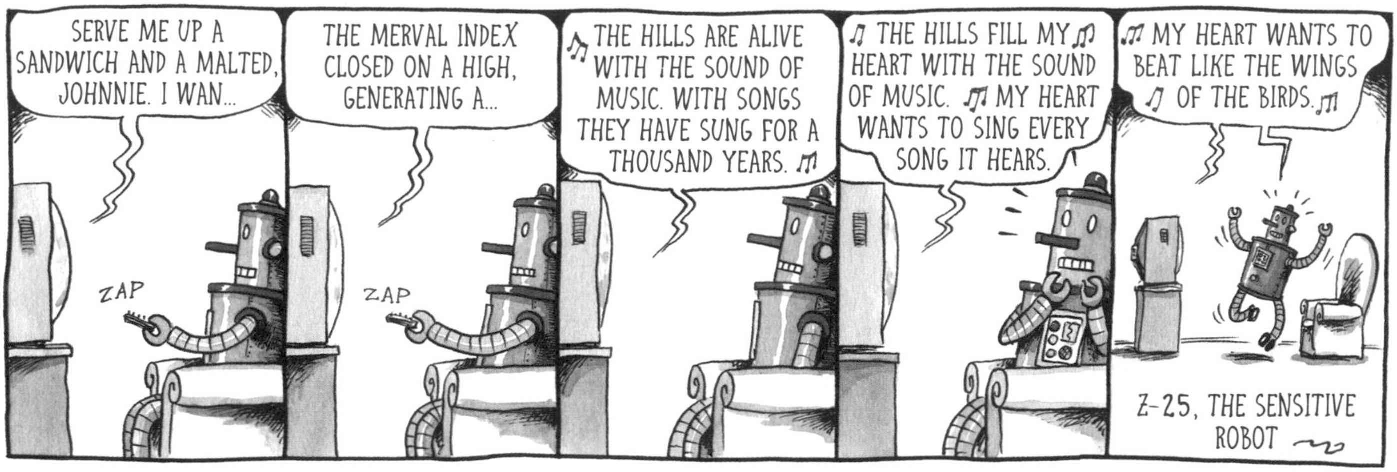
SERVE ME UP A SANDWICH AND A MALTED, JOHNNIE. I WAN...
ZAP
THE MERVAL INDEX CLOSED ON A HIGH, GENERATING A...
ZAP
THE HILLS ARE ALIVE WITH THE SOUND OF MUSIC. WITH SONGS THEY HAVE SUNG FOR A THOUSAND YEARS.
THE HILLS FILL MY HEART WITH THE SOUND OF MUSIC. MY HEART WANTS TO SING EVERY SONG IT HEARS.
MY HEART WANTS TO BEAT LIKE THE WINGS OF THE BIRDS.
Z-25, THE SENSITIVE ROBOT

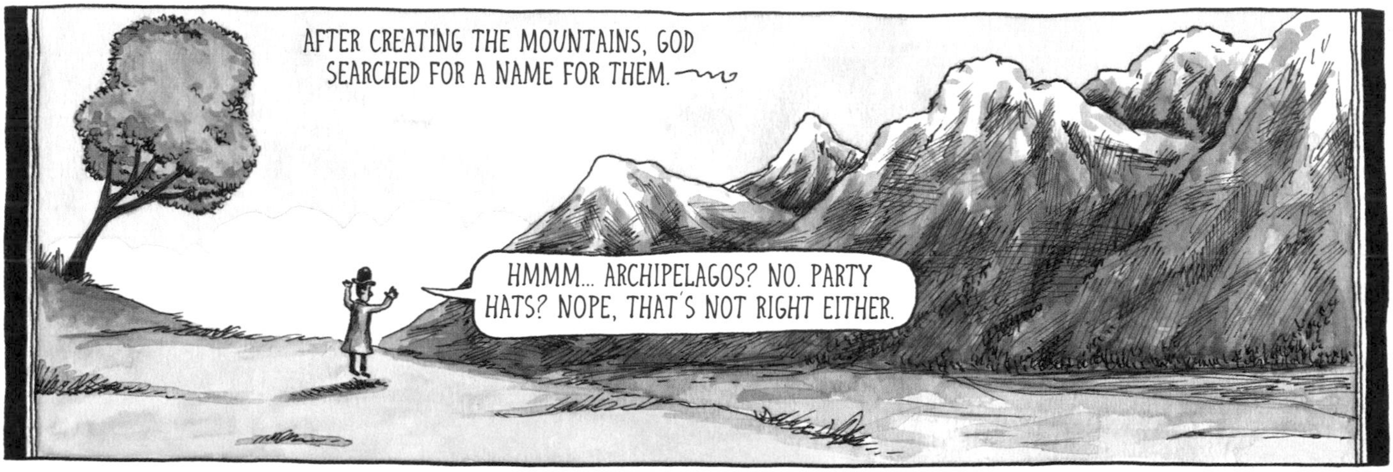
AFTER CREATING THE MOUNTAINS, GOD SEARCHED FOR A NAME FOR THEM.
HMMM... ARCHIPELAGOS? NO. PARTY HATS? NOPE, THAT'S NOT RIGHT EITHER.

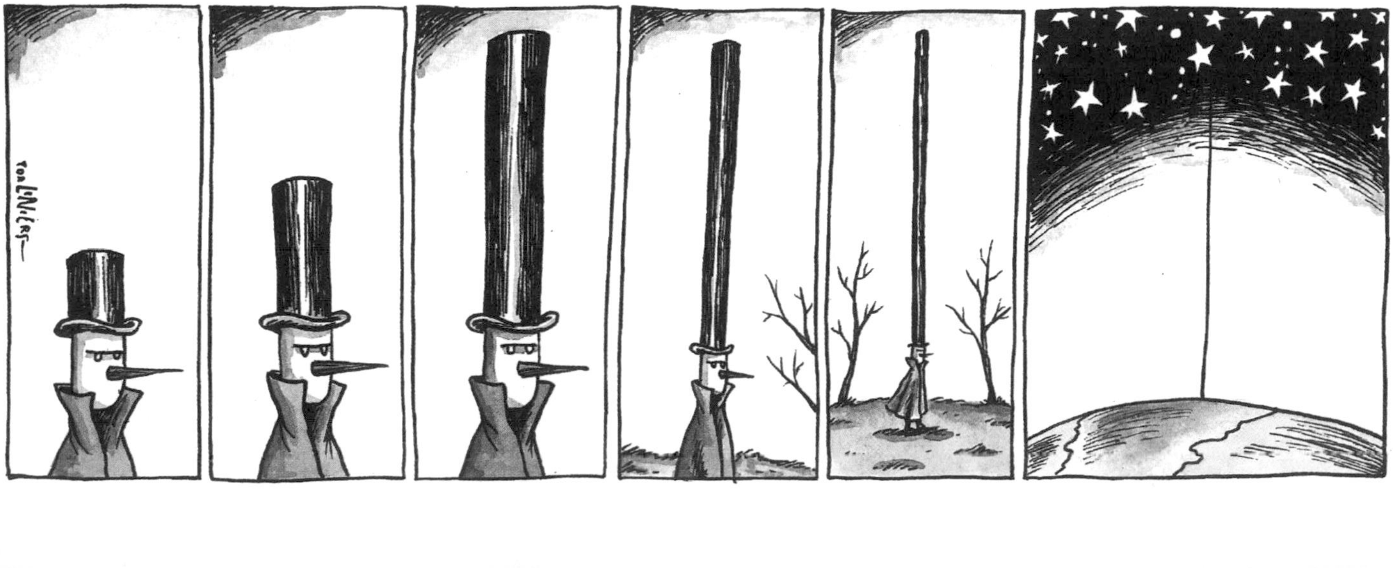

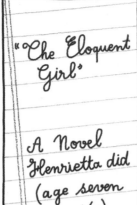

"The Eloquent Girl"

A Novel Henrietta did (age seven and 1/4)

Chapter 1

This novel it is about a very pretty very intelligent girl called

HENRIETTA!

lligent girl called Henrietta!

Chapter 2

WHAT ARE YOU WRITING?

A NOVEL, IT'S CALLED THE ELOQUENT GIRL.

IT'S ABOUT A GIRL WHO HAS A WAY WITH WORDS AND CAN GET EVERYONE TO DO HER BIDDING.

IN CHAPTER TWO SHE MAKES HER FAMILY AND FRIENDS CALL HER "YOUR MAJESTY," AND IN CHAPTER THREE SHE FIGHTS AN ALIEN.

SOON SHE'LL HAVE TO START PREPARING HER NOBEL ACCEPTANCE SPEECH....

HENRIETTA WRITES HER NOVEL.

"The Eloquent Girl" Chapter 4

The eloquent girl, who is named Henrietta and she's great, finds out that her teacher is a zombie from beyond the grave, but is still a good teacher. ~~Beesides~~, Besides she gave her an A in math, so no problem there. They just turn into friends

THERE ARE TWO POSSIBILITIES, MANDELBAUM. EITHER I'M A LITERARY GENIUS OR I LACK ALL CAPACITY FOR SELF-CRITICISM.

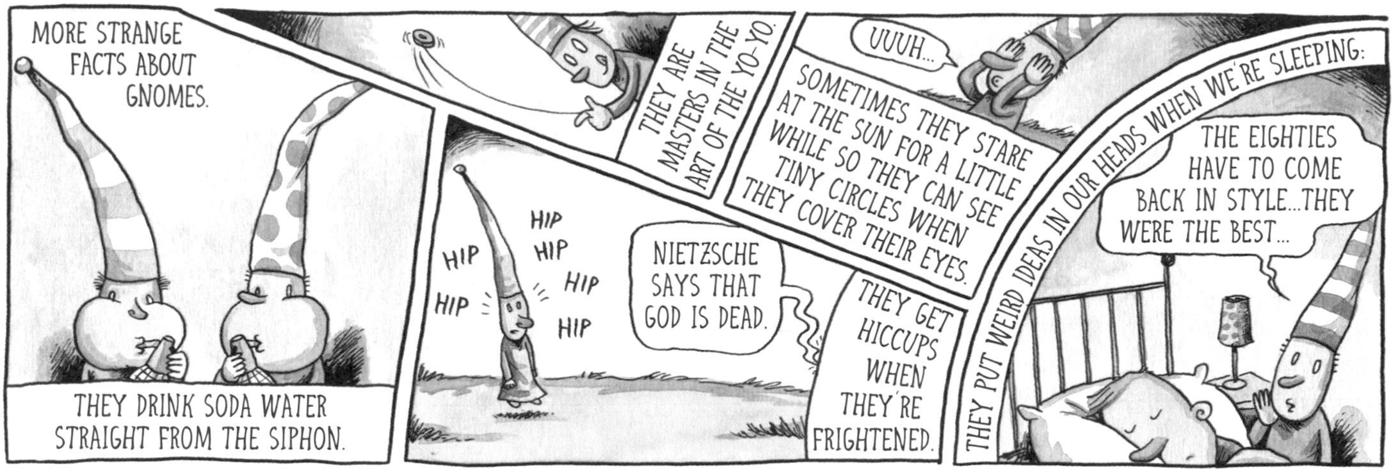
MORE STRANGE FACTS ABOUT GNOMES.
THEY DRINK SODA WATER STRAIGHT FROM THE SIPHON.
THEY ARE MASTERS IN THE ART OF THE YO-YO.
HIP HIP HIP HIP HIP HIP
NIETZSCHE SAYS THAT GOD IS DEAD.
THEY GET HICCUPS WHEN THEY'RE FRIGHTENED.
UUUH...
SOMETIMES THEY STARE AT THE SUN FOR A LITTLE WHILE SO THEY CAN SEE TINY CIRCLES WHEN THEY COVER THEIR EYES.
THEY PUT WEIRD IDEAS IN OUR HEADS WHEN WE'RE SLEEPING:
THE EIGHTIES HAVE TO COME BACK IN STYLE...THEY WERE THE BEST...

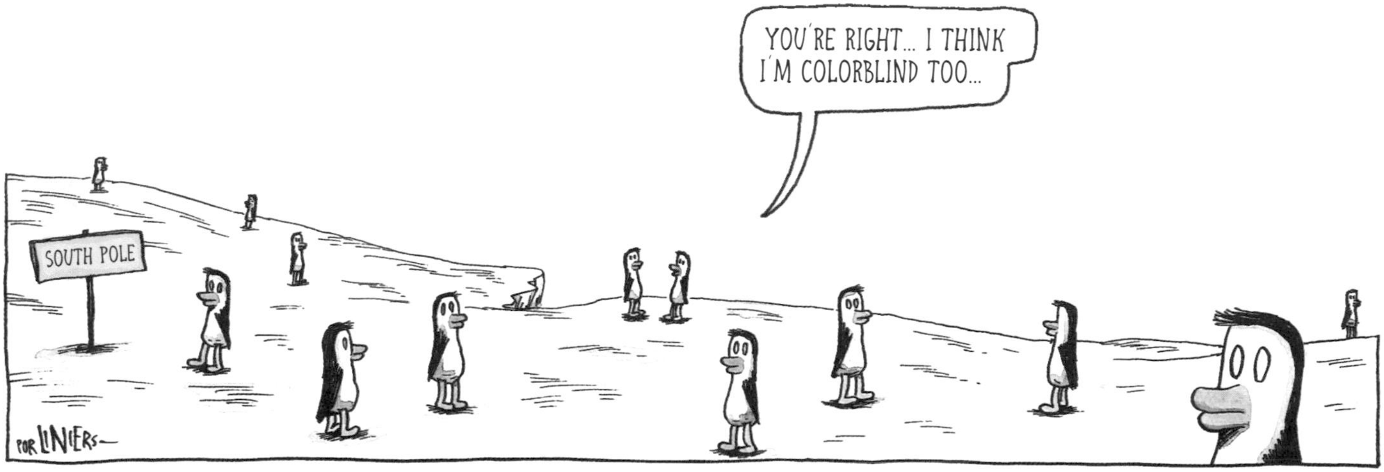
YOU'RE RIGHT... I THINK I'M COLORBLIND TOO...
SOUTH POLE
POR LINIERS

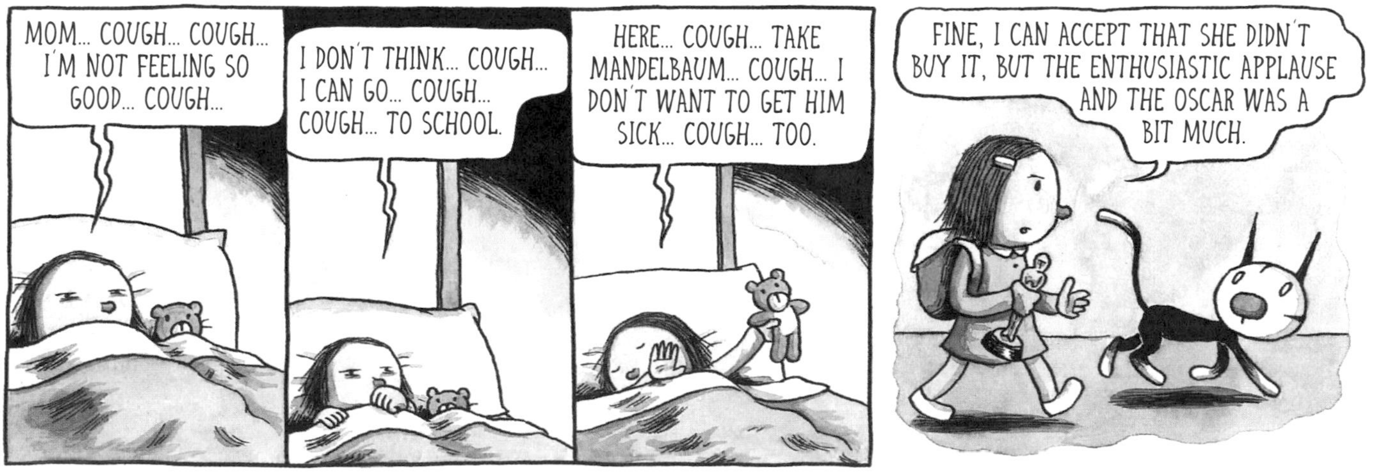
MOM... COUGH... COUGH... I'M NOT FEELING SO GOOD... COUGH...
I DON'T THINK... COUGH... I CAN GO... COUGH... COUGH... TO SCHOOL.
HERE... COUGH... TAKE MANDELBAUM... COUGH... I DON'T WANT TO GET HIM SICK... COUGH... TOO.
FINE, I CAN ACCEPT THAT SHE DIDN'T BUY IT, BUT THE ENTHUSIASTIC APPLAUSE AND THE OSCAR WAS A BIT MUCH.

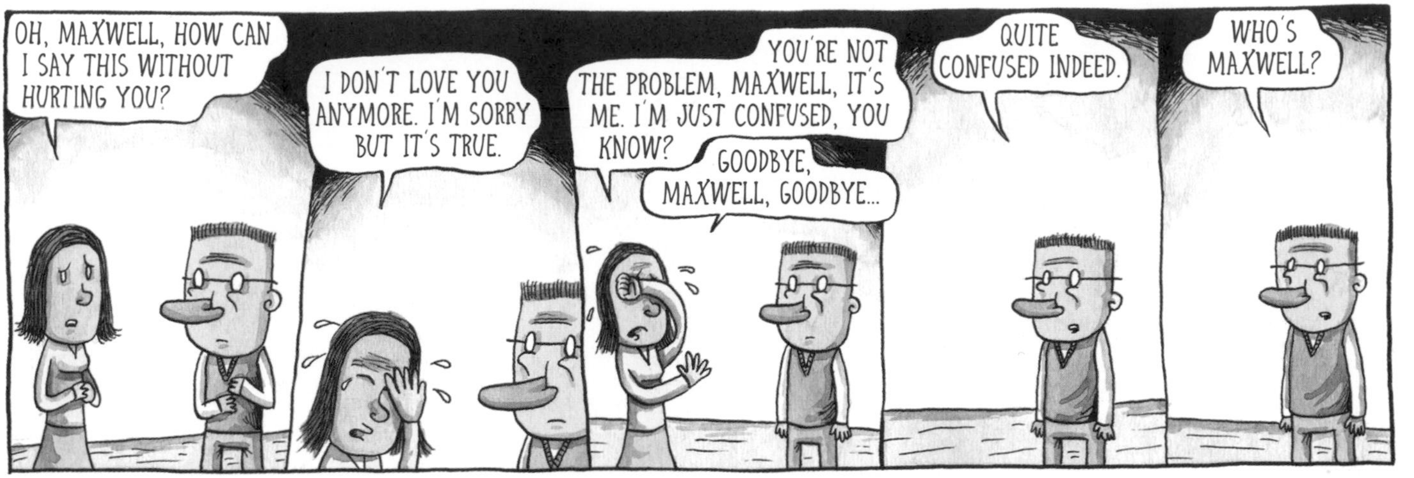
OH, MAXWELL, HOW CAN I SAY THIS WITHOUT HURTING YOU?
I DON'T LOVE YOU ANYMORE. I'M SORRY BUT IT'S TRUE.
YOU'RE NOT THE PROBLEM, MAXWELL, IT'S ME. I'M JUST CONFUSED, YOU KNOW?
GOODBYE, MAXWELL, GOODBYE...
QUITE CONFUSED INDEED.
WHO'S MAXWELL?

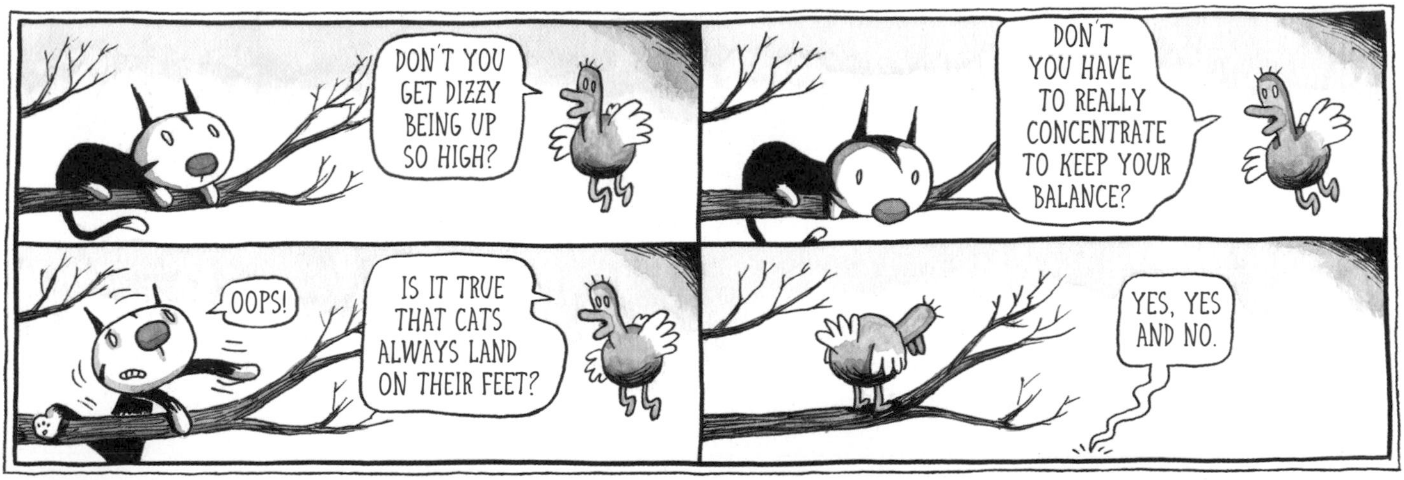
DON'T YOU GET DIZZY BEING UP SO HIGH?
DON'T YOU HAVE TO REALLY CONCENTRATE TO KEEP YOUR BALANCE?
OOPS!
IS IT TRUE THAT CATS ALWAYS LAND ON THEIR FEET?
YES, YES AND NO.

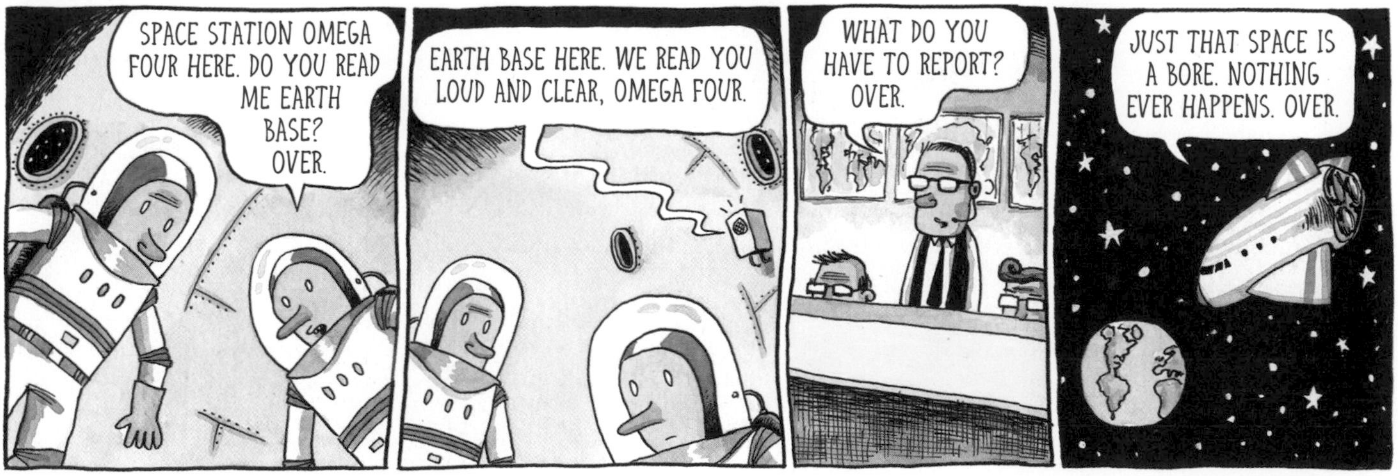
SPACE STATION OMEGA FOUR HERE. DO YOU READ ME EARTH BASE? OVER.
EARTH BASE HERE. WE READ YOU LOUD AND CLEAR, OMEGA FOUR.
WHAT DO YOU HAVE TO REPORT? OVER.
JUST THAT SPACE IS A BORE. NOTHING EVER HAPPENS. OVER.

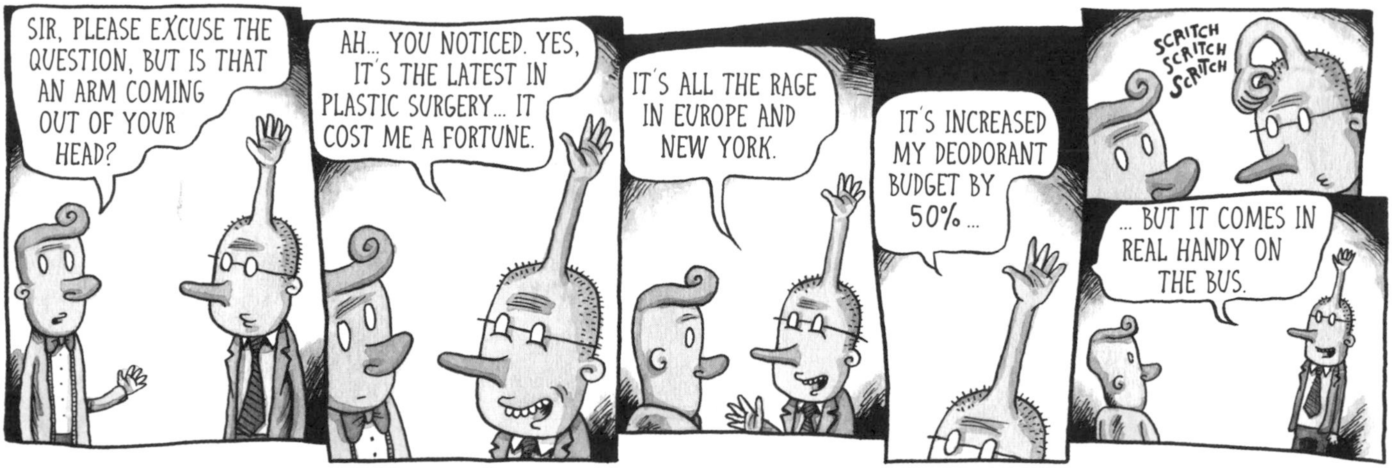
SIR, PLEASE EXCUSE THE QUESTION, BUT IS THAT AN ARM COMING OUT OF YOUR HEAD?
AH... YOU NOTICED. YES, IT'S THE LATEST IN PLASTIC SURGERY... IT COST ME A FORTUNE.
IT'S ALL THE RAGE IN EUROPE AND NEW YORK.
IT'S INCREASED MY DEODORANT BUDGET BY 50%...
SCRITCH SCRITCH SCRITCH
... BUT IT COMES IN REAL HANDY ON THE BUS.

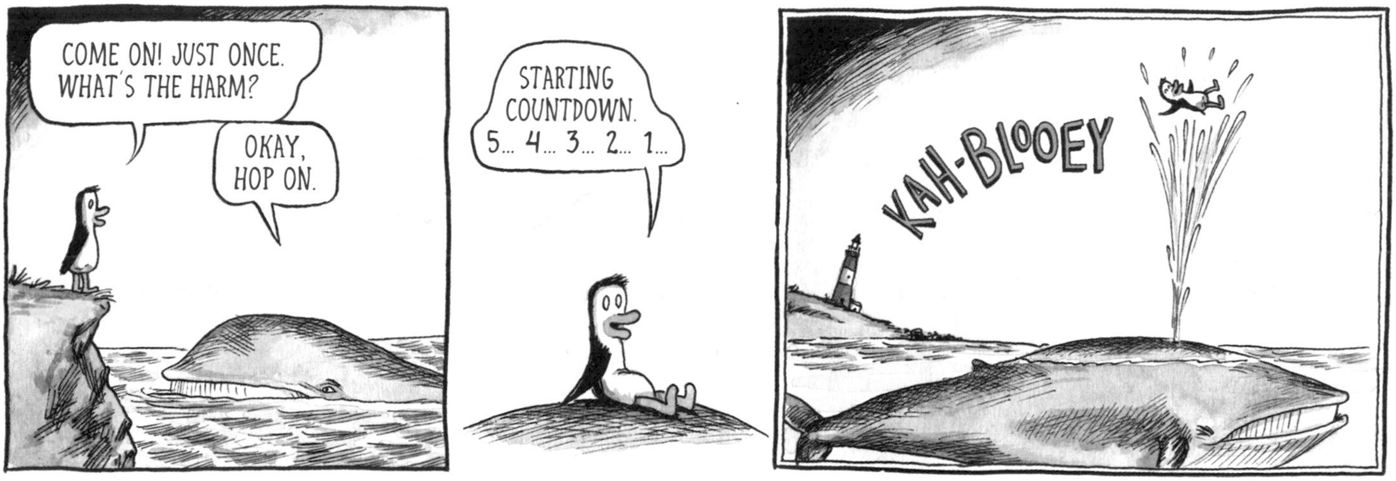
COME ON! JUST ONCE. WHAT'S THE HARM?
OKAY, HOP ON.
STARTING COUNTDOWN. 5... 4... 3... 2... 1...
KAH-BLOOEY

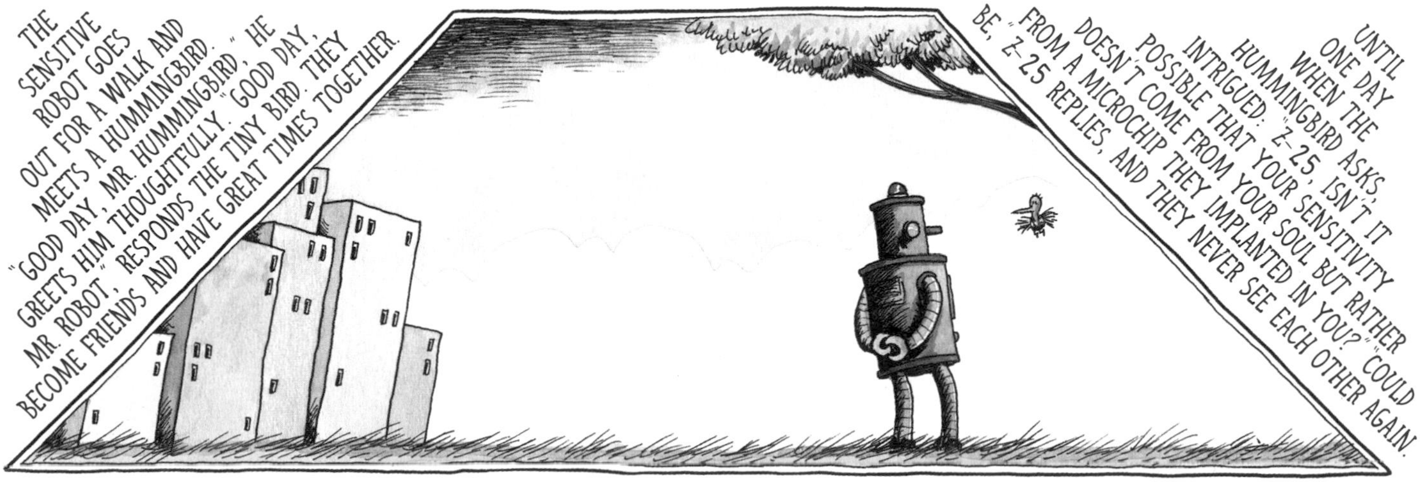
THE SENSITIVE ROBOT GOES OUT FOR A WALK AND MEETS A HUMMINGBIRD. "GOOD DAY, MR. HUMMINGBIRD," HE GREETS HIM THOUGHTFULLY. "GOOD DAY, MR. ROBOT," RESPONDS THE TINY BIRD. THEY BECOME FRIENDS AND HAVE GREAT TIMES TOGETHER.
UNTIL ONE DAY WHEN THE HUMMINGBIRD ASKS, INTRIGUED: "Z-25, ISN'T IT POSSIBLE THAT YOUR SENSITIVITY DOESN'T COME FROM YOUR SOUL BUT RATHER FROM A MICROCHIP THEY IMPLANTED IN YOU?" "COULD BE," Z-25 REPLIES, AND THEY NEVER SEE EACH OTHER AGAIN.

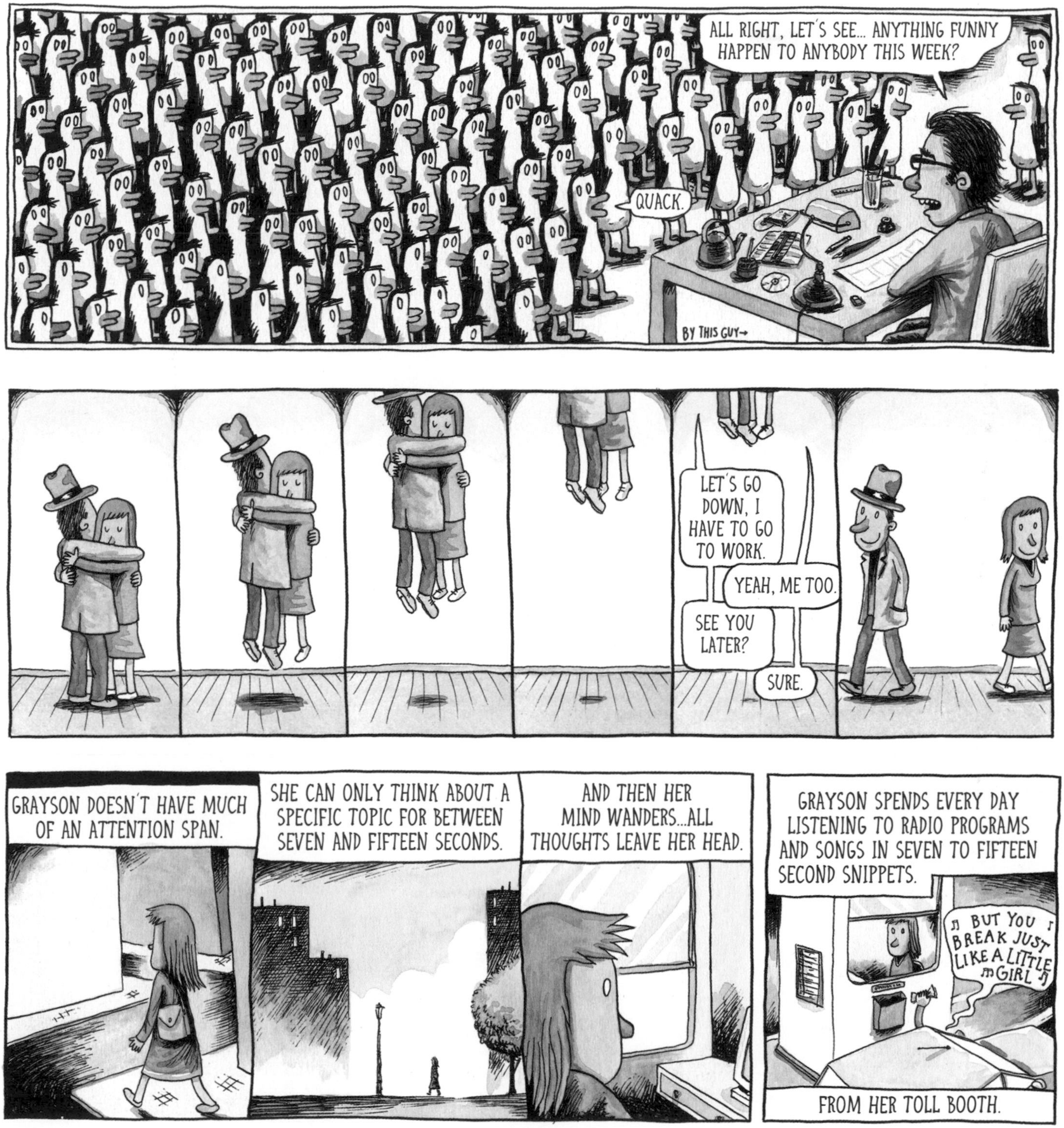
ALL RIGHT, LET'S SEE... ANYTHING FUNNY HAPPEN TO ANYBODY THIS WEEK?
QUACK.
BY THIS GUY→
LET'S GO DOWN, I HAVE TO GO TO WORK.
YEAH, ME TOO.
SEE YOU LATER?
SURE.
GRAYSON DOESN'T HAVE MUCH OF AN ATTENTION SPAN.
SHE CAN ONLY THINK ABOUT A SPECIFIC TOPIC FOR BETWEEN SEVEN AND FIFTEEN SECONDS.
AND THEN HER MIND WANDERS...ALL THOUGHTS LEAVE HER HEAD.
GRAYSON SPENDS EVERY DAY LISTENING TO RADIO PROGRAMS AND SONGS IN SEVEN TO FIFTEEN SECOND SNIPPETS.
♫ BUT YOU ♪ BREAK JUST LIKE A LITTLE ♫ GIRL ♫
FROM HER TOLL BOOTH.

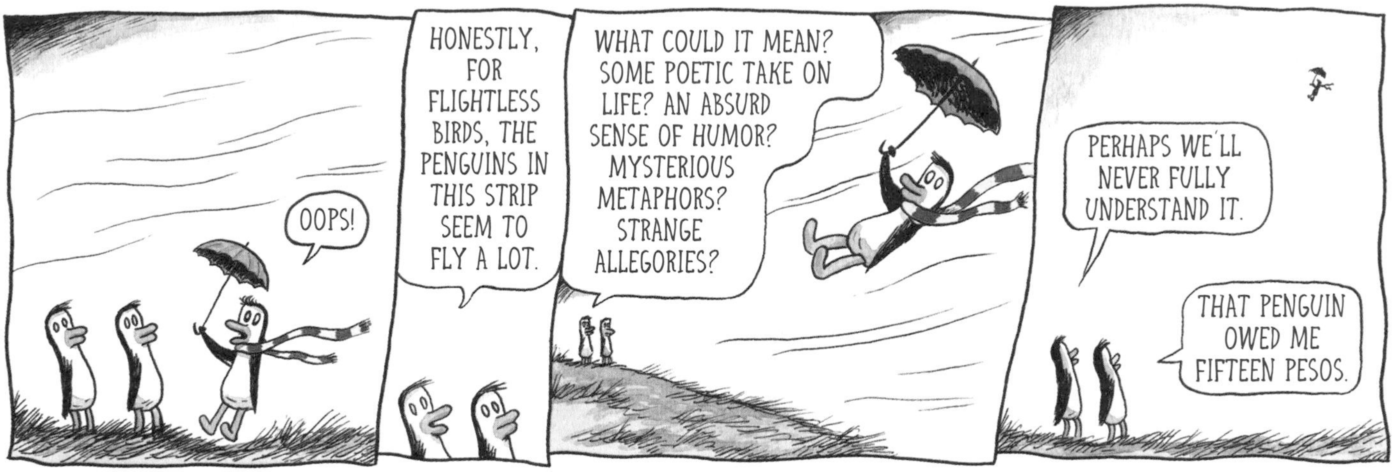
OOPS!
HONESTLY, FOR FLIGHTLESS BIRDS, THE PENGUINS IN THIS STRIP SEEM TO FLY A LOT.
WHAT COULD IT MEAN? SOME POETIC TAKE ON LIFE? AN ABSURD SENSE OF HUMOR? MYSTERIOUS METAPHORS? STRANGE ALLEGORIES?
PERHAPS WE'LL NEVER FULLY UNDERSTAND IT.
THAT PENGUIN OWED ME FIFTEEN PESOS.

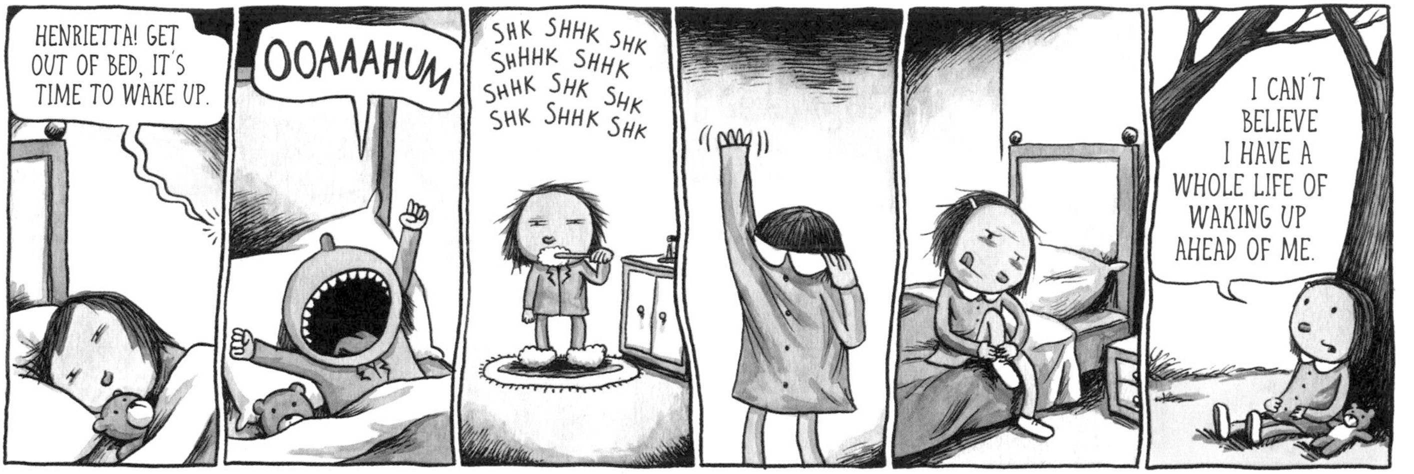
HENRIETTA! GET OUT OF BED, IT'S TIME TO WAKE UP.
OOAAAHUM
SHK SHHK SHK SHHHK SHHK SHHK SHK SHK SHK SHHK SHK
I CAN'T BELIEVE I HAVE A WHOLE LIFE OF WAKING UP AHEAD OF ME.

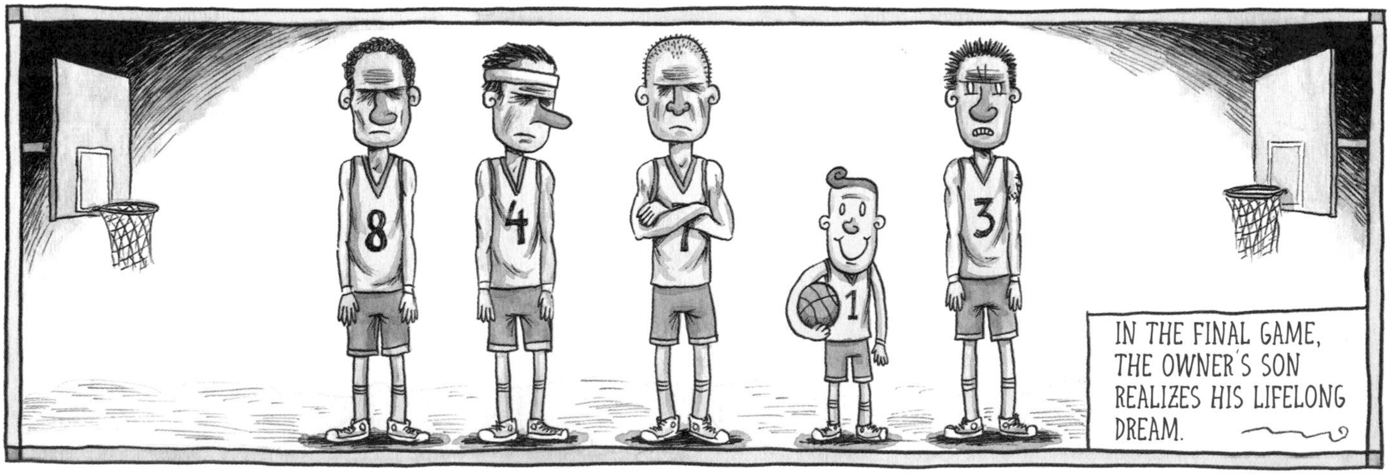
8
4
7
1
3
IN THE FINAL GAME, THE OWNER'S SON REALIZES HIS LIFELONG DREAM.

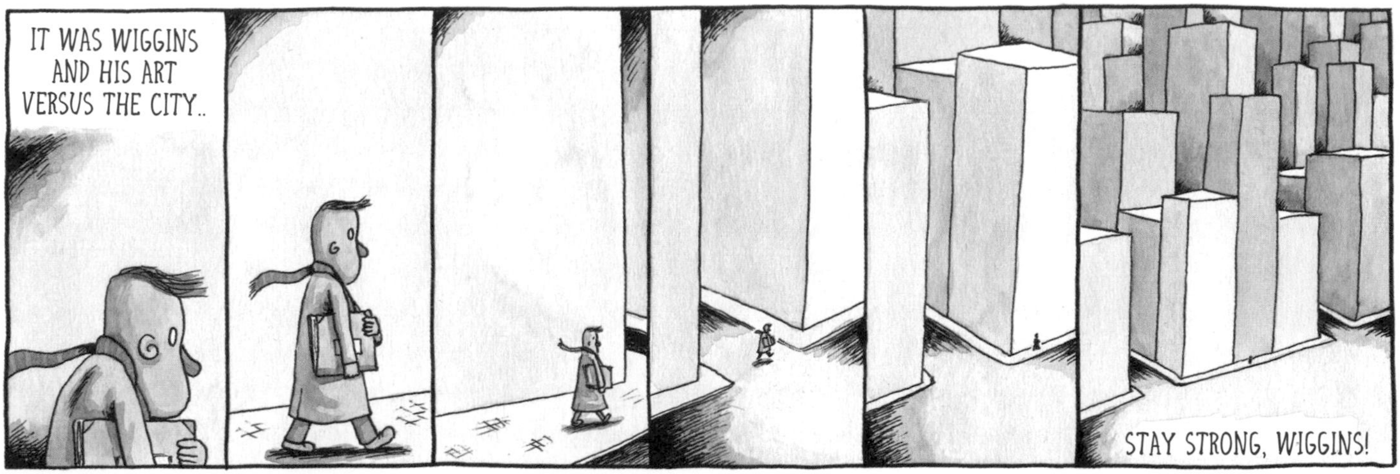
IT WAS WIGGINS AND HIS ART VERSUS THE CITY..
STAY STRONG, WIGGINS!

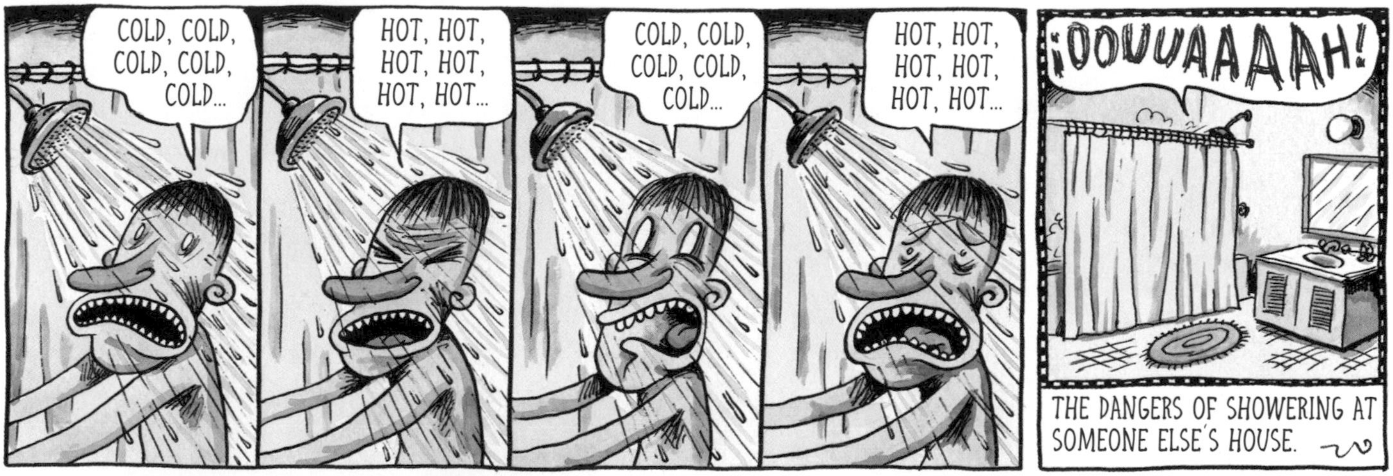
COLD, COLD, COLD, COLD, COLD...
HOT, HOT, HOT, HOT, HOT, HOT...
COLD, COLD, COLD, COLD, COLD...
HOT, HOT, HOT, HOT, HOT, HOT...
¡OOUUAAAAH!
THE DANGERS OF SHOWERING AT SOMEONE ELSE'S HOUSE.

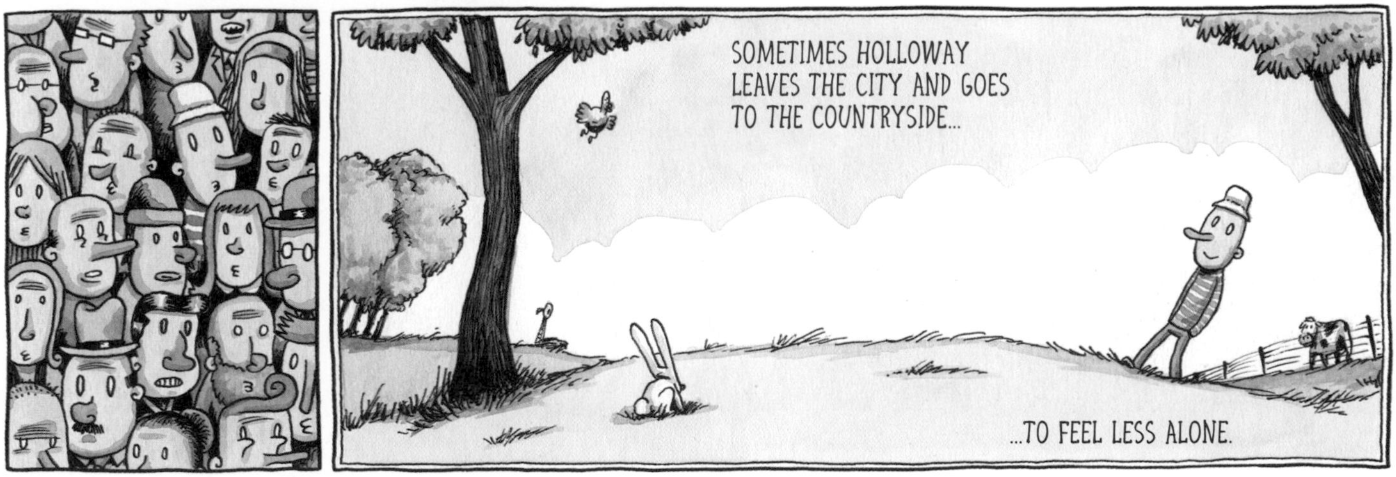
SOMETIMES HOLLOWAY LEAVES THE CITY AND GOES TO THE COUNTRYSIDE...
...TO FEEL LESS ALONE.

WOULD YOU CUT IT OUT!! IT'S SIX IN THE MORNING!
CHAN CHAN
CHAAAN CHAAAN
CHA...
WHAT ARE YOU DOING, JONATHAN?
I'M PRETENDING TO PLAY THE GUITAR BECAUSE I'M REALLY INTO THIS SONG.
AH...
HOW STUPID.
NO WAY ARE YOU GETTING A BACKSTAGE PASS!
I DON'T REALLY KNOW WHAT IT IS.
ALL I KNOW IS THAT IT APPEARED ONE DAY ON MY WINDOW SILL.
IT WATCHES ME WITHOUT SAYING OR DOING ANYTHING. THIS STRANGE CREATURE HAS BEEN WATCHING ME FOR YEARS.
SO ONE DAY I ASKED IT...
WHAT DO YOU WANT? WHAT?
IK.
...THAT'S ALL IT SAID. THAT WAS OUR ONLY CONVERSATION.

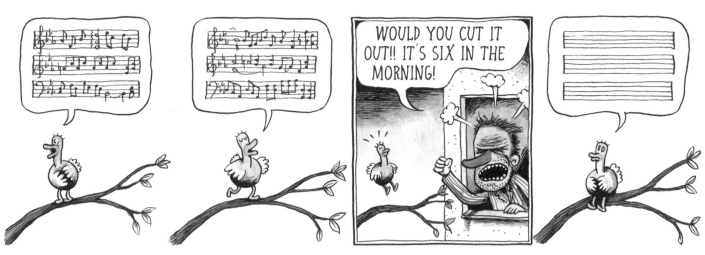

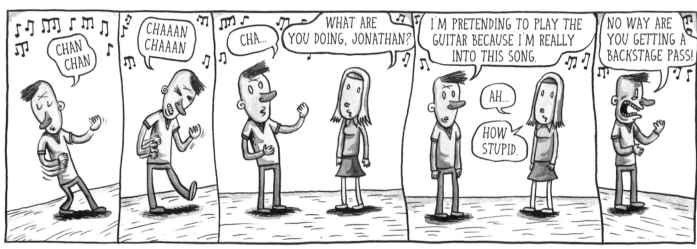

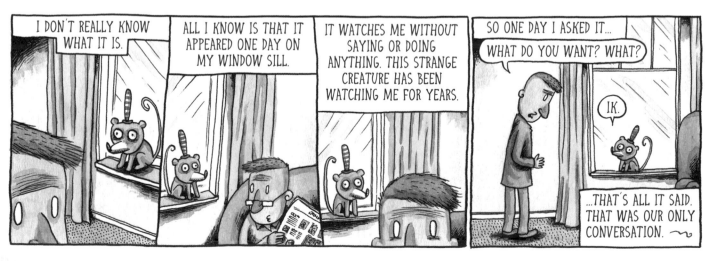

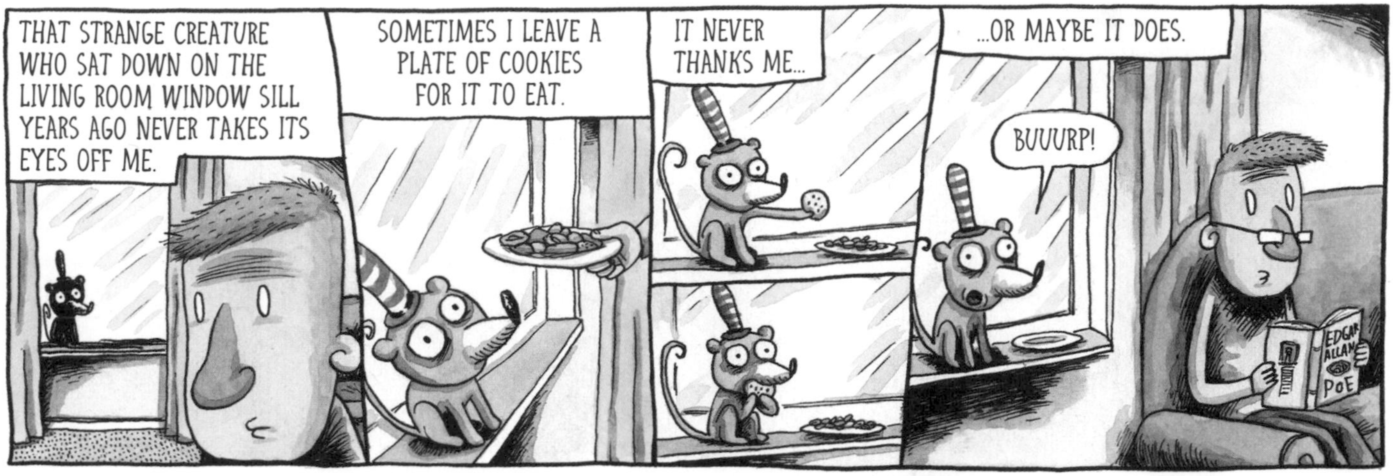
THAT STRANGE CREATURE WHO SAT DOWN ON THE LIVING ROOM WINDOW SILL YEARS AGO NEVER TAKES ITS EYES OFF ME.
SOMETIMES I LEAVE A PLATE OF COOKIES FOR IT TO EAT.
IT NEVER THANKS ME...
...OR MAYBE IT DOES.
BUUURP!
EDGAR ALLAN POE

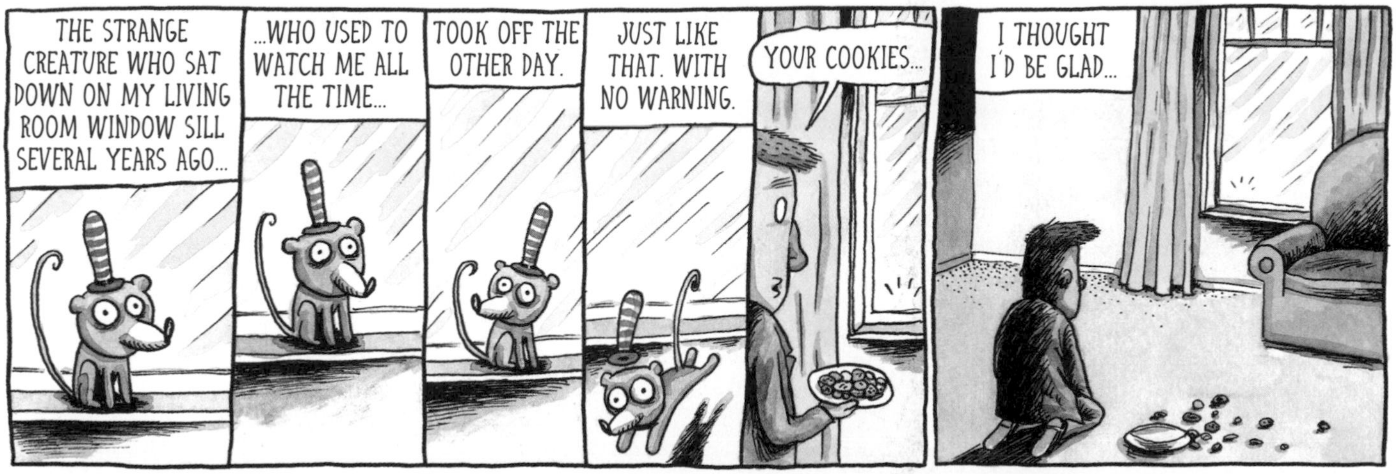
THE STRANGE CREATURE WHO SAT DOWN ON MY LIVING ROOM WINDOW SILL SEVERAL YEARS AGO...
...WHO USED TO WATCH ME ALL THE TIME...
TOOK OFF THE OTHER DAY.
JUST LIKE THAT. WITH NO WARNING.
YOUR COOKIES...
I THOUGHT I'D BE GLAD...

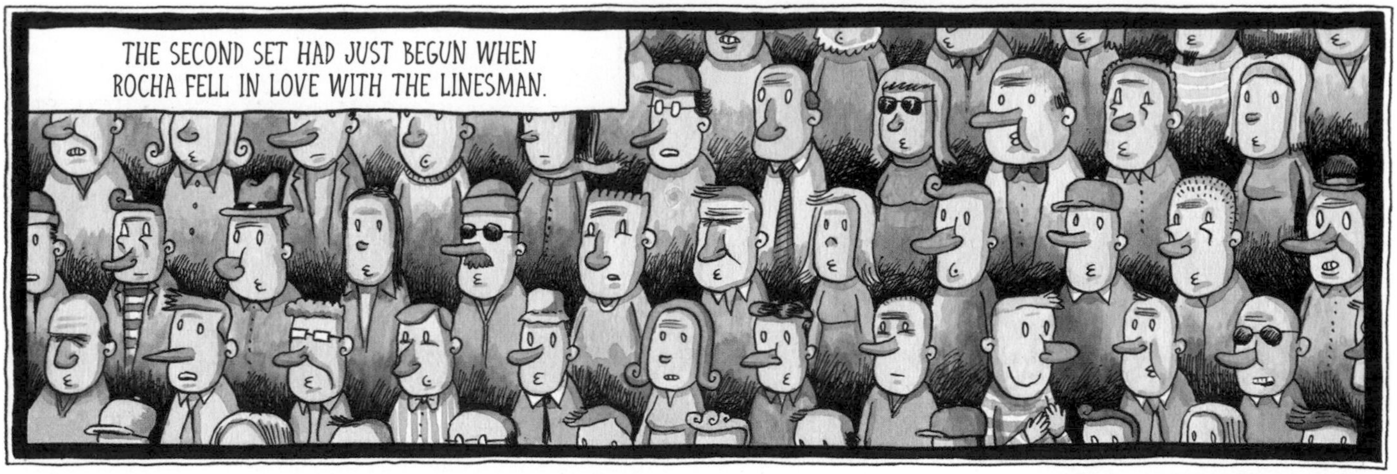
THE SECOND SET HAD JUST BEGUN WHEN ROCHA FELL IN LOVE WITH THE LINESMAN.

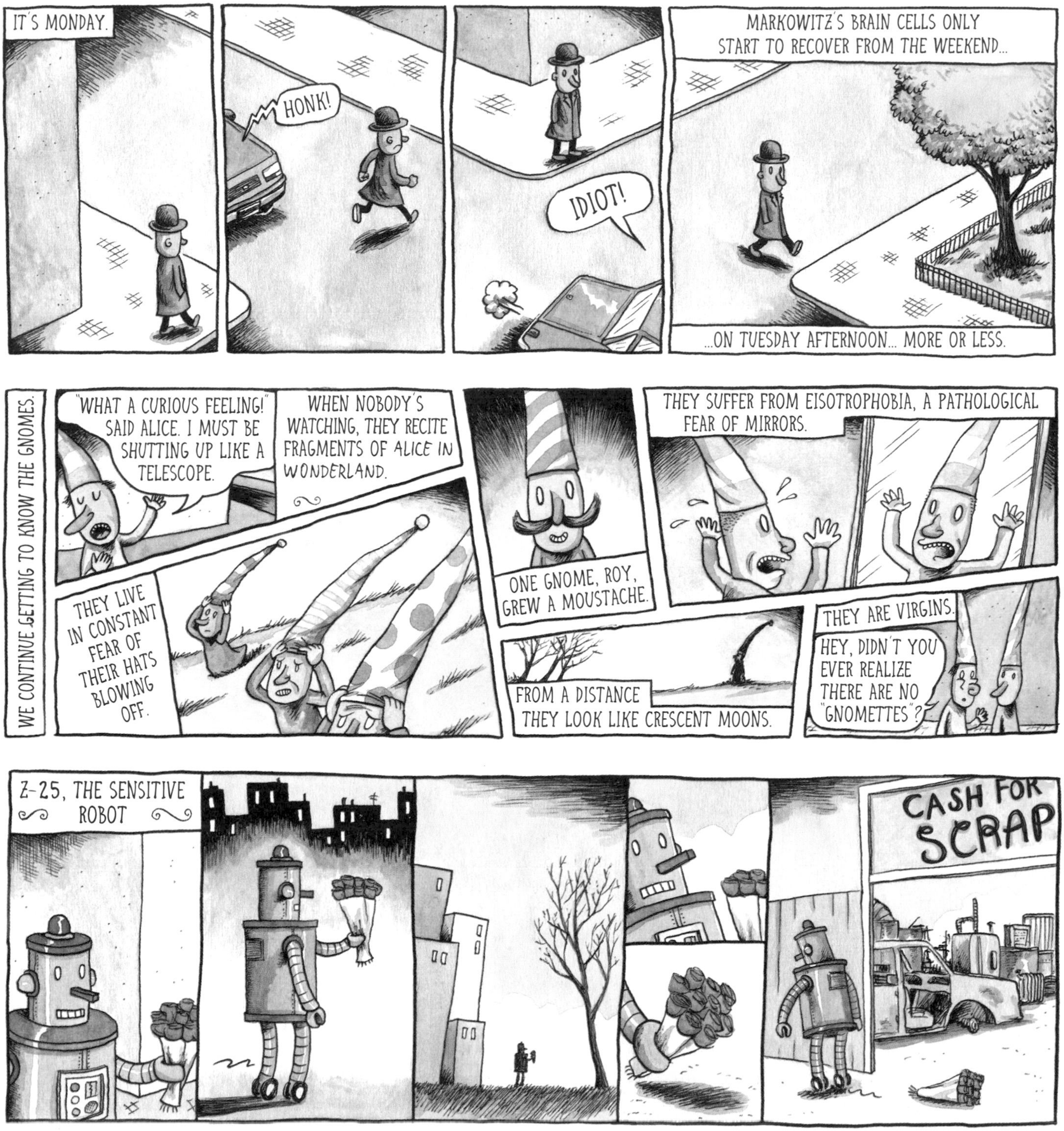
IT'S MONDAY.
HONK!
IDIOT!
MARKOWITZ'S BRAIN CELLS ONLY START TO RECOVER FROM THE WEEKEND...
...ON TUESDAY AFTERNOON... MORE OR LESS.
WE CONTINUE GETTING TO KNOW THE GNOMES.
"WHAT A CURIOUS FEELING!" SAID ALICE. I MUST BE SHUTTING UP LIKE A TELESCOPE.
WHEN NOBODY'S WATCHING, THEY RECITE FRAGMENTS OF ALICE IN WONDERLAND.
THEY LIVE IN CONSTANT FEAR OF THEIR HATS BLOWING OFF.
ONE GNOME, ROY, GREW A MOUSTACHE.
THEY SUFFER FROM EISOTROPHOBIA, A PATHOLOGICAL FEAR OF MIRRORS.
FROM A DISTANCE THEY LOOK LIKE CRESCENT MOONS.
THEY ARE VIRGINS.
HEY, DIDN'T YOU EVER REALIZE THERE ARE NO "GNOMETTES"?
Z-25, THE SENSITIVE ROBOT
CASH FOR SCRAP

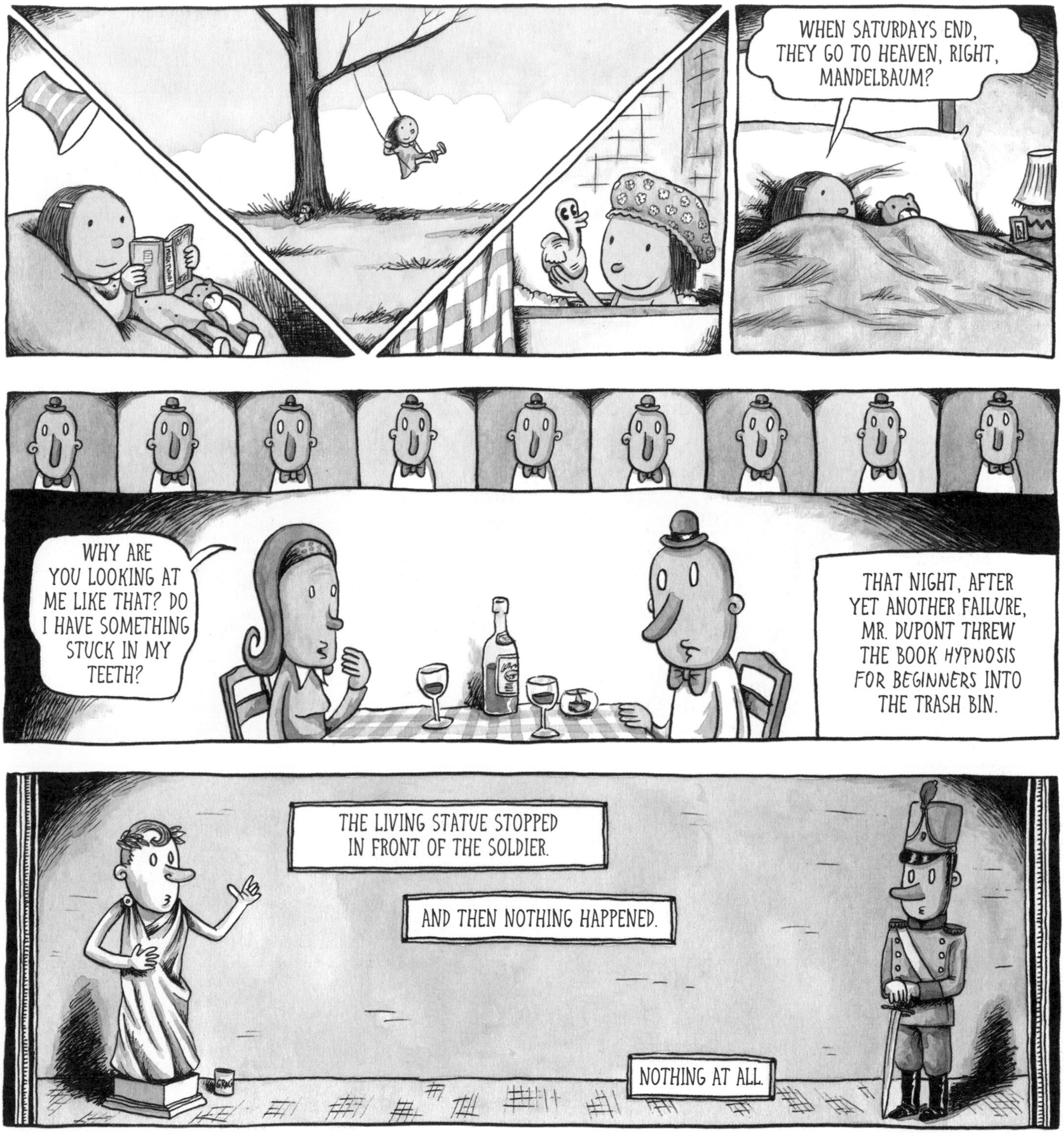
WHEN SATURDAYS END, THEY GO TO HEAVEN, RIGHT, MANDELBAUM?
WHY ARE YOU LOOKING AT ME LIKE THAT? DO I HAVE SOMETHING STUCK IN MY TEETH?
THAT NIGHT, AFTER YET ANOTHER FAILURE, MR. DUPONT THREW THE BOOK HYPNOSIS FOR BEGINNERS INTO THE TRASH BIN.
THE LIVING STATUE STOPPED IN FRONT OF THE SOLDIER.
AND THEN NOTHING HAPPENED.
NOTHING AT ALL.

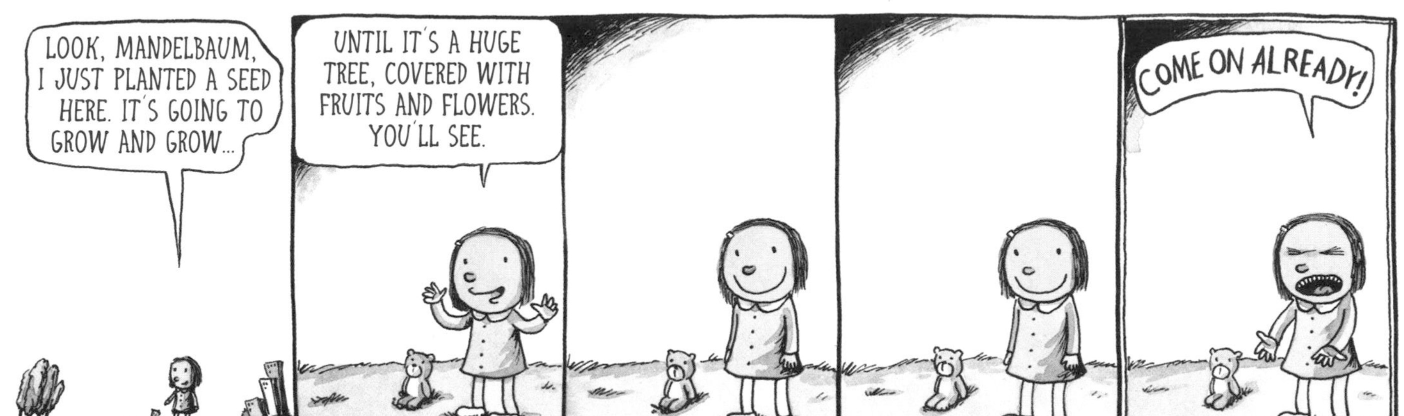
LOOK, MANDELBAUM, I JUST PLANTED A SEED HERE. IT'S GOING TO GROW AND GROW...
UNTIL IT'S A HUGE TREE, COVERED WITH FRUITS AND FLOWERS. YOU'LL SEE.
COME ON ALREADY!

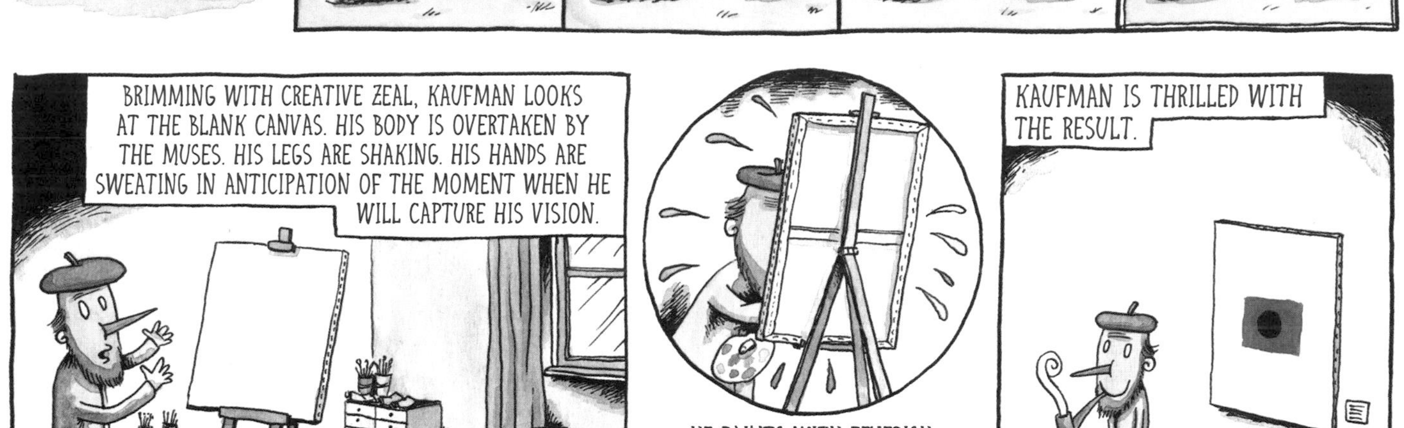
BRIMMING WITH CREATIVE ZEAL, KAUFMAN LOOKS AT THE BLANK CANVAS. HIS BODY IS OVERTAKEN BY THE MUSES. HIS LEGS ARE SHAKING. HIS HANDS ARE SWEATING IN ANTICIPATION OF THE MOMENT WHEN HE WILL CAPTURE HIS VISION.
HE PAINTS WITH FEVERISH ENTHUSIASM FOR HOURS, DAYS, AS IF POSSESSED BY THE DEVIL HIMSELF.
KAUFMAN IS THRILLED WITH THE RESULT.

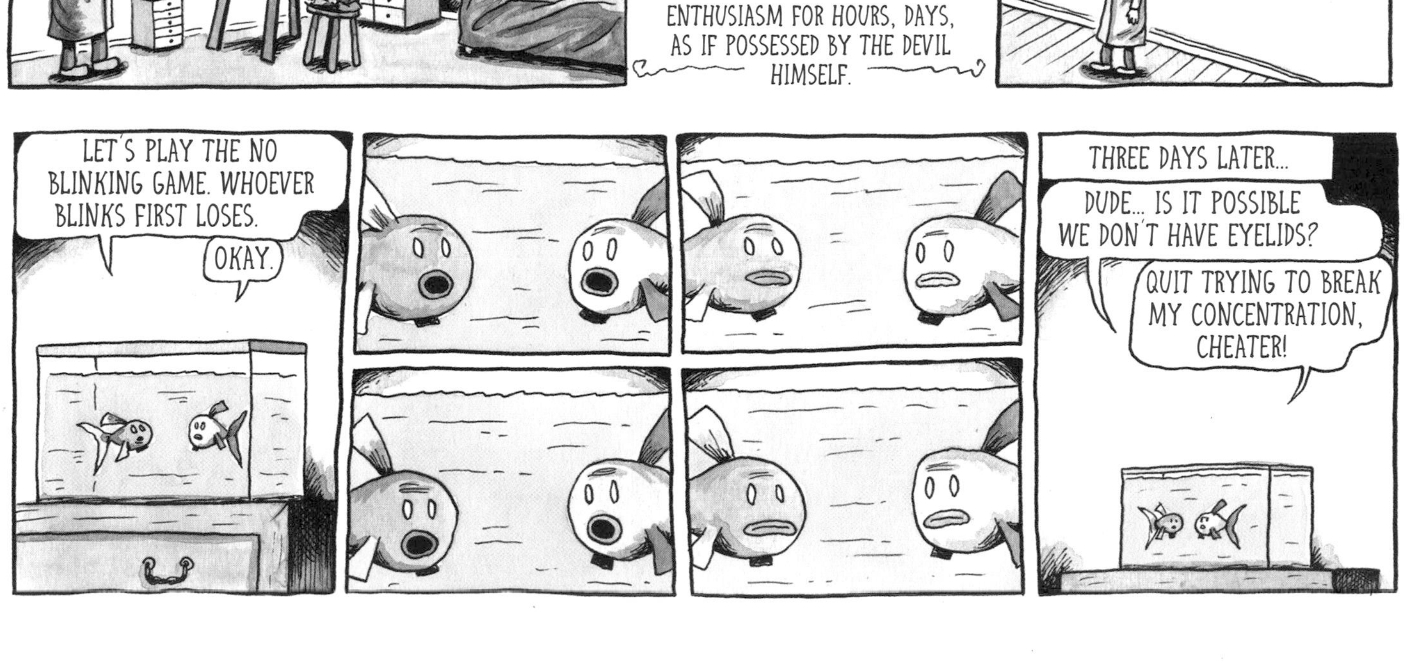
LET'S PLAY THE NO BLINKING GAME. WHOEVER BLINKS FIRST LOSES.
OKAY.
THREE DAYS LATER...
DUDE... IS IT POSSIBLE WE DON'T HAVE EYELIDS?
QUIT TRYING TO BREAK MY CONCENTRATION, CHEATER!

IN THE PAST THEY WERE FAMOUSLY BITTER ENEMIES. BUT AS TIME PASSED THEY MANAGED TO SMOOTH OVER THEIR DIFFERENCES. NOW THEY'RE SHARING THEIR GOLDEN YEARS TOGETHER, AND THEY'RE ALMOST NEVER OVERCOME BY THE DESIRE TO EAT EACH OTHER.

THEY ARE PERFECT FOR EACH OTHER. FATE BRINGS THEM FACE TO FACE. THEY COME CLOSER. NOTHING CAN GO WRONG.

SHE KNOWS THREE POEMS BY PIZARNIK BY HEART. HE CRIES EVERY TIME HE WATCHES E.T. SHE SAYS BOB DYLAN IS A GENIUS. HE LIKES TO EAT FONDUE.

OKAY, HERE COMES THE KISS, INSEPARABILITY, AND THE HAPPILY EVER AFTER.

OOPS...THEY MISSED THEIR MOMENT.

YOU ALWAYS HAVE TO KEEP MOVING FORWARD IN LIFE, HENRIETTA...

WHY? WHAT'S AHEAD?

MORE LIFE.

DEEP, FELLINI, DEEEEEEP.

77

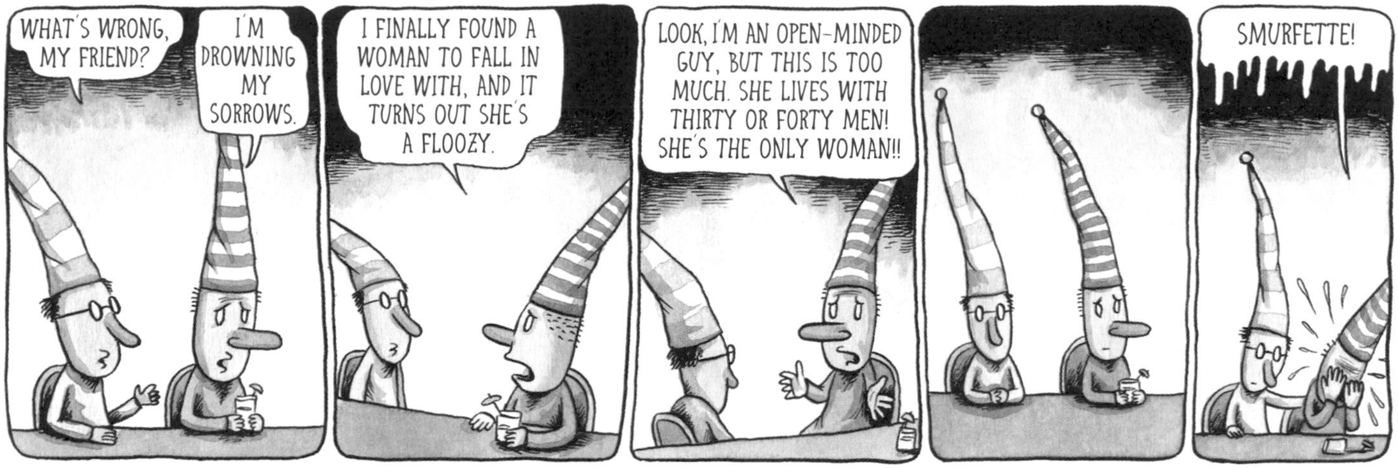
WHAT'S WRONG, MY FRIEND?
I'M DROWNING MY SORROWS.
I FINALLY FOUND A WOMAN TO FALL IN LOVE WITH, AND IT TURNS OUT SHE'S A FLOOZY.
LOOK, I'M AN OPEN-MINDED GUY, BUT THIS IS TOO MUCH. SHE LIVES WITH THIRTY OR FORTY MEN! SHE'S THE ONLY WOMAN!!
SMURFETTE!

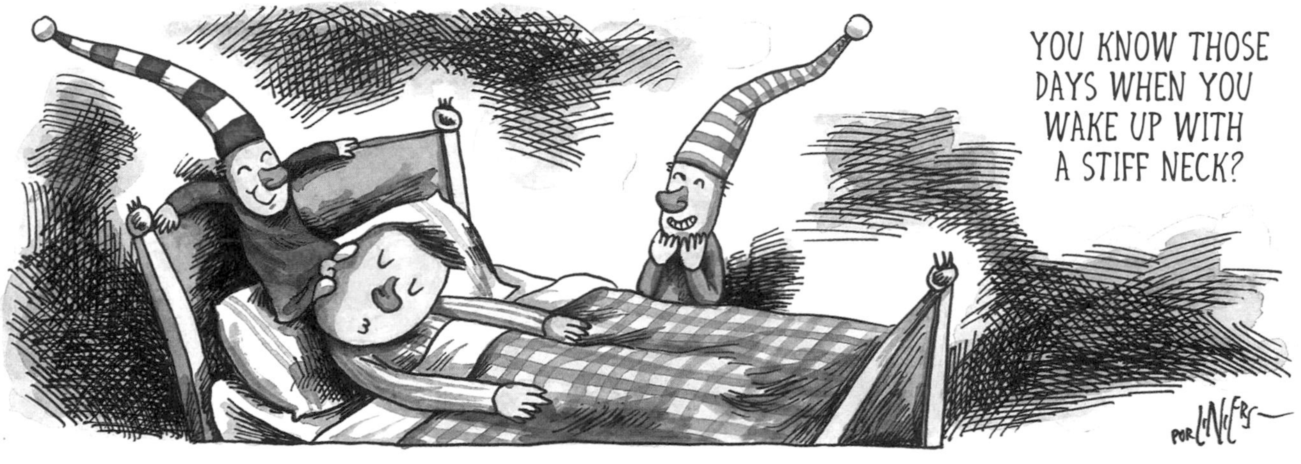
YOU KNOW THOSE DAYS WHEN YOU WAKE UP WITH A STIFF NECK?
POR LINIERS

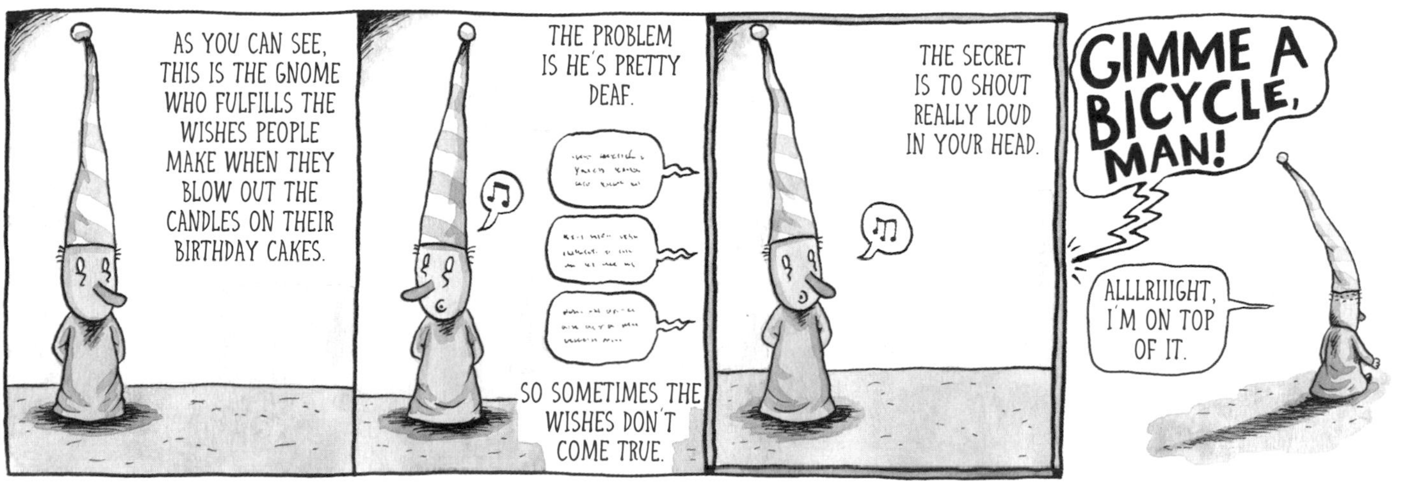
AS YOU CAN SEE, THIS IS THE GNOME WHO FULFILLS THE WISHES PEOPLE MAKE WHEN THEY BLOW OUT THE CANDLES ON THEIR BIRTHDAY CAKES.
THE PROBLEM IS HE'S PRETTY DEAF.
SO SOMETIMES THE WISHES DON'T COME TRUE.
THE SECRET IS TO SHOUT REALLY LOUD IN YOUR HEAD.
GIMME A BICYCLE, MAN!
ALLLRIIIGHT, I'M ON TOP OF IT.

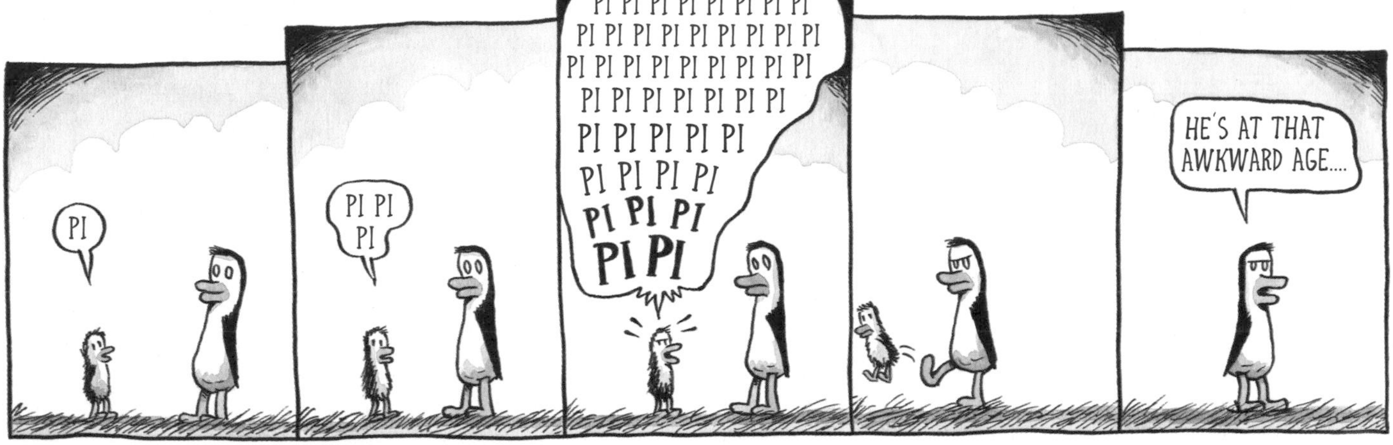
PI
PI PI PI
PI PI PI PI PI PI PI PI
PI PI PI PI PI PI PI PI PI
PI PI PI PI PI PI PI PI PI
PI PI PI PI PI PI PI
PI PI PI PI PI
PI PI PI PI
PI PI PI
PI PI
HE'S AT THAT AWKWARD AGE....

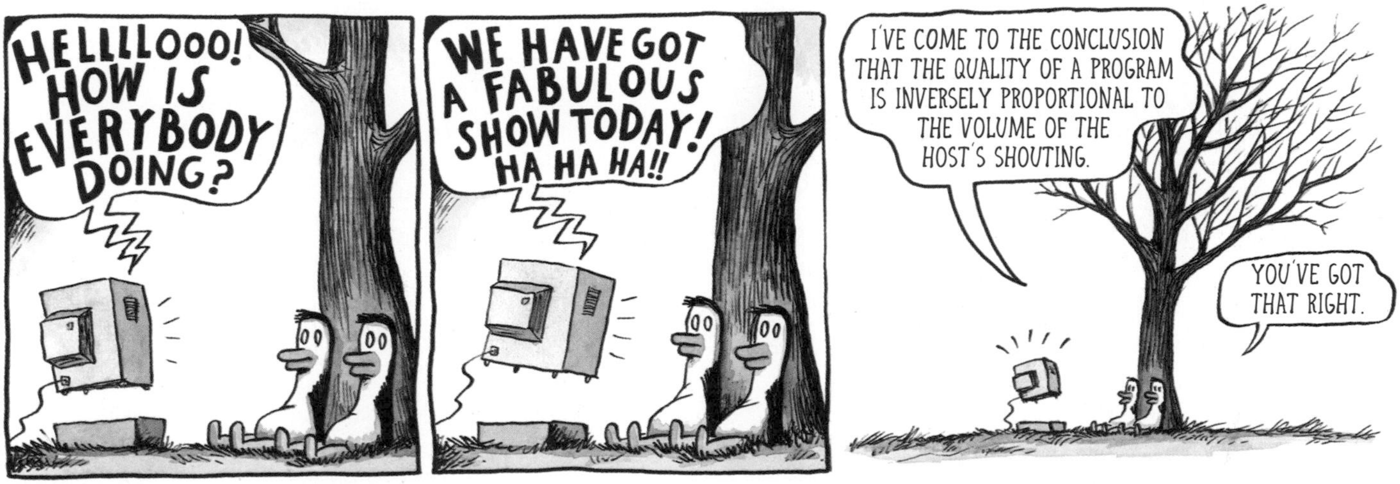
HELLLLOOO! HOW IS EVERYBODY DOING?
WE HAVE GOT A FABULOUS SHOW TODAY! HA HA HA!!
I'VE COME TO THE CONCLUSION THAT THE QUALITY OF A PROGRAM IS INVERSELY PROPORTIONAL TO THE VOLUME OF THE HOST'S SHOUTING.
YOU'VE GOT THAT RIGHT.

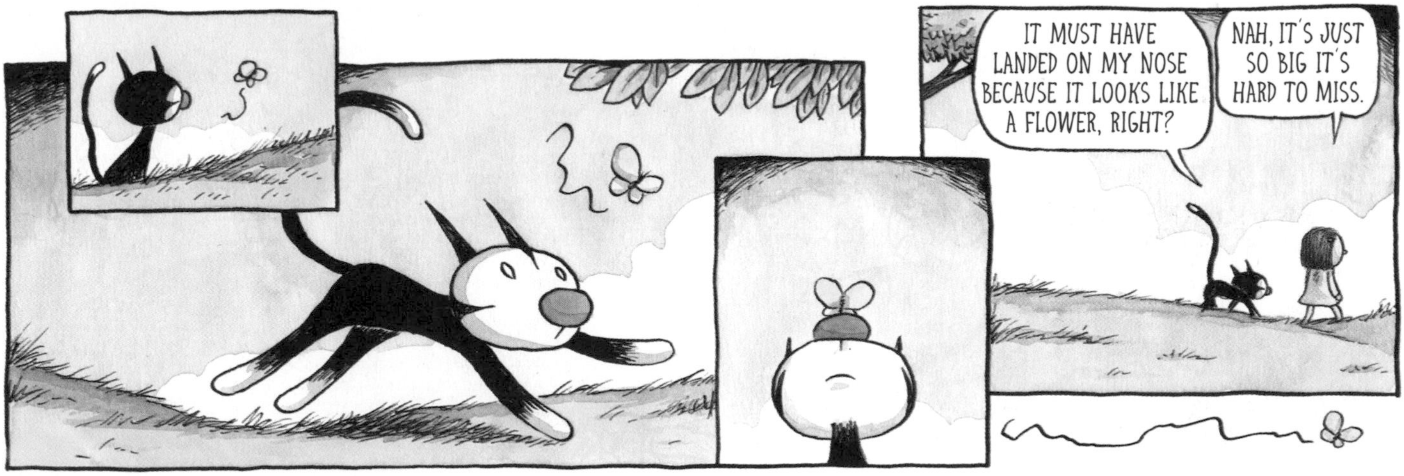
IT MUST HAVE LANDED ON MY NOSE BECAUSE IT LOOKS LIKE A FLOWER, RIGHT?
NAH, IT'S JUST SO BIG IT'S HARD TO MISS.

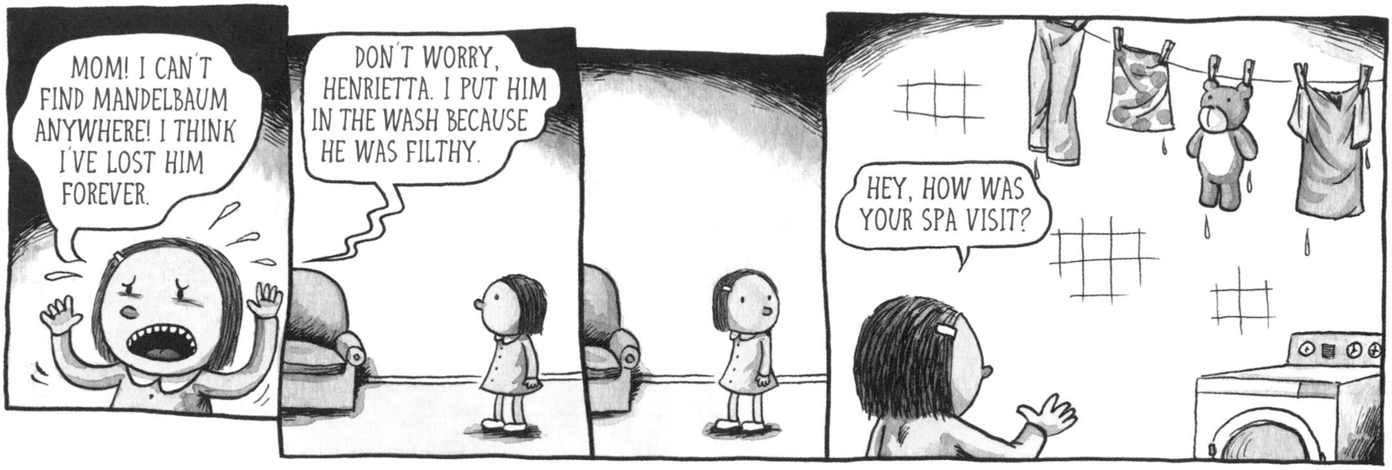
MOM! I CAN'T FIND MANDELBAUM ANYWHERE! I THINK I'VE LOST HIM FOREVER.
DON'T WORRY, HENRIETTA. I PUT HIM IN THE WASH BECAUSE HE WAS FILTHY.
HEY, HOW WAS YOUR SPA VISIT?

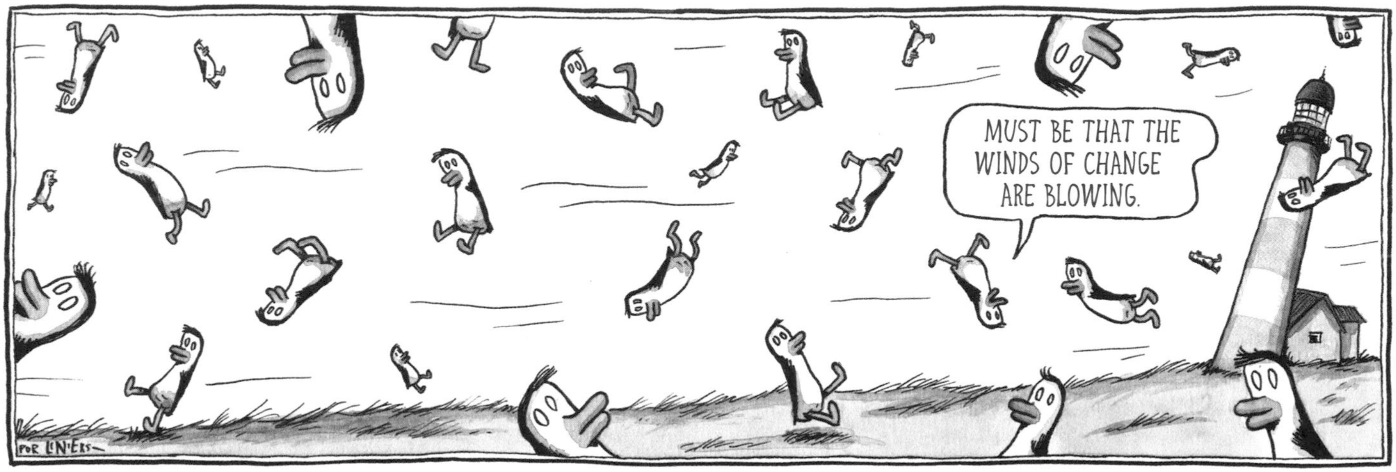
MUST BE THAT THE WINDS OF CHANGE ARE BLOWING.

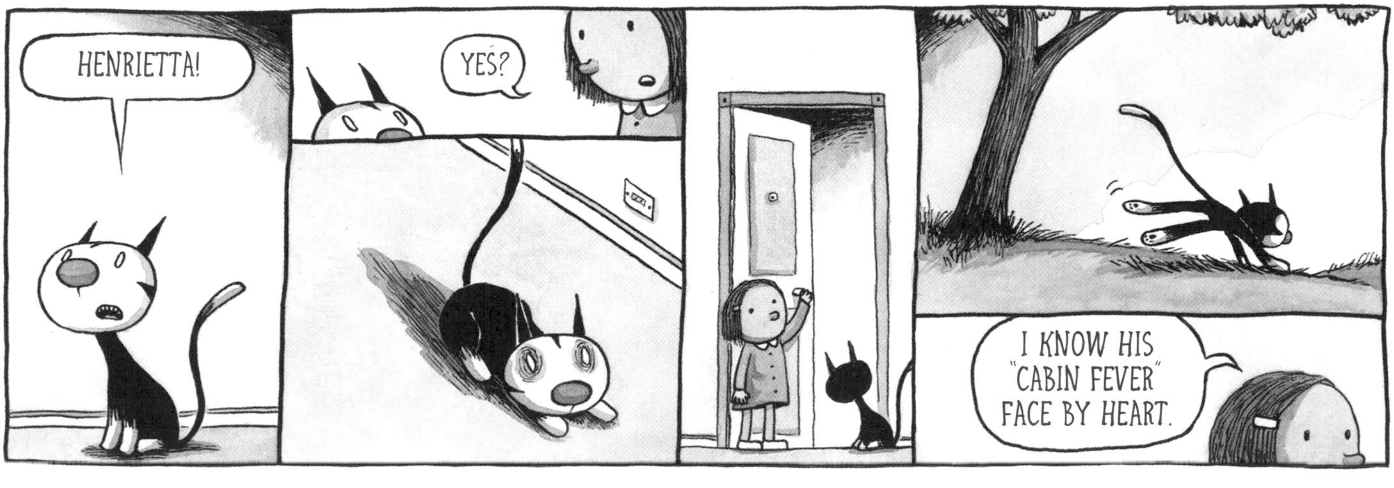
HENRIETTA!
YES?
I KNOW HIS "CABIN FEVER" FACE BY HEART.

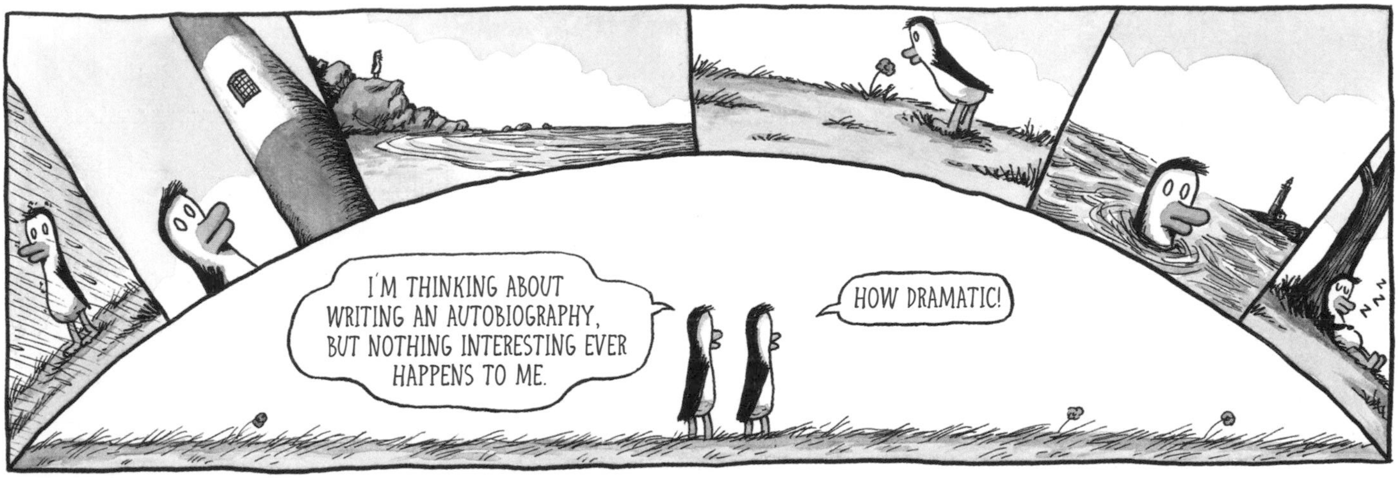
I'M THINKING ABOUT WRITING AN AUTOBIOGRAPHY, BUT NOTHING INTERESTING EVER HAPPENS TO ME.
HOW DRAMATIC!
ZZZ

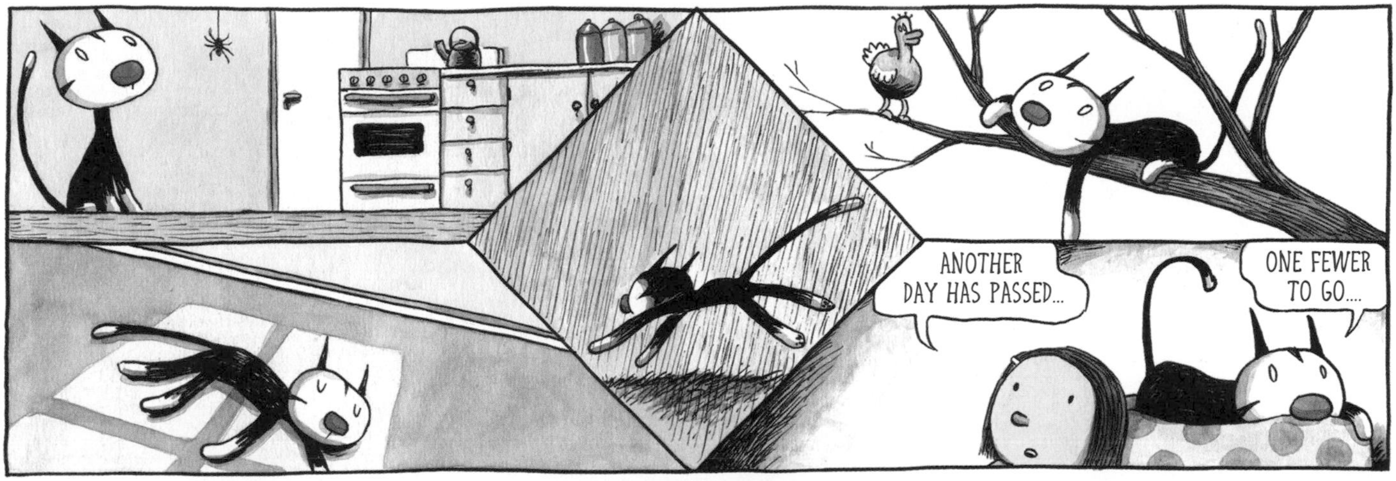
ANOTHER DAY HAS PASSED...
ONE FEWER TO GO....

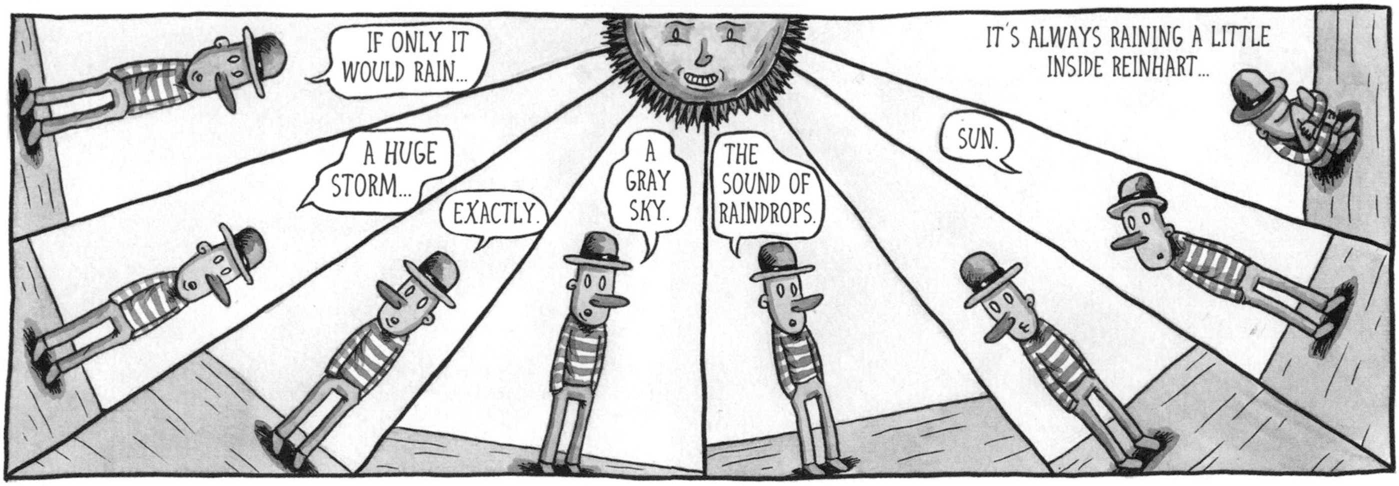
IF ONLY IT WOULD RAIN...
IT'S ALWAYS RAINING A LITTLE INSIDE REINHART...
A HUGE STORM...
EXACTLY.
A GRAY SKY.
THE SOUND OF RAINDROPS.
SUN.

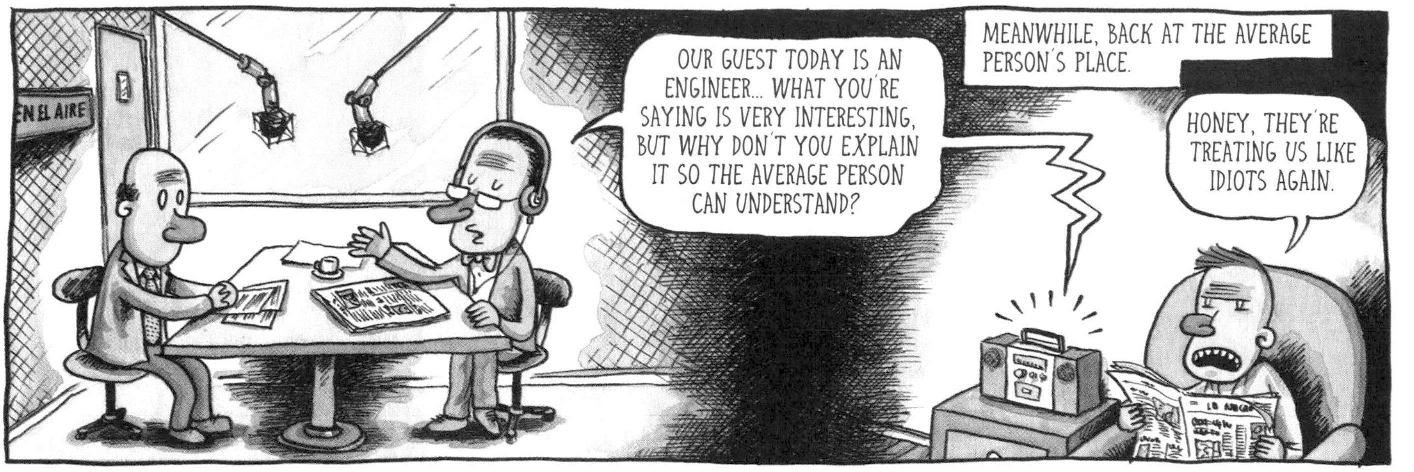
EN EL AIRE
OUR GUEST TODAY IS AN ENGINEER... WHAT YOU'RE SAYING IS VERY INTERESTING, BUT WHY DON'T YOU EXPLAIN IT SO THE AVERAGE PERSON CAN UNDERSTAND?
MEANWHILE, BACK AT THE AVERAGE PERSON'S PLACE.
HONEY, THEY'RE TREATING US LIKE IDIOTS AGAIN.

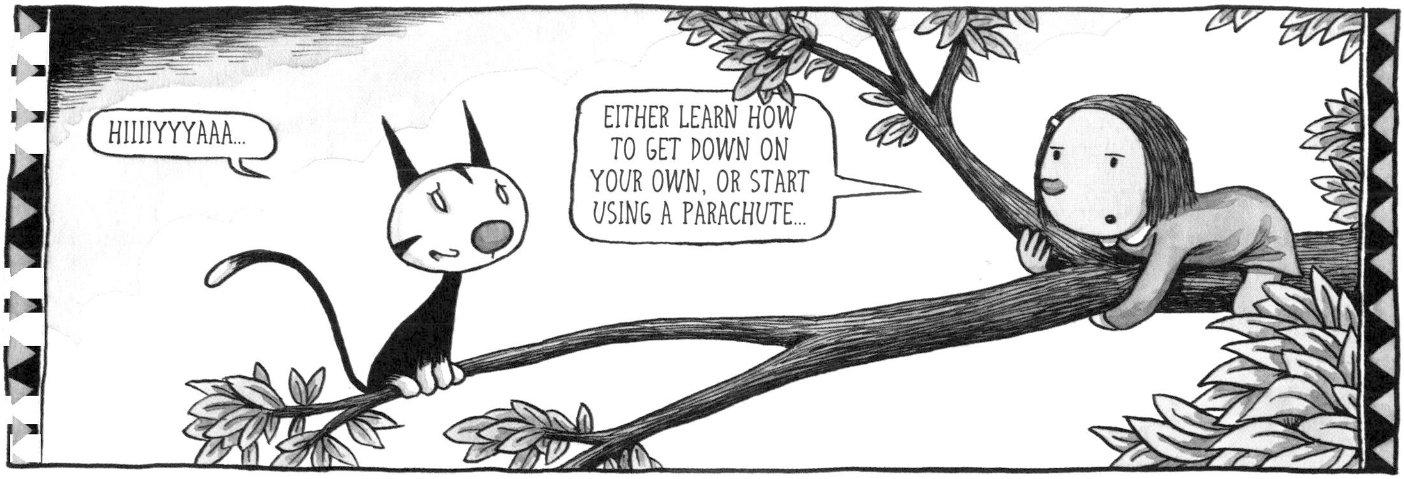
HIIIIYYYAAA...
EITHER LEARN HOW TO GET DOWN ON YOUR OWN, OR START USING A PARACHUTE...

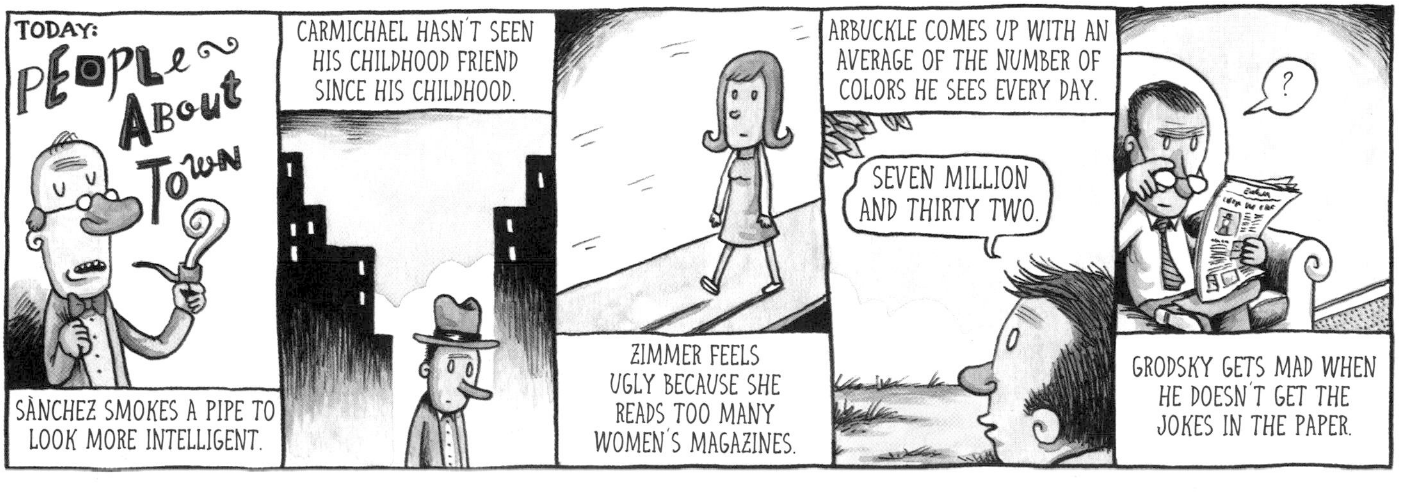
TODAY:
PEOPLE About Town
SÀNCHEZ SMOKES A PIPE TO LOOK MORE INTELLIGENT.
CARMICHAEL HASN'T SEEN HIS CHILDHOOD FRIEND SINCE HIS CHILDHOOD.
ZIMMER FEELS UGLY BECAUSE SHE READS TOO MANY WOMEN'S MAGAZINES.
ARBUCKLE COMES UP WITH AN AVERAGE OF THE NUMBER OF COLORS HE SEES EVERY DAY.
SEVEN MILLION AND THIRTY TWO.
?
GRODSKY GETS MAD WHEN HE DOESN'T GET THE JOKES IN THE PAPER.

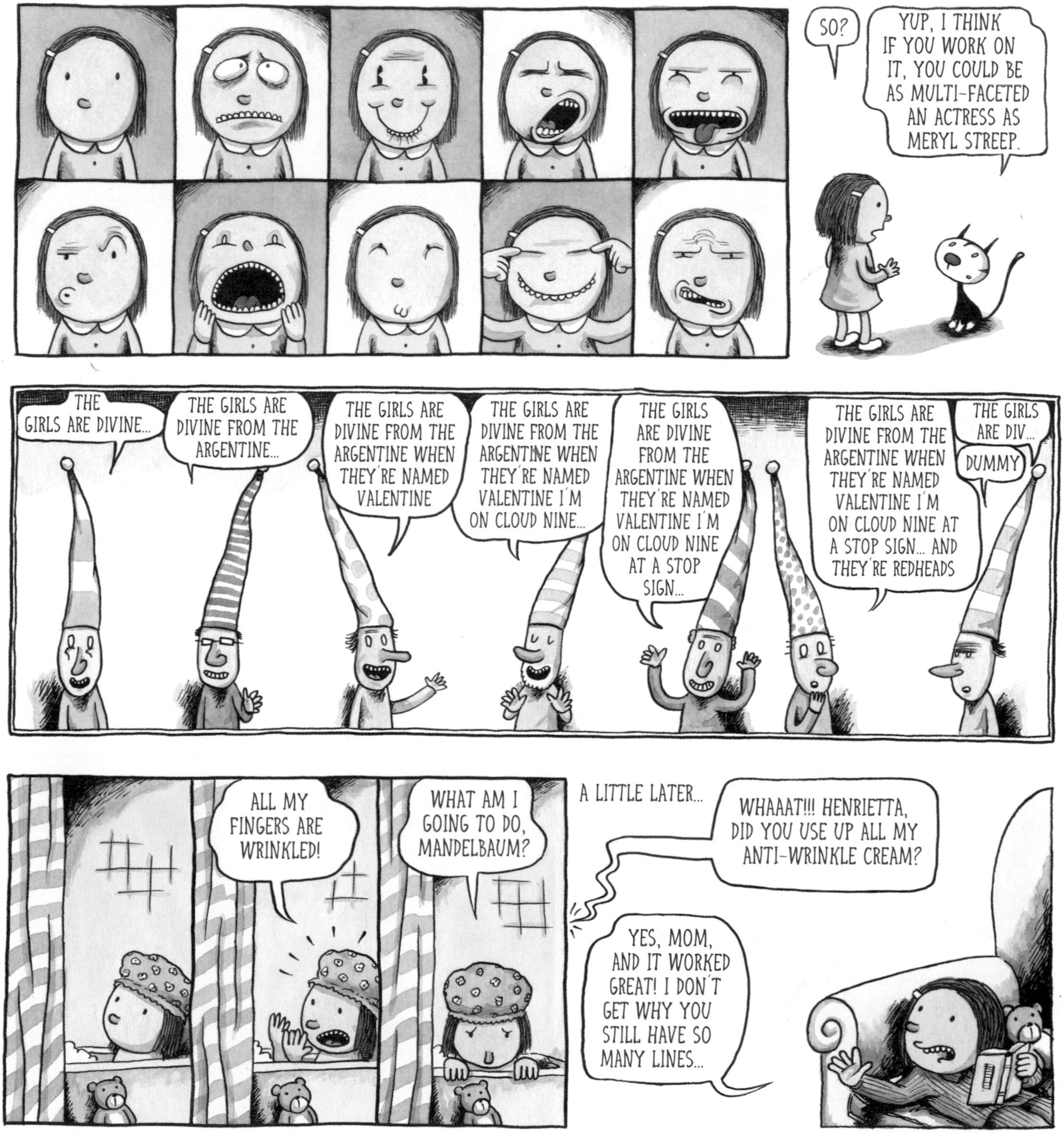
SO?
YUP, I THINK IF YOU WORK ON IT, YOU COULD BE AS MULTI-FACETED AN ACTRESS AS MERYL STREEP.
THE GIRLS ARE DIVINE...
THE GIRLS ARE DIVINE FROM THE ARGENTINE...
THE GIRLS ARE DIVINE FROM THE ARGENTINE WHEN THEY'RE NAMED VALENTINE
THE GIRLS ARE DIVINE FROM THE ARGENTINE WHEN THEY'RE NAMED VALENTINE I'M ON CLOUD NINE...
THE GIRLS ARE DIVINE FROM THE ARGENTINE WHEN THEY'RE NAMED VALENTINE I'M ON CLOUD NINE AT A STOP SIGN...
THE GIRLS ARE DIVINE FROM THE ARGENTINE WHEN THEY'RE NAMED VALENTINE I'M ON CLOUD NINE AT A STOP SIGN... AND THEY'RE REDHEADS
THE GIRLS ARE DIV...
DUMMY
ALL MY FINGERS ARE WRINKLED!
WHAT AM I GOING TO DO, MANDELBAUM?
A LITTLE LATER...
WHAAAT!!! HENRIETTA, DID YOU USE UP ALL MY ANTI-WRINKLE CREAM?
YES, MOM, AND IT WORKED GREAT! I DON'T GET WHY YOU STILL HAVE SO MANY LINES...

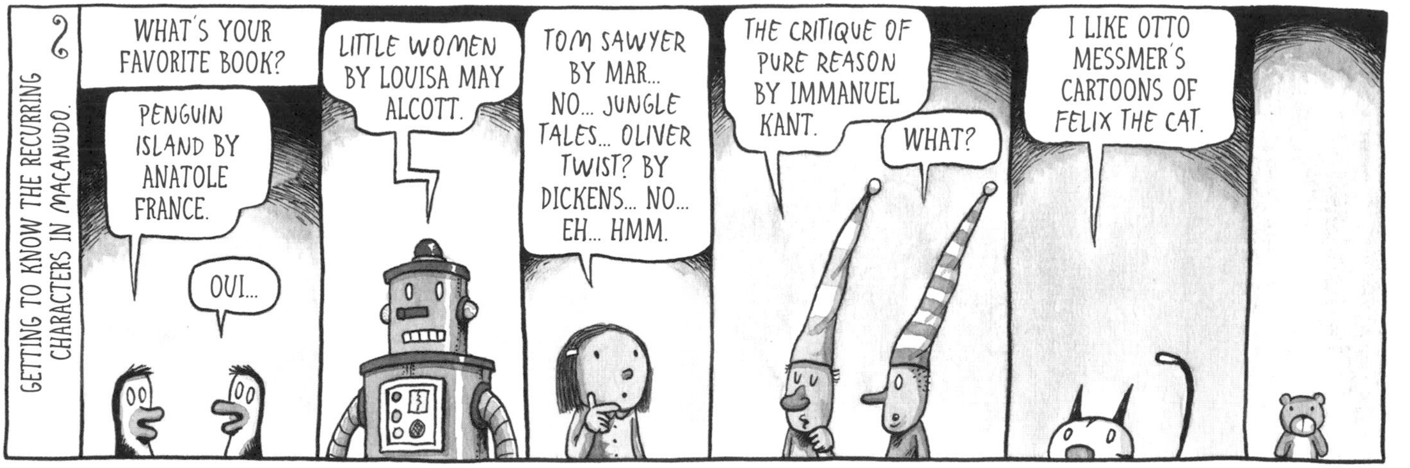
GETTING TO KNOW THE RECURRING CHARACTERS IN MACANUDO.
WHAT'S YOUR FAVORITE BOOK?
PENGUIN ISLAND BY ANATOLE FRANCE.
OUI...
LITTLE WOMEN BY LOUISA MAY ALCOTT.
TOM SAWYER BY MAR... NO... JUNGLE TALES... OLIVER TWIST? BY DICKENS... NO... EH... HMM.
THE CRITIQUE OF PURE REASON BY IMMANUEL KANT.
WHAT?
I LIKE OTTO MESSMER'S CARTOONS OF FELIX THE CAT.

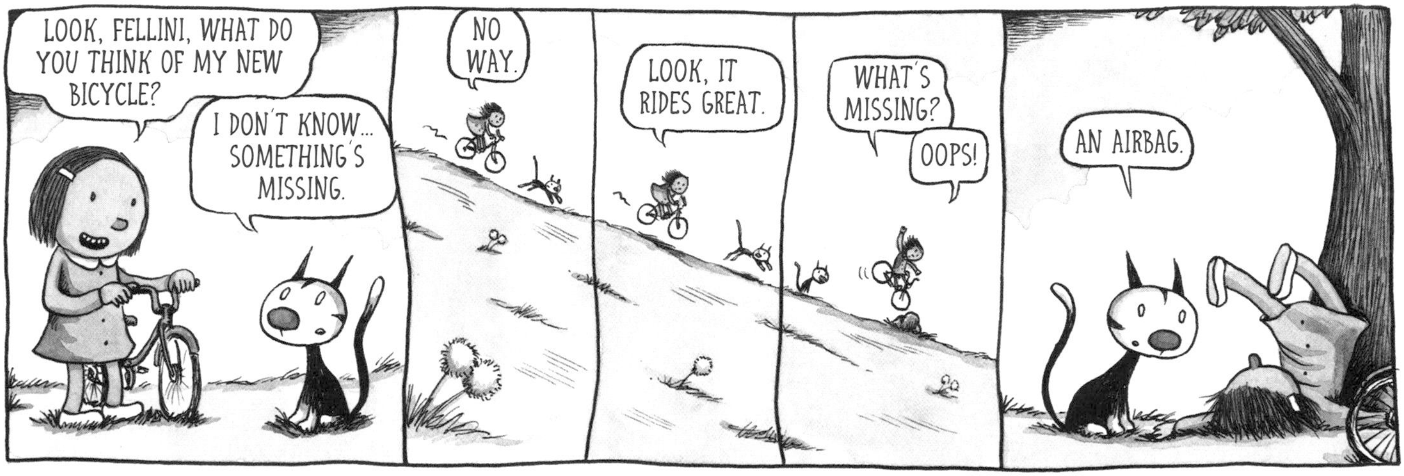
LOOK, FELLINI, WHAT DO YOU THINK OF MY NEW BICYCLE?
I DON'T KNOW... SOMETHING'S MISSING.
NO WAY.
LOOK, IT RIDES GREAT.
WHAT'S MISSING?
OOPS!
AN AIRBAG.

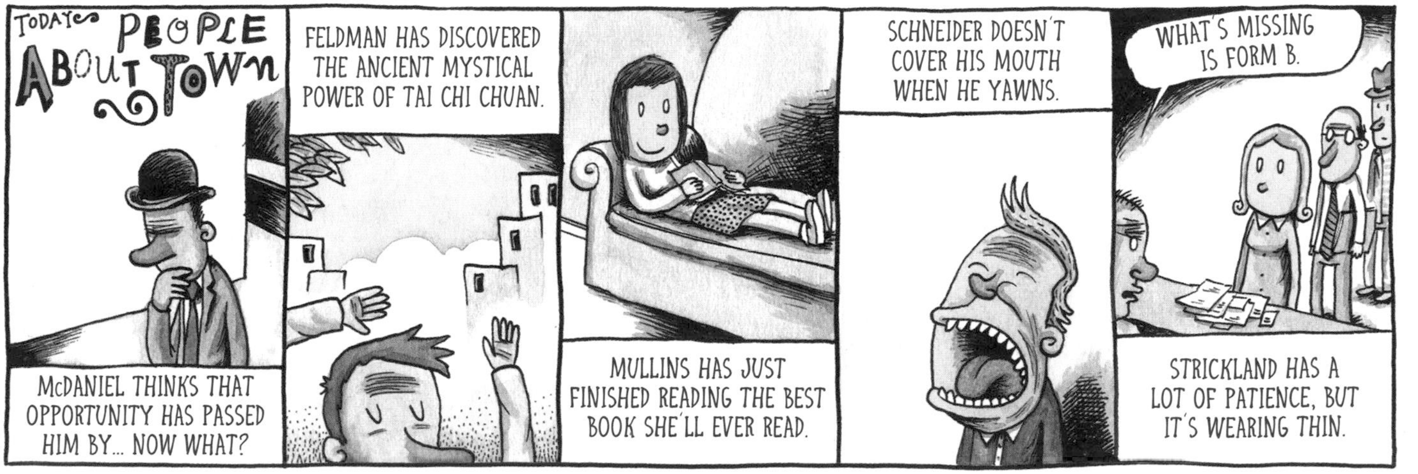
TODAY'S PEOPLE ABOUT TOWN
McDANIEL THINKS THAT OPPORTUNITY HAS PASSED HIM BY... NOW WHAT?
FELDMAN HAS DISCOVERED THE ANCIENT MYSTICAL POWER OF TAI CHI CHUAN.
MULLINS HAS JUST FINISHED READING THE BEST BOOK SHE'LL EVER READ.
SCHNEIDER DOESN'T COVER HIS MOUTH WHEN HE YAWNS.
WHAT'S MISSING IS FORM B.
STRICKLAND HAS A LOT OF PATIENCE, BUT IT'S WEARING THIN.

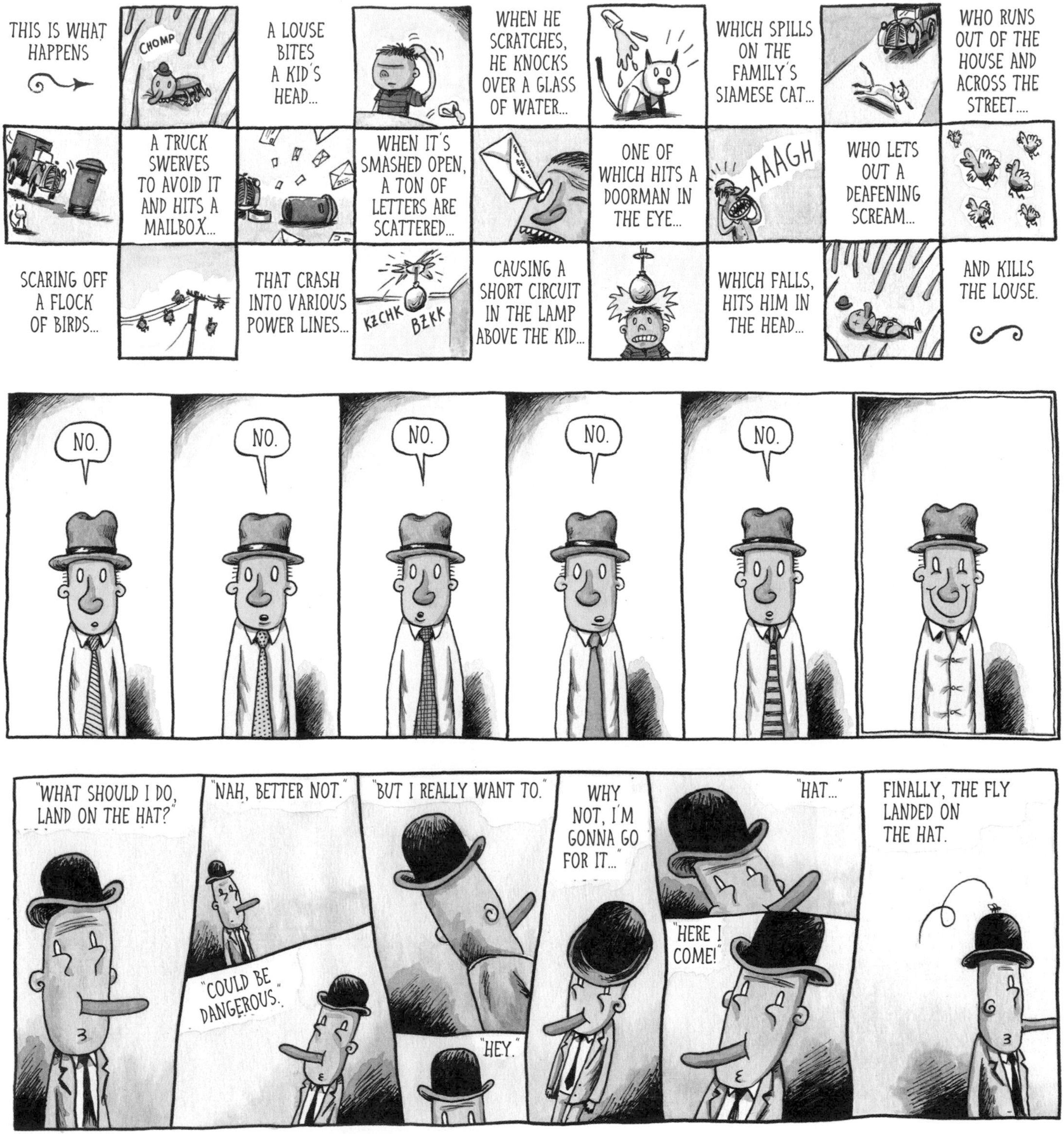
THIS IS WHAT HAPPENS
CHOMP
A LOUSE BITES A KID'S HEAD...
WHEN HE SCRATCHES, HE KNOCKS OVER A GLASS OF WATER...
WHICH SPILLS ON THE FAMILY'S SIAMESE CAT...
WHO RUNS OUT OF THE HOUSE AND ACROSS THE STREET....
A TRUCK SWERVES TO AVOID IT AND HITS A MAILBOX...
WHEN IT'S SMASHED OPEN, A TON OF LETTERS ARE SCATTERED...
ONE OF WHICH HITS A DOORMAN IN THE EYE...
AAAGH
WHO LETS OUT A DEAFENING SCREAM...
SCARING OFF A FLOCK OF BIRDS...
THAT CRASH INTO VARIOUS POWER LINES...
KZCHK
BZKK
CAUSING A SHORT CIRCUIT IN THE LAMP ABOVE THE KID...
WHICH FALLS, HITS HIM IN THE HEAD...
AND KILLS THE LOUSE.
NO.
NO.
NO.
NO.
NO.
"WHAT SHOULD I DO, LAND ON THE HAT?"
"NAH, BETTER NOT."
"COULD BE DANGEROUS."
"BUT I REALLY WANT TO."
"HEY."
WHY NOT, I'M GONNA GO FOR IT..."
"HAT..."
"HERE I COME!"
FINALLY, THE FLY LANDED ON THE HAT.

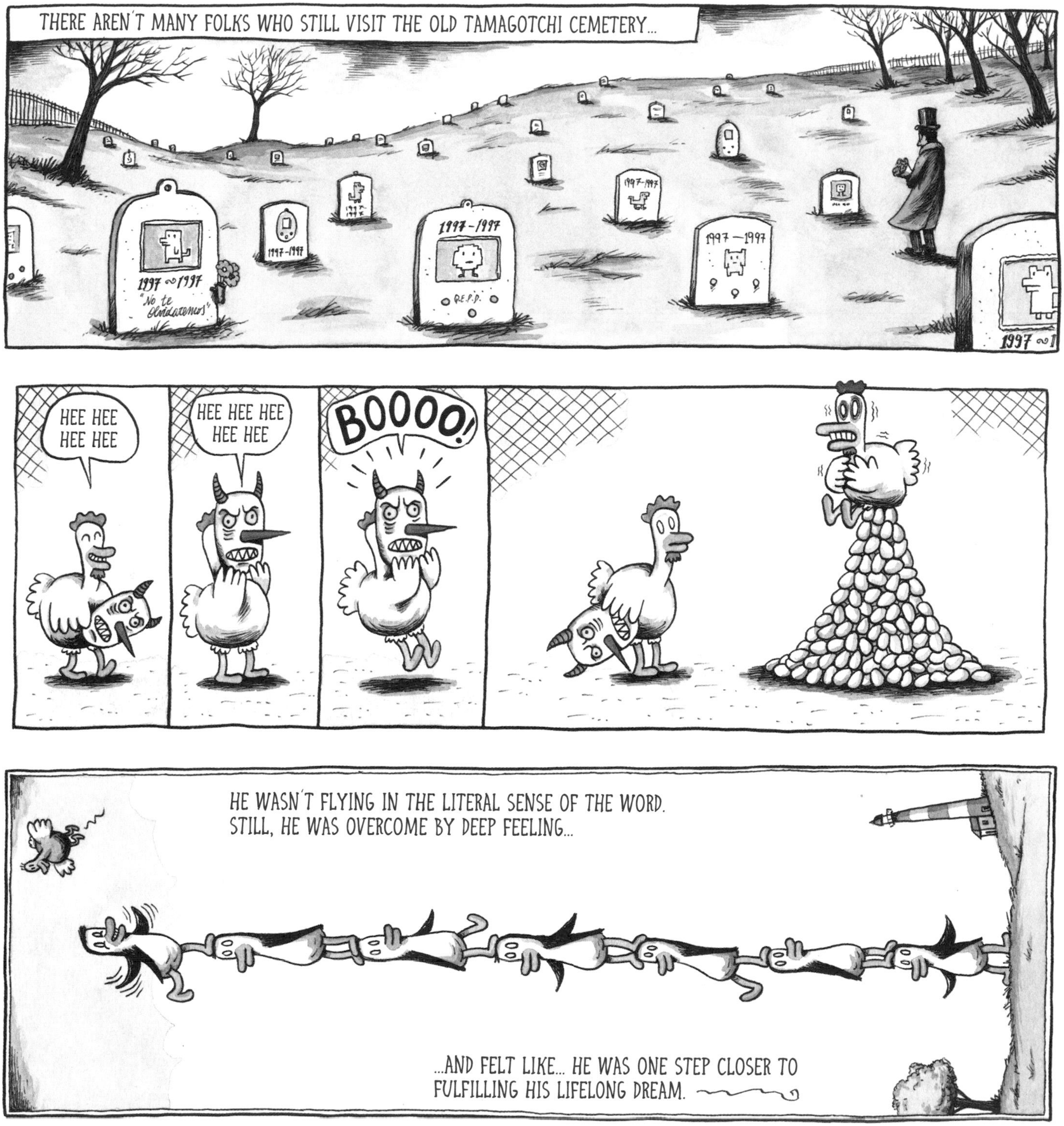
THERE AREN'T MANY FOLKS WHO STILL VISIT THE OLD TAMAGOTCHI CEMETERY...
HEE HEE HEE HEE
HEE HEE HEE HEE HEE
BOOOO!
HE WASN'T FLYING IN THE LITERAL SENSE OF THE WORD. STILL, HE WAS OVERCOME BY DEEP FEELING...
...AND FELT LIKE... HE WAS ONE STEP CLOSER TO FULFILLING HIS LIFELONG DREAM.

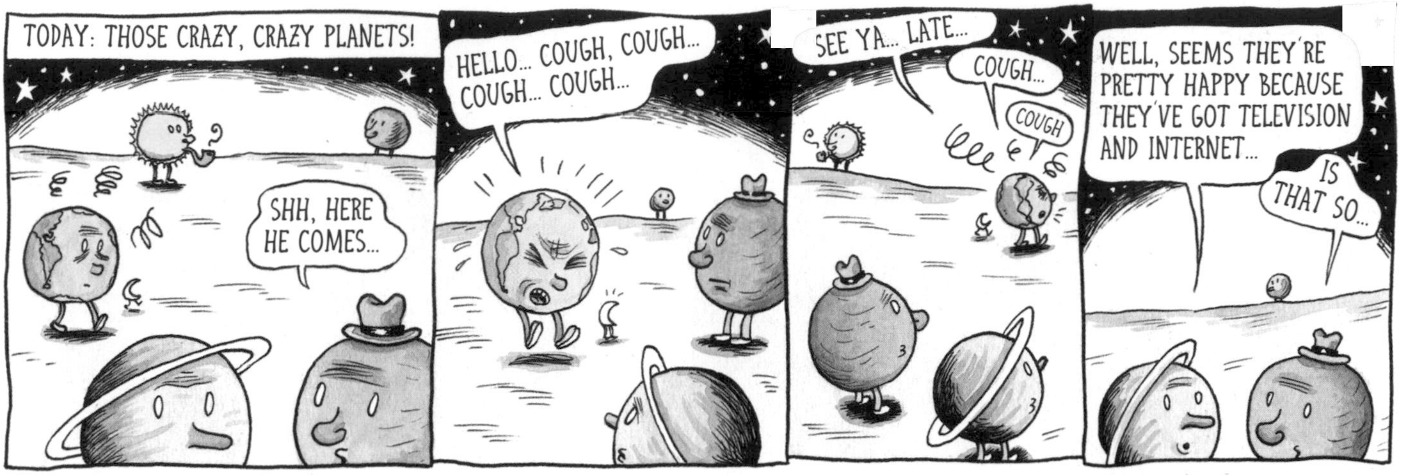
TODAY: THOSE CRAZY, CRAZY PLANETS!
SHH, HERE HE COMES...
HELLO... COUGH, COUGH... COUGH... COUGH...
SEE YA... LATE...
COUGH...
COUGH
WELL, SEEMS THEY'RE PRETTY HAPPY BECAUSE THEY'VE GOT TELEVISION AND INTERNET...
IS THAT SO...

AFTER A LONG NAP IN THE SHADE OF A TREE ON A WISCONSIN FARM, TOM CRUISE GETS UP SOMEWHAT CONFUSED AND DISCOVERS THAT IT WAS ALL JUST A DREAM...

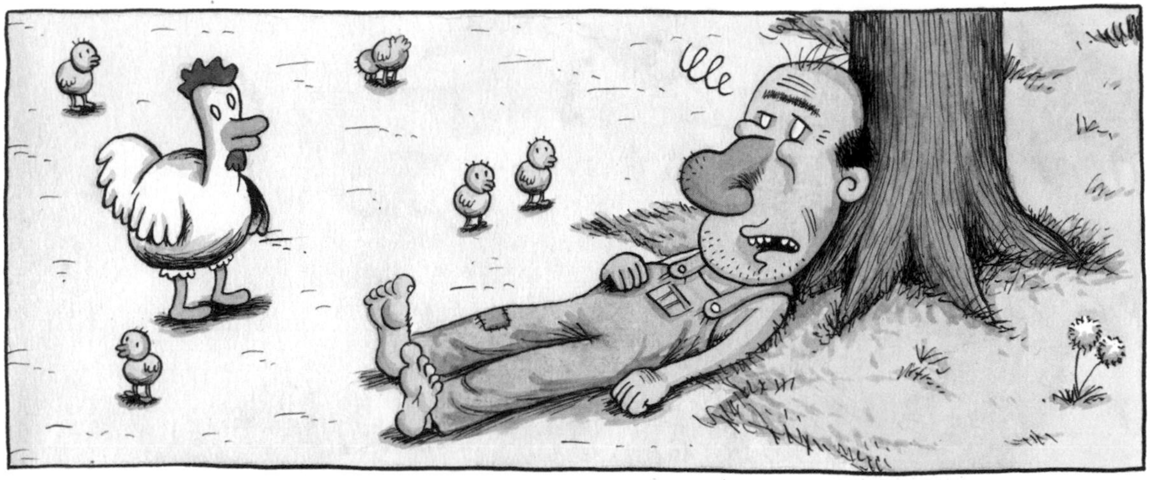

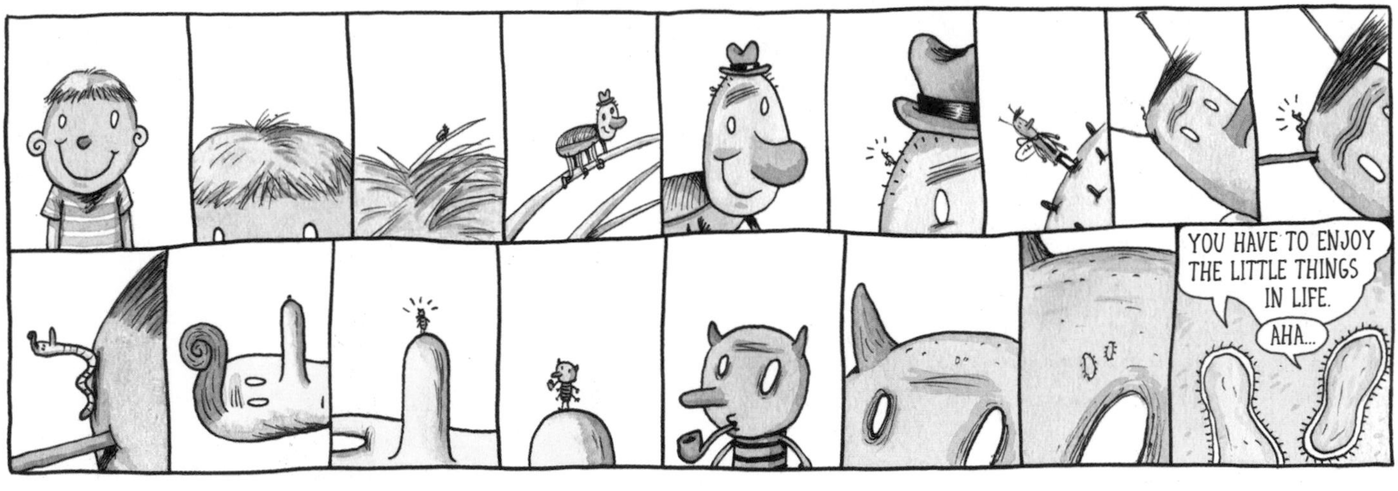
YOU HAVE TO ENJOY THE LITTLE THINGS IN LIFE.
AHA...

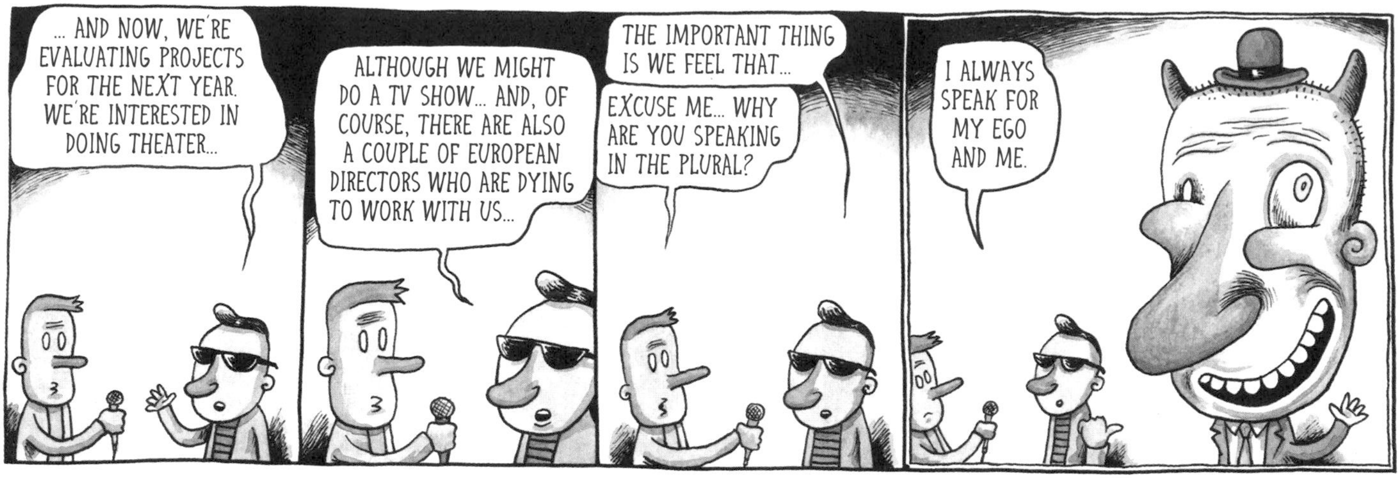
... AND NOW, WE'RE EVALUATING PROJECTS FOR THE NEXT YEAR. WE'RE INTERESTED IN DOING THEATER...
ALTHOUGH WE MIGHT DO A TV SHOW... AND, OF COURSE, THERE ARE ALSO A COUPLE OF EUROPEAN DIRECTORS WHO ARE DYING TO WORK WITH US...
THE IMPORTANT THING IS WE FEEL THAT...
EXCUSE ME... WHY ARE YOU SPEAKING IN THE PLURAL?
I ALWAYS SPEAK FOR MY EGO AND ME.

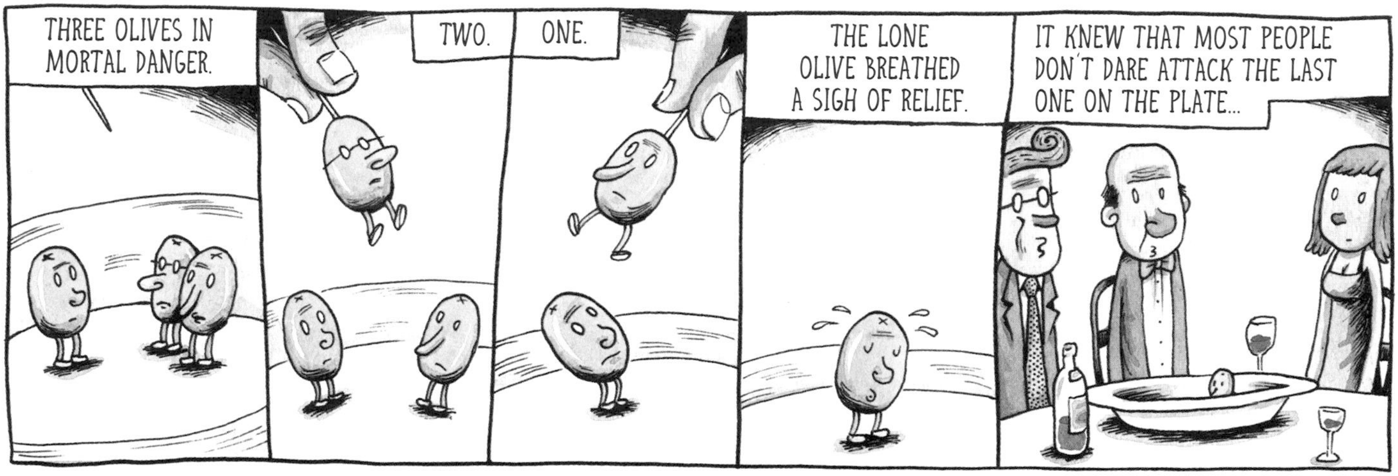
THREE OLIVES IN MORTAL DANGER.
TWO.
ONE.
THE LONE OLIVE BREATHED A SIGH OF RELIEF.
IT KNEW THAT MOST PEOPLE DON'T DARE ATTACK THE LAST ONE ON THE PLATE...

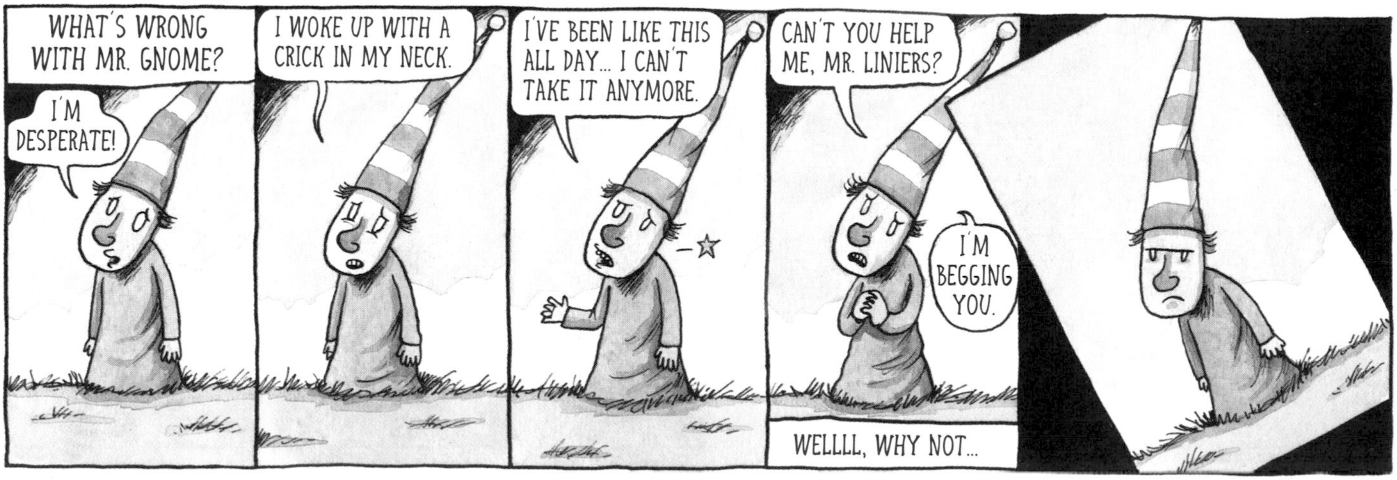
WHAT'S WRONG WITH MR. GNOME?
I'M DESPERATE!
I WOKE UP WITH A CRICK IN MY NECK.
I'VE BEEN LIKE THIS ALL DAY... I CAN'T TAKE IT ANYMORE.
CAN'T YOU HELP ME, MR. LINIERS?
I'M BEGGING YOU.
WELLLL, WHY NOT...

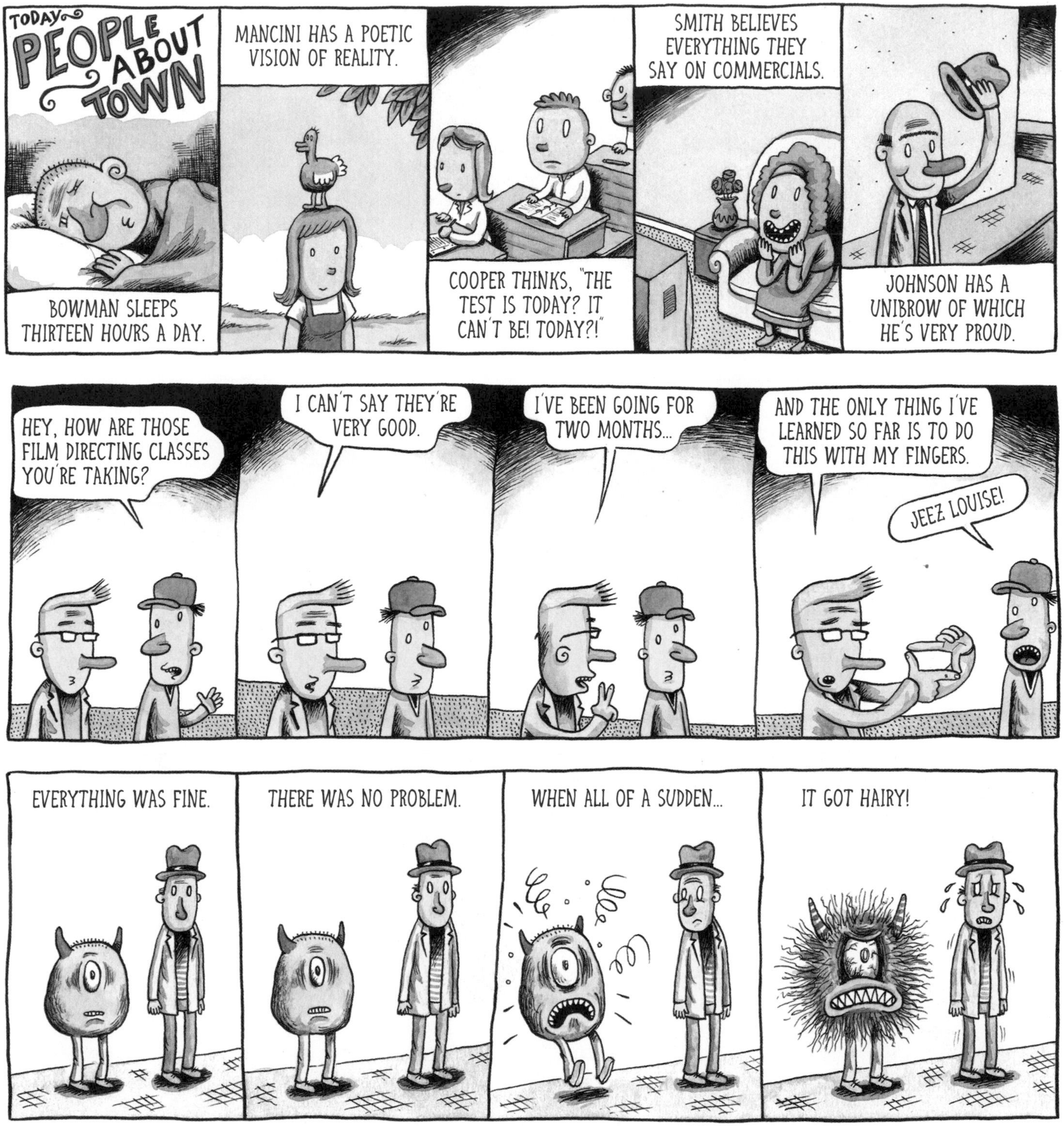
TODAY
PEOPLE ABOUT TOWN
BOWMAN SLEEPS THIRTEEN HOURS A DAY.
MANCINI HAS A POETIC VISION OF REALITY.
COOPER THINKS, "THE TEST IS TODAY? IT CAN'T BE! TODAY?!"
SMITH BELIEVES EVERYTHING THEY SAY ON COMMERCIALS.
JOHNSON HAS A UNIBROW OF WHICH HE'S VERY PROUD.
HEY, HOW ARE THOSE FILM DIRECTING CLASSES YOU'RE TAKING?
I CAN'T SAY THEY'RE VERY GOOD.
I'VE BEEN GOING FOR TWO MONTHS...
AND THE ONLY THING I'VE LEARNED SO FAR IS TO DO THIS WITH MY FINGERS.
JEEZ LOUISE!
EVERYTHING WAS FINE.
THERE WAS NO PROBLEM.
WHEN ALL OF A SUDDEN...
IT GOT HAIRY!

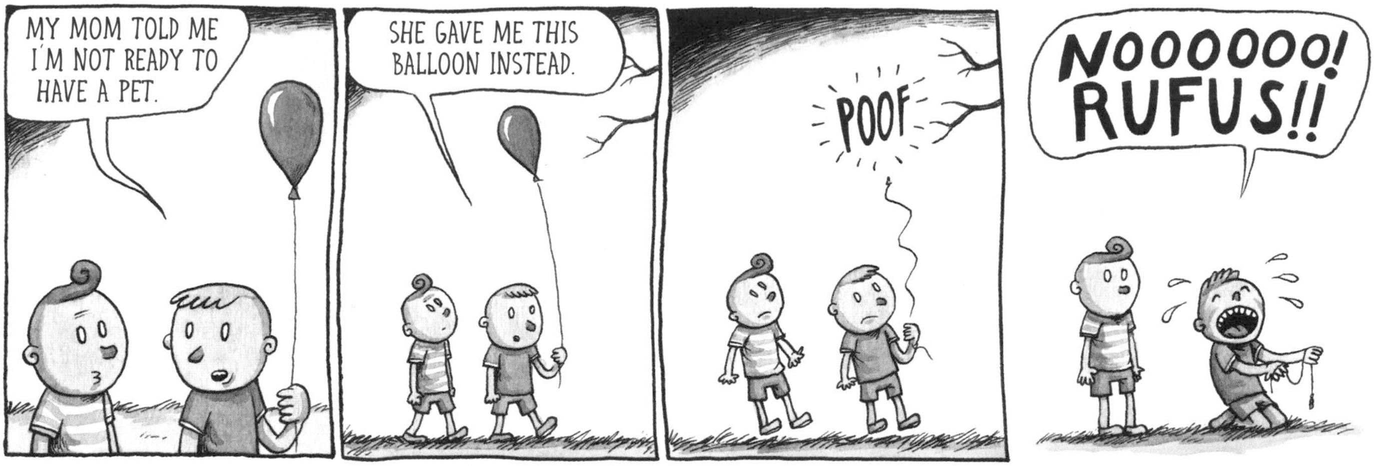
MY MOM TOLD ME I'M NOT READY TO HAVE A PET.
SHE GAVE ME THIS BALLOON INSTEAD.
POOF
NOOOOOO! RUFUS!!

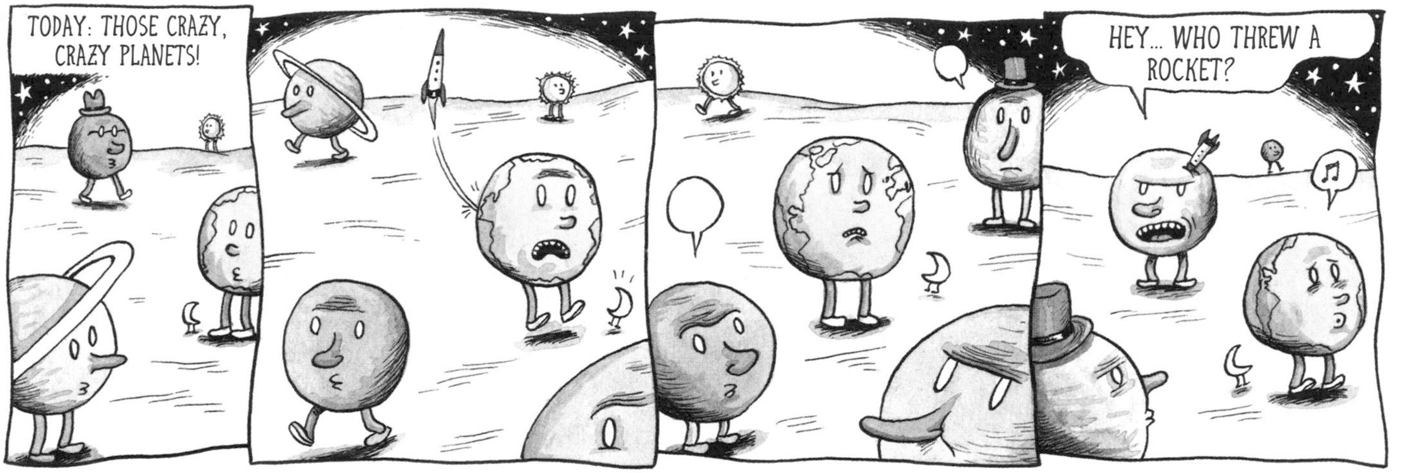
TODAY: THOSE CRAZY, CRAZY PLANETS!
HEY... WHO THREW A ROCKET?

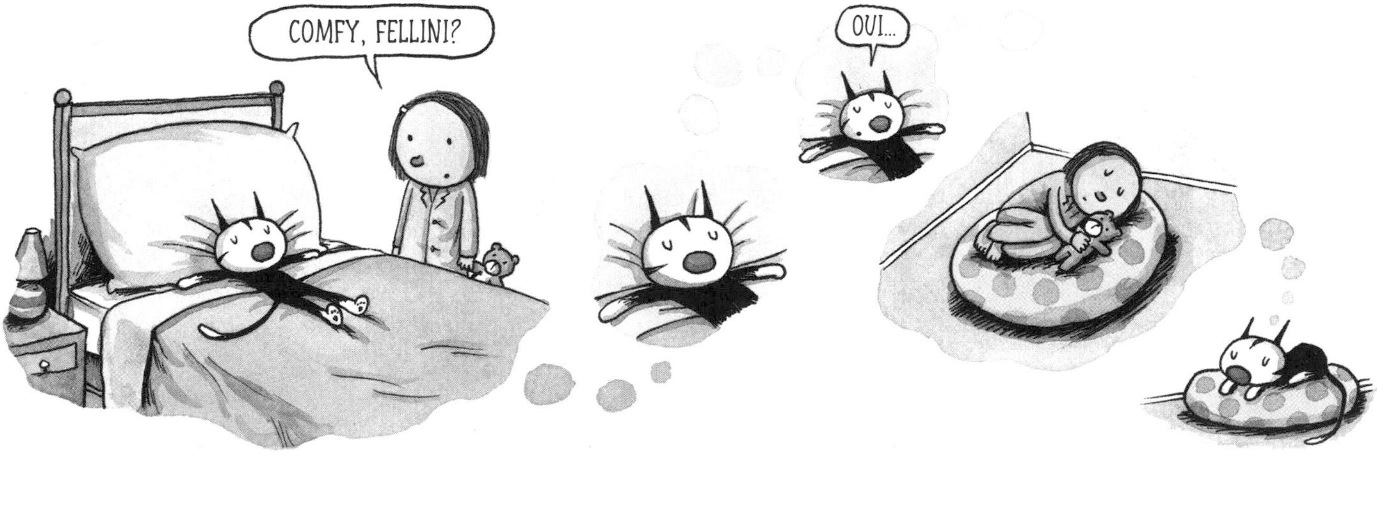
COMFY, FELLINI?
OUI...

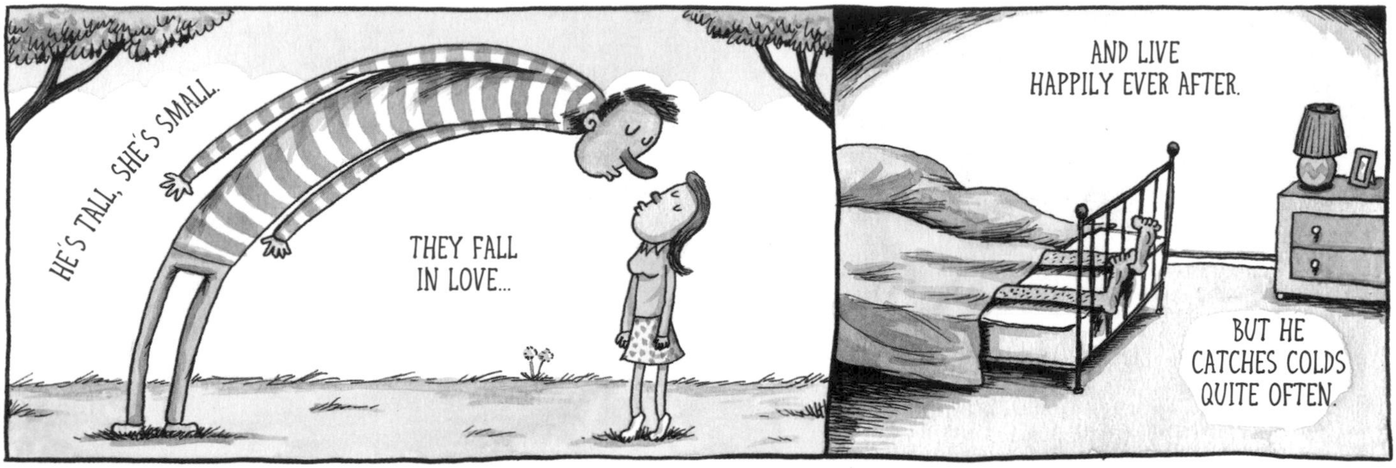
HE'S TALL, SHE'S SMALL.
THEY FALL IN LOVE...
AND LIVE HAPPILY EVER AFTER.
BUT HE CATCHES COLDS QUITE OFTEN.

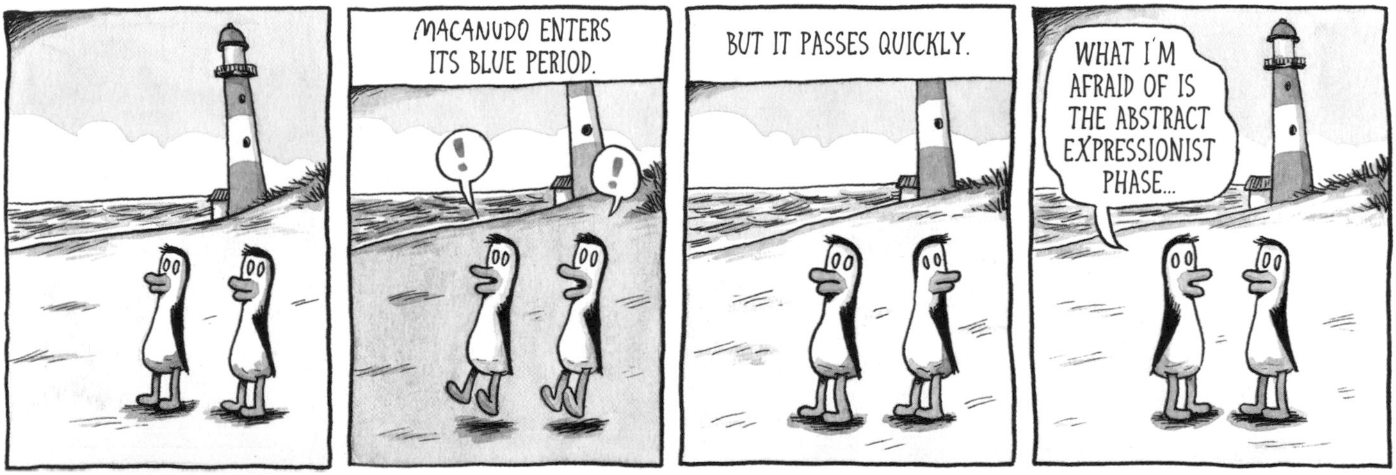
MACANUDO ENTERS ITS BLUE PERIOD.
!
!
BUT IT PASSES QUICKLY.
WHAT I'M AFRAID OF IS THE ABSTRACT EXPRESSIONIST PHASE...

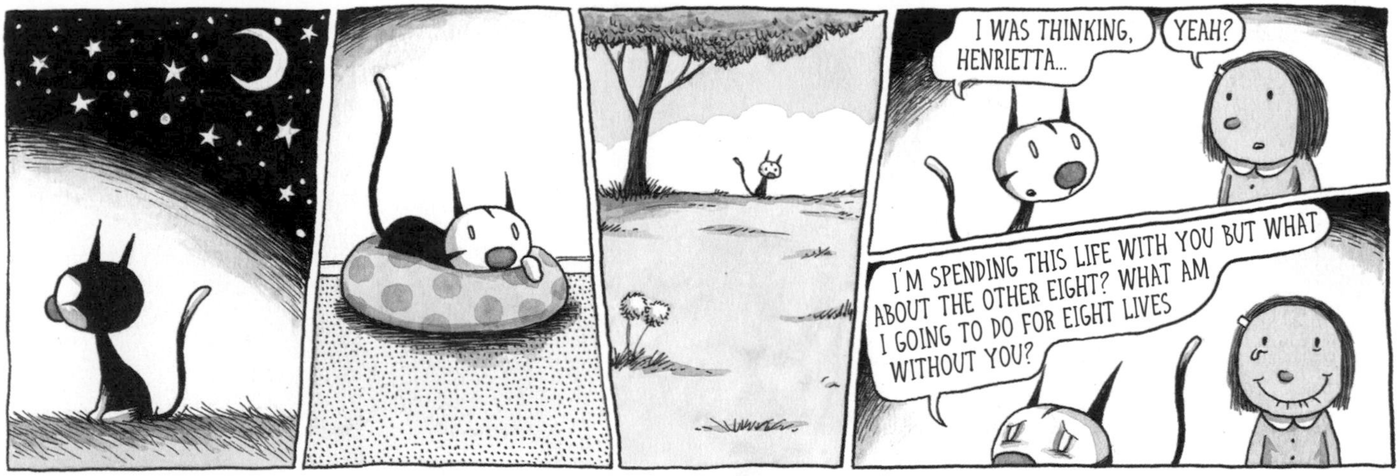
I WAS THINKING, HENRIETTA...
YEAH?
I'M SPENDING THIS LIFE WITH YOU BUT WHAT ABOUT THE OTHER EIGHT? WHAT AM I GOING TO DO FOR EIGHT LIVES WITHOUT YOU?

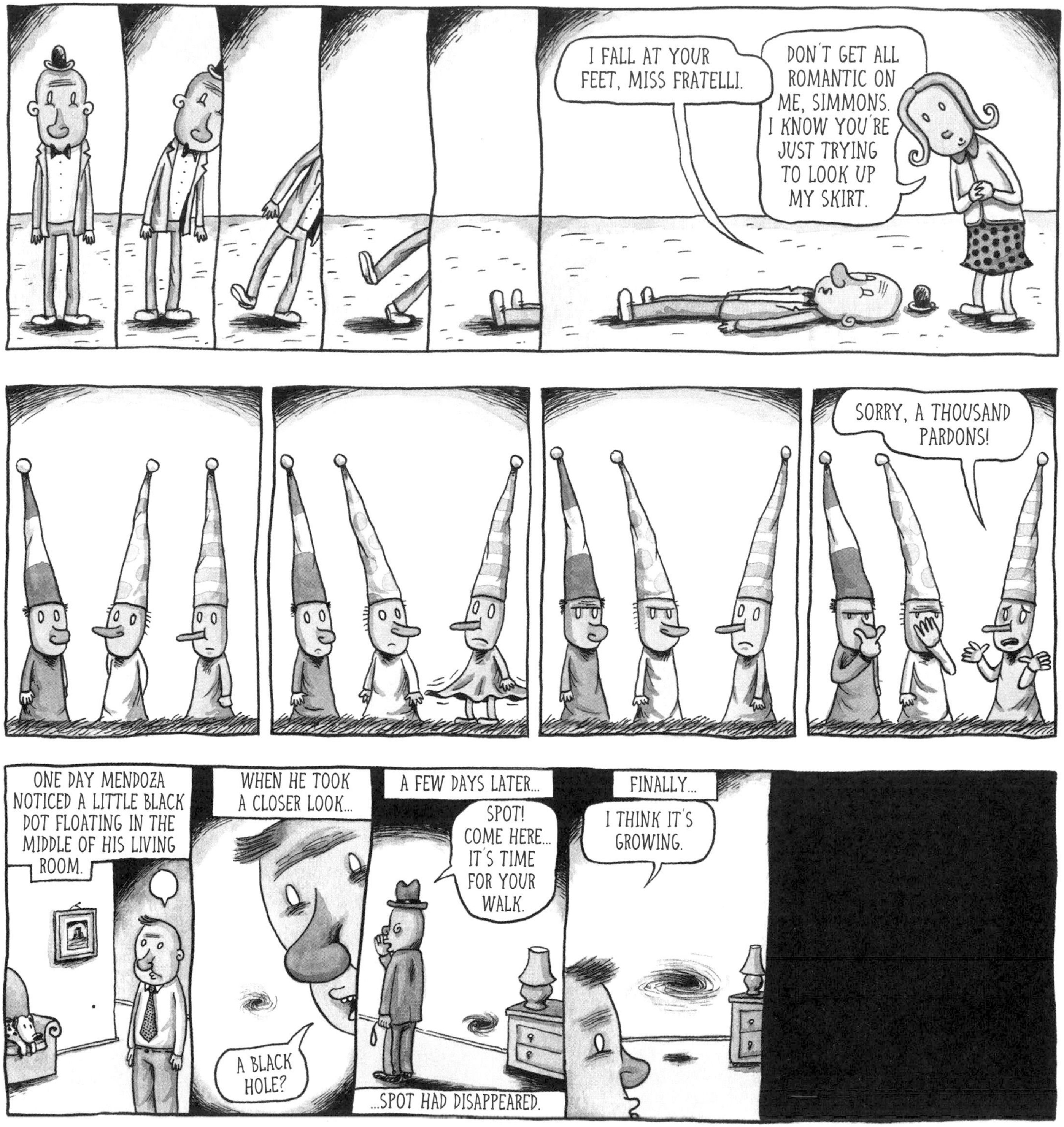
I FALL AT YOUR FEET, MISS FRATELLI.
DON'T GET ALL ROMANTIC ON ME, SIMMONS. I KNOW YOU'RE JUST TRYING TO LOOK UP MY SKIRT.
SORRY, A THOUSAND PARDONS!
ONE DAY MENDOZA NOTICED A LITTLE BLACK DOT FLOATING IN THE MIDDLE OF HIS LIVING ROOM.
WHEN HE TOOK A CLOSER LOOK...
A BLACK HOLE?
A FEW DAYS LATER...
SPOT! COME HERE... IT'S TIME FOR YOUR WALK.
...SPOT HAD DISAPPEARED.
FINALLY...
I THINK IT'S GROWING.

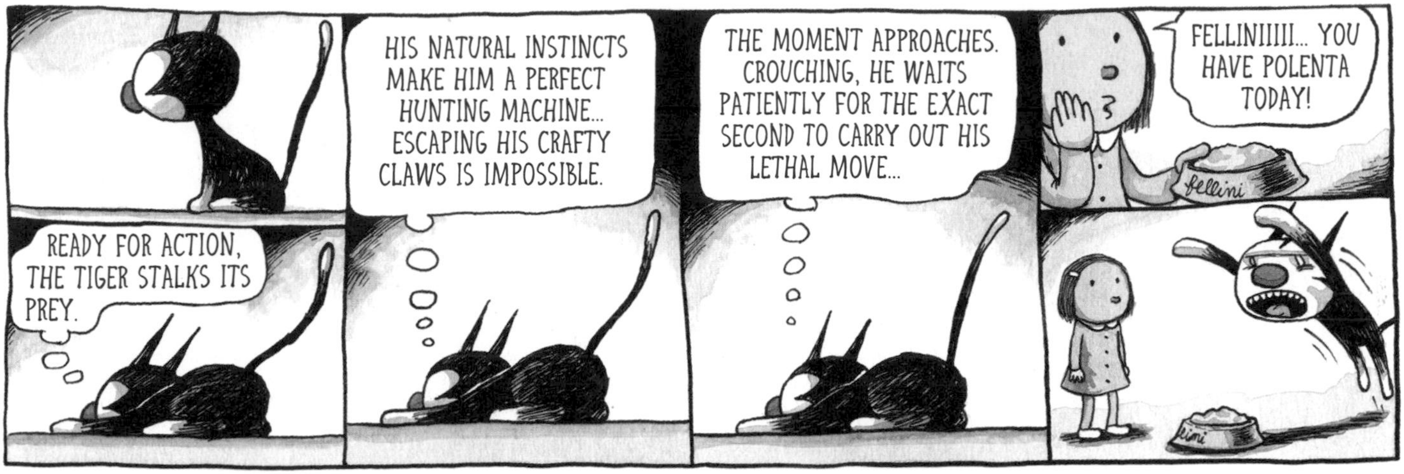
READY FOR ACTION, THE TIGER STALKS ITS PREY.
HIS NATURAL INSTINCTS MAKE HIM A PERFECT HUNTING MACHINE... ESCAPING HIS CRAFTY CLAWS IS IMPOSSIBLE.
THE MOMENT APPROACHES. CROUCHING, HE WAITS PATIENTLY FOR THE EXACT SECOND TO CARRY OUT HIS LETHAL MOVE...
FELLINIIIII... YOU HAVE POLENTA TODAY!
fellini

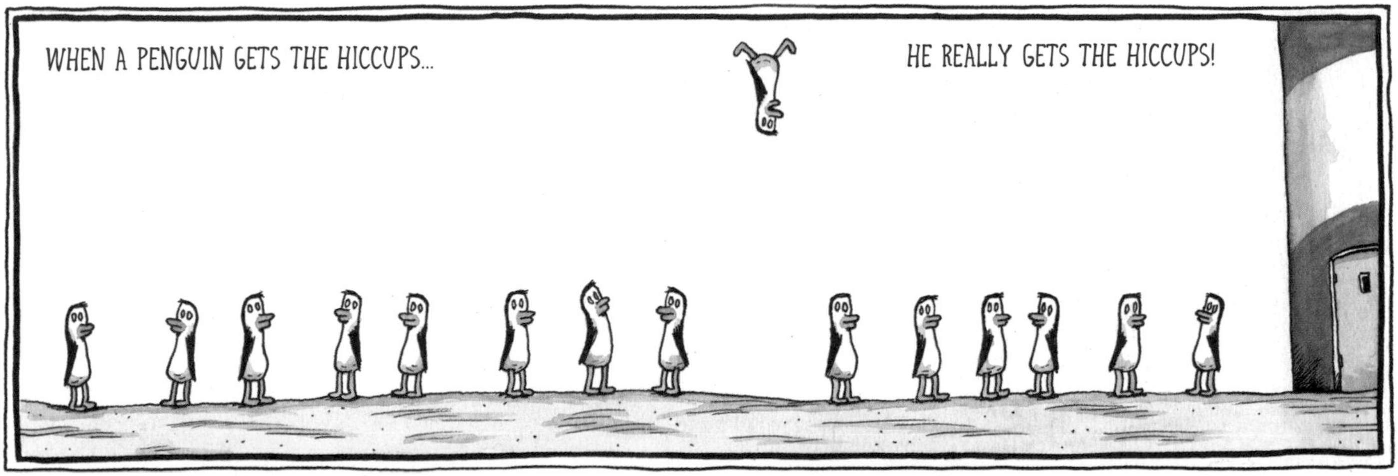
WHEN A PENGUIN GETS THE HICCUPS...
HE REALLY GETS THE HICCUPS!

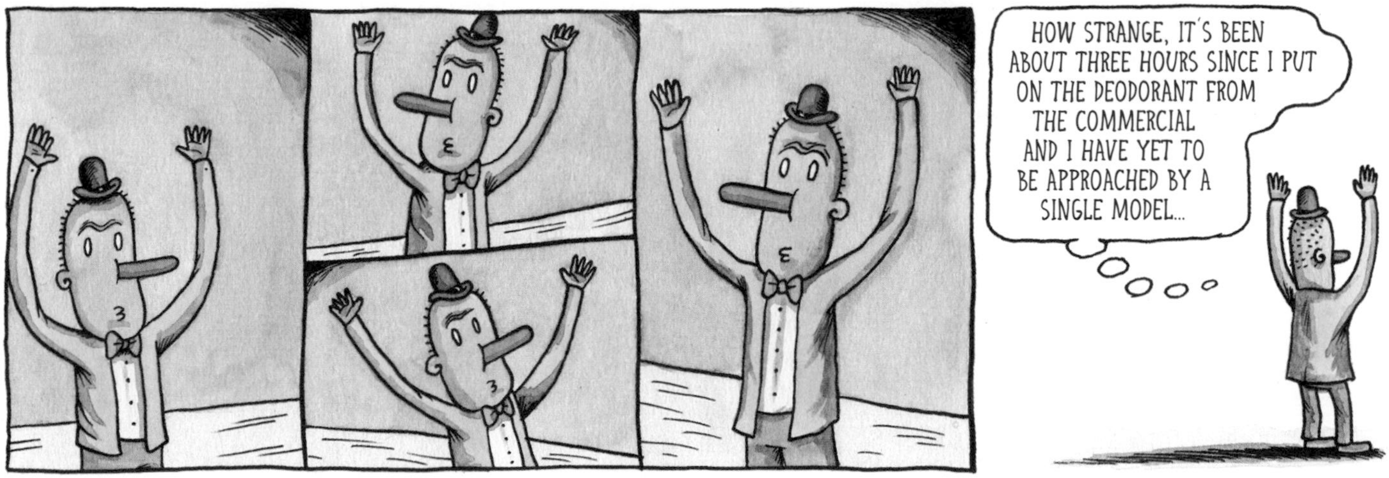
HOW STRANGE, IT'S BEEN ABOUT THREE HOURS SINCE I PUT ON THE DEODORANT FROM THE COMMERCIAL AND I HAVE YET TO BE APPROACHED BY A SINGLE MODEL...

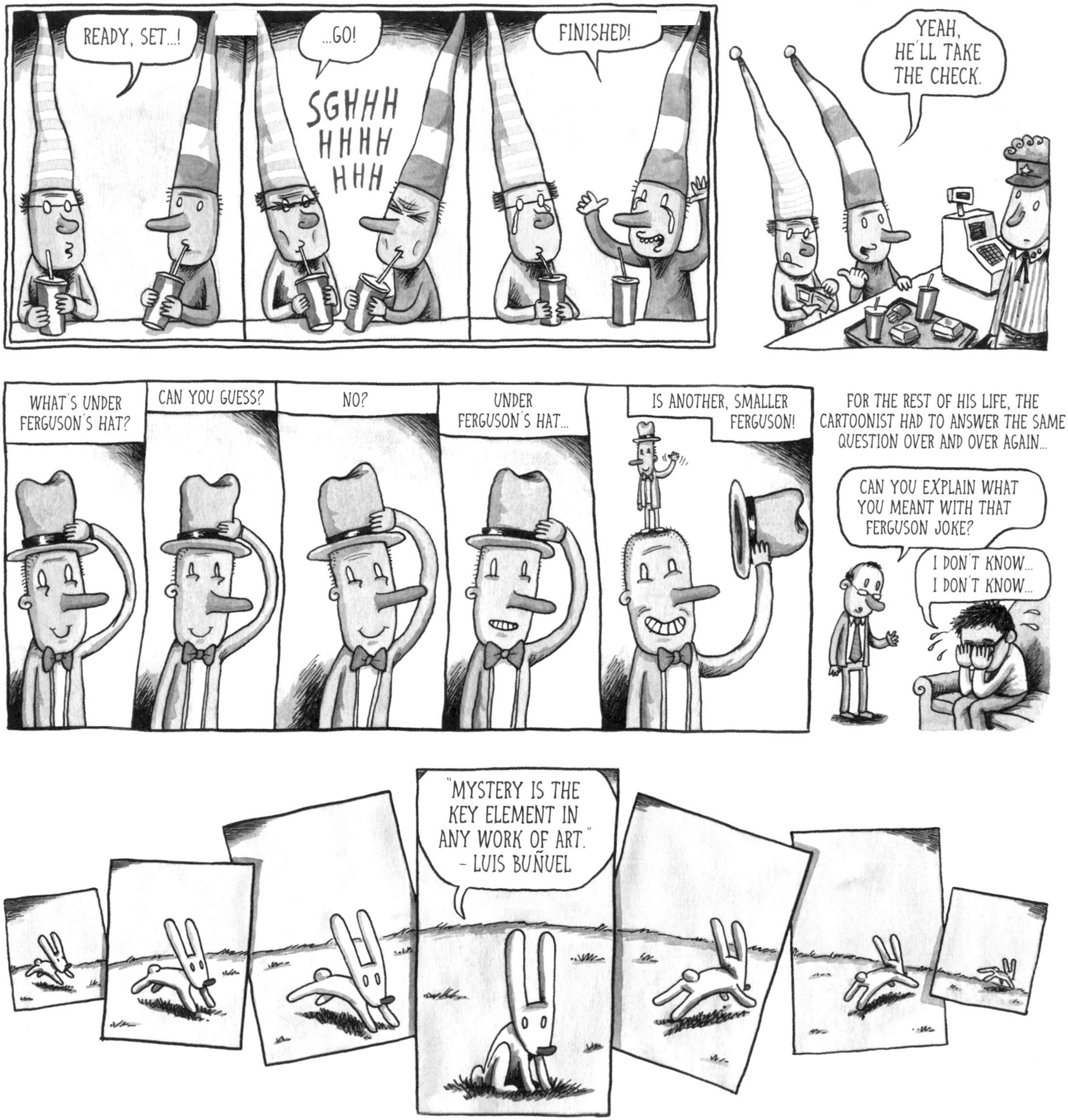
READY, SET...!
...GO!
SGHHH HHHH HHH
FINISHED!
YEAH, HE'LL TAKE THE CHECK.
WHAT'S UNDER FERGUSON'S HAT?
CAN YOU GUESS?
NO?
UNDER FERGUSON'S HAT...
IS ANOTHER, SMALLER FERGUSON!
FOR THE REST OF HIS LIFE, THE CARTOONIST HAD TO ANSWER THE SAME QUESTION OVER AND OVER AGAIN...
CAN YOU EXPLAIN WHAT YOU MEANT WITH THAT FERGUSON JOKE?
I DON'T KNOW... I DON'T KNOW...
"MYSTERY IS THE KEY ELEMENT IN ANY WORK OF ART." - LUIS BUÑUEL

ACKNOWLEDGEMENTS

Thanks to my parents.

Thanks to Maitena.

Thanks to Carlos Guyot, Carmen Piaggio,
and the newspaper *La Nación*.

Thanks to Nora Lezano and Arpe.

Thanks to Fernando Fratantoni and Pablo Cabrera.

And more than thanks to Daniel, Kuki,
Nicolás Arfeli, and Ediciones de la Flor.

Photo by Nora Lezano

Ricardo "Liniers" Siri is an acclaimed and well-beloved Argentine cartoonist, whose wildly popular daily strip *Macanudo* ("cool") has been published in the Argentine newspaper *La Nación* over the past ten years. This strip has won him fans throughout the world and comparisons to the cartoonist heavyweights Charles Schultz and Bill Watterson. Liniers also travels around the world with musician Kevin Johansen, painting on big canvases on stage while Johansen makes music. Sometimes, they switch places.

Liniers has over 3,600 published comic strips, has published over twenty-five books in Spanish, and has published more than ten books in nine countries, from Brazil to France, Italy, and the Czech Republic. His first book to be published in English, *The Big Wet Balloon* (Toon Books, September 2013) has been both a critical and popular success and was selected as a best book of 2013 by *Parents Magazine*. Moreover, the fourth volume of his *Macanudo* to appear in French was recently selected for the 2014 Angouléme Festival.

Together with his wife Angie, Liniers also founded the comics publisher *La Editorial Común*, which publishes Latin American comics and Spanish translations of European and American comics.

Liniers lives in Buenos Aires with his wife and three daughters—Matilda, Clementina, and Emma…No penguins, though…Yet.